Edward Genung

The Machinist and Tool Maker's Instructor

containing an easy method of calculating and laying out difficult work in the

machine shop

Edward Genung

The Machinist and Tool Maker's Instructor
containing an easy method of calculating and laying out difficult work in the machine shop

ISBN/EAN: 9783337392765

Printed in Europe, USA, Canada, Australia, Japan

Cover: Foto ©Andreas Hilbeck / pixelio.de

More available books at **www.hansebooks.com**

THE MACHINIST AND TOOL MAKER'S
INSTRUCTOR,

CONTAINING AN EASY METHOD OF CALCULATING AND LAYING
OUT DIFFICULT WORK IN THE MACHINE SHOP.

THE CONSTRUCTION OF GEARING AND GEAR CUTTERS.

THE UNIVERSAL MILLING MACHINE WITH PRACTICAL
EXAMPLES. · THE MAKING OF CUTTERS FOR VARIOUS
PURPOSES. ALSO A METHOD of CALCULATING GEAR-
ING FOR THE CUTTING of SPIRALS, ETC.

THE UNIVERSAL GRINDING MACHINE
WITH PRACTICAL EXAMPLES.

The ELEMENTARY PRINCIPLES of MECHANICAL POWERS.

SIMPLE AND COMPOUND GEARING.

THE TREATMENT OF STEEL.

TOGETHER WITH TABLES, RULES AND VALUABLE INFORMATION FOR
MECHANICS GENERALLY.

FULLY ILLUSTRATED ,
BY
EDWARD GENUNG,
MECHANICAL ENGINEER AND MACHINIST,
NEW YORK.

PREFACE.

IN the preparation of this work I have taken into consideration the fact that as the average machinist has not had the education necessary to understand the more advanced mechanical works, and believing myself to be in a position to know the subjects least understood, (having had the management of machine shops for the past sixteen years) and also knowing the dislike generally for mathematical problems, more especially those in algebraic formulas, I have adopted arithmetic and plane trigonometry for this work, the former in as simple a manner as possible, and in the latter treating of right angled triangles only.

I would call the reader's attention particularly to that part of the work devoted to plane trigonometry, as, by its methods we are enabled to lay out geometric figures accurately and also to measure circular and angular distances of any description or magnitude. This subject, although new to most mechanics, can, by careful study be easily comprehended. The relation of sines, cosines, tangents and secants in regard to their respective positions should be carefully studied.

I trust the reader will not only recognize the value of this work, but that he will also appreciate its subjects.

The writer gratefully acknowledges favors shown by Prof. De Volson Wood and R. H. Thurston; also to the Brown & Sharpe Manufacturing Co., and the Pratt & Whitney Company.

THE AUTHOR.

New York, July, 1896.

CHAPTER I.

The following examples have been prepared to assist the reader not conversant with arithmetic:

ADDITION OF INTEGERS OR WHOLE NUMBERS.

The sign of Addition is marked thus ($+$), and, when placed between numbers means that they are to be added together, thus, $4 + 1 + 5$ reads 4 plus 1 plus 5.

The sign $=$ means equal, and, $4 + 1 + 5 = 10$; $6 + 2 = 8$; $1 + 1 = 2$.

The sign of subtraction is marked thus ($-$), and, when placed between two numbers, means that the one after it is to be taken from the one before it, thus, $7 - 3 = 4$, or 7 minus 3 equals 4; $2 - 1 = 1$; $70 - 50 = 20$.

MULTIPLICATION.

The sign of multiplication is marked thus ($\times$), and, when placed between two numbers, means that they are to be multiplied together, thus, $4 \times 2 = 8$, or 4 times 2 are 8; $7 \times 2 \times 2 = 28$; $2 \times 3 \times 2 \times 2 \times 2 = 48$.

INTEGERS.

A Vinculum $\overline{}$, or bar, and a Parenthesis ( ), both have the same meaning; thus, $8 \times \overline{6 + 3}$ reads 8 times 6 plus 3; now $6 + 3$ are 9, and 8×9 are 72. $4 \times (6 + 2)$: $6 + 2$ are 8, and 4 times 8 are 32, Ans. $3 \times (2 + 2 + 2) = 18$, Ans., $5 \times 1 + 1 + 1 + 1 + 1 = 25$, Ans.

DIVISION.

The sign of division is marked thus (÷), and, when placed between two numbers, means that the number on the left is to be divided by the number on the right, as follows: 10 ÷ 2 means that 10 is to be divided by 2 = 5 Ans., 40 ÷ 20 = 2 Ans., 74 ÷ 2 = 37 Ans.

We sometimes place them in the following manner, thus 40 / 20, which means that 40 is to be divided by 20, which would be 2 ; 40 / 2 = 20 Ans., 1000 / 4 = 250 Ans., etc.

DECIMALS.

The word decimal means numbered by tens, and, in enumerating figures, we sometimes see a figure thus 4.6, which reads 4 and 6 tenths. The figure 6 to the right is called the decimal, or fractional number; the figure to the left, or 4, is a whole number. The point between is called the decimal point because it separates whole numbers from parts of numbers, or fractions, etc.

ADDITION OF DECIMALS.

What is the sum of 4 tenths, 5 hundredths, 52 thousandths?

```
.4      reads   4 tenths,
.05      "      5 hundredths,
.052     "      52 thousandths.
-------
```

.502, Ans., reads 502 thousandths.

Always keep the decimal point in a column, and as there are no whole numbers, consequently there are no units. Commencing at the left, enumerate as follows: tenths, hundredths, thousandths, etc.

.001 = 1 / 1000, or, 1 thousandth, .021 = 21 / 1000, or, 21 thousandths. 1.001 reads 1 and 1 thousandth.

Add the following numbers : 42.1, 421, 4, .04, .044.

```
42.1    reads   42 and 1 tenth,
421.     "      421
4.      "       4
.04     "          4 hundredths,
.044    "          44 thousandths.
--------
```

467.184   "   467 and 184 thousandths.

SUBTRACTION OF DECIMALS.

From 23.1 take 19.9, or, 23.1 — 19.9.

 23.1 reads 23 and 1 tenth,
 19.9 " 19 and 9 tenths,

 3.2 Ans., reads 3 and 2 tenths.

From 45.04 take 20.004.

 45.04 reads 45 and 4 hundredths,
 20.004 " 20 and 4 thousandths.

 25.036 Ans., reads 25 and 36 thousandths.

Keep the decimal points in a column.

431.0095 — 47.000095.

 431.0095 reads 431 and 95 ten thousandths,
 47.000095 " 47 and 95 millionths.

 384.009405 Ans., reads 384 and 9405 millionths.

MULTIPLICATION OF DECIMALS.

Multiply 3.7 by 2.6, or, 3.7 × 2.6.

 3.7 reads 3 and 7 tenths,
 2.6 " 2 and 6 tenths.

 222
 74

 9.62 Ans., reads 9 and 62 hundredths.

840 × .004.

 840 reads 840,
 .004 " 4 thousandths.

 3.360 reads 3 and 36 hundredths, or, 360 thousandths.

.004 × .000004.

  .000004 reads 4 millionths,
  .004 " 4 thousandths.

 .000000016 reads 16 billionths = product.

Always cut off as many figures in the product, or answer, as there are decimals in the multiplier and multiplicand together. There are nine in this last case.

DIVISION OF DECIMALS.

Divide 4.5 by 7.2, or, 4.5 ÷ 7.2.

```
7.2 ) 4.500 ( .62 + reads 62 hundredths.
      4.32
      ───
       180
       144
       ───
        36 +
```

4.5 in this case is the Dividend, and reads 4 and 5 tenths. 7.2 in the example is the Divisor, and reads 7 and 2 tenths.

The Dividend being the smaller number we place several ciphers to the right, which does not change the number, but makes it more convenient to divide. It now reads 4 and 500 thousandths, as 5 tenths, 50 hundredths and 500 thousandths are the same, or, means one-half, it will be seen that it remains the same. The Dividend having three decimal points and the Divisor but one, subtract one from three, we have two places or figures to cut off.

.4 ÷ 142.

```
142 ) .40000 ( 281 +
      284
      ───
      1160
      1136
      ───
       240
```

As the Dividend in this example contains five decimal figures, and none in the Divisor, the answer, or quotient, must have five decimal places also, and as we have but three figures, or as shown 281, we must annex two ciphers to the left, making it thus, .00281, Answer.

Remember that if we continue the quotient one or more figures farther, we must also, for every figure thus carried, place a cipher in the dividend, which would leave the answer the same.

471.38 ÷ 27.5.

```
        27.5 ) 471.38 ( 17.1+ Answer.   17 and 1 tenth.
        275
        ─────
        196 3
        192 5
        ─────
          3 88
          2 75
        ─────
          1 13
```

.0000050 ÷ .02

```
        .02 ) .0000050 ( .00025 Answer.
          4
        ───
         10
         10
```

In this example the Dividend reads, 50 ten millionths, and the Divisor 2 hundredths, and, as there are 7 decimals in the dividend and 2 in the divisor, subtracting 2 from 7, we have 5 decimals in the quotient, and, in a case of this kind, we have to add three ciphers, making the answer read 25 hundred thousandths.

FRACTIONS.

There are two kinds of fractions: Common and Decimal. Thus, .750 reads 750 thousandths, and is a decimal fraction, and if placed thus, 750/1000, it is a common fraction ; the meaning is not changed but still reads 750 one thousandths.

There are also simple and compound fractions, thus, ¼ of anything, 1/1000, 1/10, ¾, etc., are simple fractions.

¼ of ⅛, or ⅓ of 1/5, is a fraction of a fraction, and is called a compound fraction.

ADDITION OF FRACTIONS.

Add the following sums: ¼ + ⅓ + 1/6.

The figures above the line are the Numerators, and, those below, the Denominator. We now find the smallest number (called the Least Common Denominator) that 4, 3 and 6 will divide without any remainder, which is 12; now one-fourth of 12 is 3, one-third of 12 is 4 and one-sixth of twelve is 2, or thus,

$$12 \div 4 = 3$$
$$12 \div 3 = 4$$
$$12 \div 6 = 2$$
$$\overline{9}$$

Since these are all fractional numbers, less than one,

1/4 of 12 twelfths = 3/12
1/3 of 12   "   = 4/12
1/6 of 12   "   = 2/12

or added together the sum is 9/12 = ¾.

We can also do this in decimals, thus,

1/4 of 1000 = .250
1/3 of 1000 = .33333 +
1/6 of 1000 = .16666 +
$$\overline{}$$
.74999 +

Add together 2/5 + ⅔ + 1/7.

In an example of this kind we multiply all of the lower figures, (Denominators,) together, thus, $5 \times 3 \times 7 = 105$,

then 2/5 of 105 = 42
      2/3 of 105 = 70
      1/7 of 105 = 15
$$\overline{}$$
                   127 which means 127/105, then divid-

ing 125 by 105 = $1\frac{22}{105}$, Answer.

Add together the following fractions :

.1″ + 1/5″ + .3″ + ¼″, or fractions of an inch.
1/10 of 1.000 = .100
1/5 of 1.000 = .200
5/10 of 1.000 = .300
1/4 of 1.000 = .250
$$\overline{}$$
                .850, reads 850 thousandths of an inch.

SUBTRACTION OF FRACTIONS.

⅝ − ⅜ = 2/8 = ¼, reads ⅝ minus ⅜ equals 2/8, equals ¼.

⅞ − 2/9 = ? Multiplying the Denominators together, we have 8 times 9 are 72, and ⅞ of 72 are 63; and 2/9 of 72 are 16. Then 16 from 63 = 47. As the denominators are 72, it will read, thus, 63/72 − 16/72 = 47/72, Answer.

$4\tfrac{1}{8}'' - 2.1''$, reads, from $4\tfrac{1}{8}$ inches take 2 and one-tenth inches.

$$4\tfrac{1}{8} = 4.125$$
$$2.1 = 2.100$$

2.025, reads 2 inches and 25 thousandths.

$12\tfrac{3}{8}'' - 2.05''$?   From $12\tfrac{3}{8}''$ take 2 and 5 hundredths of an inch.

$$12\tfrac{3}{8}'' = 12.375''$$
$$2.05'' = 2.05''$$

10.325'' reads 10 inches and 325 thousandths of an inch.

$10\tfrac{1}{2} - 4\tfrac{1}{7}$. $10\tfrac{1}{2} = 21/2$

$4\tfrac{1}{7} = 29/7$, multiplying the denominators together we have $2 \times 7 = 14$, and we have

21/2 of 14 $= 147/14$
29/7 of 14 $= 58/14$

89/14, or thus, 14) 89 ($6\tfrac{5}{14}$ Answer.
                             84
                             ――
                              5

or carried out, thus,

14) 89 (6.35 +   Answer.
     84
     ――
     50
     42
     ――
     80
     70
     ――

or in decimals, $10\tfrac{1}{2} = 10.5000$
                $4\tfrac{1}{7} = 4.1428$

7) 1,0000   6.3572, Answer.
――――
,1428

Always remember that in decimals we try to reduce to thousandths, thus when we say $4\tfrac{1}{6}$, we divide 1000 by 6 ; if we say $4\tfrac{1}{9}$, we divide 1000 by 9, etc.

MULTIPLICATION OF FRACTIONS.

$\frac{1}{4} \times \frac{1}{2} = \frac{1}{8}$ reads $\frac{1}{4}$ multiplied by $\frac{1}{2}$; or $\frac{1}{2} \times \frac{1}{4} = \frac{1}{8}$ multiplied by $\frac{1}{4}$ = the same.

If we cut an apple into two equal parts, each of those parts is one-half, and, if we take one of those parts and cut it into four (4) equal parts, then there would be four (4) parts in the other half also, and as 4 and 4 are eight, or equal parts, each one of those parts would be one-eighth ($\frac{1}{8}$) the answer, and, it will be the same as saying $\frac{1}{2}$ of $\frac{1}{4}$, or, $\frac{1}{4}$ of $\frac{1}{2}$. Let us take $\frac{1}{4}$ of $\frac{1}{2}$ an inch for an example and see if we do not get $\frac{1}{8}$ of an inch.

$\frac{1}{2}$ of an inch = .500, reads 500 thousandths,

$\frac{1}{4}$) .500

.125, Answer, reads 125 thousandths, or $\frac{1}{8}''$.

1/2 × 1/6 = 1/12 Multiply the Numerator and Denominator together.
1/7 × 1/8 = 1/56
3/4 × 4/5 = 12/20
12 × 3/8 = 36/8 = $4\frac{4}{8}$ or $4\frac{1}{2}$, Answer.
12.5 × .004

12.5
.00 4

.050 0 Answer, reads 5 hundredths, or, 500 ten thousandths.

In multiplying decimals the most important thing to remember is where to place the decimal point. 12.5 in the example is the Multiplicand. 12 is a whole number and .5 is the decimal; consequently, a decimal point must be in front of it. .004 = 4/1000 is also a decimal and has three figures, together with the one above, making 4 figures to cut off in the answer. Should there not be as many figures in the answer to cut off as in the Multiplier and Multiplicand together, then always place as many (Prefix) as required to do so and place the decimal point in front as shown below.

5/12 × 7/9 = 35/108 Answer.

27 × $\frac{1}{3}$ = 27/3 = 9 Answer.

.004 × .004 reads 4 thousandths multiplied by 4 thousandths. .004
.004
___
.000016 Answer.
.000002 × .006.   .000002
.006
_____
.000000012 Answer.

DIVISION OF FRACTIONS.

1 ÷ ¼ = 4 Answer.
¼ ÷ 1/5 reads ¼ divided by 1/5.
¼ ÷ 1/5 = 5/4 = 1¼, Answer.
10⁴⁄₇ ÷ ⅓.   10⁴⁄₇ = 74/7.   Now if we had said 10⁴⁄₇ ÷ 3, we would take ⅓ of the 74/7 or 74/21 ; but we say divided by ⅓, which would be 9 times as much, since ⅓ is only 1/9 of 3, so we place the figures thus, 74/7 ÷ 3/1, or invert the ⅓ ; now multiply the numerators together and divide by the denominators, thus,   74
3
___
7) 222
___
31⁵⁄₇ Answer.

If I had said divide 12″ × ½″, or divide 12 inches by ½ inches, you would not say the answer was 6, but you would say 24 ; the answer is, however, the same, no matter what we are speaking of ; again
48 ÷ 4 = 12 Answer.
48 ÷ ¼. As there are four fourths to one, in four whole numbers there would be four times four or sixteen times as much ; now let us invert (turn upside down) the figures, and see what we get. It should be 16 times 12 or 192.
48 ÷ 4/1 = 192/1 or 192, Answer.
8 ÷ 1/3 = 24 Answer.
1 ÷ 1/10 = 10.
4 ÷ 1/10 = 40.
7 ÷ 1/7 = 49.
4½ ÷ ¼ = 18.
2½ ÷ ½ = 5.

INVOLUTION,

OR, SQUARES, CUBES, ETC.

The word Involution means the raising of a quantity to any given power.

The power of any number is obtained by using that number one or more times as a factor, thus, $2 \times 2 = 4$, means that 4 is the square of 2, or the second power of 2; the first power of the number is 2 or the number itself. Again, $4 \times 4 \times 4 = 64$.

$4 =$, the first power,

$4 \times 4 = 16$, the second power.

$4 \times 4 \times 4 = 64$, the third power.

The second power would then be the square of the number, and the third power would be the cube of the number, etc.

The squares, cubes, etc., are also indicated in another manner, thus, 4^2 means the square of 4, or $4 \times 4 = 16$, Ans.

4^3 means the cube of 4, or $4 \times 4 \times 4 = 64$ Ans.

2^5 means the fifth power of 2, or $2 \times 2 \times 2 \times 2 \times 2 = 32$

5^4 means the fourth power, or $5 \times 5 \times 5 \times 5 = 625$ Ans.

The small figure at the top of the number is called the Index, and means the power.

Remember the figure itself is always the first power.

EVOLUTION.

SQUARE AND CUBE ROOT.

The word Evolution means the reverse of Involution.

The sign of square root is the symbol $\sqrt{}$ and is always placed before the number, thus, $\sqrt{3}$, which means that the square root of 3 is wanted; they are usually made thus, $^2\sqrt{3}$, to distinguish them from cube root, which is also made in the following manner $^3\sqrt{3}$. The small figure 2 means the square root and the small figure 3 means the cube root is wanted of 3.

What is the square root of 4, or $^2\sqrt{4}$? I explained in Involution that the square of 2 was 4, and, Evolution being the reverse of Involution, the square root of any number is found by the following method.   In the example the figure 2 multiplied by itself, or $2 \times 2 = 4$, now 2 is the square root of 4, and 3 is the square root of 9 :

$^2\!\sqrt{16} = 4$, means the square root of 16 is 4,
$^2\!\sqrt{64} = 8$, means the square root of 64 is 8.

The square root of $9/25 = 3/5$; of $16/64 = 4/8$; of $\frac{25}{100} =$ 5/10; of $4/9 = 2/3$; of $4/16 = 2/4$, etc.

Find the square root of 256.

```
            2 56 ( 16 Ans.
            1
            ───
            156
      26    156
```

In square root we commence by separating into periods of two figures each; always remember to commence at the decimal point to cut of, thus, in 256 there is no decimal point, because it is a whole number, then commence from the right.

Extract the cube root of 25.4.

```
            25.40      ( 5.039 +  Answer.
            25
            ────
            4000
    1003    3009
            ─────
            99100
   10069    90621
            ─────
            8479
```

Find the square root of 18.

```
            18'00      ( 4.2426 +
            16
            ────
     82 )   2 00
            1 64
            ─────
    844 )   3600
            3376
            ──────
   8482 )  22400
           16964
           ───────
  84846 ) 543600
          509076
```

Find the greatest square that will go into 18, which is 4; 5 would be too much because the square of 5 is 25. Place the 4 in the quotient, as in division, subtract 16 from 18, we have 2, and annex the next period, or add two ciphers in the absence of other figures. Now double the figure 4 and place it on the left, as shown, to form a new divisor. Now

18.00 (4   find how many times this 8, with some other
16   figure will go into 200, which is 2; place this
─────   2 at the right of 8, making it 82, then multiply
8) 2 00   the 82 by the 2, which is supposed to go into

the quotient with the 4, and continue as before. Remember to double all figures in the quotient as fast as you proceed, except, the last named figure.

CUBE ROOT.

As square root is separated into periods of two figures each, so is cube root separated into periods of three figures each. As the cube of 2 is 8, so the cube root of 8 is 2. The cube of 3 is 27, so the cube root of 27 is 3, and the cube root of 27/64 = ¾, etc.

The cube of 1 = 1, the cube root of 1 = 1,
The cube of 2 = 8, the cube root of 2 = 1.259 + ,
The cube of 8 = 512, the cube root of 8 = 2.
The cube root of 512 = 8.
The cube root of 8 = 2.
The cube root of 1 = 1.
The cube of 1.259 + = 2.

Extract the cube root of 1420.

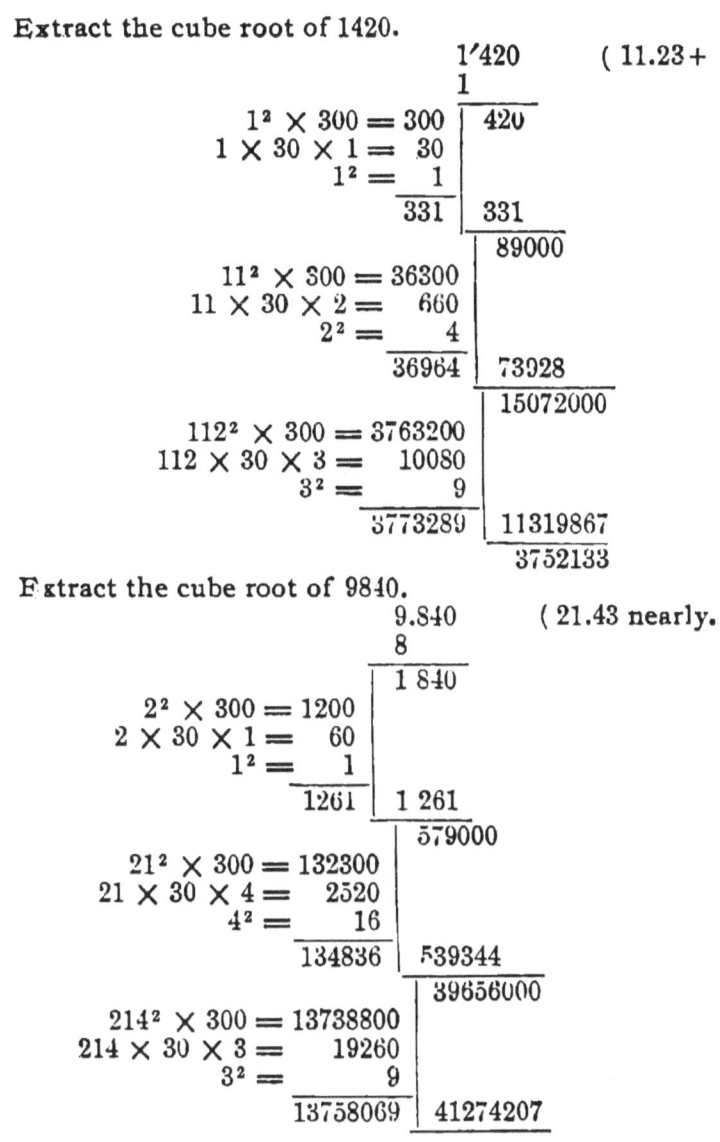

$$1'420 \qquad (\ 11.23 +$$
$$1$$

$$
\begin{array}{r}
1^2 \times 300 = 300 \\
1 \times 30 \times 1 = 30 \\
1^2 = 1 \\
\hline
331
\end{array}
\quad
\begin{array}{r}
420 \\
331 \\
\hline
89000 \\
\end{array}
$$

$$
\begin{array}{r}
11^2 \times 300 = 36300 \\
11 \times 30 \times 2 = 660 \\
2^2 = 4 \\
\hline
36964
\end{array}
\quad
\begin{array}{r}
73928 \\
\hline
15072000
\end{array}
$$

$$
\begin{array}{r}
112^2 \times 300 = 3763200 \\
112 \times 30 \times 3 = 10080 \\
3^2 = 9 \\
\hline
3773289
\end{array}
\quad
\begin{array}{r}
11319867 \\
\hline
3752133
\end{array}
$$

Extract the cube root of 9840.

$$9.840 \qquad (\ 21.43 \text{ nearly.}$$
$$8$$

$$
\begin{array}{r}
2^2 \times 300 = 1200 \\
2 \times 30 \times 1 = 60 \\
1^2 = 1 \\
\hline
1261
\end{array}
\quad
\begin{array}{r}
1\ 840 \\
1\ 261 \\
\hline
579000
\end{array}
$$

$$
\begin{array}{r}
21^2 \times 300 = 132300 \\
21 \times 30 \times 4 = 2520 \\
4^2 = 16 \\
\hline
134836
\end{array}
\quad
\begin{array}{r}
539344 \\
\hline
39656000
\end{array}
$$

$$
\begin{array}{r}
214^2 \times 300 = 13738800 \\
214 \times 30 \times 3 = 19260 \\
3^2 = 9 \\
\hline
13758069
\end{array}
\quad
\begin{array}{r}
41274207
\end{array}
$$

TO EXTRACT THE CUBE ROOT.

Commence at the Decimal point, if any; if there is none
ommence from the right, and separate the figures into periods
f three figures each, as shown in the examples; find the
iighest number that, when cubed, will go into the first period

at the left, which in the last example is 2; place this figure in the quotient, then cube it, which is 8, and place it under the figure 9 as shown ; subtract this, and we have 1840 for a remainder. We will now have to find a divisor for this 1840, which is done in the following manner: Place the same figure in the quotient, whatever it may be, to the left of the example, square it and multiply by 300; then take the same figure and multiply by 30, find how many times these figures (that is, the $2^2 \times 300 + 2 \times 30$) will go into the dividend (1840 in this instance) and we find it to be 1; then place this figure 1, which is called the last figure of the root, in the divisor, which now reads $2 \times 30 \times 1$; take the same figure 1 and square it as shown, add all together and we have 1261. Then as the last figure in the quotient is 1, we multiply 1261 by 1 and place it in the dividend under the 1840, then subtracting, we have 579 ; add the next period, or. if none, three ciphers, and we now proceed to find a new divisor, which is done in the same manner as before.

Remember when making a new divisor that we always take all the figures in the quotient, no matter how many there are and first square them, then multiply by 300 ; next take the same figures of the quotient and multiply by 30, and this again by the next figure that we will have to find the same as before explained, and proceed as shown in the example as far as desired.

MENSURATION.

The word mensuration means the process of taking dimensions, and includes lines, angles, surfaces and solids. Surface measurements have no thickness.

Example: We want to find how many yards of carpet to cover a floor that measures twenty by twelve feet ($20' \times 12'$): twenty times twelve is 240 ; this would be square feet, and as a square yard is three feet each way, which makes 9 square feet, dividing the 240 by 9 we have $26\frac{6}{9}$ or $26\frac{2}{3}$ yards.

We have a table, the top of which measures two feet each way, and two times two are four, which makes four square feet. This can easily be proved by running a line across the middle on each side and it will just divide it, leaving four equal spaces, which will measure a foot each way.

To find the length of one side of a right angled triangle, when the length of the other two sides are given.

. Example: Figure 1 represents a right angled triangle, so called because there is one right angle, or 90°. In the figure one of the sides is marked 2″ long, the other 3″; either one of these sides can be called the base and the other would then be the perpendicular. A perpendicular line always means a line at right angles to the object spoken of. If we drive a nail in the side of a building, we call it perpendicular to the wall. The hypothenuse of a right angled triangle is always the side opposite the right angle and is always the longest side. To find the length of the hypothenuse we proceed as follows: We square the base and perpendicular, separately, and add them together, then extract the square root, thus,

$$2^2 \text{ or } 2 \text{ times } 2 \text{ are } 4$$
$$3^2 \text{ or } 3 \text{ times } 3 \text{ are } 9$$

$$\begin{array}{l} \overline{13'00} \quad (\; 3''.605+ \;\; \text{Answer.} \\ 9 \\ \hline 66\;)\,4\;00 \\ 3\;96 \\ \hline 72\;)\quad 40000 \\ 36025 \\ \hline 7205\;) \end{array}$$

Figure 2 is similar to figure 1. In this case we have decimals to deal with, otherwise it is the same.

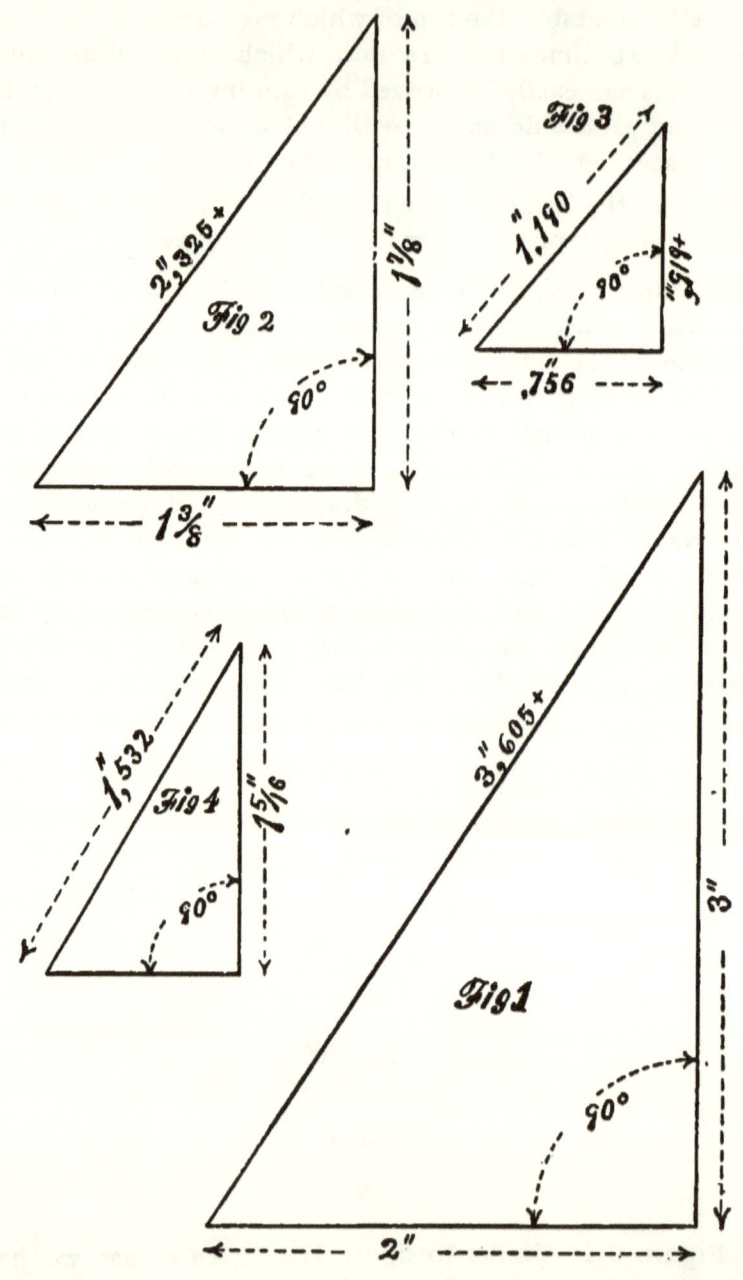

Example, Figure 2: Let us call the bottom of the figure the base, then $1\frac{3}{8}'' = 1.375''$:

$$\begin{array}{r} 1.375 \\ 1.375 \\ \hline 6\ 875 \\ 96\ 25 \\ 412\ 5 \qquad \bullet \\ 1375 \\ \hline \end{array}$$

$1\frac{7}{8}'' = 1.875$, which squared

equals 3.515625, and both added

$$\begin{array}{r} 1.890\ 625 \\ 3.515\ 625 \\ \end{array}$$

together $= 5.406\ 250\ (\ 2.325'' +$ Ans.
  4

$$\begin{array}{r} 43\ )\ 1\ 40 \\ 1\ 29 \\ \hline 462\ )\ 1162 \\ 924 \\ \hline 4645\ )\ 23850 \\ 23225 \\ \hline \end{array}$$

In Figure 3 we have given the base as .756″ in length, the hypothenuse as 1.190 in length. In examples of this kind, figures 3 and 4, we square both numbers as before, but subtract the less from the greater and then extract the square root; the quotient is then the answer. Thus, figure 3 $=$

$$\begin{array}{ccc} .756 & 1.190 & 1.416100 \\ .756 & 1.190 & .571536 \\ \hline 4536 & 10.710 & .844564\ (\ .919 + \quad \text{Ans.} \\ 3780 & 11\ 90 & 81 \qquad \bullet \\ 5292 & 119\ 0 & 181\ )\ 345 \\ \hline & & 181 \\ .571536 & 1.41\ 610 & \overline{\qquad} \\ & & 1829\ )\ 16464 \\ & & 16461 \\ \end{array}$$

Figure 4 is done in the same manner as figure 3.

To find how long a piece of wire it will take to make a spiral spring, or, what is the same thing, to find the length of a spiral groove, sometimes called a helix.

Example: A spring 2″ in diameter, 1/4″ pitch = 4 to the inch, 12″ long. Diameter 2″, the circumference would be:

```
        3.1416                    1/4″ pitch = .250″
             2                              .250
     ─────────                        ─────────
        6.2832 squared                  12500
        6.2832                        . 500
     ─────────                        ─────────
       12.5664                         .062500
      188 496                        39.478602
     5026 56                         ─────────
    12566 4                          39.541102 ( 6.288 +
   376992                            36
     ─────────                       ─────────
      39.4786 0224               122 ) 3 54
                                      2 44
                                    ─────────
                                 1248 )1 1011
                                      9984
                                    ─────────
                                12568 ) 102702
                                      100544
Length of one coil
    = 6.288″
        48 coils
     ─────────
     50 304
    251 52
   ─────────
 12)301.824″
   ─────────
```

25.152 Ans., in feet and decimal of a foot.

To understand how to figure the contents of solid bodies is of the greatest importance to any mechanic. Frequently we wish to get some particular size and shape forged in the blacksmith shop and not having anything on hand of that particular shape, we have to take something smaller, larger, or, the shape may be quite different. It sometimes happens that we want a square block forged and we have to take a piece of round material to make it. The question then arises how long a piece will have to be cut off, so that we may get

what we want without waste of material, or without having it
too large, etc.   Figure 5
is a block, we will say of
steel, as shown, 5″ square
and 3″ thick, and, as
shown before, the sur-
face measure would be
thus,

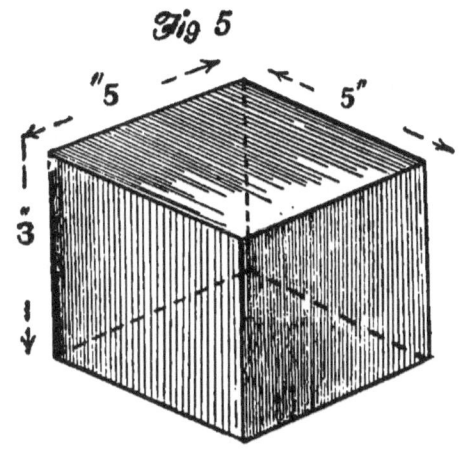

Fig 5

5″
5″
—
25″   this would be the
 3   number of square
——— inches, on the end
 75   only, and if it is
three inches deep or thick, we multiply this by three inches(3″)
giving 75.   This is the number of cubic inches in the block.
Or, the rule would be, to multiply the three dimensions together; if the figures given were inches, the answer would be
inches, and if they were feet, the answer would be feet, etc.
If the answer obtained were feet, multiplying by 1728 would
give the number of cubic inches.   Figure 5 therefore has 75
cubic inches.

Now Figure 7 is a round piece of 4″
diameter; let us see how many inches
of this it would take to make figure 5.
In any round piece we square the diameter and multiply by .7854; this gives the
surface of one end only, thus,

$4^2 = 4$ ·   .7854
          4   16
         ———   ———
          16   47124
                       7854
                      ———
                      12.5664

Always remember to cut off as many figures in the answer
as there are decimals, which is four in this case.   Now there

are a little more than twelve and a half inches (12½″), and dividing the seventy-five (75) by the twelve and a half, will give the length of a round piece of 4″ diameter, as shown in Figure 7.

```
12.56 ) 75.000 ( 5.97″+   Ans.
        62.80

        12 200
        11 304

           8960
           8792
           ────
```

Now if we were to get this forged to finish we would have to change our sizes or we would not get what we wanted; instead of calling the block that we intended to finish 5″, we would say 5.2″ square, or more, and 3¼″, or more, in length, depending upon the accuracy of the forging. There is also a little waste in the forging of anything in the fire, but that does not usually amount to much on small pieces.

Figure 6 is 2½″ × 3½″ and 5½″ long; what is the contents in cubic inches ?

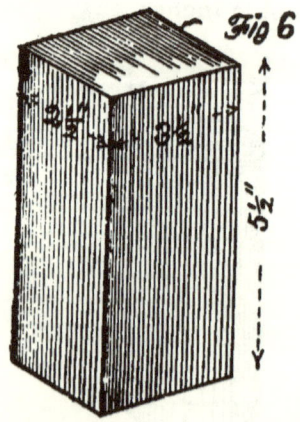

Fig 6

```
3.5
2.5
──
17 5
70
──
8.75 square inches.
5.5 long.
──
4375
4375
────
48.125 cubic inches.
```

Figure 8 represents a round ball, say 4¼″ in diameter What is the number of cubic inches in the ball?

Cube the diameter and multiply by .5236 :

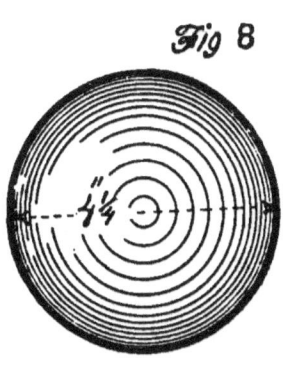

Fig 8

```
        4.25
        4.25

       21 25
       85 0
      1700

      18.06 25
       4.25

      903125
      361250
      722500

      76.765625
       .5236

      460593750
      230296875
      153531250
      383828125

      40.1944812500    Answer.
```

Figure 9 represents a ring of round steel or iron, say 12″ inside diameter and made of 2½″ iron; what is the number of cubic inches in the piece? To the inside diameter of the ring, which is 12″, add the thickness of metal 2½″ which makes 14½″, and this sum multiplied by 3.1416 :

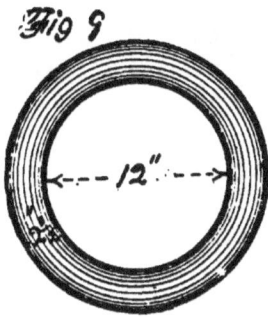

Fig 9

3.1416
14.5
———
157080
125664
31416
———
45.55320 = the length of ring.
4.908+
———
36442560
40997880
18221280
———
223.57510560   Answer.

2.5 Diameter of ring
2.5
———
125
50
———
6.25
.7854
6.25
———
39270
15708
47124
———
4.908750 sq. inches at end of ring; if cut open and this multiplied by the length of ring, it will give the answer in Cubic inches.

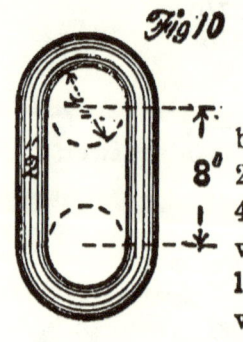

Fig 10

Figure 10.   This is an eliptical ring, 8″ between centers, 4″ inside diameter, and 2″ iron; what is the cubic contents of link? 4 + 2 = 6″, the average diameter of link, which multiplied by 3.1416 will give the length of the two ends if placed together with the center (8″) taken out.

3.1416
6
———
18.8496   Now add the two center pieces of 8″ or 16″
16
———
34.8496 = the whole length of piece.

The area of the ring is 2 × 2 × .7854 = 3.1416 and this again multiplied by the length, thus, 34.849+ × 3.1416 = 109.427 cubic inches in the ring.

Figure 11 represents a cone 6″ diameter at the base and 14″ high. What is the number of cubic inches in the piece? 6″ Diameter of base. The height is 14″

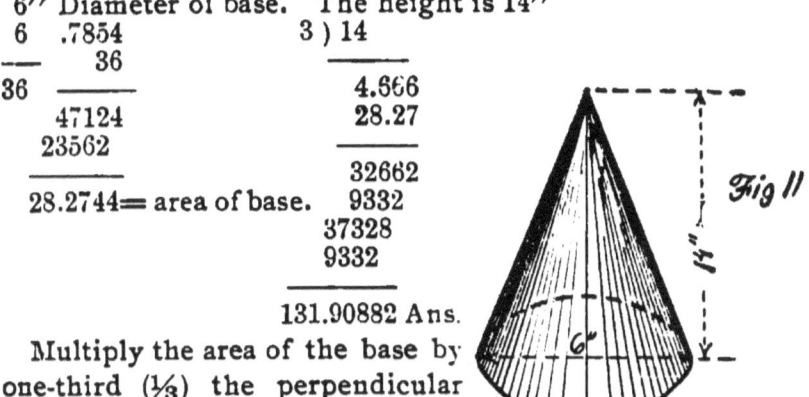

Fig 11

6	.7854		3) 14
36			
36	47124		4.666
	23562		28.27
			32662
28.2744= area of base.			9332
			37328
			9332

131.90882 Ans.

Multiply the area of the base by one-third (⅓) the perpendicular height.

The following two examples are similar (in shape) although not round, to figure 9. Suppose we want to make a ring gear that is to be shrunk on a cast iron center, or flange. The ring is to finish 24¼ inches outside diameter and 22⅞ inches inside diameter and 1¼ inches wide. In a ring as large as this there should not be less than ⅛ of an inch all over to finish. The best way to do a piece of work of this kind is to cut from a bar a piece that, when split through the center and opened up round, there will be no weld, leaving the ring solid throughout. The question now is, how large a piece shall we use to make this ring?

If we make it ⅛″ large all over, then the ring forged would be 24½″ diameter outside and 22⅝″ diameter inside and 1½″ wide; then 22⅝ from 24½ leaves 1⅞″, and one-half of this will be the right thickness of the ring when forged. But if we can get a bar 1⅞″ × 1½″, it will be just right when opened up, for there is very little waste in this kind of work. The ring when forged will be about 1⅓″ × 1½″ (in section). We will now have to find the solid contents or cubic inches in this ring before we cut off the bar, for we might make a mistake and cut it off an inch or two too long or too short. We first find the diameter of the ring midway between the inside and outside diameters, which would be about 23¹³⁄₁₆″ or 23.812 inches diameter, and multiplied by 3.1416 = 74.8 + inches long. As a section of the ring be ¹⁵⁄₁₆″ by 1½″, we multiply this together, thus, ¹⁵⁄₁₆ = .938 and 1½ = 1.5, then .938 × 1.5= 1.4 + square inches of section in the ring. We then multiply the length by the area or section, thus, 74.8 × 1.4 = 104.7 cubic inches in the forged ring. Now, as the rough bar is 1⅞″ × 1½ inches, we will have to find the area (or cross section), thus, 1⅞ = 1.875 and 1½ = 1.5, then 1.875 × 1.5 = 2.8 + inches area. We now divide the cubic contents of the forged ring by the area of the rough bar, thus, 104.7 ÷ 2.8 = 37.2 + inches in length, or, say 37½″ that we would have to cut from a bar 1⅞ × 1½ to make the ring.

We want to make a steel ring that will finish 16½″ outside diameter and 14¾″ inside diameter and 1¼″ wide. What size bar shall we use and what should be its length?

Allowing ⅛″ all over to finish, then the forged ring will be 16¾ × 14½ inches, and, measured as before through the center of its section, will be about 15⅝″ diameter; then 15.875 × 3.1416 = 49.87 + inches for the length of ring. As the forged ring should be 1½″ wide, the cross section of this ring would be one-half (½) the difference between the inside and outside diameter, multiplied by 1½, or thus, 1.12 + × 1.5 = 1.68 + square inches of section. Then, 49.87 × 1.68 = 83.7 + cubic inches in the ring when forged. Our bar should then be the difference between the outside and the inside diameter, or 2.25 inches by 1½″; then the area will be 2.25 × 1.5 = 3.37 + inches. Then 83.7 ÷ 3.37 = 24.8″ Answer.

TRIGONOMETRY.

Trigonometry is the science of determining the sides and angles of triangles by means of certain parts which are given.

It is of the greatest importance that every machinist, and more especially those who work to close measurements, should fully understand this science.

In this work I propose to treat of right angled triangles only, as I believe this will be sufficient for all purposes.

An angle is the opening between two lines that meet each other. The point at which they meet is called the Vertex; thus in Figure 12, A is the vertex of the angle.

In Figure 21, when speaking of the angle A, or whose vertex is at A, remember to always say the angle B A C or C A B ; in other words, the letter that is placed between the other two is the angle to be considered. If at any time we see on a drawing an angle similar to Figure 21, with the words written, the angle A C B, or B C A, we would know without asking any questions that the angle was 90 degrees, as shown.

The size of an angle does not depend on any length, but the rapidity with which the lines separate from each other.

Adjacent angles are so called from their having a common vertex ; thus, in Figure 17 B is the vertex of both angles and B D a side of both angles ; consequently either angle is adjacent to the other, that is, the angle C B D is adjacent to the angle D B A.

Angles are measured by making their vertex the center of a circle, and computing the arc that is included between its sides.

The circumference of any circle is divided into 360 equal parts, called degrees, each degree into 60 equal parts, called minutes, and each minute into 60 equal parts, called seconds.

TANGENTS.

A tangent is a straight line that touches a curve. In connection with an angle, the tangent of an angle is a straight line that touches the circumference of a circle at one end, and extending out to and meeting a secant at the other. It is always at right angles (or perpendicular) to the radius.

A secant is a straight line that is drawn from the center of a circle and, proceeding through the circumference, meets with a tangent to the same circle.

A sine is a straight line drawn from the end of an arc and

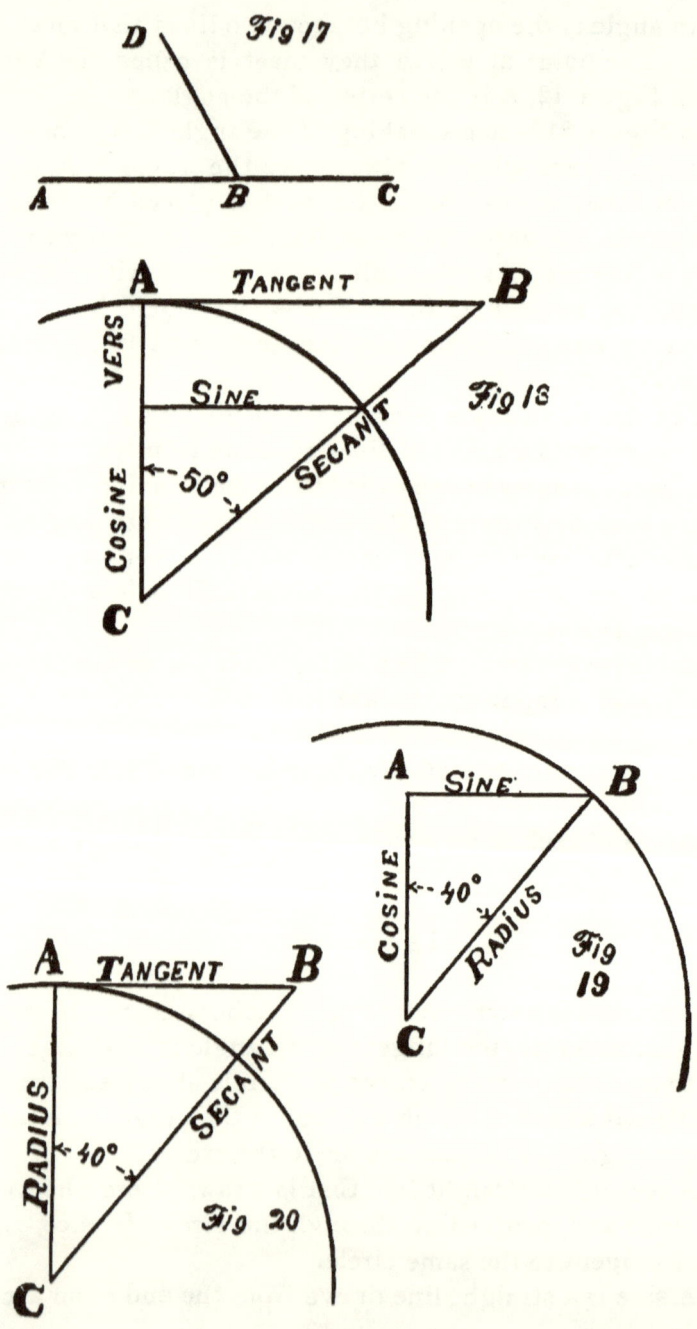

touching a line perpendicular to the diameter at the other end.

The cosine of an arc or angle is a line extending from the sine to the center.

The versed sine of an arc or angle is a continuation of that part of the radius from the cosine to the circumference.

Figure 18 will more fully explain the positions of the tangents, sines, cosines, secants, etc., with reference to the arc and angle, and always refers to the angle at the center of the circle, or as shown at C, which in this case is 50 degrees. In any triangle, right angled or otherwise, there are always two (2) right angles; consequently in Figure 18 the angle A C B being 50 degrees, then the other acute angle (there are always two in every right angled triangle), whose vertex is at B, is the difference between 50 and 90 degrees, which is 40 degrees, and this is always called the complement of the angle; that is, in speaking of any right angled triangle, suppose we find one of the acute angles to be 20 degrees, then the complement of that angle would be 70 degrees.

A Chord is a straight line joining the extremities of the arc of a circle, and when passing through the center is equal to the diameter of that circle.

The Chord of an angle is found by doubling the sine of half that angle; that is, if we want to know the chord of 50° we find the sine of 25° and double it.

A tangent is always outside of the arc or circle, as shown in Figure 18, and the sine is always within the circle.

In Figure 19 I have shown a right angled triangle, in which the radius of the circle corresponds to one of the sides of the angle.

Now, let it be remembered that when the distance C B (which is the longest line) of any right angled triangle is known, then the line A B is always the sine, and A C is always the cosine of the angle.

Remember, also, that if the arc was removed that either C or B may be used as the vertex of the angle. In the figure (19) C is the vertex of the angle A C B, then the lines

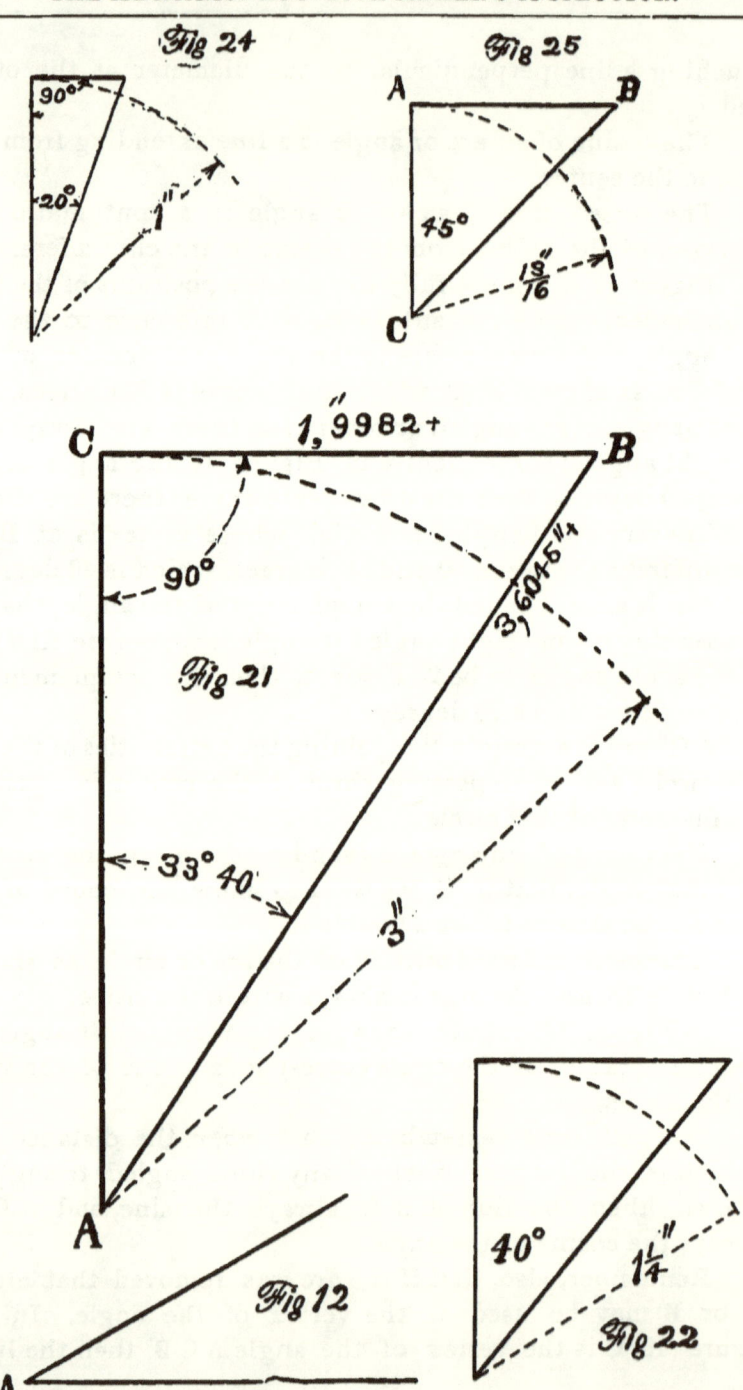

Fig 24

90°

20°

1"

Fig 25

A

B

45°

13/16"

C

1,9982+"

C

B

90°

3,6045 1/4"

Fig 21

33° 40'

3"

A

Fig 12

A

40°

1 1/4"

Fig 22

marked sine and cosine are correct, but if we were to figure the complement of this angle, then the vertex of the angle would be at B, the sine and cosine would then exchange places, because the sine never touches the vertex of the angle while the cosine always does.

Remember that when the longest line of the angle is known that it is then called radius, and that the other two sides are always sine and cosine.

In Figure 20, which is similar to Figure 19 (as regards the angle), when the distance A C is known, then A B becomes tangent, and B C the secant of the angle.

Remember that when the longest line is not known it is always the secant of the angle.

Remember, also, that if the arc of the circle was removed that either A B or A C can be called radius (that is, if the distance of either one of them was known). The length or distance of the one known is called radius; thus, when the distance A C is known it is called radius, and A. B. becomes the tangent of the angle, but if A. B. was known it would be called radius, and A C the tangent of the angle A B C.

In other words, where we figure tangents, the longest line of the angle is always the secant.

And when we figure sines, the longest line of the angle is always the radius.

Also that radius and tangent are perpendicular, or at right angles to each other.

And that the sine and cosine of an angle are always at right angles to each other.

In the trigonometric tables that will follow this chapter we take the radius of 1 and, for convc ience, we usually say one (1) inch.

In Figure 21 the radius of the angle is marked 3 inches, and the angle is 33° 40'. In the table of tangents we find that the angle 33° 40' corresponds with the decimal .666+, which means that for every inch in length of the radius, that the tangent is .666+ inches in length; therefore, multiplying this decimal by 3, we have 1.998+ for the length of the tangent.

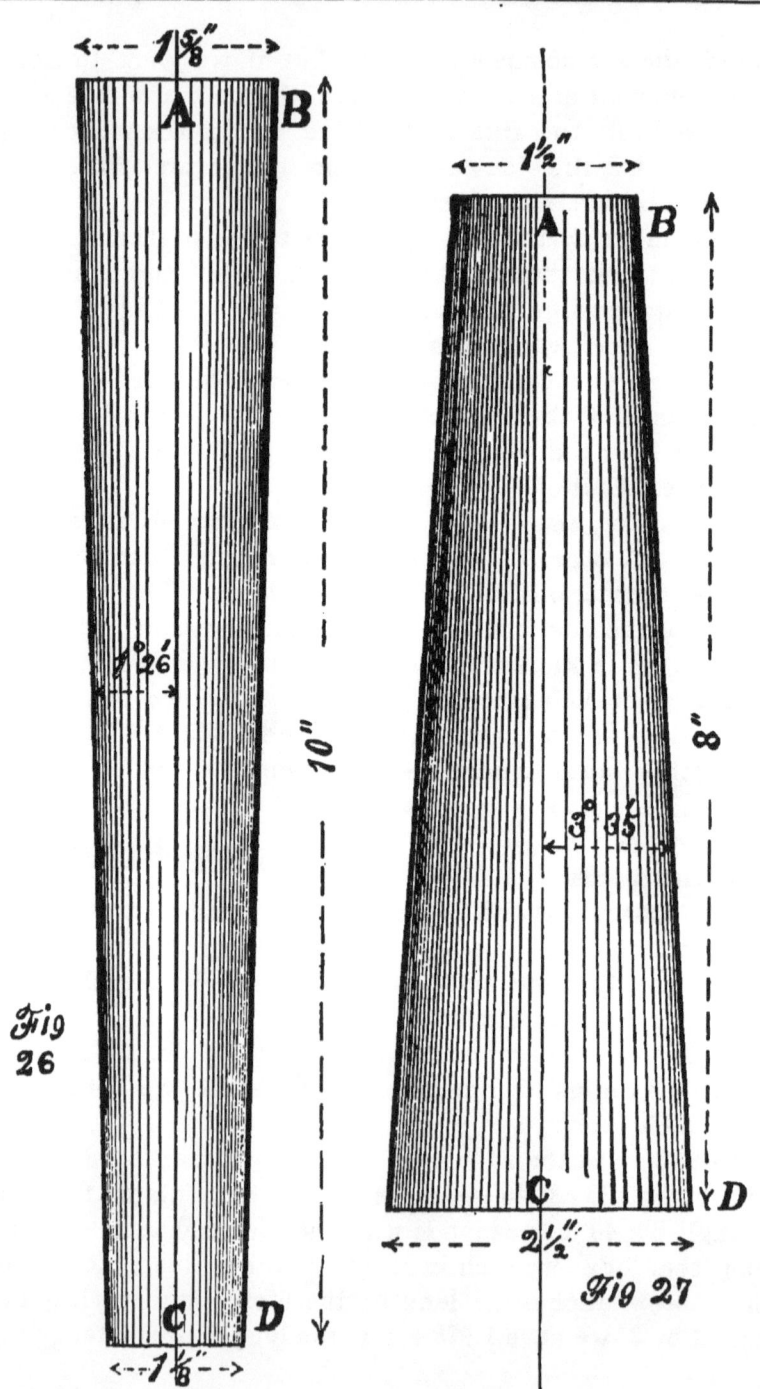

Fig 26

Fig 27

In the table of secants we find the number 1.201 + opposite 33° 40′, which means that for every inch in length of the radius that the secant is 1.201+ inches; therefore, multiplying this number by 3, we have 3.603+ inches for the length of A B.

As the angle C A B is 33° 40′, the complement of this angle must be 90° — 33° 40′ = 56° 20′.

Figures 22, 24 and 25 are respectively 60°, 20° and 45°. Find the lengths of their tangents and secants. You will find in the table of tangents for 45° that 1 is the number given, which always means that the tangent is equal in length to radius.

In Figures 26 and 27 we have two pieces of taper work, which is a very common thing in the machine shop. Figure 26 represents a piece 10 inches long (through its axis), and tapers from 1⅛″ to 1⅝″, which is just ½″ taper in its whole length. Then, dividing ½″ or .500″ by 10 inches, we have .050″ for one inch long; but we only want one side of the taper and, consequently the taper for one inch would be .025″. In the table of tangents we find the angle 1° 26′ to correspond with this number (.025), and this would be the angle to turn or grind the piece.

In Figure 27 the taper is from 1½″ to 2½″, or one inch to 8 inches in length; this would equal .125 to each inch, or .0625 inches for one side, and the tangent .0625 corresponds to the angle 3° 35′, which is the correct angle to set over the table on the Universal Grinding machine, or the taper attachment on the lathe, as the case may be.

It must not be forgotten that if told to turn or grind a piece of work 2° taper, that in the machine you would set it for 1° only; the taper of Figure 27 is, therefore, 7° 10′.

Now, if you were given a piece of work, say like figure 27, to turn 8 inches long and 1½″ diameter at the small end, the other end not being given, you would naturally want to know, the first thing, how large the piece would be on the other end. As the angle given would be 7° 10′, take ½ of this, or 3° 35′. In the table of tangents opposite 3° 35′ you will find the

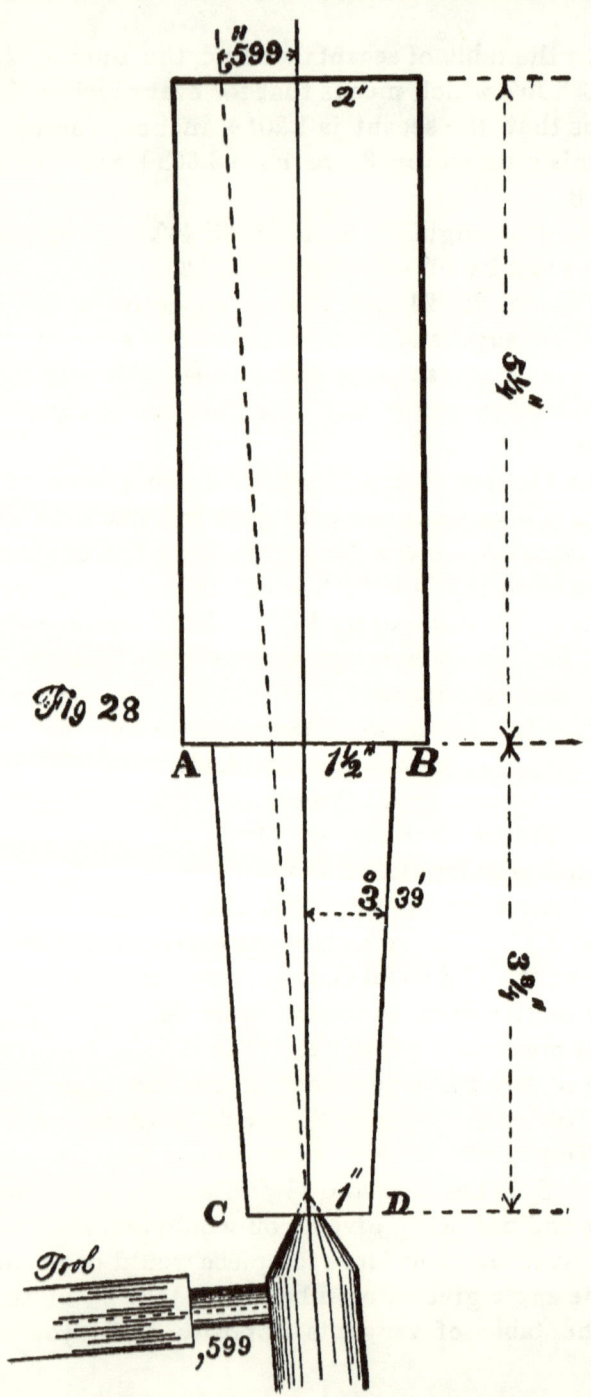

Fig 28

decimal .0626, which, multiplied by the length, 8″, = .5008, then double this and it will tell you how much larger the piece must be on the other end.

Figure 28 is also a piece of taper work quite common in the machine shop. In this case the taper does not extend the whole length of the piece.

In turning with a taper attachment or grinding by swiveling the table of a Universal Grinding machine, the angle of the piece is all that is required; that is, if the piece is longer or shorter, it makes no difference in the angle. But if turned in the lathe by setting the tail stock over, then, if a number of pieces are turned taper, they will all have to be the same length, otherwise their tapers will vary. The tail stock should not be set over (out of alignment) if possible, as it is hard to get a piece of work accurate in this manner, for the reason that the center has but little bearing surface. If such is required, however, Figure 28 will show a very good way to do it if accuracy is desired.

The drawing shows that the taper is to be ½″ to 3¾″ in length, or ¼″ for one side; then, dividing ¼″ or .250 by 3.75, we have the decimal number .0666 + for the taper to one inch in length, and multiplying this by the whole length of the piece, which is 9 inches, we have .5994″, which is the distance that the tail stock center will have to be moved over. Now file a piece of wire to the micrometer caliper of this length, and, placing a tool with a smooth end in the tool post, with this piece between it and the center, then slack the screws and first take out the piece of wire (.599″), then move the center over until it just touches the tool, then clamp the center firmly, and you will have but little trouble in fitting the piece by filing.

POLYGONS.

We now come to a class of work that is almost an everyday occurrence, at least in some shops. Suppose that we want to turn a piece of work that will be large enough to mill a hexigon 3½″ across the flat sides. In Figure 29 the distance A B is, of course, 1¾ inches, and is the radius of the angle A B C of 30°; then B C is the secant, and in the table of secants we find that the secant of 30° is 1.154 +, which, multiplied by the radius and doubled, or by the diameter, thus, 1.154 × 3.5 = 4.039 inches, the diameter across the corners. In

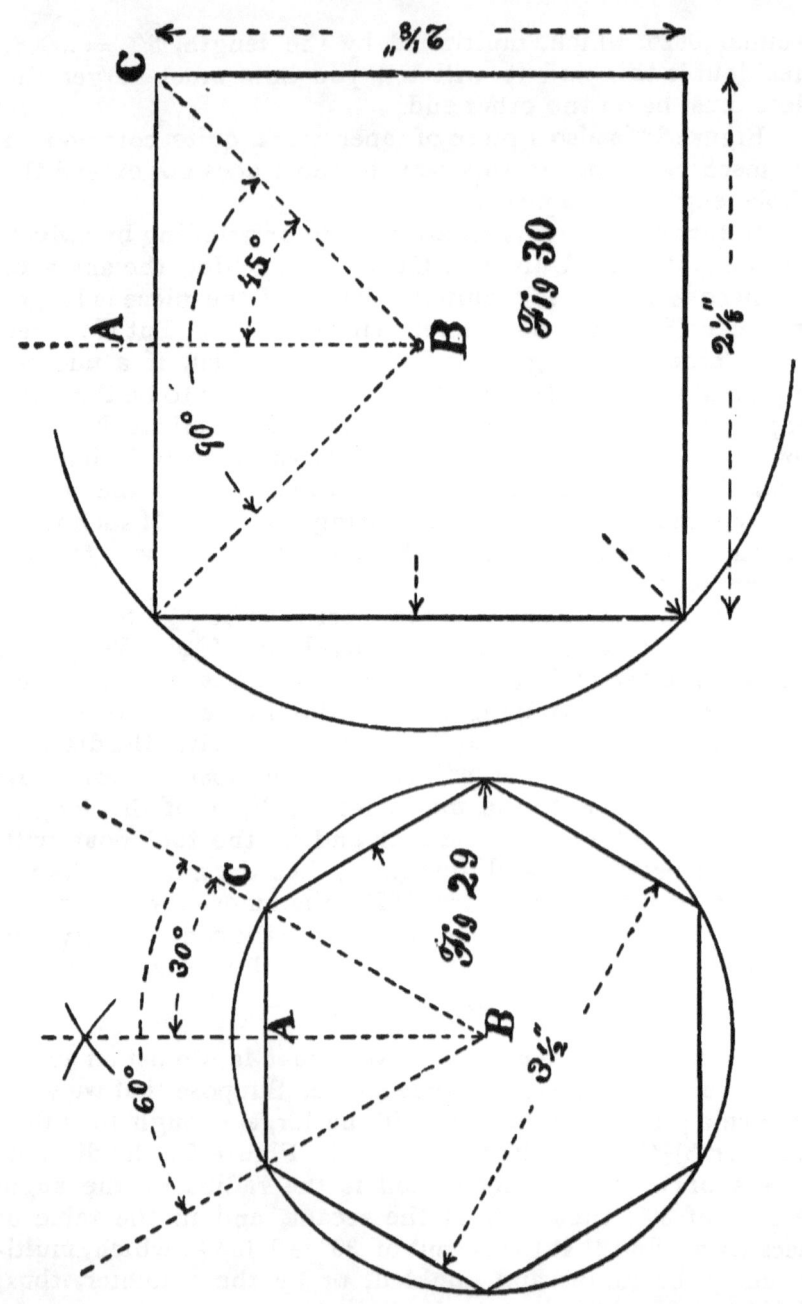

other words, to find the diameter across the corners of any size of hexagon (six sides), multiply the secant of 30° by the diameter across the short side (or flat).

Or, if you have a round piece of steel and want to know how large a hexagon you can mill on it, multiply the cosine of 30° by the diameter of the piece, and the result is the width across the flat side.

Figure 30 represents a piece 2⅛ inches square.

To find the diameter across the corners of any given square, multiply the secant of 45° by the diameter required across the flat side. Thus, in Figure 30 the square required is 2⅛ inches, and the secant of 45° is 1.414, which, multiplied by 2⅛, = 3.003, the answer across corners.

To find how large a square we can make from any piece of round material: Multiply the cosine of 45° (.707 +) by the diameter of the piece given, and the result is the width across the flat side, or the size of square.

Figure 31 represents an octagon or eight sided figure (or polygon).

To find the diameter across the corners of any size octagno: Multiply the secant of 22½ degrees = 1.082 + by the diameter required across the flat side. Thus, suppose that Figure 31 was to be 3 ins. across the flat side, then 1.082 × 3″ = 3.246 inches across corners etc.; or, suppose that we have a round piece of stock and we want to mill it to the shape of an octagon. Then multiply the cosine of 22½° = .9239, by the diameter of the stock, and the result is the diameter across the flat (sometimes called the short diameter. Thus, if we have a piece of round stock 2″ in diameter, .9239 × 2 = 1.847 + for the size of octagon that could be made from a round piece 2 ins. in diam.

Figure 32 is also a polygon of ten sides, generally called a decagon.

Example: We want to mill a piece 2½″ across the flat

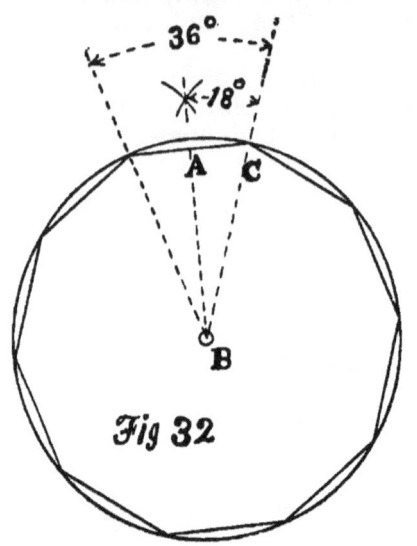

Fig 32

side (the short diameter). How large a piece of round stock will be required to make it? Multiply the secant of 18° = 1.051 + by the flat diameter required; thus, if we want it to measure 2½″ across the flat sides, 1.051 × 2.5 = 2.628, for the diameter across the corners, etc.

To find the diameter across the flat side of any decagon that many be required, multiply the cosine of 18° = .951 by the diameter of the round piece; thus, a piece of round stock two inches in diameter will make a decagon .951 × 2 = 1.902 inches for the short diameter.

Figure 33 is a polygon of twelve sides (called a dodecagon. Having the short diameter (across the flat sides), to find the diameter across the corners multiply the secant of 15° = 1.035 by the diameter across the flat side.

To find how large a dodecagon we can make from a round piece of any given size, multiply the cosine of 15° = .966 by the diameter of the round piece required.

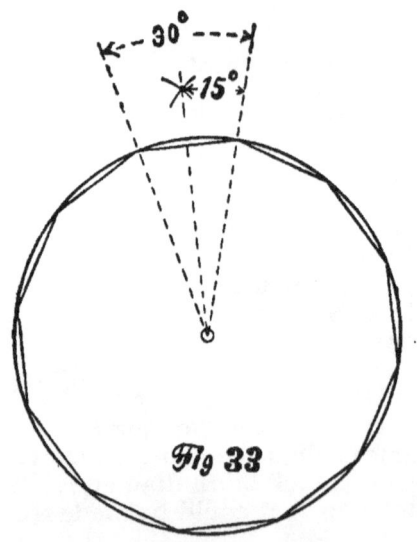

Fig 33

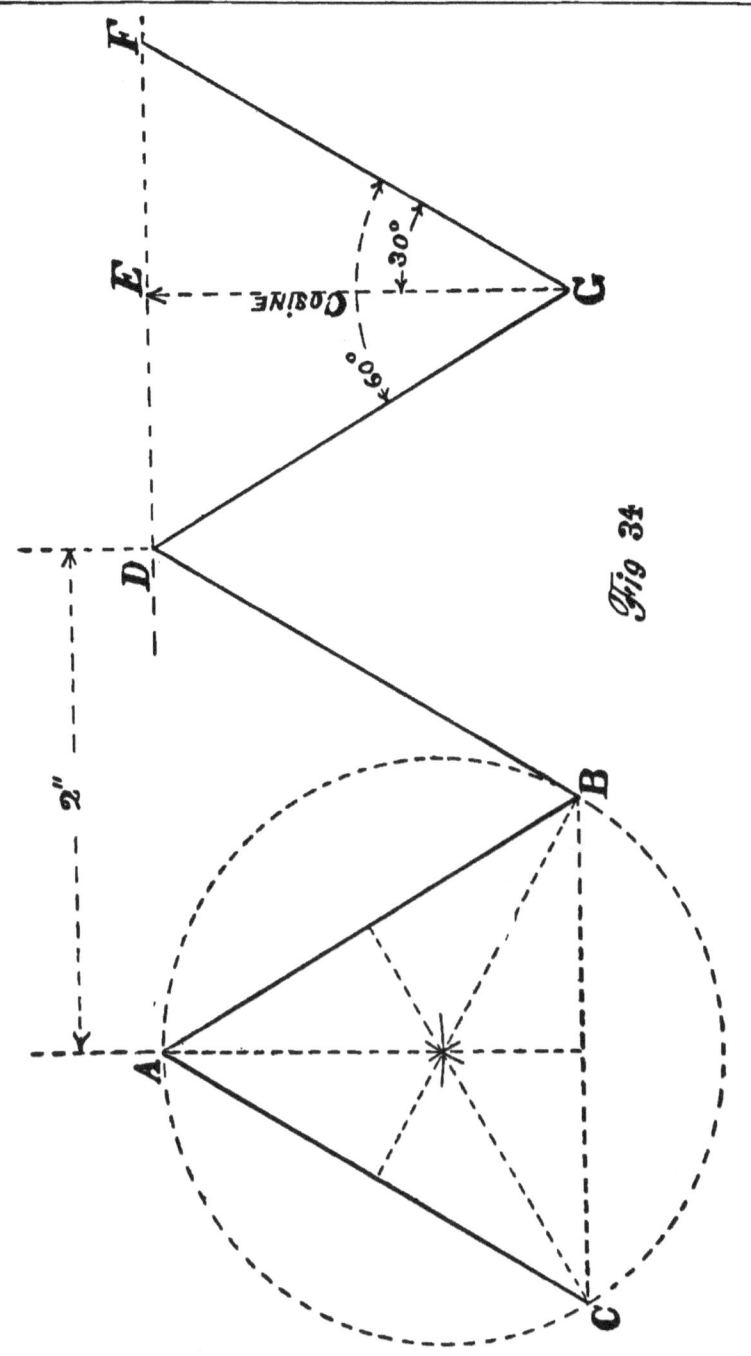

Fig 34

SCREW THREADS.

There are three forms of screw threads now generally used in making taps, dies, machine screws, etc., and it is very important at times to know the exact depth of the thread.

In Figure 34, I have shown the common sharp V thread, in which the surfaces are inclined toward each other at an angle of 60°. A section of this thread, A B C, forms an equilateral triangle, each side of it being equal to the pitch of the thread (that is, in the figure the pitch A D is of the same length as A B or B C), and its depth, measured perpendicular to the axis, is found by multiplying the cosine of the angle of 30° = .866 by the pitch of the thread; thus, in a tap of eight threads per inch the pitch of the thread (or distance between two consecutive threads) is ⅛ inch, or .125″, then .866 × .125 = .10825″; this, then, is the depth on one side only, so that in any thread of ⅛″ pitch, or eight threads per inch, the depth of both sides together would be twice this, or .2165″.

The most convenient way, however, to find the depth of both sides is to double the cosine .866, and we then have the constant number 1.732, and this number divided by the number of threads per inch of any V shape threads, will be the answer; thus, 1.732 ÷ 10 threads per inch = .173″ for ten threads; 1.732 ÷ 40 = .043 for 40 threads.

Suppose we have a screw 6 inches diameter and we want a thread of 1 inch pitch cut on it (sharp V style), what will be the diameter of the screw at the bottom of thread? 1.732 ÷ 1 = 1.732; then 6″ − 1.732 = 4.268″, Answer.

If we have a tap one inch in diameter and ten threads per inch, then 1.732 ÷ 10 = .1732; and 1″ − .1732 = .826, the answer (or diameter at root of thread).

Figure 35 is the shape of the United States standard, or the Franklin Institute thread (sometimes called the Seller's system), and the depths of threads are found in the same manner as the sharp V, and then subtracting ¼ of the whole

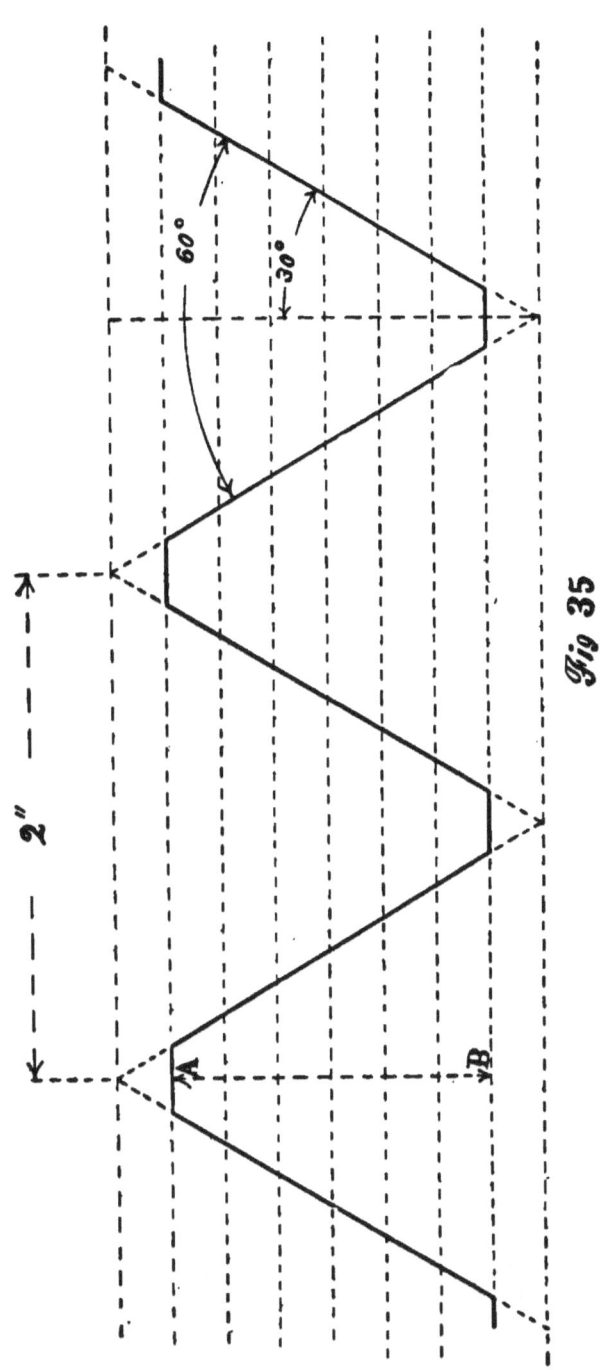

Fig 35

depth; thus, in the sharp V thread, four threads per inch, the depth on both sides is .433″, and for the U. S. standard it will be .433″ — ¼ = .325″, Answer.

Figure 36 represents the Whitworth or English Standard shape of thread, the angle of which is 55°, as shown. We cannot find the depth of C B in this shape of thread in the same manner as shown in the previous examples, for the reason that the distance, A B, is not the same as A D and, consequently, we have only the angle and distance C A (which, of course, is one-half the pitch) to work from ; we therefore call the distance C A of the right angled triangle the tangent, and C B the radius. Now, in the table of tangents for 27° 30′ we find the decimal .5205 for the length C A, when C B or radius is one inch, and as C A in the figure is just one inch, then we know that C B is nearly two inches, or just what .5205 will go into 1. Thus, 1 ÷ .5205 = 1.921 for the depth C B. In the Whitworth threads 1/6 is rounded off on the top and bottom of the threads, so that we will have to deduct ⅓ of this full depth; thus, 1.921 — ⅓ = 1.281 inches for one side, as shown in the figure.

In Figure 37, which is a departure from the original intention of confining to right angled triangles, I have shown a class of work that you may be called upon to perform at any time, that is, to key a pair of levers on a shaft so that they will stand at an angle of 80° to each other (or anything similar).

Now, if the angle A B D is 80°, then we can easily see that by making the small acute angle B A C we will have a right angled triangle, A C D. The object now is to find the length of A D (between centers). If we know this distance, by placing a pin in each of the holes A D we can make an end gauge by means of the micrometer caliper or vernier, and get it almost exact to the proper angle.

We know the lengths A B and D B, but as we are now confined to a right angled triangle we must know the distances A C and D C, and to do this we must calculate the sides A C and B C of the right angled triangle B A C. As the

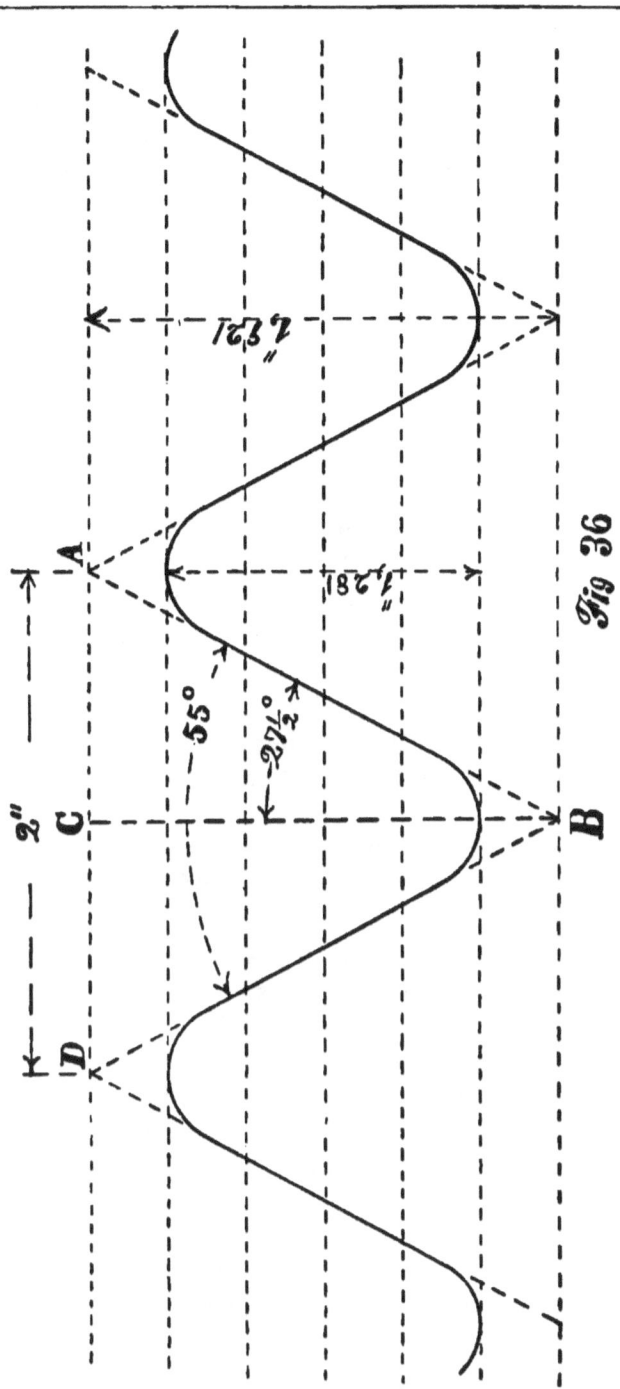

Fig 36

longest side, A B, is given as 4″, then B C is sine, and C A cosine of the angle of 10°. In the table of sines we find the number .1736 opposite 10°, then multiplying thus, .1736 × 4 the radius = .694, the distance B to C; and in the table of cosines we find the number .985 nearly which, multiplied by the radius (A B) 4″ = 3.94 as the distance A C.

The distance D C is now 5½″ — .694 = 4.806 inches.

The length A C is 3.94 inches, as before explained; we now have a right angled triangle, but we do not know what either of the acute angles are, and we can call D C or A C radius; one of these sides will be radius and the other tangent. Let us call D C radius, then A C is tangent to the angle A D C.

We now divide the tangent A C (or 3.94) by the radius D C, or 4.806, which = .8198, or the tangent to the radius of 1 inch, and in the table of tangents we find this number to correspond with the angle 39° 21′.

Having found the angle, we now find the secant of 39° 21′, which is 1.2932, which, multiplied by the radius 4.806 = 6.214+, the answer, or distance between centers D A.

The following is another method, provided great accuracy is not required.

In the same example, where two levers are to be keyed on a shaft, let Figure 38 represent the end of the shaft, which has a fine line lengthwise, say at B, and we want to make another line lengthwise at D, that will be just 80 degrees from B.

The object now is to find the exact distance in a straight line from B to D in order to get the line lengthwise on the shaft at D.

As the shaft is 2½″ in diameter, then in the angle A C B the radius is 1¼″, and A B is the sine of the angle (40°.)

The sine of 40° = .6428, and multiplied by the radius 1¼ = .8033, or the distance A B in a straight line; twice this = 1.6066 inches, or the distance required D B. Having center lines on the two levers, and using a good new scale and a magnifying glass, very good results can be obtained in this manner.

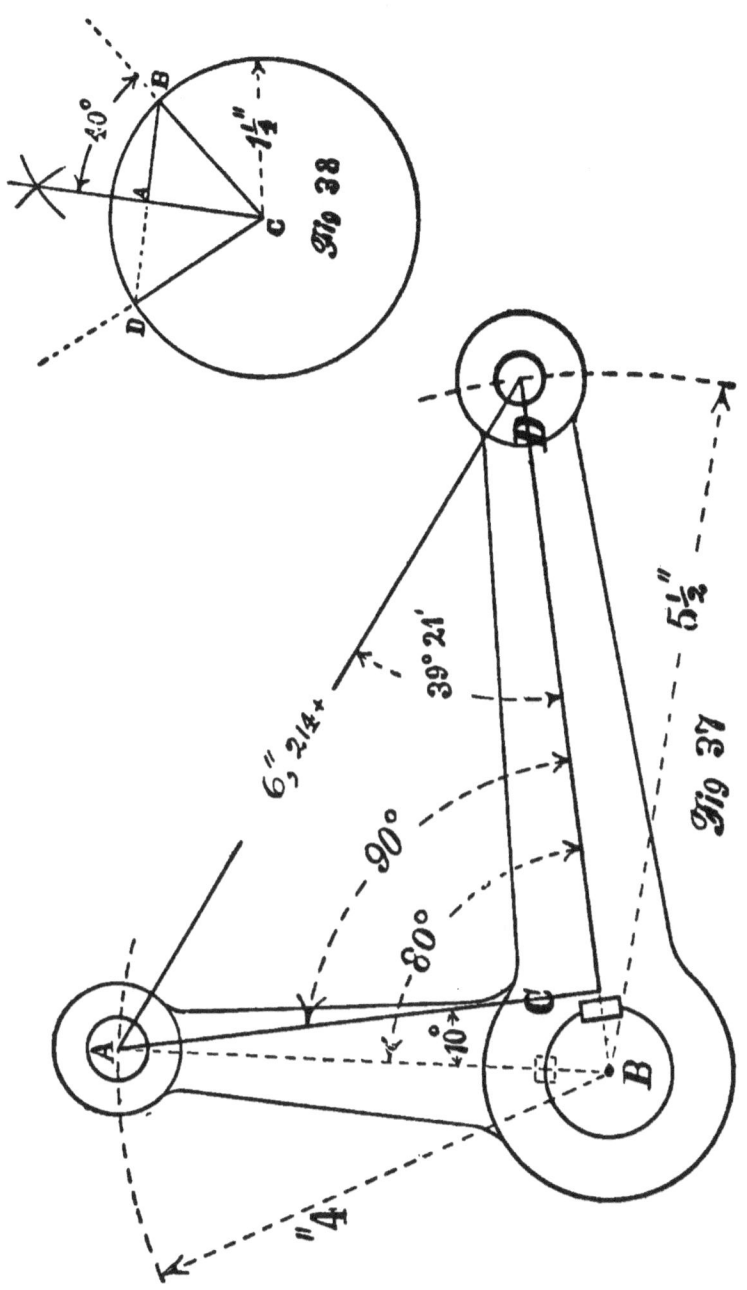

Figure 40 is similar to Figure 37, except that in the latter the two levers form an acute angle, while in the former (Figure 40) they form an obtuse angle. Suppose these two levers are to be keyed on the shaft F and at an angle of 120 degrees, as shown. How shall we proceed to get this accurate? We will first get a surface plate and level up one of the levers (A) by means of parallels, so that a line through the center, C D, will be parallel with the surface plate, as shown. And as 180° form a half circle, we know that the lever, B, should be 60° from D, then, as the length of the lever B is 6½'' (between centers), which is radius to the angle E F G, the line E G becomes the sine of that angle. The sine of 60° = .866, which, multiplied by the radius 6½ = 5.629 inches, and, adding this to the height (whatever it may be raised) from the center of the shaft to the surface plate, (in this case 2¾''), it will make exactly 8.379 inches; now place a pin in the lever at E, 1¼ inches diameter, and with an end gauge 8.379 less one-half the diameter of this pin, or 7.754 inches (total length) will be the exact distance between the plate and the pin at E. Another way is to take the distance from the side of the shaft shown at I by means of a square and finding the distance, I E; now, as F G is the cosine of the angle E F G and the cosine of 60° = .5, then the distance F G is one-half the length of radius or 3¼''', and, added to one-half the diameter of the shaft, will be 4.500 inches, or the distance from the center of E to I, as shown.

Figure 41 is an example of lathe work that is impossible for anyone to do correctly who does not understand plain trigonometry, and yet it is very simple, as I will show you, by that process.

Suppose we have a plate and want to turn a groove on one side of it just large enough so that eleven (11) balls, each one-quarter (¼) inch in diameter, will lie in the groove neatly or just fill it. How large will it be?

A great many not accustomed to work of this kind would, at first thought, naturally think that the circumference through the center of the balls would be eleven one-quarter

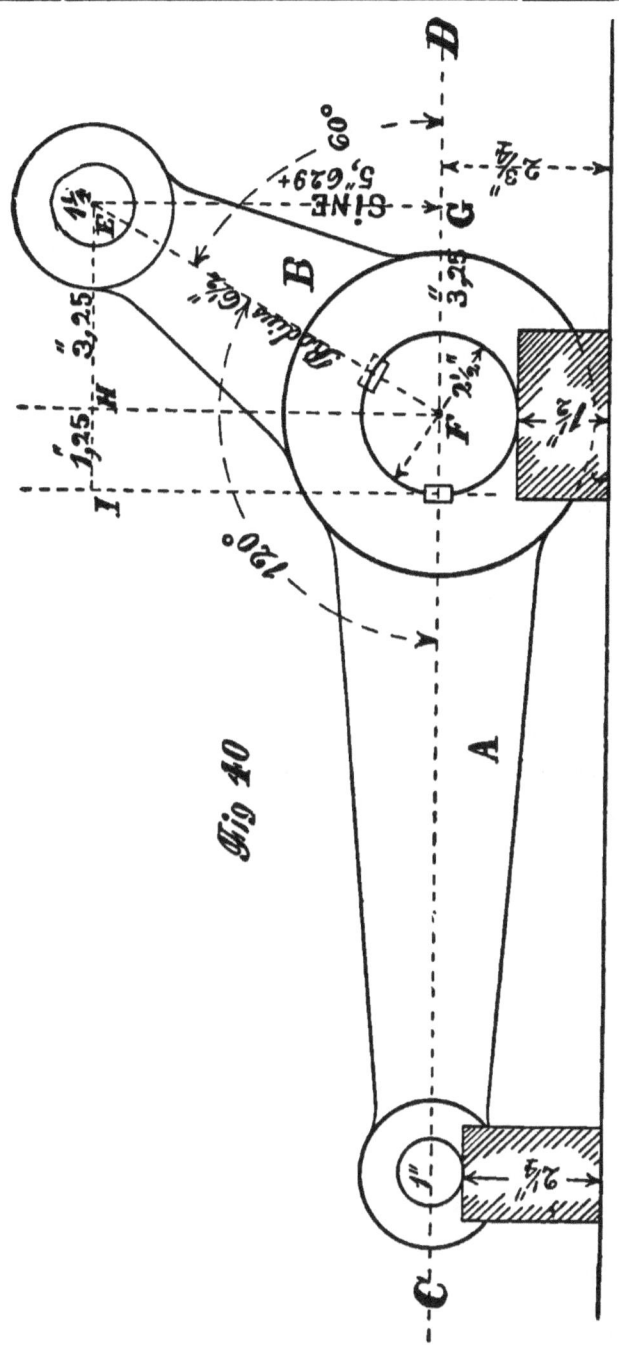

Fig 40

inches, but this is a mistake, as a glance at the figure, which is greatly enlarged, will show that the balls will touch only on the line A C and not on the circle D E.

In an example of this kind no drawing is necessary. In any circle there are 360 degrees and, dividing this by twice the number of balls required, we produce a right angled triangle, as shown.

In this example, dividing 360° by twice the number of balls (22) = 16° 22′ nearly.

We now have an angle of 16° 22′, and we know the sine to be one-half the diameter of the ball, or .125; then, in the table of sines and opposite 16° 22′, we find the decimal .2817, which means that A C would be .2817 to every inch of B C, and 1 × .125 ÷ .2817 = .4437, or the length B C; then twice this = .8874, and the diameter of the ball added to this = 1.137 inches for the outside diameter of the groove.

Required the outside diameter of a groove that will admit 12 1½ inch balls without play.

360° ÷ 24 = 15° for the angle; as the balls are 1½″, then the sine of this angle = .750. In the table of sines and opposite 15° we find the decimal .259; then .750 ÷ .259 = 2.895 + ″ for the distance from the center of the circle to the center of the balls; then, 2.895 × 2 = 5.790 and the diameter of the ball added = 7.290 inches, the answer.

Figure 42 will show how to find the length of a (cross) belt when the size of the pulleys and their center distances are known. One side only of the belt is shown, and by drawing a line, A B, parallel from B, we form the angle C B A. As the distance A B is known we call it radius, and the belt, C B, the secant, and A C the tangent of the angle; we know the tangent, because it is equal to one-half of the diameter of the large pulley added to one-half the diameter of the small pulley = 28 inches, and 28 ÷ 74 (the radius) = .3784 + = the tangent to radius of 1, and in the table of tangents we find this number to correspond with the angle 20° 44′; then the secant of this angle equals 1.069, which, multiplied by the radius (74″) = 79.121 nearly ; twice this length added to one-half

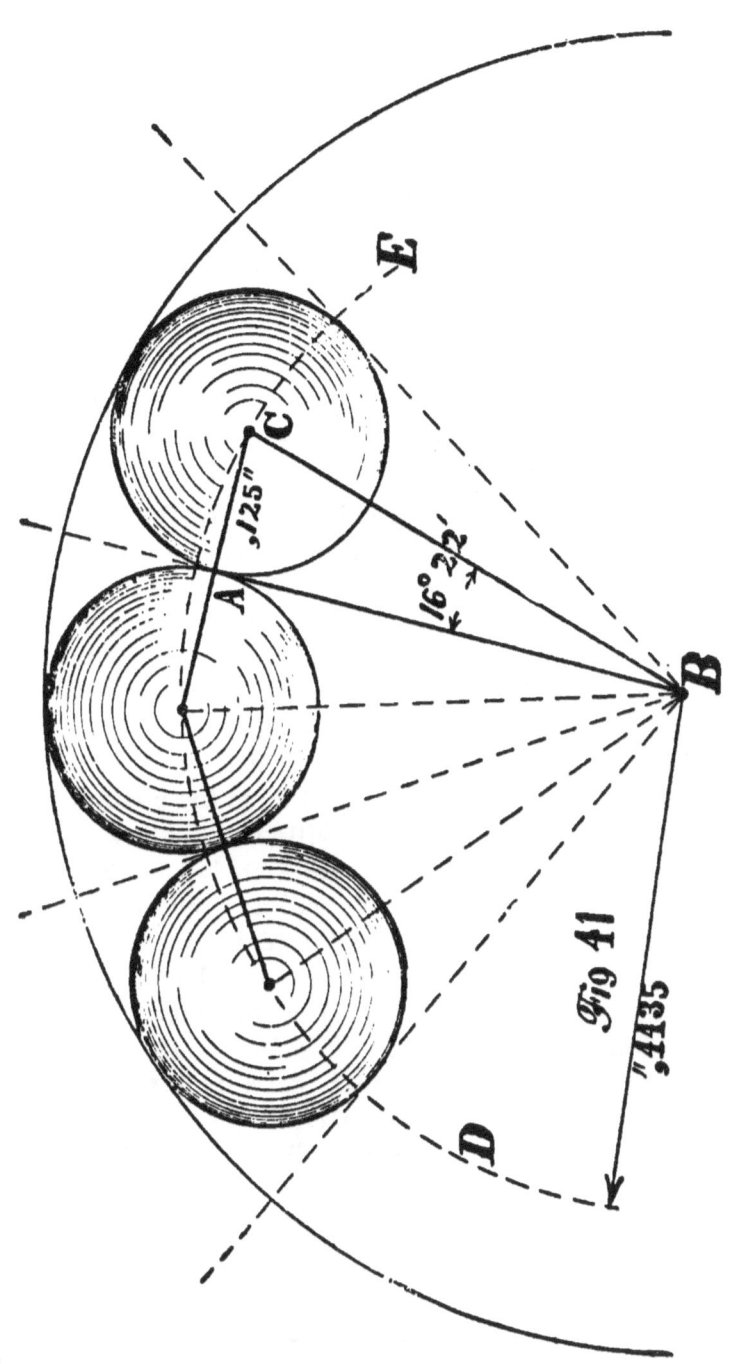

Fig 41

the circumference of both pulleys = 246,206 inches for the total length of the belt. It will be seen from the figure that the belt does not meet at the center of the pulleys, B C, but this slight difference need not be noticed.

Figure 43 is similar to Figure 42, except that the former is an open belt, but otherwise the dimensions are found in the same manner. Thus, the dotted line, B C, is parallel to the centers of the two pulleys and is the radius to the angle C B A; the difference between half the diameters of the pulleys equals the tangent, which is 8″; then 8″ ÷ 74″ = .1081 or the tangent to a radius of 1 inch, and in the table we find this number to correspond to the angle 6° 10′, and the secant of this angle = 1.0058, which, multiplied by the radius 74 = 74.429 for the length of one side or A B; then twice this length, added to one-half the circumference of both pulleys =236.8 inches for the answer, or total length of the belt.

In nearly all our modern machine tools the cones on the feed shafts, that are usually but a short distance from the cone on the main spindle, have their steps turned, as shown in Figure 44; that is, each step is made ¼″, ⅜″, ½″, or uniformly increasing in diameters, and it can easily be seen by the figure that if the belt is changed from the position shown to the center of the cones that it will be too slack.

The dimensions of the cones are each 4, 6 and 8 inches for the diameters of their steps. We will now find the difference in the length of belt required for the center speed and the end of the cones. The difference between one half the diameters of the smallest step and one-half the diameter of the largest step is 2 inches, as shown; then 2″ ÷ 16″ = .125″, or the tangent of the angle A B C, which corresponds to the angle 7° 8′ ; the secant of this angle, as per table, is 1.0078, which, multiplied by the radius (16″) = 16.124″ for one side or A B, and twice this = 32.250 inches nearly, or about one-fourth inch too long for the center speeds. On long belts this little difference would not make any trouble, but when they are very short they should be made so that the tension of the belt will be the same throughout. It is very easy to see that

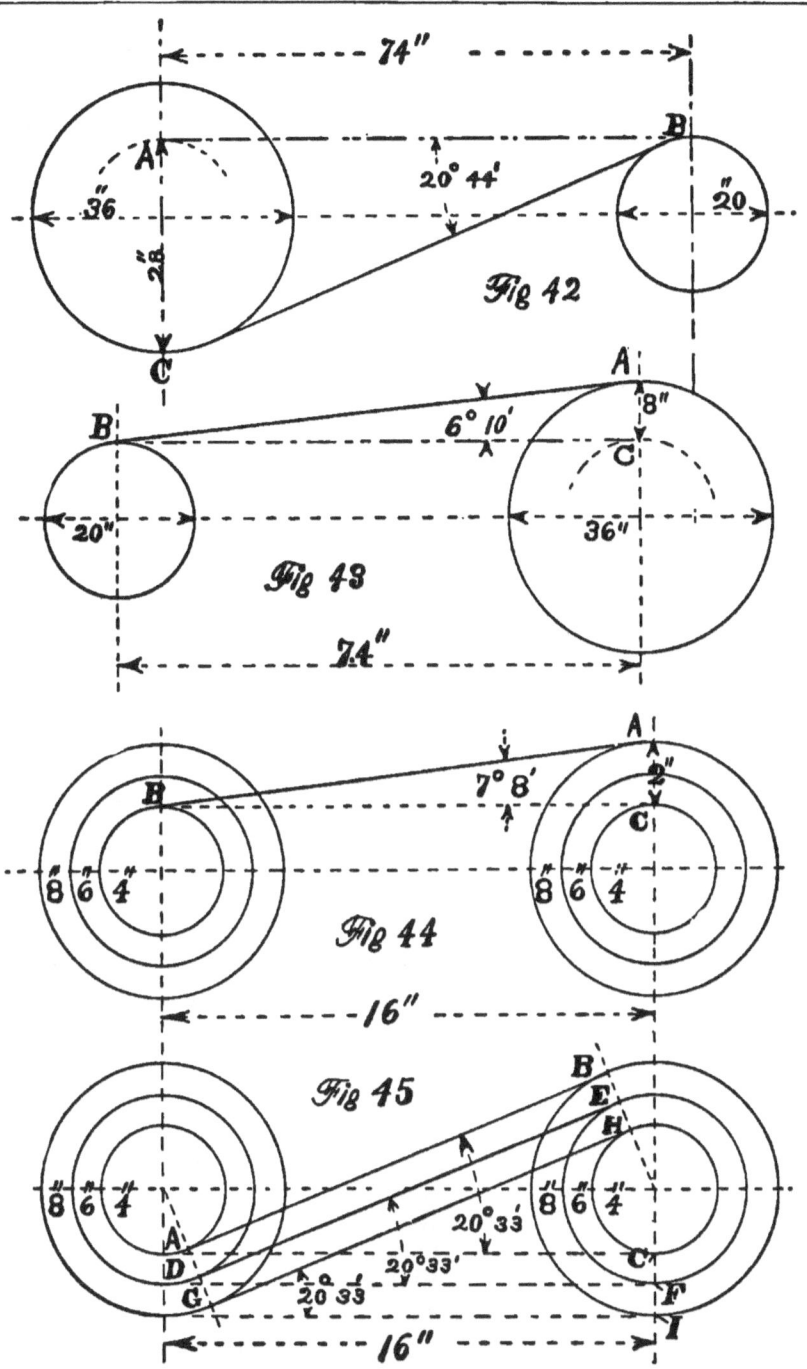

Fig 42

Fig 43

Fig 44

Fig 45

in this case (Figure 44) that one-half of the circumference of both center steps ought to be exactly .125 of an inch longer, or .250″ in the whole circumference greater than shown in the figure. Thus, the circumference of 6″ = 18.849, and adding .250 we have 19.1 nearly, and dividing by 3.1416 = 6.079″, or about $6\frac{5}{64}$ for the diameter.

Figure 45 represents the same dimensions of cone and distances as in Figure 44, but in the former we have a cross belt; it can readily be seen that wherever the belt is placed that the angles are the same; when the diameters are uniform as shown, the radius of the angles are 16 inches and the tangents are each 6 inches; then 6 ÷ 16 = .375, or the tangent to radius of one inch, which in the table corresponds with the angle 20° 33′, and the secant of this angle = 1.068 nearly, which, multiplied by the radius 16″ = 17.086″ for the length of one side, as A B, etc.; then twice this length, added to one-half the circumference of any pair of steps, as shown, will be the total length of belt, or about 53.02″, the answer.

This answer will not be strictly correct, for the reason (shown in diagram) that the belt will not be in a straight line to the center of the steps and, consequently, it will be a little longer than the figures given, but this need not be taken into consideration, except when the differences of their diameters are very great, which seldom happens in practice.

It sometimes happens that in an example like Figure 44 that the middle steps are not of the same diameter; thus, suppose we have .250″ to be divided proportionately between the center steps of two cone pulleys, the diameter of which are 8 and 10 inches respectively; then 8 + 10 = 18, and one should have 8/18 and the other 10/18, or, what is the same thing, 4/9 and 5/9 each of the .250″. Generally it would not make any difference if the whole amount were to be added to either one of the pair. It will be seen from Figure 45 that in making cone pulleys for similar purposes shown that the diameters of their steps may increase uniformly if cross belts are to be used, but not for open belts, to secure good results.

In making jigs and templates it is sometimes necessary (in order to obtain good results) that we know the distances in straight lines and in different directions between holes, etc.

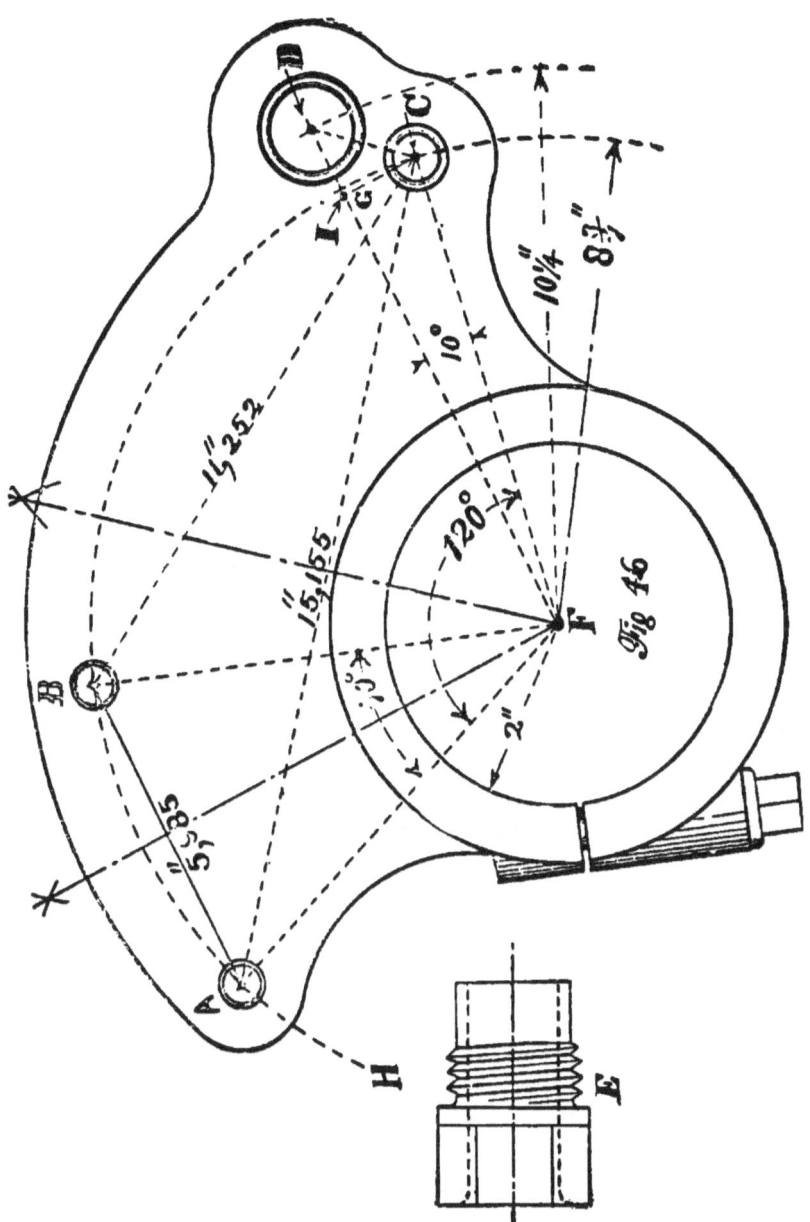

Fig 46

In Figure 46 I have shown a template in which three sets of holes, A B D, are to be drilled and reamed in a flange (nine holes in all); the flange has a hub 4 inches diameter, and the template is bored to suit this hub and is fitted with a binding screw, as shown, to hold it securely in any position.

As there are to be three sets of holes, A, B, D, then after the first set is finished we will have to slack the binding screw and turn the template exactly 120°. But in order to know when it is exactly at that angle and at the same time to hold it in that position, we will make an extra hole (C); then, after the holes, A B D, are completed in the flange, a pin in the template at C is fitted to the hole in the flange at A, and it is then ready to drill the next three holes, etc.

This is very easy to do when the template is at hand, but the first thing to do is to make the template and to know how to make it correctly; it makes no difference what hole we start from to get the 120°. If we start from B we will have to make the template larger, and if we start from D we would have to build up on the template above A and to the left of it; by starting from A, as shown, we have less to add to the template than from any other place. Now, in boring holes in jigs and templates, if not too large, they should always be done in the lathe, if accuracy is required, because it is almost impossible in any drill press to bore a hole and find it true (at right angles to the surface of the plate being drilled or bored), and even when the drill press is in good condition when new, after using it for some time it will get out of shape. But, wherever done, in the lathe or drill press, a piece of cast iron (or something similar) should be turned four inches diameter to fit the template at F, and a plug to fit the spindle in place of the center, projecting outside of the face plate an inch or two, and turned true and of some exact size; for convenience only, suppose this to be one inch, then as the holes, A B C, are 8¾ inches from the center, our block at F, which supports the template, can, by means of an end gauge 6.250 inches long placed between them, set the template in proper position to get this radius of 8¾″ correct. This is the first operation; the template should in the meantime have these holes laid off by dividers, etc. roughly (so that we may know about where to start the first hole). We will now drill and bore the hole at A. Never depend upon a drill to finish holes in tools of this kind, and if these holes are to be tapped, never depend on an ordinary tap to run straight, because they never will. Special taps with a pilot on the end that fits the hole closely should be used, or the thread should be finished or very nearly so with a tool in the tool post. If the thread is roughed out so that the tap will about enter, then it may be finished in this way, but the less you take out with the tap the better, and finishing with a tool is the best of all.   The hole, A, is now supposed to be finished and, before moving the template, fit a plug neatly in it (A).   The distance in a straight line, A B, or the chord A B of 40° is found by doubling the sine of half that angle; thus, the sine of 20° = .342, and multiplied by the radius = .342 × 8.75 = 2.9925, and twice this = 5.985, or the distance between the centers, A B.   If these two holes are to be the same size we will make an end gauge 5.985 inches long, and placing one end against the plug in A and the other end towards H., we will secure a block firmly on the face plate of the lathe and, touching this end gauge near H, now take away the end gauge and swing the template so that the plug at A will just touch the block near H, and bore the hole B.

If the template is ¾″ thick, then the block will have to be raised high enough to let it pass under.

The hole C can also be bored in a similar manner.   The distance, C B, in a straight line is found in the following manner: As A C is 120° and A B 40°, then B C is the difference between these two angles, or 80°, and the sine of 40° = .643, which, multiplied by the radius (8¾) = 5.626, and twice this = the chord of 80° = 11.252″ for the distance B C, as shown.   The hole D is 10° from C and is 10¼″ from the center.   We will move the center piece upon which the template is held at F and set it by an end gauge as before.   We will now find the distance in a straight line from the center of C to G, which is on the line D F; then, as C F is the longest line of the angle G F C and is 8¾ inches long, it is the radius of this angle, and G C is the sine; as the sine of 10° =

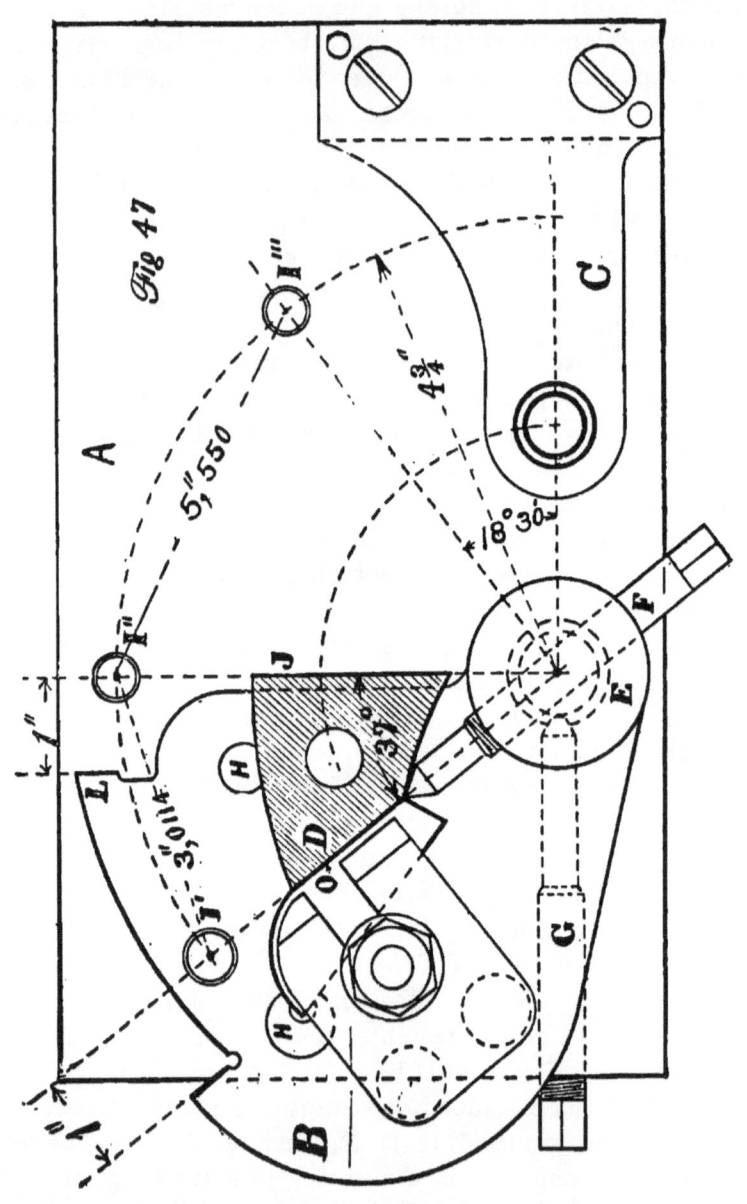

Fig 47

.1736, then multiplied by the radius $(8\frac{3}{4}) = 1.519$ inches for the answer.

A better way, perhaps, for locating the distances in this case would be to place the plug in the tail stock spindle (made to some standard size), as described, for the reason that it can always be moved out of the way, or brought up to the work just as close as occasion may require; the end gauge may then be used between this and a piece fitted in one of the holes already made, for the next operation, etc.

It is well known that close, accurate work cannot be done by the most skillful hand without accurate measuring tools, as, for instance, in making the end gauges just mentioned I would recommend that they be made of $\frac{3}{8}''$ or $\frac{1}{2}''$ round steel. Drill rods are the most convenient for this purpose, and an instrument that will measure 6 inches will be sufficient for most purposes, as we can sometimes use two or three pieces together to get the necessary length required.

In figure 46, E represents a bush, sometimes used for these templates. It is sometimes more convenient to have two or more of them fitted to the same hole, and by using threaded bushes (of standard sizes) we are enabled to use one with a plain hole, or we may want one with a tapped hole. The latter is far the better when tapping holes, and in this case the bushes should be made of extra length, and special taps would also wear better if made longer in the thread, and fluted for as short a distance as possible; the extra length of the bush will guide the tap better and will also prevent its wearing away so rapidly; they may be used without tempering.

Figure 47 represents a jig made for shaping the piece D, and also for drilling it, the surface shaded only being finished, including the two edges to form the angle of 37°.

The plate A is held in the vise of the shaper, while B, on which D is clamped, is free to swivel on A. The three successive positions, two to shape, and the third to drill (the last being the second operation after they are all shaped) are shown by the three holes I, I, I, in which a taper pin is used to hold the plate B in the proper position on A; there is also a pin E, with a large head, as shown, on which B swivels, and this pin is forced down hard by the screw G, the point of which bears on one side only of a V groove; this binds the two plates B and A firmly together after the dowel-pin is in place; the manner of holding D is shown by the screw F pressing it against the two pins H H, and also the clamp, as shown. The plate C is raised high enough to let D pass under to be drilled.

The work, D, as shown, is in the proper position for finishing the edge, shown at J. In taking the finishing cut an end gauge, one inch long, is placed against the finished surface L, and the tool set so as to touch the other end of this gauge. After this operation the taper pin is withdrawn and B is swiveled to the next hole I; while in this position the shaded surface is finished as well as the edge, shown at O.

Now, in boring these holes in the plate A, it should be swung from a pin on the face plate through the hole E, and the holes should be bored with a tool in the tool post, using the taper attachment; a taper plug should be used for sizing the holes. After both plates are bored in this manner, and put together, they may, by being careful, be slightly reamed to suit the taper pin.

If we know the distance in a straight line between these holes, by means of gauges, as before stated, we can, with very little trouble, make the jig accurate enough for most any purpose. As the angle calls for 37°, we first find the sine of 18° 30′, which is .317, then $.317 \times 4\frac{3}{4}'' = 1.5057$, and twice this $= 3.0114$ or the distance I' I''; and if the hole through C is parallel with E, as shown, and the hole through D is to be in the center, then I''' C, should be 18° 30′. The drawing is wrong, for it shows 37°, but the figures are right, and the angle I'' I''' or the opening between these lines will be the difference between 90° and 18° 30′ which is 71° 30′; the sine of half this angle which is 35° 45′ $= .584$, and multiplied by the radius $(4\frac{3}{4}) = 2.775$, then twice this sum $= 5.550$ for the answer, as shown.

Figure 48 shows a method of finding the size of a pulley (or anything similar) from a piece of the broken rim A B. Place the rim on a piece of paper and make the arc of a circle, as shown, A B, and in this arc make three or more circles, and at the points of intersection of these circles draw lines, and the point C, where these lines cross, is the center of the pulley, etc.

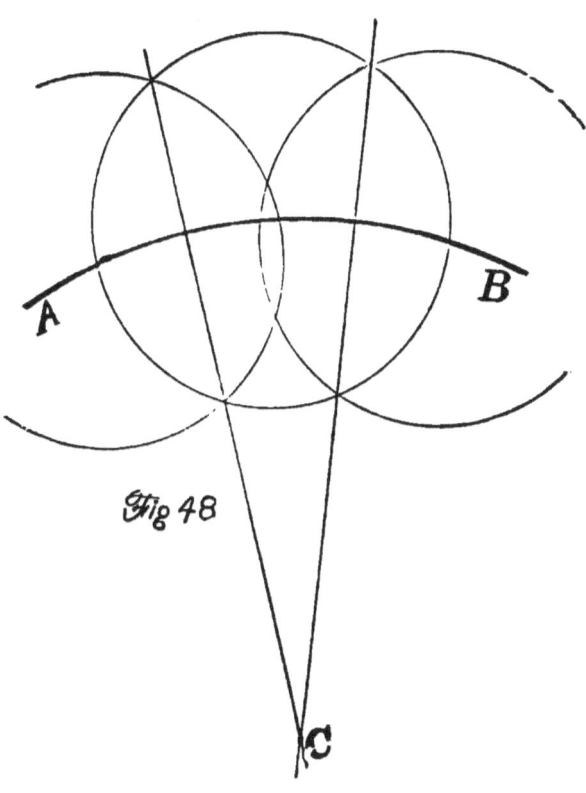

Fig 48

Figure 49 shows a method of setting a machine at right angles to the main shaft.

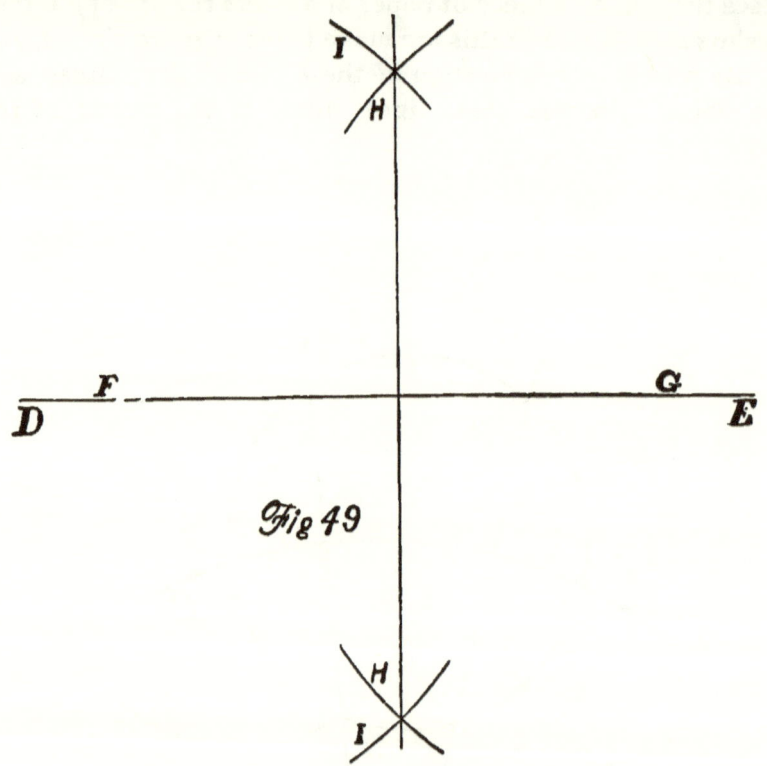

Fig 49

Drop a plumb line from the main shaft to the floor, and make a mark, D; from ten to twenty feet drop the line again and make another mark, E; with a good chalk line make the line D E on the floor; from two points on this line F G (anywhere to suit) make the arcs H H, I I, and, where these lines cross each other draw a line, then this line will be at right angles to the line D E, as shown.

Figure 50 represents a plate that is to have a number of holes bored through it, and two of these holes should be exactly six inches center to center, as shown, so that a pair of gears will run neatly on studs that are fitted to these holes. How shall we do this and know it to be correct?

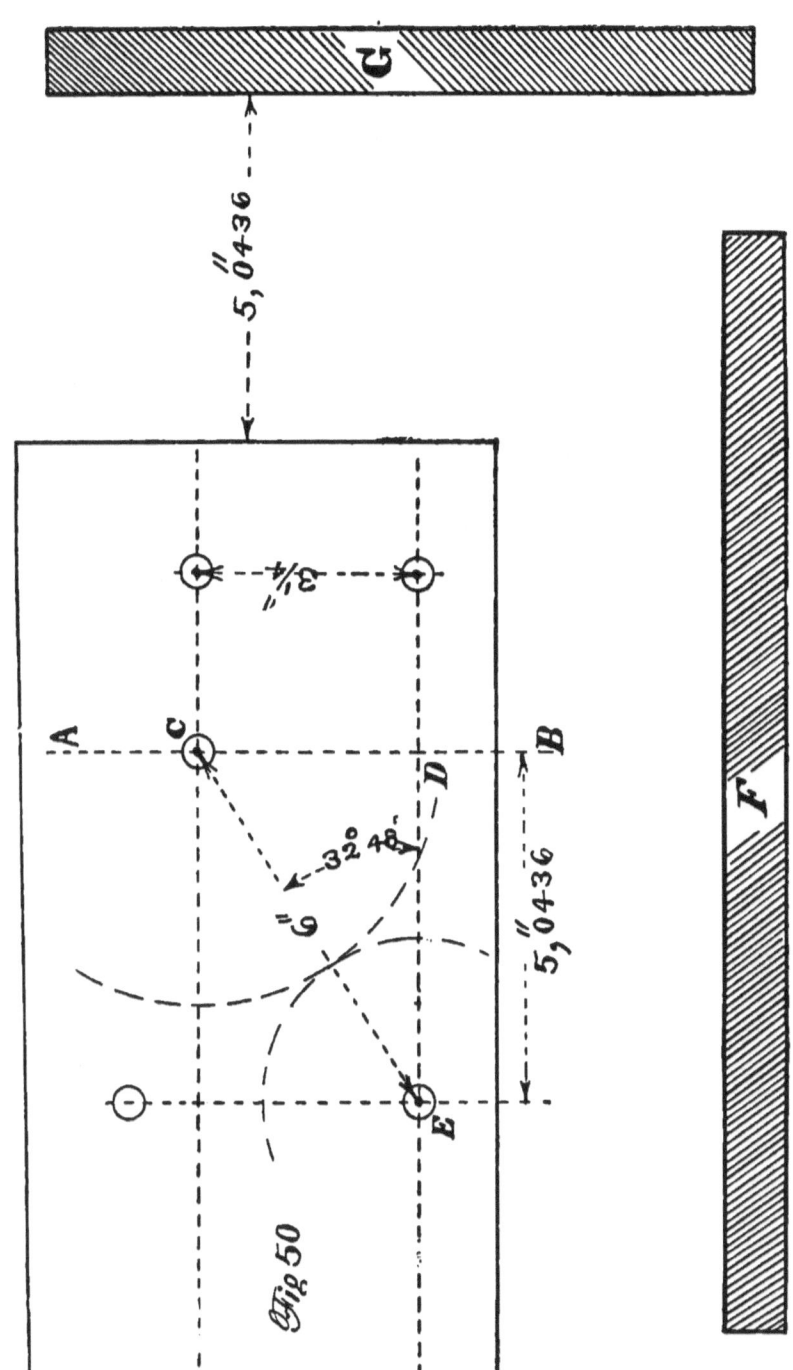

Fig 50

We have only to draw the line A B, and we have a right angled triangle C E D, the radius of which is six inches, and C D is the sine of the angle; dividing 3¼ by 6 we have the decimal .5416 which equals the sine to a radius of one inch. In the table of sines we find this number to correspond with the angle 32° 48′, nearly; then as C D is the sine, E D becomes cosine to this angle, and the cosine of the angle 32° 48′, as per table, is .8406, and multiplied by the radius (6″) = 5.0436 inches, as shown.

Now, if we know these dimensions, by clamping parallels F G either on the drill press table or the face plate of a lathe, and then letting the plate rest on the parallel F, with an end gauge 5.043″ long placed between the end and the parallel G, it will be in the proper position for boring the hole C; then move the plate against the parallel G, and with two end gauges made of good sized wire (or another parallel) placed between the plate and the parallel F, just 3¼″ long, it will then be in the proper position for boring the hole, shown at E, etc.

NATURAL SINES, TANGENTS, COSINES AND SECANTS.

		O Deg.					I Deg.		
MIN	SINE.	TANG.	COSINE.	SEC.	MIN	SINE.	TANG.	COSINE.	SEC.
0	.0	.0	1.	1.	0	.01745	.01745	.99984	1.0001
2	.00058	.00058	1.	1.	2	.01803	.01803	.99984	1.0001
4	.00116	.00116	1.	1.	4	.01861	.01862	.99983	1.0002
6	.00174	.00174	.99999	1.	6	.01919	.01920	.99982	1.0002
8	.00233	.00233	.99999	1.	8	.01978	.01978	.99980	1.0002
10	.00291	.00291	.99999	1.	10	.02036	.02036	.99979	1.0002
12	.00349	.00349	.99999	1.	12	.02094	.02095	.99978	1.0002
14	.00407	.00407	.99999	1.	14	.02152	.02153	.99977	1.0002
16	.00465	.00465	.99999	1.	16	.02210	.02211	.99975	1.0002
18	.00524	.00524	.99998	1.	18	.02269	.02269	.99974	1.0002
20	.00582	.00582	.99998	1.	20	.02327	.02327	.99973	1.0003
22	.00640	.00640	.99998	1.	22	.02385	.02386	.99971	1.0003
24	.00698	.00698	.99997	1.	24	.02443	.02444	.99970	1.0003
26	.00756	.00756	.99997	1.	26	.02501	.02502	.99969	1.0003
28	.00814	.00814	.99997	1.	28	.02560	.02560	.99967	1.0003
30	.00872	.00872	.99996	1.	30	.02617	.02618	.99966	1.0003
32	.00931	.00931	.99996	1.	32	.02676	.02677	.99964	1.0003
34	.00989	.00989	.99995	1.	34	.02734	.02735	.99962	1.0004
36	.01047	.01047	.99995	1.0001	36	.02792	.02793	.99961	1.0004
38	.01105	.01105	.99994	1.0001	38	.02850	.02851	.99959	1.0004
40	.01163	.01164	.99993	1.0001	40	.02908	.02909	.99958	1.0004
42	.01222	.01222	.99992	1.0001	42	.02966	.02968	.99956	1.0004
44	.01279	.01280	.99992	1.0001	44	.03025	.03026	.99954	1.0004
46	.01338	.01338	.99991	1.0001	46	.03083	.03084	.99952	1.0005
48	.01396	.01396	.99990	1.0001	48	.03141	.03142	.99951	1.0005
50	.01454	.01454	.99989	1.0001	50	.03199	.03201	.99949	1.0005
52	.01513	.01513	.99988	1.0001	52	.03257	.03259	.99947	1.0005
54	.01571	.01571	.99988	1.0001	54	.03315	.03317	.99945	1.0005
56	.01629	.01629	.99987	1.0001	56	.03374	.03375	.99943	1.0006
58	.01687	.01687	.99986	1.0001	58	.03432	.03434	.99941	1.0006

NATURAL SINES, TANGENTS, COSINES AND SECANTS.

	2 Deg.					3 Deg.			
MIN	SINE.	TANG.	COSINE.	SEC.	MIN	SINE.	TANG.	COSINE.	SEC.
0	.03489	.03492	.99939	1.0006	0	.05233	.05241	.99863	1.0014
2	.03548	.03550	.99937	1.0006	2	.05292	.05299	.99859	1.0014
4	.03606	.03608	.99935	1.0006	4	.05349	.05357	.99857	1.0014
6	.03664	.03667	.99934	1.0007	6	.05408	.05416	.99853	1.0015
8	03722	.03725	.99931	1.0007	8	.05466	.05474	.99850	1.0015
10	.03780	.03783	.99928	1.0007	10	.05524	.05532	.99847	1.0015
12	.03839	.03841	.99926	1.0007	12	.05582	.05591	.99844	1.0016
14	.03897	.03899	.99924	1.0008	14	.05640	.05649	.99841	1.0016
16	.03955	.03958	.99922	1.0008	16	.05698	.05707	.99837	1.0016
18	.04013	.04016	.99919	1.0008	18	.05756	.05766	.99834	1.0017
20	.04071	.04074	.99917	1.0008	20	.05814	.05824	.99831	1.0017
22	.04129	.04133	.99915	1.0008	22	.05872	.05883	.99827	1.0017
24	.04187	.04191	.99912	1.0009	24	.05930	.05941	.99824	1.0018
26	.04245	.04249	.99909	1.0009	26	.05989	.05999	.99820	1.0018
28	.04304	.04308	.99907	1.0009	28	.06047	.06058	.99817	1.0018
30	.04362	.04366	.99905	1.0009	30	.06104	.06116	.99813	1.0019
32	.04420	.04424	.99902	1.0010	32	.06163	.06174	.99810	1.0019
34	.04478	.04482	.99900	1.0010	34	.06221	.06233	.99806	1.0019
36	.04536	.04541	.99897	1.0010	36	.06279	.06291	.99803	1.0020
38	.04594	.04599	.99894	1.0010	38	.06337	.06349	.99799	1.0020
40	.04652	.04657	.99892	1.0011	40	.06395	.06408	.99795	1.0020
42	.04711	.04716	.99889	1.0011	42	.06453	.06467	.99791	1.0021
44	.04768	.04774	.99886	1.0011	44	.06511	.06525	.99788	1.0021
46	.04827	.04832	.99883	1.0012	46	.06569	.06583	.99784	1.0022
48	.04885	.04891	.99880	1.0012	48	.06627	.06642	.99780	1.0022
50	.04943	.04949	.99877	1.0012	50	.06685	.06700	.99776	1.0022
52	.05001	.05007	.99875	1.0012	52	.06743	.06759	.99772	1.0023
54	.05059	.05065	.99872	1.0013	54	.06801	.06817	.99768	1.0023
56	.05117	.05124	.99869	1.0013	56	.06859	.06876	.99764	1.0024
58	.05175	.05182	.99866	1.0013	58	.06917	.06934	.99760	1.0024

NATURAL SINES, TANGENTS, COSINES AND SECANTS.

	4 DEG.				5 DEG.		
MIN	SINE.	TANG.	COSINE.	SEC.	MIN	SINE.	TANG.	COSINE.	SEC.
0	.06975	.06992	.99756	1.0024	0	.08715	.08749	.99619	1.0038
2	.07034	.07051	.99752	1.0025	2	.08773	.08807	.99614	1.0039
4	.07091	.07109	.99748	1.0025	4	.08831	.08866	.99609	1.0039
6	.07150	.07168	.99744	1.0026	6	.08889	.08925	.99604	1.0040
8	.07208	.07226	.99740	1.0026	8	.08947	.08983	.99599	1.0040
10	.07266	.07285	.99736	1.0026	10	.09005	.09042	.99594	1.0041
12	.07324	.07343	.99731	1.0027	12	.09063	.09100	.99588	1.0041
14	.07382	.07402	.99727	1.0027	14	.09121	.09159	.99583	1.0042
16	.07440	.07460	.99723	1.0027	16	.09179	.09218	.99578	1.0042
18	.07498	.07519	.99718	1.0028	18	.09237	.09276	.99572	1.0043
20	.07556	.07577	.99714	1.0029	20	.09295	.09335	.99567	1.0043
22	.07614	.07636	.99709	1.0029	22	.09353	.09394	.99562	1.0044
24	.07672	.07694	.99705	1.0029	24	.09411	.09453	.99556	1.0044
26	.07730	.07753	.99701	1.0030	26	.09468	.09511	.99551	1.0045
28	.07788	.07811	.99696	1.0030	28	.09526	.09570	.99545	1.0046
30	.07846	.07870	.99692	1.0031	30	.09584	.09629	.99539	1.0046
32	.07904	.07929	.99687	1.0031	32	.09642	.09687	.99534	1.0047
34	.07962	.07987	.99682	1.0032	34	.09700	.09746	.99528	1.0047
36	.08020	.08076	.99678	1.0032	36	.09758	.09805	.99523	1.0048
38	.08078	.08104	.99673	1.0033	38	.09816	.09863	.99517	1.0048
40	.08136	.08163	.99668	1.0033	40	.09874	.09922	.99511	1.0049
42	.08194	.08221	.99664	1.0034	42	.09932	.09981	.99505	1.0050
44	.08252	.08280	.99659	1.0034	44	.09990	.10040	.99499	1.0050
46	.08310	.08338	.99654	1.0035	46	.10047	.10099	.99494	1.0051
48	.08368	.08397	.99649	1.0035	48	.10105	.10157	.99488	1.0051
50	.08426	.08456	.99644	1.0036	50	.10163	.10216	.99482	1.0052
52	.08484	.08514	.99639	1.0036	52	.10221	.10275	.99476	1.0053
54	.08542	.08573	.99634	1.0037	54	.10279	.10334	.99470	1.0053
56	.08599	.08632	.99629	1.0037	56	.10337	.10393	.99464	1.0054
58	.08657	.08690	.99624	1.0038	58	.10395	.10451	.99458	1.0054

NATURAL SINES, TANGENTS, COSINES AND SECANTS.

	6 Deg.					7 Deg.			
MIN	SINE.	TANG.	COSINE.	SEC.	MIN	SINE.	TANG.	COSINE.	SEC.
0	.10453	.10510	.99452	1.0055	0	.12187	.12278	.99254	1.0075
2	.10511	.10569	.99446	1.0056	2	.12245	.12337	.99247	1.0076
4	.10568	.10628	.99440	1.0056	4	.12302	.12396	.99240	1.0076
6	.10626	.10687	.99434	1 0057	6	.12360	.12455	.99233	1.0077
8	.10684	.10746	.99427	1.0057	8	.12418	.12515	.99226	1.0078
10	.10742	.10804	.99421	1.0058	10	.12475	.12574	.99219	1.0079
12	.10800	.10863	.99415	1.0059	12	.12533	.12633	.99211	1.0079
14	.10857	.10922	.99409	1.0059	14	.12591	.12692	.99204	1.0080
16	.10915	.10981	.99402	1.0060	16	.12648	.12751	.99197	1.0081
18	.10973	.11040	.99396	1.0060	18	.12706	.12810	.99189	1.0082
20	.11031	.11099	.99389	1.0061	20	.12764	.12869	.99182	1.0082
22	.11089	.11158	.99383	1.0062	22	.12822	.12928	.99174	1.0083
24	.11147	.11217	.99377	1.0063	24	.12879	.12987	.99167	1.0084
26	.11205	.11276	.99370	1.0063	26	.12937	.13045	.99159	1.0085
28	.11262	.11334	.99363	1.0064	28	.12995	.13106	.99152	1.0085
30	.11320	.11393	.99357	1.0065	30	.13052	.13165	.99144	1.0086
32	.11378	.11452	.99350	1.0065	32	.13110	.13224	.99137	1.0087
34	.11436	.11511	.99344	1.0066	34	.13168	.13283	.99129	1.0088
36	.11494	.11570	.99337	1.0066	36	.13225	.13342	.99121	1.0089
38	.11551	.11629	.99331	1.0067	38	.13283	.13402	.99114	1.0089
40	.11609	.11688	.99324	1.0068	40	.13341	.13461	.99106	1.0090
42	.11667	.11747	.99317	1.0069	42	.13398	.13520	.99098	1.0091
44	.11725	.11806	.99310	1.0069	44	.13456	.13580	.99090	1.0092
46	.11782	.11865	.99303	1 0070	46	.13514	.13639	.99082	1.0092
48	.11840	.11924	.99296	1.0071	48	.13571	.13698	.99075	1.0093
50	.11898	.11983	.99289	1.0071	50	.13629	.13757	.99067	1.0094
52	.11956	.12042	.99283	1.0072	52	.13687	.13817	.99059	1.0095
54	.12014	.12101	.99276	1.0073	54	.13744	.13876	.99051	1.0096
56	.12071	.12160	.99269	1.0074	56	.13802	.13935	.99043	1.0097
58	.12129	.12219	.99262	1.0074	58	.13859	.13995	.99035	1.0097

NATURAL SINES, TANGENTS, COSINES AND SECANTS.

	8 DEG.				9 DEG.			
MIN	SINE.	TANG.	COSINE.	SEC.	MIN	SINE.	TANG.	COSINE.	SEC.
0	.13917	.14054	.99027	1.0098	0	.15643	.15838	.98769	1.0125
2	.13975	.14113	.99018	1.0099	2	.15700	.15898	.98759	1.0125
4	.14032	.14172	.99010	1.0100	4	.15758	.15957	.98750	1.0126
6	.14090	.14232	.99002	1.0101	6	.15816	.16017	.98741	1.0127
8	.14148	.14291	.98994	1.0102	8	.15873	.16077	.98732	1.0128
10	.14205	.14351	.98986	1.0102	10	.15930	.16136	.98723	1.0129
12	.14263	.14410	.98977	1.0103	12	.15988	.16196	.98713	1.0130
14	.14320	.14469	.98969	1.0104	14	.16045	.16256	.98704	1.0131
16	.14378	.14529	.98961	1.0105	16	.16103	.16316	.98695	1.0132
18	.14435	.14588	.98952	1.0106	18	.16160	.16375	.98685	1.0133
20	.14493	.14648	.98944	1.0107	20	.16218	.16435	.98676	1.0134
22	.14551	.14707	.98935	1.0107	22	.16275	.16495	.98666	1.0135
24	.14608	.14766	.98927	1.0108	24	.16332	.16555	.98657	1.0136
26	.14666	.14826	.98918	1.0109	26	.16390	.16614	.98647	1.0137
28	.14723	.14885	.98910	1.0110	28	.16447	.16674	.98638	1.0138
30	.14781	.14945	.98901	1.0111	30	.16504	.16734	.98628	1.0139
32	.14838	.15004	.98893	1.0112	32	.16562	.16794	.98619	1.0140
34	.14896	.15064	.98884	1.0113	34	.16619	.16854	.98609	1.0141
36	.14953	.15123	.98875	1.0114	36	.16677	.16913	.98599	1.0142
38	.15011	.15183	.98867	1.0115	38	.16734	.16973	.98590	1.0143
40	.15068	.15242	.98858	1.0115	40	.16791	.17033	.98580	1.0144
42	.15126	.15302	.98849	1.0116	42	.16849	.17093	.98570	1.0145
44	.15183	.15362	.98840	1.0117	44	.16906	.17153	.98560	1.0146
46	.15241	.15421	.98832	1.0118	46	.16963	.17213	.98551	1.0147
48	.15298	.15481	.98823	1.0119	48	.17021	.17273	.98541	1.0148
50	.15356	.15540	.98814	1.0120	50	.17078	.17333	.98531	1.0149
52	.15413	.15600	.98805	1.0121	52	.17135	.17393	.98521	1.0150
54	.15471	.15659	.98796	1.0122	54	.17193	.17452	.98511	1.0151
56	.15528	.15719	.98787	1.0123	56	.17250	.17512	.98501	1.0152
58	.15586	.15779	.98778	1.0124	58	.17307	.17572	.98491	1.0153

NATURAL SINES, TANGENTS, COSINES AND SECANTS.

	10 DEG.					11 DEG.			
MIN	SINE.	TANG.	COSINE.	SEC.	MIN	SINE.	TANG.	COSINE.	SEC.
0	.17365	.17633	.98481	1.0154	0	.19081	.19438	.98162	1.0187
2	.17422	.17693	.98471	1.0155	2	.19138	.19498	.98151	1.0188
4	.17479	.17753	.98460	1.0156	4	.19195	.19559	.98140	1.0189
6	.17536	.17813	.98450	1.0157	6	.19252	.19619	.98129	1.0191
8	.17594	.17873	.98440	1.0158	8	.19309	.19679	.98118	1.0192
10	.17651	.17933	.98430	1.0159	10	.19366	.19740	.98107	1.0193
12	.17708	.17993	.98419	1.0160	12	.19423	.19800	.98095	1.0194
14	.17766	.18053	.98409	1.0162	14	.19480	.19861	.98084	1.0195
16	.17823	.18113	.98399	1.0163	16	.19537	.19921	.98073	1.0196
18	.17880	.18173	.98388	1.0164	18	.19594	.19982	.98061	1.0198
20	.17937	.18233	.98378	1.0165	20	.19652	.20042	.98050	1.0199
22	.17994	.18293	.98367	1.0166	22	.19709	.20103	.98038	1.0200
24	.18052	.18353	.98357	1.0167	24	.19766	.20163	.98027	1.0201
26	.18109	.18413	.98347	1.0168	26	.19823	.20224	.98015	1.0202
28	.18166	.18474	.98336	1.0169	28	.19880	.20285	.98004	1.0204
30	.18223	.18534	.98325	1.0170	30	.19937	.20345	.97992	1.0205
32	.18281	.18594	.98315	1.0171	32	.19994	.20406	.97981	1.0206
34	.18338	.18654	.98304	1.0172	34	.20051	.20466	.97969	1.0207
36	.18395	.18714	.98293	1.0174	36	.20108	.20527	.97957	1.0208
38	.18452	.18775	.98283	1.0175	38	.20165	.20587	.97946	1.0210
40	.18509	.18835	.98272	1.0176	40	.20222	.20648	.97934	1.0211
42	.18567	.18895	.98261	1.0177	42	.20279	.20709	.97922	1.0212
44	.18624	.18955	.98250	1.0178	44	.20336	.20769	.97910	1.0213
46	.18681	.19016	.98239	1.0179	46	.20393	.20830	.97898	1.0215
48	.18738	.19076	.98229	1.0180	48	.20449	.20891	.97887	1.0216
50	.18795	.19136	.98218	1.0181	50	.20506	.20952	.97875	1.0217
52	.18852	.19196	.98207	1.0182	52	.20563	.21012	.97863	1.0218
54	.18909	.19257	.98196	1.0184	54	.20620	.21073	.97851	1.0220
56	.18967	.19317	.98185	1.0185	56	.20677	.21134	.97839	1.0221
58	.19024	.19377	.98174	1.0186	58	.20734	.21195	.97827	1.0222

NATURAL SINES, TANGENTS, COSINES AND SECANTS.

	12 Deg.					13 Deg.			
MIN	SINE.	TANG.	COSINE.	SEC.	MIN	SINE.	TANG.	COSINE.	SEC.
0	.20791	.21255	.97815	1.0223	0	.22495	.23087	.97437	1.0263
2	.20848	.21316	.97802	1.0225	2	.22552	.23148	.97424	1.0264
4	.20905	.21377	.97790	1.0226	4	.22608	.23209	.97411	1.0266
6	.20962	.21438	.97778	1.0227	6	.22665	.23271	.97397	1.0267
8	.21019	.21499	.97766	1.0228	8	.22722	.23332	.97384	1.0268
10	.21075	.21560	.97754	1.0230	10	.22778	.23393	.97371	1.0270
12	.21132	.21620	.97742	1.0231	12	.22835	.23455	.97358	1.0271
14	.21189	.21681	.97729	1.0232	14	.22892	.23516	.97345	1.0273
16	.21246	.21742	.97717	1.0234	16	.22948	.23577	.97331	1.0274
18	.21303	.21803	.97704	1.0235	18	.23005	.23639	.97318	1.0276
20	.21360	.21864	.97692	1.0236	20	.23062	.23700	.97304	1.0277
22	.21417	.21925	.97679	1.0237	22	.23118	.23762	.97291	1.0278
24	.21473	.21986	.97667	1.0239	24	.23175	.23823	.97277	1.0280
26	.21530	.22047	.97654	1.0240	26	.23231	.23885	.97264	1.0281
28	.21587	.22108	.97642	1.0241	28	.23288	.23946	.97250	1.0283
30	.21644	.22169	.97629	1.0243	30	.23344	.24008	.97237	1.0284
32	.21700	.22230	.97617	1.0244	32	.23401	.24069	.97223	1.0285
34	.21757	.22291	.97604	1.0245	34	.23458	.24131	.97209	1.0287
36	.21814	.22352	.97592	1.0247	36	.23514	.24192	.97196	1.0288
38	.21871	.22414	.97579	1.0248	38	.23571	.24254	.97182	1.0290
40	.21928	.22475	.97566	1.0249	40	.23627	.24316	.97168	1.0291
42	.21984	.22536	.97553	1.0251	42	.23684	.24377	.97155	1.0293
44	.22041	.22597	.97540	1.0252	44	.23740	.24439	.97141	1.0294
46	.22098	.22658	.97528	1.0253	46	.23797	.24500	.97127	1.0296
48	.22155	.22719	.97515	1.0255	48	.23853	.24562	.97113	1.0297
50	.22211	.22780	.97502	1.0256	50	.23910	.24624	.97099	1.0299
52	.22268	.22842	.97489	1.0257	52	.23966	.24686	.97085	1.0300
54	.22325	.22903	.97476	1.0259	54	.24023	.24747	.97071	1.0302
56	.22382	.22964	.97463	1.0260	56	.24079	.24809	.97057	1.0303
58	.22438	.23025	.97450	1.0262	58	.24136	.24871	.97043	1.0305

NATURAL SINES, TANGENTS, COSINES AND SECANTS.

		14 Deg.					15 Deg.		
MIN	SINE.	TANG.	COSINE.	SEC.	MIN	SINE.	TANG.	COSINE.	SEC.
0	.24192	.24933	.97029	1.0306	0	.25882	.26795	.96593	1.0353
2	.24248	.24994	.97015	1.0308	2	.25938	.26857	.96577	1.0354
4	.24305	.25056	.97001	1.0309	4	.25994	.26919	.96562	1.0356
6	.24361	.25118	.96987	1.0311	6	.26050	.26982	.96547	1.0358
8	.24418	.25180	.96973	1.0312	8	.26106	.27044	.96532	1.0359
10	.24474	.25242	.96959	1.0314	10	.26163	.27107	.96517	1.0361
12	.24531	.25304	.96944	1.0315	12	.26219	.27169	.96501	1.0362
14	.24587	.25366	.96930	1.0317	14	.26275	.27232	.96486	1.0364
16	.24643	.25427	.96916	1.0318	16	.26331	.27294	.96471	1.0366
18	.24700	.25489	.96901	1.0320	18	.26387	.27357	.96456	1.0367
20	.24756	.25551	.96887	1.0321	20	.26443	.27419	.96440	1.0369
22	.24812	.25613	.96873	1.0323	22	.26499	.27482	.96425	1.0371
24	.24869	.25675	.96858	1.0324	24	.26555	.27544	.96409	1.0372
26	.24925	.25737	.96844	1.0326	26	.26612	.27607	.96394	1.0374
28	.24982	.25800	.96829	1.0327	28	.26668	.27670	.96379	1.0376
30	.25038	.25862	.96814	1.0329	30	.26724	.27732	.96363	1.0377
32	.25094	.25924	.96800	1.0330	32	.26780	.27795	.96347	1.0379
34	.25150	.25986	.96785	1.0332	34	.26836	.27858	.96332	1.0381
36	.25207	.26048	.96771	1.0333	36	.26892	.27920	.96316	1.0382
38	.25263	.26110	.96756	1.0335	38	.26948	.27983	.96300	1.0384
40	.25319	.26172	.96741	1.0337	40	.27004	.28046	.96285	1.0385
42	.25376	.26234	.96727	1.0338	42	.27060	.28108	.96269	1.0387
44	.25432	.26297	.96712	1.0340	44	.27116	.28171	.96253	1.0389
46	.25488	.26359	.96697	1.0341	46	.27172	.28204	.96237	1.0391
48	.25544	.26421	.96682	1.0343	48	.27228	.28297	.96222	1.0393
50	.25600	.26483	.96667	1.0345	50	.27284	.28360	.96206	1.0394
52	.25657	.26545	.96652	1.0346	52	.27340	.28423	.96190	1.0396
54	.25713	.26608	.96637	1.0348	54	.27396	.28486	.96174	1.0398
56	.25769	.26670	.96622	1.0349	56	.27452	.28548	.96158	1.0399
58	.25826	.26732	.96607	1.0351	58	.27508	.28611	.96142	1.0401

NATURAL SINES, TANGENTS, COSINES AND SECANTS.

	16 DEG.					17 DEG.			
MIN	SINE.	TANG.	COSINE.	SEC.	MIN	SINE.	TANG.	COSINE.	SEC.
0	.27564	.28674	.96126	1.0403	0	.29237	.30573	.95630	1.0457
2	.27619	.28737	.96110	1.0405	2	.29293	.30637	.95613	1.0459
4	.27675	.28800	.96094	1.0406	4	.29348	.30700	.95596	1.0461
6	.27731	.28863	.96078	1.0408	6	.29404	.30764	.95579	1.0463
8	.27787	.28926	.96062	1.0410	8	.29459	.30827	.95562	1.0464
10	.27843	.28989	.96045	1.0412	10	.29515	.30891	.95545	1.0466
12	.27899	.29052	.96029	1.0413	12	.29571	.30955	.95528	1.0468
14	.27955	.29116	.96013	1.0415	14	.29626	.31019	.95510	1.0470
16	.28011	.29179	.95997	1.0417	16	.29682	.31082	.95493	1.0472
18	.28066	.29242	.95980	1.0419	18	.29737	.31146	.95476	1.0474
20	.28122	.29305	.95964	1.0420	20	.29793	.31210	.95459	1.0476
22	.28178	.29368	.95948	1.0422	22	.29848	.31274	.95441	1.0478
24	.28234	.29431	.95931	1.0424	24	.29904	.31338	.95424	1.0479
26	.28290	.29495	.95915	1.0426	26	.29959	.31402	.95406	1.0481
28	.28346	.29558	.95898	1.0428	28	.30015	.31466	.95389	1.0483
30	.28401	.29621	.95882	1.0429	30	.30070	.31530	.95372	1.0485
32	.28457	.29684	.95865	1.0431	32	.30126	.31594	.95354	1.0487
34	.28513	.29748	.95849	1.0433	34	.30181	.31658	.95336	1.0489
36	.28569	.29811	.95832	1.0435	36	.30237	.31722	.95319	1.0491
38	.28624	.29874	.95815	1.0437	38	.30292	.31786	.95301	1.0493
40	.28680	.29938	.95799	1.0438	40	.30348	.31850	.95284	1.0495
42	.23736	.30001	.95782	1.0440	42	.30403	.31914	.95266	1.0497
44	.28792	.30065	.95765	1.0442	44	.30458	.31978	.95248	1.0499
46	.28847	.30128	.95749	1.0444	46	.30514	.32042	.95231	1.0501
48	.28903	.30192	.95732	1.0446	48	.30569	.32106	.95213	1.0503
50	.28959	.30255	.95715	1.0448	50	.30625	.32170	.95195	1.0505
52	.29014	.30318	.95698	1.0449	52	.30680	.32235	.95177	1.0507
54	.29070	.30382	.95681	1.0451	54	.30735	.32299	.95159	1.0509
56	.29126	.30446	.95664	1.0453	56	.30791	.32363	.95141	1.0511
58	.29181	.30509	.95647	1.0455	58	.30846	.32427	.95123	1.0513

NATURAL SINES, TANGENTS, COSINES AND SECANTS.

	18 DEG.					19 DEG.			
MIN	SINE.	TANG.	COSINE.	SEC.	MIN	SINE.	TANG.	COSINE.	SEC.
0	.30902	.32492	.95105	1.0515	0	.32557	.34433	.94552	1.0576
2	.30957	.32556	.95088	1.0517	2	.32612	.34498	.94533	1.0578
4	.31012	.32620	.95069	1.0519	4	.32667	.34563	.94514	1.0580
6	.31067	.32685	.95051	1.0521	6	.32722	.34628	.94495	1.0582
8	.31123	.32749	.95033	1.0523	8	.32777	.34693	.94476	1.0585
10	.31178	.32814	.95015	1.0525	10	.32832	.34758	.94457	1.0587
12	.31233	.32878	.94997	1.0527	12	.32886	.34823	.94437	1.0589
14	.31289	.32943	.94979	1.0529	14	.32941	.34889	.94418	1.0591
16	.31344	.33007	.94961	1.0531	16	.32996	.34954	.94399	1.0593
18	.31399	.33072	.94942	1.0533	18	.33051	.35019	.94380	1.0595
20	.31454	.33136	.94924	1.0535	20	.33106	.35085	.94361	1.0598
22	.31509	.33200	.94906	1.0537	22	.33161	.35150	.94341	1.0600
24	.31565	.33265	.94887	1.0539	24	.33216	.35215	.94322	1.0602
26	.31620	.33330	.94869	1.0541	26	.33271	.35281	.94303	1.0604
28	.31675	.33395	.94851	1.0543	28	.33326	.35346	.94283	1.0606
30	.31730	.33459	.94832	1.0545	30	.33381	.35412	.94264	1.0608
32	.31785	.33524	.94814	1.0547	32	.33435	.35477	.94245	1.0611
34	.31841	.33589	.94795	1.0549	34	.33490	.35543	.94225	1.0613
36	.31896	.33654	.94777	1.0551	36	.33545	.35608	.94206	1.0615
38	.31951	.33718	.94758	1.0553	38	.33599	.35674	.94186	1.0617
40	.32006	.33783	.94739	1.0555	40	.33655	.35739	.94166	1.0619
42	.32061	.33848	.94721	1.0557	42	.33709	.35805	.94147	1.0621
44	.32116	.33913	.94702	1.0559	44	.33764	.35871	.94127	1.0624
46	.32171	.33978	.94683	1.0561	46	.33819	.35936	.94108	1.0626
48	.32226	.34043	.94665	1.0563	48	.33874	.36002	.94088	1.0628
50	.32282	.34108	.94646	1.0566	50	.33928	.36068	.94068	1.0630
52	.32337	.34172	.94627	1.0568	52	.33983	.36134	.94048	1.0633
54	.32392	.34237	.94608	1.0570	54	.34038	.36199	.94029	1.0635
56	.32447	.34302	.94589	1.0572	56	.34092	.36265	.94009	1.0637
58	.32502	.34368	.94571	1.0574	58	.34147	.36331	.93989	1.0639

NATURAL SINES, TANGENTS, COSINES AND SECANTS.

	20 DEG.					21 DEG.			
MIN	SINE.	TANG.	COSINE.	SEC.	MIN	SINE.	TANG.	COSINE.	SEC.
0	.34202	.36397	.93969	1.0642	0	.35837	.38386	.93358	1.0711
2	.34257	.36463	.93949	1.0644	2	.35891	.38453	.93337	1 0714
4	.34311	.36529	.93929	1.0646	4	.35945	.38520	.93316	1.0716
6	.34366	.36595	.93909	1.0648	6	.36000	.38587	.93295	1.0719
8	.34420	.36661	.93889	1.0651	8	.36054	.38653	.93274	1.0721
10	.34475	.36727	.93869	1.0653	10	.36108	.38720	.93253	1.0723
12	.34530	.86793	.93849	1.0655	12	.36162	.38787	.93232	1.0726
14	.34584	.36859	.93829	1.0658	14	.36217	.38854	.93211	1.0728
16	.34639	.36925	.93809	1.0660	16	.36271	.38921	.93190	1.0731
18	.34693	.36991	.93789	1.0662	18	.36325	.38988	.93169	1.0733
20	.34748	.37057	.93769	1.0664	20	.36379	.39055	.93148	1.0736
22	.34803	.37123	.93748	1.0667	22	.36433	.39122	.93127	1.0738
24	.34857	.37189	.93728	1.0669	24	.36488	.39189	.93105	1.0740
26	.34912	.37256	.93708	1.0672	26	.36542	.39257	.93084	1.0743
28	.34966	.37322	.93687	1.0674	28	.36596	.39324	.93063	1.0745
30	.35021	.37388	.93667	1.0676	30	.36650	.39390	.93042	1.0748
32	.35075	.37455	.93647	1.0678	32	.36704	.39458	.93020	1.0750
34	.35129	.37521	.93626	1.0681	34	.36758	.39525	.92999	1.0753
36	.35184	.37587	.93606	1.0683	36	.36812	.39593	.92977	1.0755
38	.35238	.37654	.93585	1.0685	38	.36866	.39660	.92956	1.0758
40	.35293	.87720	.93565	1.0688	40	.36920	.39727	.92935	1.0760
42	.35347	.37787	.93544	1.0690	42	.36975	.39795	.92913	1.0762
44	.35402	.37853	.93524	1.0692	44	.37029	.39862	.92892	1.0765
46	.35456	.379_0	.93503	1.0695	46	.37083	.39929	.92870	1.0768
48	.35511	.37986	.93483	1.0697	48	.37137	.39997	.92848	1.0770
50	.35565	.38053	.94462	1.0699	50	.37191	.40064	.92827	1.0773
52	.35619	.38119	.93441	1.0702	52	.37245	.40132	.92805	1.0775
54	.35674	.38186	.93420	1.0704	54	.37299	.40199	.92783	1.0778
56	.35728	.38253	.93399	1.0707	56	.37353	.40267	.92762	1.0780
58	.35782	.38319	.93379	1.0709	58	.37406	.40335	.92740	1.0783

NATURAL SINES, TANGENTS, COSINES AND SECANTS.

	22 Deg.					23 Deg.			
MIN	SINE.	TANG.	COSINE.	SEC.	MIN	SINE.	TANG.	COSINE.	SEC.
0	.37460	.40402	.92718	1.0785	0	.39073	.42447	.92050	1.0864
2	.37514	.40470	.92697	1.0788	2	.39126	.42516	.92028	1.0866
4	.37568	.40538	.92674	1.0790	4	.39180	.42585	.92005	1.0869
6	.37622	.40606	.92653	1.0793	6	.39234	.42653	.91982	1.0872
8	.37676	.40673	.92631	1.0795	8	.39287	.42722	.91959	1.0874
10	.37730	.40741	.92609	1.0798	10	.39341	.42791	.91936	1.0877
12	.37784	.40809	.92587	1.0801	12	.39394	.42860	.91913	1.0880
14	.37838	.40877	.92565	1.0803	14	.39447	.42929	.91890	1.0882
16	.37892	.40945	.92543	1.0806	16	.39501	.42998	.91867	1.0885
18	.37945	.41013	.92521	1.0808	18	.39554	.43067	.91845	1.0888
20	.37999	.41081	.92499	1.0811	20	.39608	.43136	.91821	1.0891
22	.38053	.41149	.92477	1.0813	22	.39661	.43205	.91798	1.0893
24	.38107	.41217	.92454	1.0816	24	.39715	.43274	.91775	1.0896
26	.38161	.41285	.92432	1.0819	26	.39768	.43343	.91752	1.0899
28	.38214	.41353	.92410	1.0821	28	.39821	.43412	.91729	1.0902
30	.38268	.41421	.92388	1.0824	30	.39875	.43481	.91706	1.0904
32	.38322	.41489	.92366	1.0826	32	.39928	.43550	.91683	1.0907
34	.38376	.41558	.92343	1.0829	34	.39981	.43619	.91659	1.0910
36	.38429	.41626	.92321	1.0832	36	.40035	.43689	.91636	1.0913
38	.38483	.41694	.92298	1.0834	38	.40088	.43758	.91613	1.0915
40	.38537	.41762	.92276	1.0837	40	.40141	.43827	.91589	1.0918
42	.38590	.41831	.92254	1.0840	42	.40195	.43897	.91566	1.0921
44	.38644	.41899	.92231	1.0842	44	.40248	.43966	.91543	1.0924
46	.38698	.41967	.92208	1.0845	46	.40301	.44036	.91519	1.0927
48	.38751	.42036	.92186	1.0847	48	.40354	.44105	.91496	1.0929
50	.38805	.42104	.92164	1.0850	50	.40407	.44175	.91472	1.0932
52	.38859	.42173	.92141	1.0853	52	.40461	.44244	.91449	1.0935
54	.38912	.42241	.92118	1.0855	54	.40514	.44314	.91425	1.0938
56	.38966	.42310	.92096	1.0858	56	.40567	.44383	.91402	1.0941
58	.39019	.42379	.92073	1.0861	58	.40620	.44453	.91378	1.0943

NATURAL SINES, TANGENTS, COSINES AND SECANTS.

	24 DEG.				25 DEG.			
MIN	SINE.	TANG.	COSINE.	SEC.	MIN	SINE.	TANG.	COSINE.	SEC.
0	.40674	.44523	.91354	1.0946	0	.42262	.46631	.90631	1.1034
2	.40727	.44592	.91331	1.0949	2	.42314	.46701	.90606	1.1037
4	.40780	.44662	.91307	1.0952	4	.42367	.46772	.90581	1.1040
6	.40833	.44732	.91283	1.0955	6	.42420	.46843	.90557	1.1043
8	.40886	.44802	.91259	1.0958	8	.42472	.46914	.90532	1.1046
10	.40939	.44872	.91236	1.0961	10	.42525	.46985	.90507	1.1049
12	.40992	.44941	.91212	1.0963	12	.42578	.47056	.90482	1.1052
14	.41045	.45012	.91188	1.0966	14	.42630	.47127	.90458	1.1055
16	.41098	.45081	.91164	1.0969	16	.42683	.47198	.90433	1.1058
18	.41151	.45152	.91140	1.0972	18	.42736	.47270	.90408	1.1061
20	.41204	.45221	.91116	1.0975	20	.42788	.47341	.90383	1.1064
22	.41257	.45292	.91092	1.0978	22	.42841	.47412	.90358	1.1067
24	.41310	.45362	.91068	1.0981	24	.42893	.47483	.90333	1.1070
26	.41363	.45432	.91044	1.0984	26	.42946	.47555	.90308	1.1073
28	.41416	.45502	.91020	1.0987	28	.42999	.47626	.90283	1.1076
30	.41469	.45572	.90996	1.0989	30	.43051	.47697	.90258	1.1079
32	.41522	.45643	.90972	1.0992	32	.43103	.47769	.90233	1.1082
34	.41575	.45713	.90948	1.0995	34	.43156	.47840	.90208	1.1085
36	.41628	.45783	.90923	1.0998	36	.43209	.47912	.90183	1.1088
38	.41681	.45854	.90899	1.1001	38	.43261	.47983	.90158	1.1092
40	.41734	.45924	.90875	1.1004	40	.43313	.48055	.90133	1.1095
42	.41787	.45995	.90851	1.1007	42	.43366	.48127	.90107	1.1098
44	.41839	.46065	.90826	1.1010	44	.43418	.48198	.90082	1.1101
46	.41892	.46136	.90802	1 1013	46	.43471	.48270	.90057	1.1104
48	.41945	.46206	.90778	1.1016	48	.43523	.48342	.90032	1.1107
50	.41998	.46277	.90753	1.1019	50	.43575	.48413	.90006	1.1110
52	.42051	.46348	.90729	1.1022	52	.43628	.48485	.89981	1.1113
54	.42104	.46418	.90704	1.1025	54	.43680	.48557	.89956	1.1116
56	.42156	.46489	.90680	1.1028	56	.43732	.48629	.89930	1.1119
58	.42209	.46560	.90655	1.1031	58	.43785	.48701	.89905	1.1123

NATURAL SINES, TANGENTS, COSINES AND SECANTS.

	26 Deg.					27 Deg.			
MIN	SINE.	TANG.	COSINE.	SEC.	MIN	SINE.	TANG.	COSINE.	SEC.
0	.43837	.48773	.89879	1.1126	0	.45400	.50952	.89100	1.1223
2	.43889	.48845	.89854	1.1129	2	.45451	.51026	.89087	1.1226
4	.43941	.48917	.89828	1.1132	4	.45503	.51099	.89048	1.1229
6	.43994	.48989	.89803	1.1135	6	.45554	.51172	.89021	1.1233
8	.44046	.49062	.89777	1.1138	8	.45606	.51246	.88995	1.1237
10	.44098	.49134	.89751	1.1142	10	.45658	.51319	.88968	1.1240
12	.44150	.49206	.89726	1.1145	12	.45710	.51393	.88941	1.1243
14	.44203	.49278	.89700	1.1148	14	.45761	.51466	.88915	1.1247
16	.44255	.49351	.89674	1.1151	16	.45813	.51540	.88888	1.1250
18	.44307	.49423	.89648	1.1155	18	.45865	.51614	.88862	1.1253
20	.44359	.49495	.89623	1.1158	20	.45916	.51687	.88835	1.1257
22	.44411	.49568	.89597	1.1161	22	.45968	.51761	.88808	1.1260
24	.44463	.49640	.89571	1.1164	24	.46020	.51835	.88781	1.1264
26	.44515	.49713	.89545	1.1167	26	.46071	.51909	.88755	1.1267
28	.44568	.49785	.89519	1.1171	28	.46123	.51983	.88728	1.1270
30	.44620	.49858	.89493	1.1174	30	.46175	.52057	.88701	1.1274
32	.44672	.49931	.89467	1.1177	32	.46226	.52130	.88674	1.1277
34	.44724	.50003	.89441	1.1180	34	.46278	.52204	.88647	1.1281
36	.44776	.50076	.89415	1.1184	36	.46329	.52279	.88620	1.1284
38	.44828	.50149	.89389	1.1187	38	.46381	.52353	.88593	1.1287
40	.44880	.50222	.89363	1.1190	40	.46433	.52427	.88566	1.1291
42	.44932	.50295	.89337	1.1193	42	.46484	.52501	.88539	1.1294
44	.44984	.50367	.89311	1.1197	44	.46536	.52575	.88512	1.1298
46	.45036	.50440	.89285	1.1200	46	.46587	.52649	.88485	1.1301
48	.45088	.50513	.89258	1.1203	48	.46639	.52724	.88458	1.1305
50	.45139	.50586	.89232	1.1207	50	.46690	.52798	.88431	1.1308
52	.45191	.50660	.89206	1.1210	52	.46741	.52873	.88404	1.1312
54	.45243	.50733	.89179	1.1213	54	.46793	.52947	.88376	1.1315
56	.45295	.50806	.89153	1.1217	56	.46844	.53022	.88349	1.1319
58	.45347	.50879	.89127	1.1220	58	.46896	.53096	.88322	1.1322

NATURAL SINES, TANGENTS, COSINES AND SECANTS.

	28 Deg.					29 Deg.			
MIN	SINE.	TANG.	COSINE.	SEC·	MIN	SINE.	TANG.	COSINE.	SEC.
0	.46947	.53171	.88295	1.1326	0	.48481	.55431	.87462	1.1433
2	.46998	.53245	.88267	1.1329	2	.48532	.55507	.87434	1 1437
4	.47050	.53320	.88240	1.1333	4	.48582	.55583	.87405	1.1441
6	.47101	.53395	.88213	1.1336	6	.48633	.55659	.87377	1.1445
8	.47152	.53470	.88185	1.1339	8	.48684	.55735	.87349	1.1448
10	.47204	.53544	.88158	1.1343	10	.48735	.55812	.87321	1.1452
12	.47255	.53619	.88130	1.1347	12	.48786	.55888	.87292	1.1456
14	.47306	.53694	.88103	1.1350	14	.48836	.55964	.87264	1.1459
16	.47357	.53769	.88075	1.1354	16	.48887	.56041	.87235	1.1463
18	.47409	.53844	.88047	1.1357	18	.48938	.56117	.87207	1.1467
20	.47460	.53919	.88020	1.1361	20	.48989	.56194	.87178	1.1471
22	.47511	.53994	.87992	1.1365	22	.49040	.56270	.87150	1.1474
24	.47562	.54070	.87965	1.1368	24	.49090	.56347	.87121	1.1478
26	.47613	.54145	.87937	1.1372	26	.49141	.56424	.87093	1.1482
28	.47664	.54220	.87909	1.1375	28	.49191	.56500	.87064	1.1486
30	.47716	.54295	.87881	1.1379	30	.49242	.56577	.87035	1.1489
32	.47767	.54371	.87854	1.1382	32	.49293	.56654	.87007	1.1493
34	.47818	.54446	.87826	1.1386	34	.49343	.56731	.86978	1.1497
36	.47869	.54522	.87798	1.1390	36	.49394	.56808	.86949	1.1502
38	.47920	.54597	.87770	1.1393	38	.49445	.56885	.86920	1.1505
40	.47971	.54673	.87742	1.1397	40	.49495	.56962	.86892	1.1508
42	.48022	.54748	.87714	1.1401	42	.49546	.57039	.86863	1.1512
44	.48073	.54824	.87686	1.1404	44	.49596	.57116	.86834	1.1516
46	.48124	.54899	.87659	1.1408	46	.49647	.57193	.86805	1.1520
48	.48175	.54975	.87631	1.1411	48	.49697	.57270	.86776	1.1524
50	.48226	.55051	.87602	1.1415	50	.49748	.57348	.86747	1.1528
52	.48277	.55127	.87574	1.1419	52	.49798	.57425	.86718	1.1531
54	.48328	.55203	.87546	1.1422	54	.49849	.57502	.86689	1.1535
56	.48379	.55279	.87518	1.1426	56	.49899	.57580	.86660	1.1539
58	.48430	.55355	.87490	1.1430	58	.49949	.57657	.86631	1.1543

NATURAL SINES, TANGENTS, COSINES AND SECANTS.

	30 Deg.					31 Deg.			
MIN	SINE.	TANG.	COSINE.	SEC.	MIN	SINE.	TANG.	COSINE.	SEC.
0	.50000	.57735	.86602	1.1547	0	.51504	.60086	.85717	1.1666
2	.50050	.57812	.86573	1.1551	2	.51554	.60165	.85687	1.1670
4	.50100	.57890	.86544	1.1555	4	.51603	.60244	.85657	1.1674
6	.50151	.57968	.86515	1.1559	6	.51653	.60324	.85627	1.1678
8	.50201	.58046	.86486	1.1562	8	.51703	.60403	.85596	1.1683
10	.50252	.58123	.86456	1.1566	10	.51753	.60482	.85566	1.1687
12	.50302	.58201	.86427	1.1570	12	.51803	.60562	.85536	1.1691
14	.50352	.58279	.86398	1.1574	14	.51852	.60642	.85506	1.1695
16	.50402	.58357	.86369	1.1578	16	.51902	.60721	.85476	1.1699
18	.50453	.58435	.86339	1.1582	18	.51952	.60801	.85446	1.1703
20	.50503	.58513	.86310	1.1586	20	.52001	.60880	.85415	1.1707
22	.50553	.58591	.86281	1.1590	22	.52051	.60960	.85385	1.1712
24	.50603	.58669	.86251	1.1594	24	.52101	.61040	.85355	1.1716
26	.50653	.58748	.86222	1.1598	26	.52150	.61120	.85325	1.1720
28	.50703	.58826	.86192	1.1602	28	.52200	.61200	.85294	1.1724
30	.50754	.58904	.86163	1.1606	30	.52250	.61280	.85264	1.1728
32	.50804	.58983	.86133	1.1610	32	.52300	.61360	.85233	1.1732
34	.50854	.59061	.86104	1.1614	34	.52349	.61440	.85203	1.1737
36	.50904	.59140	.86074	1.1618	36	.52398	.61520	.85173	1.1741
38	.50954	.59218	.86044	1.1622	38	.52448	.61600	.85142	1.1745
40	.51004	.59297	.86015	1.1626	40	.52498	.61681	.85112	1.1749
42	.51054	.59375	.85985	1.1630	42	.52547	.61761	.85081	1.1753
44	.51104	.59454	.85955	1.1634	44	.52597	.61841	.85050	1.1758
46	.51154	.59533	.85925	1.1638	46	.52646	.61922	.85020	1.1762
48	.51204	.59612	.85896	1.1642	48	.52696	.62002	.84989	1.1766
50	.51254	.59691	.85866	1.1646	50	.52745	.62083	.84958	1.1770
52	.51304	.59770	.85836	1.1650	52	.52794	.62164	.84928	1.1775
54	.51354	.59848	.85806	1.1654	54	.52844	.62244	.84897	1.1779
56	.51404	.59928	.85776	1.1658	56	.52893	.62325	.84866	1.1783
58	.51454	.60007	.85746	1.1662	58	.52943	.62406	.84835	1.1787

NATURAL SINES, TANGENTS, COSINES AND SECANTS.

	32 Deg.					33 Deg.			
MIN	SINE.	TANG.	COSINE.	SEC.	MIN	SINE.	TANG.	COSINE.	SEC.
0	.52992	.62487	.84805	1.1792	0	.54464	.64941	.83867	1.1924
2	.53041	.62568	.84774	1.1796	2	.54513	.65023	.83835	1.1928
4	.53090	.62649	.84743	1.1800	4	.54561	.65106	.83803	1.1933
6	.53140	.62730	.84712	1.1805	6	.54610	.65189	.83772	1.1937
8	.53189	.62811	.84681	1.1809	8	.54659	.65272	.83740	1.1942
10	.53238	.62892	.84650	1.1813	10	.54707	.65355	.83708	1.1946
12	.53287	.62970	.84619	1.1818	12	.54756	.65438	.83676	1.1951
14	.53337	.63054	.84588	1.1822	14	.54805	.65521	.83644	1.1955
16	.53386	.63135	.84557	1.1826	16	.54853	.65604	.83612	1.1960
18	.53435	.63217	.84526	1.1831	18	.54902	.65687	.83581	1.1964
20	.53484	.63299	.84495	1.1835	20	.54951	.65771	.83549	1.1969
22	.53533	.63380	.84464	1.1840	22	.54999	.65854	.83517	1.1974
24	.53583	.63462	.84433	1.1844	24	.55048	.65938	.83485	1.1978
26	.53632	.63543	.84401	1.1848	26	.55096	.66021	.83453	1.1983
28	.53681	.63625	.84370	1.1852	28	.55145	.66105	.83421	1.1987
30	.53730	.63707	.84339	1.1857	30	.55194	.66188	.83389	1.1992
32	.53779	.63789	.84308	1.1861	32	.55242	.66272	.83356	1.1997
34	.53828	.63870	.84276	1.1866	34	.55291	.66356	.83324	1.2001
36	.53877	.63952	.84245	1.1870	36	.55339	.66440	.83292	1.2006
38	.53926	.64034	.84214	1.1874	38	.55387	.66523	.83260	1.2010
40	.53975	.64117	.84182	1.1879	40	.55436	.66607	.83228	1.2015
42	.54024	.64199	.84151	1.1883	42	.55484	.66692	.83195	1.2020
44	.54073	.64281	.84119	1.1888	44	.55533	.66776	.83163	1.2024
46	.54122	.64363	.84088	1.1892	46	.55581	.66860	.83131	1.2029
48	.54171	.64445	.84056	1.1897	48	.55629	.66944	.83098	1.2034
50	.54220	.64528	.84025	1.1901	50	.55678	.67028	.83066	1.2039
52	.54268	.64610	.83993	1.1906	52	.55726	.67113	.83033	1.2043
54	.54317	.64693	.83962	1.1910	54	.55774	.67197	.83001	1.2048
56	.54366	.64775	.83930	1.1915	56	.55823	.67281	.82969	1.2053
58	.54415	.64858	.83898	1.1919	58	.55871	.67366	.82936	1.2057

NATURAL SINES, TANGENTS, COSINES AND SECANTS.

	34 Deg.					35 Deg.			
MIN	SINE.	TANG.	COSINE.	SEC.	MIN	SINE.	TANG.	COSINE.	SEC.
0	.55919	.67451	.82903	1.2062	0	.57357	.70021	.81915	1.2208
2	.55967	.67535	.82871	1.2067	2	.57405	.70107	.81882	1.2213
4	.56016	.67620	.82838	1.2072	4	.57453	.70194	.81848	1.2218
6	.56064	.67705	.82806	1.2076	6	.57500	.70281	.81815	1.2223
8	.56112	.67790	.82773	1.2081	8	.57548	.70368	.81781	1.2228
10	.56160	.67875	.82741	1.2086	10	.57596	.70455	.81748	1.2233
12	.56208	.67960	.82708	1.2091	12	.57643	.70542	.81714	1.2238
14	.56256	.68045	.82675	1.2095	14	.57691	.70629	.81681	1.2243
16	.56304	.68130	.82642	1.2100	16	.57738	.70716	.81647	1.2248
18	.56352	.68215	.82610	1.2105	18	.57786	.70804	.81614	1.2253
20	.56400	.68300	.82577	1.2110	20	.57833	.70891	.81580	1.2258
22	.56449	.68386	.82544	1.2115	22	.57881	.70979	.81546	1.2263
24	.56497	.68471	.82511	1.2119	24	.57928	.71066	.81513	1.2268
26	.56545	.68557	.82478	1.2124	26	.57975	.71154	.81479	1.2273
28	.56593	.68642	.82445	1.2129	28	.58023	.71241	.81445	1.2278
30	.56640	.68728	.82412	1.2134	30	.58070	.71329	.81411	1.2283
32	.56688	.68814	.82379	1.2139	32	.58117	.71417	.81378	1.2288
34	.56736	.68900	.82346	1.2144	34	.58165	.71505	.81344	1.2293
36	.56784	.68985	.82313	1.2149	36	.58212	.71593	.81310	1.2298
38	.56832	.69071	.82280	1.2153	38	.58260	.71681	.81276	1.2304
40	.56880	.69157	.82247	1.2158	40	.58307	.71769	.81242	1.2309
42	.56928	.69243	.82214	1.2163	42	.58354	.71857	.81208	1.2314
44	.56976	.69329	.82181	1.2168	44	.58401	.71945	.81174	1.2319
46	.57023	.69415	.82148	1.2173	46	.58449	.72034	.81140	1.2324
48	.57071	.69502	.82115	1.2178	48	.58496	.72122	.81106	1.2329
50	.57119	.69588	.82082	1.2183	50	.58543	.72211	.81072	1.2335
52	.57167	.69674	.82048	1.2188	52	.58590	.72299	.81038	1.2340
54	.57214	.69761	.82015	1.2193	54	.58637	.72388	.81004	1.2345
56	.57262	.69847	.81982	1.2198	56	.58684	.72476	.80970	1.2350
58	.57310	.69934	.81948	1.2203	58	.58731	.72565	.80936	1.2355

NATURAL SINES, TANGENTS, COSINES AND SECANTS.

	36 DEG.					37 DEG.			
MIN	SINE.	TANG.	COSINE.	SEC.	MIN	SINE.	TANG.	COSINE.	SEC.
0	.58778	.72654	.80902	1.2361	0	.60181	.75355	.79863	1.2521
2	.58825	.72743	.80867	1.2366	2	.60228	.75446	.79828	1 2527
4	.58872	.72832	.80833	1.2371	4	.60274	.75538	.79793	1.2532
6	.58919	.72921	.80799	1.2376	6	.60321	.75629	.79758	1.2538
8	.58966	.73010	.80765	1.2382	8	.60367	.75721	.79723	1.2543
10	.59013	.73099	.80730	1.2387	10	.60413	.75812	.79688	1.2549
12	.59060	.73189	.80696	1.2392	12	.60460	.75904	.79653	1.2554
14	.59107	.73278	.80662	1.2397	14	.60506	.75996	.79618	1.2560
16	.59154	.73367	.80627	1.2403	16	.60552	.76087	.79583	1.2565
18	.59201	.73457	.80593	1.2408	18	.60599	.76179	.79547	1.2571
20	.59248	.73547	.80558	1.2413	20	.60645	.76271	.79512	1.2577
22	.59295	.73636	.80524	1.2419	22	.60691	.76363	.79477	1.2582
24	.59342	.73726	.80489	1.2424	24	.60738	.76456	.79441	1.2588
26	.59389	.73816	.80455	1.2429	26	.60784	.76548	.79406	1.2593
28	.59435	.73906	.80420	1.2435	28	.60830	.76640	.79371	1.2599
30	.59482	.73996	.80386	1.2440	30	.60876	.76733	.79335	1.2605
32	.59529	.74086	.80351	1.2445	32	.60922	.76825	.79300	1.2610
34	.59576	.74176	.80316	1.2451	34	.60968	.76918	.79264	1.2616
36	.59622	.74266	.80282	1.2456	36	.61014	.77010	.79229	1.2622
38	.59669	.74357	.80247	1.2461	38	.61060	.77103	.79193	1.2627
40	.59716	.74447	.80212	1.2466	40	.61107	.77196	.79158	1.2633
42	.59762	.74538	.80177	1.2472	42	.61153	.77289	.79122	1.2639
44	.59809	.74628	.80143	1.2478	44	.61198	.77382	.79087	1.2644
46	.59856	.74719	.80108	1.2483	46	.61245	.77475	.79051	1.2650
48	.59902	.74809	.80073	1.2488	48	.61291	.77568	.79015	1.2656
50	.59949	.74900	.80038	1.2494	50	.61337	.77661	.78980	1.2661
52	.59995	.74991	.80003	1.2499	52	.61382	.77754	.78944	1.2667
54	.60042	.75082	.79968	1.2505	54	.61428	.77848	.78908	1.2673
56	.60088	.75173	.79933	1.2510	56	.61474	.77941	.78872	1.2679
58	.60135	.75264	.79898	1.2516	58	.61520	.78035	.78837	1.2684

NATURAL SINES, TANGENTS, COSINES AND SECANTS.

	38 Deg.					39 Deg.			
MIN	SINE.	TANG.	COSINE.	SEC.	MIN	SINE.	TANG.	COSINE.	SEC.
0	.61566	.78128	.78801	1.2690	0	.62932	.80978	.77714	1.2867
2	.61612	.78222	.78765	1.2696	2	.62977	˙81075	.77678	1.2874
4	.61658	.78316	.78729	1.2702	4	.63022	.81171	.77641	1.2880
6	.61703	.78410	.78693	1.2707	6	.63067	.81268	.77604	1.2886
8	.61749	.78504	.78657	1.2713	8	.63113	.81364	.77568	1.2892
10	.61795	.78598	.78621	1.2719	10	.63158	.81461	.77531	1.2898
12	.61841	.78692	.78586	1.2725	12	.63203	.81558	.77494	1.2904
14	.61886	.78786	.78550	1.2731	14	.63248	.81655	.77458	1.2910
16	.61932	.78881	.78514	1.2737	16	.63293	.81752	.77421	1.2916
18	.61978	.78975	.78477	1.2742	18	.63338	.81849	.77384	1.2922
20	.62023	.79070	.78441	1.2748	20	.63383	.81946	.77347	1.2929
22	.62069	.79164	.78405	1.2754	22	.63428	.82043	.77310	1.2935
24	.62115	.79259	.78369	1.2760	24	.63473	.82141	.77273	1.2941
26	.62160	.79354	.78333	1.2766	26	.63518	.82238	.77236	1.2947
28	.62206	.79448	.78297	1.2772	28	.63563	.82336	.77199	1.2953
30	.62251	.79543	.78261	1.2778	30	.63608	.82433	.77162	1.2960
32	.62297	.79638	.78224	1.2784	32	.63653	.82531	.77125	1.2966
34	.62342	.79734	.78188	1.2790	34	.63697	.82629	.77088	1.2972
36	.62388	.79829	.78152	1.2796	36	.63742	.82727	.77051	1.2978
38	.62433	.79924	.78115	1.2801	38	.63787	.82825	.77014	1.2985
40	.62479	.80019	.78079	1.2807	40	.63832	.82923	.76977	1.2991
42	.62524	.80115	.78043	1.2813	42	.63877	.83021	.76940	1.2997
44	.62570	.80210	.78006	1.2819	44	.63921	.83120	.76903	1.3003
46	.62615	.80306	.77970	1.2825	46	.63966	.83218	.76865	1.3010
48	.62660	.80402	.77934	1.2831	48	.64011	.83317	.76828	1.3016
50	.62706	.80498	.77897	1.2837	50	.64055	.83415	.76791	1.3022
52	.62751	.80594	.77861	1.2843	52	.64100	.83514	.76754	1.3029
54	.62796	.80690	.77824	1.2849	54	.64145	.83613	.76716	1.3035
56	.62841	.80786	.77788	1.2855	56	.64190	.83712	.76679	1.3041
58	.62887	.80882	.77751	1.2861	58	.64234	.83811	.76642	1.3048

NATURAL SINES, TANGENTS, COSINES
AND SECANTS.

	40 Deg.				41 Deg.			
MIN	SINE.	TANG.	COSINE.	SEC.	MIN	SINE.	TANG.	COSINE.	SEC.
0	.64279	.83910	.76604	1.3054	0	.65606	.86928	.75471	1.3250
2	.64323	.84009	.76567	1.3060	2	.65650	.87031	.75433	1 3257
4	.64368	.84108	.76529	1.3067	4	.65694	.87133	.75394	1.3263
6	.64412	.84208	.76492	1.3073	6	.65737	.87235	.75356	1.3270
8	.64457	.84307	.76455	1.3080	8	.65781	.87338	.75318	1.3277
10	.64501	.84407	.76417	1.3086	10	.65825	.87440	.75280	1.3284
12	.64546	.84506	.76379	1.3092	12	.65869	.87543	.75241	1.3290
14	.64590	.84606	.76342	1.3099	14	.65913	.87646	.75203	1.3297
16	.64634	.84706	.76304	1.3105	16	.65956	.87749	.75165	1.3304
18	.64679	.84806	.76267	1.3112	18	.66000	.87852	.75126	1.3311
20	.64723	.84906	.76229	1.3118	20	.66044	.87955	.75088	1.3318
22	.64768	.85006	.76191	1.3125	22	.66087	.88058	.75049	1.3324
24	.64812	.85106	.76154	1.3131	24	.66131	.88162	.75011	1.3331
26	.64856	.85207	.76116	1.3138	26	.66175	.88265	.74972	1.3338
28	.64900	.85307	.76078	1.3144	28	.66218	.88369	.74934	1.3345
30	.64945	.85408	.76040	1.3151	30	.66262	.88472	.74895	1.3352
32	.64989	.85509	.76003	1.3157	32	.66305	.88576	.74857	1.3359
34	.65033	.85609	.75965	1.3164	34	.66348	.88680	.74818	1.3366
36	.65077	.85710	.75927	1.3170	36	.66392	.88784	.74780	1.3372
38	.65121	.85811	.75889	1.3177	38	.66436	.88888	.74741	1.3379
40	.65166	.85912	.75851	1.3184	40	.66479	.88992	.74702	1.3386
42	.65210	.86013	.75813	1.3190	42	.66523	.89097	.74664	1.3393
44	.65254	.86115	.75775	1.3197	44	.66566	.89201	.74625	1.3400
46	.65298	.86216	.75737	1.3202	46	.66610	.89305	.74586	1.3407
48	.65342	.86317	.75699	1.3210	48	.66653	.89410	.74547	1.3414
50	.65386	.86419	.75661	1.3217	50	.66696	.89515	.74509	1.3421
52	.65430	.86521	.75623	1.3223	52	.66740	.89620	.74470	1.3428
54	.65474	.86623	.75585	1.3230	54	.66783	.89725	.74431	1.3435
56	.65518	.86724	.75547	1.3237	56	.66826	.89830	.74392	1.3442
58	.65562	.86826	.75509	1.3243	58	.66870	.89935	.74353	1.3449

NATURAL SINES, TANGENTS, COSINES AND SECANTS.

	42 Deg.					43 Deg.			
MIN	SINE.	TANG.	COSINE.	SEC.	MIN	SINE.	TANG.	COSINE.	SEC.
0	.66913	.90040	.74314	1.3456	0	.68200	.93251	.73135	1.3673
2	.66956	.90146	.74275	1.3463	2	.68242	.93360	.73096	1.3681
4	.66999	.90251	.74236	1.3470	4	.68285	.93469	.73066	1.3688
6	.67043	.90357	.74197	1.3477	6	.68327	.93578	.73016	1.3695
8	.67086	.90462	.74158	1.3485	8	.68370	.93687	.72976	1.3703
10	.67129	.90568	.74119	1.3492	10	.68412	.93797	.72937	1.3710
12	.67172	.90674	.74080	1.3499	12	.68455	.93906	.72897	1.3718
14	.67215	.90780	.74041	1.3506	14	.68497	.94016	.72857	1.3725
16	.67258	.90887	.74002	1.3513	16	.68539	.94125	.72817	1.3733
18	.67301	.90993	.73963	1.3520	18	.68582	.94235	.72777	1.3740
20	.67344	.91099	.73924	1.3527	20	.68624	.94345	.72737	1.3748
22	.67387	.91206	.73885	1.3534	22	.68666	.94455	.72697	1.3756
24	.67430	.91312	.73845	1.3542	24	.68709	.94565	.72657	1.3763
26	.67473	.91419	.73806	1.3549	26	.68751	.94675	.72617	1.3771
28	.67516	.91526	.73767	1.3556	28	.68793	.94786	.72577	1.3778
30	.67559	.91633	.73728	1.3563	30	.68835	.94896	.72537	1.3786
32	.67602	.91740	.73688	1.3571	32	.68877	.95007	.72497	1.3794
34	.67645	.91847	.73649	1.3578	34	.68920	.95118	.72457	1.3801
36	.67687	.91955	.73609	1.3585	36	.68962	.95228	.72417	1.3809
38	.67730	.92062	.73570	1.3592	38	.69004	.95339	.72377	1.3816
40	.67773	.92169	.73531	1.3600	40	.69046	.95451	.72337	1.3824
42	.67816	.92277	.73491	1.3607	42	.69088	.95562	.72297	1.3832
44	.67859	.92385	.73452	1.3614	44	.69130	.95673	.72256	1.3839
46	.67901	.92493	.73412	1.3622	46	.69172	.95785	.72216	1.3847
48	.67944	.92601	.73373	1.3629	48	.69214	.95896	.72176	1.3855
50	.67987	.92709	.73333	1.3636	50	.69256	.96008	.72136	1.3863
52	.68029	.92817	.73294	1.3644	52	.69298	.96120	.72095	1.3870
54	.68072	.92926	.73254	1.3651	54	.69340	.96232	.72055	1.3878
56	.68114	.93034	.73215	1.3658	56	.69382	.96344	.72015	1.3886
58	.68157	.93143	.73175	1.3666	58	.69424	.96456	.71974	1.3894

NATURAL SINES, TANGENTS, COSINES AND SECANTS.

	44 Deg.					45 Deg.			
MIN	SINE.	TANG.	COSINE.	SEC.	MIN	SINE.	TANG.	COSINE.	SEC.
0	.69466	.96569	.71934	1.3902	0	.70711	1.	.70711	1.4142
2	.69507	.96681	.71893	1.3909	2	.70752	1.0012	.70669	1.4150
4	.69549	.96794	.71853	1.3917	4	.70793	1.0023	.70628	1.4159
6	.69591	.96906	.71812	1.3925	6	.70834	1.0035	.70587	1.4167
8	.69633	.97019	.71772	1.3933	8	.70875	1.0047	.70546	1.4175
10	.69675	.97132	.71732	1.3941	10	.70916	1.0058	.70505	1.4183
12	.69716	.97246	.71691	1.3949	12	.70957	1.0070	.70463	1.4192
14	.69758	.97359	.71650	1.3957	14	.70998	1.0082	.70422	1.4200
16	.69800	.97472	.71610	1.3964	16	.71039	1.0093	.70381	1.4208
18	.69841	.97586	.71569	1.3972	18	.71080	1.0105	.70339	1.4217
20	.69883	.97699	.71528	1.3980	20	.71121	1.0117	.70298	1.4225
22	.69925	.97813	.71488	1.3988	22	.71162	1.0129	.70257	1.4233
24	.69966	.97927	.71447	1.3996	24	.71202	1.0141	.70215	1.4242
26	.70008	.98041	.71406	1.4004	26	.71243	1.0152	.70174	1.4250
28	.70049	.98155	.71366	1.4012	28	.71284	1.0164	.70132	1.4259
30	.70091	.98270	.71325	1.4020	30	.71325	1.0176	.70091	1.4267
32	.70132	.98384	.71284	1.4028	32	.71366	1.0188	.70049	1.4276
34	.70174	.98499	.71243	1.4036	34	.71406	1.0200	.70008	1.4284
36	.70215	.98613	.71202	1.4044	36	.71447	1.0212	.69966	1.4292
38	.70257	.98728	.71162	1.4052	38	.71488	1.0223	.69925	1.4301
40	.70298	.98843	.71121	1.4060	40	.71528	1.0235	.69883	1.4310
42	.70339	.98958	.71080	1.4069	42	.71569	1.0247	.69841	1.4318
44	.70381	.99073	.71039	1.4077	44	.71610	1.0259	.69800	1.4327
46	.70422	.99189	.70998	1.4085	46	.71650	1.0271	.69758	1.4335
48	.70463	.99304	.70957	1.4093	48	.71691	1.0283	.69716	1.4344
50	.70505	.99420	.70916	1.4101	50	.71732	1.0295	.69675	1.4352
52	.70546	.99535	.70875	1.4109	52	.71772	1.0307	.69633	1.4361
54	.70587	.99651	.70834	1.4117	54	.71812	1.0319	.69591	1.4370
56	.70628	.99767	.70793	1.4126	56	.71853	1.0331	.69549	1.4378
58	.70669	.99884	.70752	1.4134	58	.71893	1.0343	.69507	1.4387

NATURAL SINES, TANGENTS, COSINES AND SECANTS.

	46 Deg.					47 Deg.			
MIN	SINE.	TANG.	COSINE.	SEC.	MIN	SINE.	TANG.	COSINE.	SEC.
0	.71984	1.0355	.69466	1.4395	0	.73135	1.0724	.68200	1.4663
2	.71974	1.0367	.69424	1.4404	2	.73175	1.0736	.68157	1.4672
4	.72015	1.0379	.69382	1.4413	4	.73215	1.0748	.68115	1.4681
6	.72055	1.0391	.69340	1.4422	6	.73254	1.0761	.68072	1.4690
8	.72095	1.0403	.69298	1.4430	8	.73294	1.0774	.68029	1.4699
10	72136	1.0416	.69256	1.4439	10	.73333	1.0786	.67987	1.4709
12	.72176	1.0428	.69214	1.4448	12	.73373	1.0799	.67944	1.4718
14	.72216	1.0440	.69172	1.4457	14	.73412	1.0812	.67901	1.4727
16	.72256	1.0452	.69130	1.4465	16	.73452	1.0824	.67859	1.4736
18	.72297	1.0464	.69088	1.4474	18	.73491	1.0837	.67816	1.4745
20	.72337	1.0476	.69046	1.4483	20	.73531	1.0849	.67773	1.4755
22	.72377	1.0489	.69004	1.4492	22	.73570	1.0862	.67730	1.4764
24	.72417	1.0501	.68962	1.4501	24	.73610	1.0875	.67687	1.4774
26	.72457	1.0513	.68920	1.4510	26	.73649	1.0887	.67645	1.4783
28	.72497	1.0525	.68878	1.4518	28	.73688	1.0900	.67602	1.4792
30	.72537	1.0538	.68835	1.4527	30	.73728	1.0913	.67559	1.4802
32	.72577	1.0550	.68793	1.4536	32	.73767	1.0926	.67516	1.4811
34	.72617	1.0562	.68751	1.4545	34	.73806	1.0938	.67473	1.4821
36	.72657	1.0575	.68709	1.4554	36	.73845	1.0951	.67430	1.4830
38	.72697	1.0587	.68666	1.4563	38	.73885	1.0964	.67387	1.4839
40	.72737	1.0599	.68624	1.4572	40	.73924	1.0977	.67344	1.4849
42	.72777	1.0612	.68582	1.4581	42	.73963	1.0990	.67301	1.4858
44	.72817	1.0624	.68539	1.4590	44	.74002	1.1003	.67258	1.4868
46	.72857	1.0636	.68497	1.4599	46	.74041	1.1015	.67215	1.4877
48	.72897	1.0649	.68455	1.4608	48	.74080	1.1028	.67172	1.4887
50	.72937	1.0661	.68412	1.4617	50	.74119	1.1041	.67129	1.4897
52	.72976	1.0674	.68370	1.4626	52	.74158	1.1054	.67086	1.4906
54	.73016	1.0686	.68327	1.4635	54	.74197	1.1067	.67043	1.4916
56	.73056	1.0699	.68285	1.4644	56	.74236	1.1080	.66999	1.4925
58	.73096	1.0711	.68242	1.4654	58	.74275	1.1093	.66956	1.4935

NATURAL SINES, TANGENTS, COSINES AND SECANTS.

	48 Deg.					49 Deg.			
MIN	SINE.	TANG.	COSINE.	SEC.	MIN	SINE.	TANG.	COSINE.	SEC.
0	.74314	1.11061	.66913	1.4946	0	.75471	1.15037	.65606	1.5242
2	.74353	1.11191	.66870	1.4954	2	.75509	1.15172	.65562	1 5253
4	.74392	1.11321	.66827	1.4964	4	.75547	1.15308	.65518	1.5263
6	.74431	1.11452	.66783	1.4974	6	.75585	1.15443	.65474	1.5273
8	.74470	1.11582	.66740	1.4983	8	.75623	1.15579	.65430	1.5283
10	.74509	1.11713	.66697	1.4993	10	.75661	1.15715	.65386	1.5294
12	.74548	1.11844	.66653	1.5003	12	.75700	1.15851	.65342	1.5304
14	.74586	1.11975	.66610	1.5013	14	.75738	1.15987	.65298	1.5314
16	.74625	1.12106	.66566	1.5022	16	.75775	1.16124	.65254	1.5325
18	.74664	1.12238	.66523	1.5032	18	.75813	1.16261	.65210	1.5335
20	.74703	1.12369	.66480	1.5042	20	.75851	1.16398	.65166	1.5345
22	.74741	1.12501	.66436	1.5052	22	.75889	1.16535	.65122	1.5356
24	.74780	1.12633	.66393	1.5062	24	.75927	1.16672	.65077	1.5366
26	.74818	1.12765	.66349	1.5072	26	.75965	1.16809	.65033	1.5377
28	.74857	1.12897	.66306	1.5082	28	.76003	1.16947	.64989	1.5387
30	.74896	1.13029	.66262	1.5092	30	.76041	1.17085	.64945	1.5398
32	.74934	1.13162	.66218	1.5101	32	.76078	1.17223	.64901	1.5408
34	.74973	1.13295	.66175	1.5111	34	.76116	1.17361	.64856	1.5419
36	.75011	1.13428	.66131	1.5121	36	.76154	1.17500	.64812	1.5429
38	.75050	1.13561	.66088	1.5131	38	.76192	1.17638	.64768	1.5440
40	.75088	1.13694	.66044	1.5141	40	.76229	1.17776	.64723	1.5450
42	.75126	1.13828	.66000	1.5151	42	.76267	1.17916	.64679	1.5461
44	.75165	1.13961	.65956	1.5161	44	.76304	1.18055	.64635	1.5471
46	.75203	1.14095	.65913	1.5171	46	.76342	1.18194	.64590	1.5482
48	.75241	1.14229	.65869	1.5182	48	.76380	1.18334	.64546	1.5493
50	.75280	1.14363	.65825	1.5192	50	.76417	1.18474	.64501	1.5503
52	.75318	1.14498	.65781	1.5202	52	.76455	1.18614	.64457	1.5514
54	.75356	1.14632	.65738	1.5212	54	.76492	1.18754	.64412	1.5525
56	.75395	1.14767	.65694	1.5222	56	.76530	1.18894	.64368	1.5536
58	.75433	1.14902	.65650	1.5232	58	.76567	1.19035	.64323	1.5546

NATURAL SINES, TANGENTS, COSINES AND SECANTS.

	50 DEG.					51 DEG.			
MIN	SINE.	TANG.	COSINE.	SEC.	MIN	SINE.	TANG.	COSINE.	SEC.
0	.76604	1.19175	.64279	1.5557	0	.77715	1.23490	.62932	1.5890
2	.76642	1.19316	.64234	1.5568	2	.77751	1.23637	.62887	1.5901
4	.76679	1.19457	.64190	1.5579	4	.77788	1.23784	.62842	1.5913
6	.76717	1.19599	.64145	1.5590	6	.77824	1.23931	.62796	1.5924
8	.76754	1.19740	.64100	1.5600	8	.77861	1.24079	.62751	1.5936
10	.76791	1.19882	.64056	1.5611	10	.77897	1.24227	.62706	1.5947
12	.76828	1.20024	.64011	1.5622	12	.77934	1.24375	.62660	1.5959
14	.76866	1.20166	.63966	1.5633	14	.77970	1.24523	.62615	1.5971
16	.76903	1.20308	.63922	1.5644	16	.78007	1.24672	.62570	1.5982
18	.76940	1.20451	.63877	1.5655	18	.78043	1.24820	.62524	1.5994
20	.76977	1.20593	.63832	1.5666	20	.78079	1.24969	.62479	1.6005
22	.77014	1.20736	.63787	1.5677	22	.78116	1.25118	.62433	1.6017
24	.77051	1.20879	.63742	1.5688	24	.78152	1.25268	.62388	1.6029
26	.77088	1.21023	.63698	1.5699	26	.78188	1.25417	.62342	1.6040
28	.77125	1.21166	.63653	1.5710	28	.78225	1.25567	.62297	1.6052
30	.77162	1.21310	.63608	1.5721	30	.78261	1.25717	.62251	1.6064
32	.77199	1.21454	.63563	1.5732	32	.78296	1.25867	.62206	1.6077
34	.77236	1.21598	.63518	1.5743	34	.78333	1.26018	.62160	1.6088
36	.77273	1.21742	.63473	1.5755	36	.78369	1.26169	.62115	1.6099
38	.77310	1.21885	.63428	1.5766	38	.78405	1.26319	.62069	1.6111
40	.77347	1.22031	.63383	1.5777	40	.78442	1.26471	.62024	1.6123
42	.77384	1.22176	.63338	1.5788	42	.78478	1.26622	.61978	1.6135
44	.77421	1.22321	.63293	1.5799	44	.78514	1.26775	.61932	1.6147
46	.77458	1.22467	.63248	1.5811	46	.78550	1.26925	.61887	1.6159
48	.77494	1.22612	.63203	1.5822	48	.78586	1.27077	.61841	1.6170
50	.77531	1.22758	.63158	1.5833	50	.78622	1.27230	.61795	1.6182
52	.77568	1.22904	.63113	1.5845	52	.78658	1.27382	.61749	1.6194
54	.77605	1.23050	.63068	1.5856	54	.78694	1.27535	.61704	1.6206
56	.77641	1.23196	.63022	1.5867	56	.78729	1.27688	.61658	1.6218
58	.77677	1.23343	.62977	1.5879	58	.78765	1.27841	.61612	1.6231

NATURAL SINES, TANGENTS, COSINES AND SECANTS.

		52 Deg.				53 Deg.		
MIN	SINE.	TANG.	COSINE.	SEC·	MIN	SINE.	TANG.	COSINE.	SEC.
0	.78801	1.27994	.61566	1.6243	0	.79864	1.32704	.60182	1.6618
2	.78837	1.28148	.61520	1.6255	2	.79899	1.32865	.60135	1 6629
4	.78873	1.28302	.61474	1.6267	4	.79934	1.33026	.60089	1.6642
6	.78908	1.28456	.61429	1.6279	6	.79968	1.33187	.60042	1.6655
8	.78944	1.28610	.61383	1.6291	8	.80003	1.33349	.59994	1.6668
10	.78980	1.28764	.61337	1.6303	10	.80038	1.33511	.59949	1.6681
12	.79016	1.28919	.61291	1.6316	12	.80073	1.33673	.59902	1.6694
14	.79051	1.29074	.61245	1.6328	14	.80108	1.33835	.59856	1.6707
16	.79087	1.29229	.61199	1.6340	16	.80143	1.33998	.59809	1.6720
18	.79122	1.29385	.61153	1.6352	18	.80178	1.34160	.59763	1.6733
20	.79158	1.29541	.61107	1.6365	20	.80212	1.34323	.59716	1.6746
22	.79193	1.29696	.61061	1.6377	22	.80247	1.34487	.59669	1.6759
24	.79229	1.29853	.61015	1.6389	24	.80282	1.34650	.59622	1.6772
26	.79264	1.30009	.60968	1.6402	26	.80316	1.34814	.59576	1.6785
28	.79300	1.30166	.60922	1.6414	28	.80351	1.34978	.59529	1.6798
30	.79335	1.30323	.60876	1.6427	30	.80386	1.35142	.59482	1.6812
32	.79371	1.30480	.60830	1.6439	32	.80420	1.35307	.59436	1.6825
34	.79406	1.30637	.60784	1.6452	34	.80455	1.35472	.59389	1.6838
36	.79441	1.30795	.60738	1.6464	36	.80489	1.35637	.59342	1.6851
38	.79477	1.30952	.60691	1.6477	38	.80524	1.35802	.59295	1.6865
40	.79512	1.31110	.60645	1.6489	40	.80558	1.35968	.59248	1.6878
42	.79547	1.31269	.60599	1.6502	42	.80593	1.36134	.59201	1.6891
44	.79583	1.31427	.60553	1.6514	44	.80627	1.36300	.59154	1.6905
46	.79618	1.31586	.60506	1.6527	46	.80662	1.36466	.59108	1.6918
48	.79653	1.31745	.60460	1.6540	48	.80696	1.36633	.59061	1.6932
50	.79688	1.31904	.60414	1.6552	50	.80730	1.36800	.59014	1.6945
52	.79723	1.32064	.60367	1.6565	52	.80765	1.36967	.58967	1.6959
54	.79758	1.32224	.60321	1.6578	54	.80799	1.37134	.58920	1.6972
56	.79793	1.32384	.60274	1.6591	56	.80833	1.37302	.58873	1.6986
58	.79829	1.32544	.60228	1.6603	58	.80867	1.37470	.58826	1.6999

NATURAL SINES, TANGENTS, COSINES AND SECANTS.

	54 DEG.				55 DEG.		
MIN	SINE.	TANG.	COSINE.	SEC.	MIN	SINE.	TANG.	COSINE.	SEC.
0	.80902	1.37638	.58779	1.7013	0	.81915	1.42815	.57358	1.7434
2	.80936	1.37807	.58731	1.7027	2	.81949	1.42992	.57310	1.7449
4	.80970	1.37976	.58684	1.7040	4	.81982	1.43169	.57262	1.7463
6	.81004	1.38145	.58637	1.7054	6	.82015	1.43347	.57215	1.7478
8	.81038	1.38314	.58590	1.7068	8	.82048	1.43525	.57167	1.7493
10	.81072	1.38484	.58543	1.7081	10	.82082	1.43703	.57119	1.7507
12	.81106	1.38653	.58496	1.7095	12	.82115	1.43881	.57071	1.7522
14	.81140	1.38824	.58449	1.7109	14	.82148	1.44060	.57024	1.7537
16	.81174	1.38994	.58401	1.7123	16	.82181	1.44239	.56976	1.7551
18	.81208	1.39165	.58354	1.7137	18	.82214	1.44418	.56928	1.7566
20	.81242	1.39336	.58307	1.7151	20	.82248	1.44598	.56880	1.7581
22	.81276	1.39507	.58260	1.7164	22	.82281	1.44778	.56832	1.7596
24	.81310	1.39679	.58212	1.7178	24	.82314	1.44958	.56784	1.7610
26	.81344	1.39850	.58165	1.7192	26	.82347	1.45189	.56736	1.7625
28	.81378	1.40022	.58118	1.7206	28	.82380	1.45320	.56689	1.7640
30	.81412	1.40195	.58070	1.7220	30	.82413	1.45501	.56641	1.7655
32	.81445	1.40367	.58023	1.7234	32	.82446	1.45682	.56593	1.7670
34	.81479	1.40540	.57976	1.7249	34	.82478	1.45864	.56545	1.7685
36	.81513	1.40714	.57928	1.7263	36	.82511	1.46046	.56497	1.7700
38	.81546	1.40887	.57881	1.7277	38	.82544	1.46229	.56449	1.7715
40	.81580	1.41061	.57833	1.7291	40	.82577	1.46411	.56401	1.7730
42	.81614	1.41235	.57786	1.7305	42	.82610	1.46595	.56353	1.7745
44	.81647	1.41409	.57738	1.7319	44	.82643	1.46778	.56305	1.7760
46	.81681	1.41584	.57691	1.7334	46	.82675	1.46962	.56256	1.7775
48	.81714	1.41759	.57643	1.7348	48	.82708	1.47146	.56208	1.7791
50	.81748	1.41934	.57596	1.7362	50	.82741	1.47330	.56160	1.7806
52	.81782	1.42110	.57548	1.7377	52	.82773	1.47514	.56112	1.7821
54	.81815	1.42286	.57501	1.7391	54	.82806	1.47699	.56064	1.7837
56	.81848	1.42462	.57453	1.7405	56	.82839	1.47885	.56016	1.7852
58	.81882	1.42638	.57405	1.7420	58	.82871	1.48070	.55968	1.7867

NATURAL SINES, TANGENTS, COSINES AND SECANTS.

	56 Deg.					57 Deg.			
MIN	SINE.	TANG.	COSINE.	SEC.	MIN	SINE.	TANG.	COSINE.	SEC.
0	.82904	1.48256	.55919	1.7883	0	.83867	1.53986	.54464	1.8361
2	.82936	1.48442	.55871	1.7898	2	.83899	1.54183	.54415	1.8377
4	.82969	1.48629	.55823	1.7914	4	.83930	1.54379	.54366	1.8394
6	.83001	1.48816	.55775	1.7929	6	.83962	1.54576	.54317	1.8410
8	.83034	1.49003	.55726	1.7945	8	.83994	1.54774	.54269	1.8427
10	.83066	1.49190	.55678	1.7960	10	.84025	1.54972	.54220	1.8443
12	.83098	1.49378	.55630	1.7976	12	.84057	1.55170	.54171	1.8460
14	.83131	1.49566	.55581	1.7992	14	.84088	1.55368	.54122	1.8477
16	.83163	1.49755	.55533	1.8007	16	.84120	1.55567	.54073	1.8493
18	.83195	1.49944	.55484	1.8023	18	.84151	1.55766	.54024	1.8510
20	.83228	1.50133	.55436	1.8039	20	.84182	1.55966	.53975	1.8527
22	.83260	1.50322	.55388	1.8054	22	.84214	1.56165	.53926	1.8544
24	.83292	1.50512	.55339	1.8070	24	.84245	1.56366	.53877	1.8561
26	.83324	1.50702	.55291	1.8086	26	.84277	1.56566	.53828	1.8578
28	.83356	1.50893	.55242	1.8102	28	.84308	1.56767	.53779	1.8595
30	.83389	1.51084	.55194	1.8118	30	.84339	1.56969	.53730	1.8611
32	.83421	1.51275	.55145	1.8134	32	.84370	1.57170	.53681	1.8629
34	.83453	1.51466	.55097	1.8150	34	.84402	1.57372	.53632	1.8646
36	.83485	1.51658	.55048	1.8166	36	.84433	1.57575	.53583	1.8663
38	.83517	1.51850	.54999	1.8182	38	.84464	1.57778	.53534	1.8680
40	.83549	1.52043	.54951	1.8198	40	.84495	1.57981	.53484	1.8697
42	.83581	1.52235	.54902	1.8214	42	.84526	1.58184	.53435	1.8714
44	.83613	1.52429	.54854	1.8230	44	.84557	1.58388	.53386	1.8731
46	.83645	1.52622	.54805	1.8246	46	.84588	1.58593	.53337	1.8749
48	.83676	1.52816	.54756	1.8263	48	.84619	1.58797	.53288	1.8766
50	.83708	1.53010	.54708	1.8279	50	.84650	1.59002	.53238	1.8783
52	.83740	1.53205	.54659	1.8295	52	.84681	1.59208	.53189	1.8801
54	.83772	1.53400	.54610	1.8311	54	.84712	1.59414	.53140	1.8818
56	.83804	1.53595	.54561	1.8328	56	.84743	1.59620	.53091	1.8836
58	.83835	1.53791	.54513	1.8344	58	.84774	1.59826	.53041	1.8853

NATURAL SINES, TANGENTS, COSINES AND SECANTS.

MIN	SINE.	TANG.	COSINE.	SEC.	MIN	SINE.	TANG.	COSINE.	SEC.
		58 Deg.					**59 Deg.**		
0	.84805	1.60033	.52992	1.8871	0	.85717	1.66428	.51504	1.9416
2	.84836	1.60241	.52943	1.8888	2	.85747	1.66647	.51454	1.9435
4	.84866	1.60449	.52893	1.8906	4	.85777	1.66867	.51404	1.9454
6	.84897	1.60657	.52844	1.8924	6	.85806	1.67088	.51354	1.9473
8	.84928	1.60865	.52794	1.8941	8	.85836	1.67309	.51304	1.9491
10	.84959	1.61074	.52745	1.8959	10	.85866	1.67530	.51254	1.9510
12	.84989	1.61283	.52696	1.8977	12	.85896	1.67752	.51204	1.9530
14	.85020	1.61493	.52646	1.8995	14	.85926	1.67974	.51154	1.9549
16	.85051	1.61703	.52597	1.9013	16	.85956	1.68196	.51104	1.9568
18	.85081	1.61914	.52547	1.9030	18	.85985	1.68419	.51054	1.9587
20	.85112	1.62125	.52498	1.9048	20	.86015	1.68643	.51004	1.9606
22	.85142	1.62336	.52448	1.9066	22	.86045	1.68866	.50954	1.9625
24	.85173	1.62548	.52399	1.9084	24	.86074	1.69091	.50904	1.9645
26	.85203	1.62760	.52349	1.9102	26	.86104	1.69316	.50854	1.9664
28	.85234	1.62972	.52299	1.9121	28	.86133	1.69541	.50804	1.9683
30	.85264	1.63185	.52250	1.9139	30	.86163	1.69766	.50754	1.9703
32	.85294	1.63398	.52200	1.9157	32	.86192	1.69992	.50704	1.9722
34	.85325	1.63612	.52151	1.9175	34	.86222	1.70219	.50654	1.9742
36	.85355	1.63826	.52101	1.9193	36	.86251	1.70446	.50603	1.9761
38	.85385	1.64041	.52051	1.9212	38	.86281	1.70673	.50553	1.9781
40	.85416	1.64256	.52002	1.9230	40	.86310	1.70901	.50503	1.9801
42	.85446	1.64471	.51952	1.9248	42	.86340	1.71129	.50453	1.9820
44	.85476	1.64687	.51902	1.9267	44	.86369	1.71358	.50403	1.9840
46	.85506	1.64903	.51852	1.9285	46	.86398	1.71588	.50352	1.9860
48	.85536	1.65120	.51803	1.9304	48	.86427	1.71817	.50302	1.9880
50	.85567	1.65337	.51753	1.9322	50	.86457	1.72047	.50252	1.9900
52	.85597	1.65554	.51703	1.9341	52	.86486	1.72278	.50201	1.9920
54	.85627	1.65772	.51653	1.9360	54	.86515	1.72509	.50151	1.9940
56	.85657	1.65990	.51604	1.9378	56	.86544	1.72741	.50101	1.9960
58	.85487	1.66209	.51554	1.9397	58	.86573	1.72973	.50050	1.9980

NATURAL SINES, TANGENTS, COSINES AND SECANTS.

MIN	SINE.	TANG.	COSINE.	SEC.	MIN	SINE.	TANG.	COSINE.	SEC.
	60 Deg.					**61 Deg.**			
0	.86603	1.73205	.5	2.	0	.87462	1.80405	.48481	2.063
2	.86632	1.73438	.49950	2.002	2	.87490	1.80653	.48430	2 065
4	.86661	1.73671	.49899	2.004	4	.87518	1.80901	.48379	2.067
6	.86690	1.73905	.49849	2.006	6	.87546	1.81150	.48328	2.069
8	.86719	1.74140	.49798	2.008	8	.87575	1.81399	.48277	2.071
10	.86748	1.74375	.49748	2.010	10	.87603	1.81649	.48226	2.073
12	.86777	1.74610	.49697	2.012	12	.87631	1.81899	.48175	2.076
14	.86805	1.74846	.49647	2.014	14	.87659	1.82150	.48124	2.078
16	.86834	1.75082	.49596	2.016	16	.87687	1.82402	.48073	2.080
18	.86863	1.75319	.49546	2.018	18	.87715	1.82654	.48022	2.082
20	.86892	1.75556	.49495	2.020	20	.87743	1.82906	.47971	2.085
22	.86921	1.75794	.49445	2.022	22	.87770	1 83159	.47920	2.087
24	.86949	1.76032	.49394	2.024	24	.87798	1.83413	.47869	2.089
26	.86978	1.76271	.49344	2.026	26	.87826	1.83667	.47818	2.091
28	.87007	1.76510	.49293	2.029	28	.87854	1.83922	.47767	2.093
30	.87036	1.76749	.49242	2.031	30	.87882	1.84177	.47716	2.096
32	.87064	1.76990	.49192	2.033	32	.87909	1.84433	.47665	2.098
34	.87093	1.77230	.49141	2.035	34	.87937	1.84689	.47614	2.100
36	.87121	1.77471	.49090	2.037	36	.87965	1.84946	.47562	2.102
38	.87150	1.77713	.49040	2.039	38	.87993	1.85204	.47511	2.105
40	.87178	1.77955	.48999	2.041	40	.88020	1.85462	.47460	2.107
42	.87207	1.78198	.48938	2.043	42	.88048	1.85720	.47409	2.109
44	.87235	1.78441	.48888	2.045	44	.88075	1.85979	.47358	2.112
46	.87264	1.78685	.48837	2.047	46	.88103	1.86239	.47306	2.114
48	.87292	1.78929	.48786	2.050	48	.88130	1.86499	.47255	2.116
50	.87321	1.79174	.48735	2.052	50	.88158	1.86760	.47204	2.118
52	.87349	1.79419	.48684	2.054	52	.88185	1.87021	.47153	2.121
54	.87377	1.79665	.48634	2.056	54	.88213	1.87283	.47101	2.123
56	.87406	1.79911	.48583	2.058	56	.88240	1.87546	.47050	2.125
58	.87434	1.80158	.48532	2.060	58	.88267	1.87809	.46999	2.128

NATURAL SINES, TANGENTS, COSINES AND SECANTS.

		62 Deg.					63 Deg.		
MIN	SINE.	TANG.	COSINE.	SEC.	MIN	SINE.	TANG.	COSINE.	SEC.
0	.88295	1.88073	.46947	2.130	0	.89101	1.96261	.45399	2.203
2	.88322	1.88337	.46896	2.132	2	.89127	1.96544	.45347	2.205
4	.88349	1.88602	.46844	2.135	4	.89153	1.96827	.45295	2.208
6	.88377	1.88867	.46793	2.137	6	.89180	1.97111	.45243	2.210
8	88404	1.89133	.46742	2.139	8	.89206	1.97395	.45192	2.213
10	.88431	1.89400	.46690	2.142	10	.89232	1.97681	.45140	2.215
12	.88458	1.89667	.46639	2.144	12	.89259	1.97966	.45088	2.218
14	.88485	1.89935	.46587	2.146	14	.89285	1.98253	.45036	2.220
16	.88512	1.90203	.46536	2.149	16	.89311	1.98540	.44984	2.223
18	.88539	1.90472	.46484	2.151	18	.89337	1.98828	.44932	2.226
20	.88566	1.90741	.46433	2.154	20	.89363	1.99116	.44880	2.228
22	.88593	1.91012	.46381	2.156	22	.89389	1.99406	.44828	2.231
24	.88620	1.91282	.46330	2.158	24	.89415	1.99695	.44776	2.233
26	.88647	1.91554	.46278	2.161	26	.89441	1.99986	.44724	2.236
28	.88674	1.91826	.46226	2.163	28	.89467	2.00277	.44672	2.238
30	.88701	1.92098	.46175	2.166	30	.89493	2.00569	.44620	2.241
32	.88728	1.92371	.46123	2.168	32	.89519	2.00862	.44568	2.244
34	.88755	1.92645	.46072	2.170	34	.89545	2.01155	.44516	2.246
36	.88782	1.92920	.46020	2.173	36	.89571	2.01449	.44464	2.249
38	.88808	1.93195	.45968	2.175	38	.89597	2.01743	.44411	2.252
40	.88835	1.93470	.45917	2.178	40	.89623	2.02039	.44359	2.254
42	.88862	1.93746	.45865	2.180	42	.89649	2.02335	.44307	2.257
44	.88888	1.94023	.45813	2.183	44	.89674	2.02631	.44255	2.260
46	.88915	1.94301	.45762	2.185	46	.89700	2.02929	.44203	2.262
48	.88942	1.94579	.45710	2.188	48	.89726	2.03227	.44151	2.265
50	.88968	1.94858	.45658	2.190	50	.89752	2.03526	.44098	2.268
52	.88995	1.95137	.45606	2.193	52	.89777	2.03825	.44046	2.270
54	.89021	1.95417	.45554	2.195	54	.89803	2.04125	.43994	2.273
56	.89048	1.95698	.45503	2.198	56	.89828	2.04426	.43942	2.276
58	.89074	1.95979	.45451	2.200	58	.89854	2.04728	.43889	2.278

NATURAL SINES, TANGENTS, COSINES AND SECANTS.

		64 DEG.					65 DEG.		
MIN	SINE.	TANG.	COSINE.	SEC.	MIN	SINE.	TANG.	COSINE.	SEC.
0	.89879	2.0503	.43837	2.281	0	.90631	.21445	.42262	2.366
2	.89905	2.0533	.43785	2.284	2	.90655	.21478	.42209	2.369
4	.89930	2.0564	.43733	2.287	4	.90680	.21510	.42156	2.372
6	.89956	2.0594	.43680	2 289	6	.90704	.21543	.42104	2.375
8	.89981	2.0625	.43628	2.292	8	.90729	.21576	.42051	2.378
10	.90007	2.0655	.43575	2.295	10	.90753	.21609	.41998	2.381
12	.90032	2.0686	.43523	2.297	12	.90778	.21642	.41945	2.384
14	.90057	2.0717	.43471	2.300	14	.90802	.21675	.41892	2.887
16	.90082	2.0747	.43418	2.303	16	.90826	.21708	.41840	2.390
18	.90108	2.0778	.43366	2.306	18	.90851	.21742	.41787	2.393
20	.90133	2.0809	.43313	2.309	20	.90875	.21775	.41734	2.396
22	.90158	2.0840	.43261	2.311	22	.90899	.21808	.41681	2.399
24	.90183	2.0872	.43209	2.314	24	.90924	.21842	.41628	2.402
26	.90208	2.0903	.43156	2.317	26	.90948	.21875	.41575	2.405
28	.90233	2.0934	.43104	2.320	28	.90972	.21909	.41522	2.408
30	.90259	2.0965	.43051	2.323	30	.90996	.21943	.41469	2.411
32	.90284	2.0997	.42999	2.326	32	.91020	.21977	.41416	2.414
34	.90309	2.1028	.42946	2.328	34	.91044	.22011	.41363	2.417
36	.90334	2.1060	.42894	2.331	36	.91068	.22045	.41840	2.421
38	.90358	2.1092	.42841	2.334	38	.91092	.22079	.41257	2.424
40	.90383	2.1123	.42788	2.337	40	.91116	.22113	.41204	2.427
42	.90408	2.1155	.42736	2.340	42	.91140	.22147	.41151	2.430
44	.90433	2.1187	.42683	2.343	44	.91164	.22182	.41098	2.433
46	.90458	2.1219	.42631	2 346	46	.91188	.22216	.41045	2.436
48	.90483	2.1251	.42578	2.349	48	.91212	.22251	.40992	2.439
50	.90507	2.1283	.42525	2.351	50	.91236	.22286	.40939	2.443
52	.90532	2.1315	.42473	2.354	52	.91260	.22320	.40886	2.446
54	.90557	2.1348	.42420	2.357	54	.91283	.22355	.40833	2.449
56	.90582	2.1380	.42367	2.360	56	.91307	.22390	.40780	2.452
58	.90606	2.1412	.42315	2.363	58	.91331	.22425	.40727	2.455

NATURAL SINES, TANGENTS, COSINES AND SECANTS.

	66 Deg.					67 Deg.			
MIN	SINE.	TANG.	COSINE.	SEC.	MIN.	SINE.	TANG.	COSINE.	SEC.
0	.91355	2.2460	.40674	2.458	0	.92050	2.3558	.39073	2.559
2	.91378	2.2495	.40621	2.462	2	.92073	2.3597	.39020	2.563
4	.91402	2.2531	.40567	2.465	4	.92096	2.3635	.38966	2.566
6	.91425	2.2566	.40514	2.468	6	.92119	2.3673	.38912	2.570
8	.91449	2.2602	.40461	2.471	8	.92141	2.3712	.38859	2.573
10	.91472	2.2637	.40408	2.475	10	.92164	2.3750	.38805	2.577
12	.91496	2.2673	.40355	2.478	12	.92186	2.3789	.38752	2.580
14	.91519	2.2709	.40301	2.481	14	.92209	2.3828	.38698	2.584
16	.91543	2.2745	.40248	2.485	16	.92231	2.3867	.38644	2.588
18	.91566	2.2781	.40195	2.488	18	.92254	2.3906	.38591	2.591
20	.91590	2.2816	.40141	2.491	20	.92276	2.3945	.38537	2.595
22	.91613	2.2853	.40088	2.494	22	.92299	2.3984	.38483	2.598
24	.91636	2.2889	.40035	2.498	24	.92321	2.4023	.38430	2.602
26	.91660	2.2925	.39982	2.501	26	.92343	2.4063	.38376	2.606
28	.91683	2.2962	.39928	2.504	28	.92366	2.4102	.38322	2.609
30	.91706	2.2998	.39875	2.508	30	.92388	2.4142	.38268	2.613
32	.91729	2.3035	.39822	2.511	32	.92410	2.4182	.38215	2.617
34	.91752	2.3072	.39768	2.515	34	.92432	2.4222	.38161	2.620
36	.91775	2.3108	.39715	2.518	36	.92455	2.4262	.38107	2.624
38	.91799	2.3145	.39661	2.521	38	.92477	2.4302	.38053	2.628
40	.91822	2.3183	.39608	2.525	40	.92499	2.4342	.37999	2.632
42	.91845	2.3219	.39555	2.528	42	.92521	2.4382	.37946	2.635
44	.91868	2.3257	.39501	2.532	44	.92543	2.4423	.37892	2.639
46	.91891	2.3294	.39448	2.535	46	.92565	2.4464	.37838	2.643
48	.91914	2.3332	.39394	2.538	48	.92587	2.4504	.37784	2.647
50	.91936	2.3369	.39341	2.542	50	.92609	2.4545	.37730	2.650
52	.91959	2.3407	.39287	2.545	52	.92631	2.4586	.37676	2.654
54	.91982	2.3445	.39234	2.549	54	.92653	2.4627	.37622	2.658
56	.92005	2.3482	.39180	2.552	56	.92675	2.4668	.37569	2.662
58	.92028	2.3520	.39127	2.556	58	.92697	2.4709	.37515	2.666

NATURAL SINES, TANGENTS, COSINES
AND SECANTS.

MIN	SINE.	TANG.	COSINE.	SEC.	MIN	SINE.	TANG.	COSINE.	SEC.
	68 Deg.					**69 Deg.**			
0	.92718	2.4751	.37461	2.669	0	.93358	2.6051	.35837	2.790
2	.92740	2.4792	.37407	2.673	2	.93379	2.6096	.35782	2 795
4	.92762	2.4834	.37353	2.677	4	.93400	2.6142	.35728	2.799
6	.92784	2.4876	.37299	2.681	6	.93420	2.6187	.35674	2.803
8	.92805	2.4918	.37245	2.685	8	.93441	2.6233	.35619	2.807
10	.92827	2.4960	.37191	2.689	10	.93462	2.6279	.35565	2.812
12	.92849	2.5002	.37137	2.693	12	.93483	2.6325	.35511	2.816
14	.92870	2.5044	.37083	2.697	14	.93503	2.6371	.35456	2.820
16	.92892	2.5086	.37029	2.700	16	.93524	2.6418	.35402	2.825
18	.92913	2.5129	.36975	2.704	18	.93544	2.6464	.35347	2.829
20	.92935	2.5171	.36921	2.708	20	.93565	2.6511	.35293	2.833
22	.92956	2.5214	.36867	2.712	22	.93585	2 6557	.35239	2.838
24	.92978	2.5257	.36812	2.716	24	.93606	2.6604	.35184	2.842
26	.92999	2.5300	.36758	2.720	26	.93626	2.6651	.35130	2.847
28	.93020	2.5343	.36704	2.724	28	.93647	2.6699	.35075	2.851
30	.93042	2.5386	.36650	2.728	30	.93667	2.6746	.35021	2.855
32	.93063	2.5430	.36596	2.732	32	.93688	2.6794	.34966	2.860
34	.93084	2.5473	.36542	2.737	34	.93708	2.6841	.34912	2.864
36	.93106	2.5517	.36488	2.741	36	.93728	2.6889	.34857	2.869
38	.93127	2.5561	.36434	2.745	38	.93748	2.6937	.34803	2.873
40	.93148	2.5604	.36379	2.749	40	.93769	2.6985	.34748	2.878
42	.93169	2.5649	.36325	2.753	42	.93789	2.7033	.34694	2.882
44	.93190	2.5693	.36271	2.757	44	.93809	2.7082	.34639	2.887
46	.93211	2.5737	.36217	2.761	46	.93829	2.7130	.34584	2.891
48	.93232	2.5781	.36162	2.765	48	.93849	2.7179	.34530	2.896
50	.93253	2.5826	.36108	2.769	50	.93869	2.7228	.34475	2.900
52	.93274	2.5871	.36054	2.773	52	.93889	2.7277	.34421	2.905
54	.93295	2.5915	.36000	2.778	54	.93909	2.7326	3.4366	2.910
56	.93316	2.5960	.35945	2.782	56	.93929	2.7375	3.4311	2.914
58	.93337	2.6005	.35891	2.786	58	.93949	2.7425	3.4257	2.919

NATURAL SINES, TANGENTS, COSINES AND SECANTS.

	70 Deg.					71 Deg.			
MIN	SINE.	TANG.	COSINE.	SEC.	MIN	SINE.	TANG.	COSINE.	SEC.
0	.93969	2.7475	.34202	2.924	0	.94552	2.9042	.32557	3.071
2	.93989	2.7524	.34147	2.928	2	.94571	2.9097	.32502	3.077
4	.94009	2.7575	.34093	2.933	4	.94590	2.9152	.32447	3.082
6	.94029	2.7625	.34038	2.938	6	.94609	2.9207	.32392	3.087
8	.94049	2.7675	.33983	2.943	8	.94627	2.9263	.32337	3.092
10	.94068	2.7725	.33929	2.947	10	.94646	2.9319	.32282	3.098
12	.94088	2.7776	.33874	2.952	12	.94665	2.9375	.32227	3.103
14	.94108	2.7827	.33819	2.957	14	.94684	2 9431	.32171	3 108
16	.94127	2.7878	.33764	2.962	16	.94702	2.9487	.32116	3.114
18	.94147	2.7929	.33710	2.966	18	.94721	2.9544	.32061	3.119
20	.94167	2.7980	.83655	2.971	20	.94740	2.9600	.32006	3.124
22	.94186	2.8032	.33600	2.976	22	.94758	2.9657	.31951	3.130
24	.94206	2.8083	.33545	2.981	24	.94777	2.9714	.31896	3.135
26	.94225	2.8135	.33490	2.986	26	.94795	2.9772	.31841	3.141
28	.94245	2.8187	.33436	2.991	28	.94814	2.9829	.31786	3.146
30	.94264	2.8239	.33381	2.996	30	.94832	2.9887	.31730	3.151
32	.94284	2.8291	.33326	3.	32	.94851	2.9945	.31675	3.157
34	.94303	2.8344	.33271	3.005	34	.94869	3.0003	.31620	3.162
36	.94322	2.8396	.33216	3 011	36	.94888	3.0061	.31565	3.168
38	.94342	2.8449	.33161	3.016	38	.94906	3.0119	.31510	3.174
40	.94361	2.8502	.83106	3.021	40	.94924	3.0178	.31454	3.179
42	.94380	2.8555	.33051	3.026	42	.94943	3.0237	.31399	3.185
44	.94399	2.8609	.32997	3.031	44	.94961	3.0296	.31344	3.190
46	.94418	2.8662	.32942	3.036	46	.94979	3.0356	.31289	3.196
48	.94438	2.8716	.32887	3.041	48	.94997	3.0415	.31233	3.202
50	.94457	2.8770	.32832	3.046	50	.95015	3.0475	.31178	3.207
52	.94476	2.8824	.32777	3.051	52	.95033	3.0535	.31123	3.213
54	.94495	2.8878	.32722	3.056	54	.95052	3.0595	.31068	3.219
56	.94514	2.8933	.32667	3.061	56	.95070	3.0655	.31012	3.224
58	.94533	2.8987	.32612	3.066	58	.95088	3.0716	.30957	3.230

NATURAL SINES, TANGENTS, COSINES AND SECANTS.

	72 Deg.					73 Deg.			
MIN	SINE.	TANG.	COSINE.	SEC.	MIN	SINE.	TANG.	COSINE.	SEC.
0	.95106	3.0777	.30902	3.236	0	.95630	.32708	.29237	3.420
2	.95124	3.0838	.30846	3.242	2	.95647	.32777	.29182	3.427
4	.95142	3.0899	.30791	3.248	4	.95664	.32845	.29126	3.433
6	.95159	3.0961	.30736	3.253	6	.95681	.32914	.29070	3.440
8	.95177	3.1022	.30680	3.259	8	.95698	.32983	.29015	3.446
10	.95195	3.1084	.30625	3.265	10	.95715	.33052	.28959	3.453
12	.95213	3.1146	.30570	3.271	12	.95732	.33122	.28903	3.460
14	.95231	3.1209	.30514	3.277	14	.95749	.33191	.28847	3.466
16	.95248	3.1271	.30459	3.283	16	.95766	.33261	.28792	3.473
18	.95266	3.1334	.30403	3.289	18	.95782	.33332	.28736	3.480
20	.95284	3.1397	.30348	3.295	20	.95799	.33402	.28680	3.487
22	.95301	3.1460	.30292	3.301	22	.95816	.33473	.28625	3.493
24	.95319	3.1524	.30237	3.307	24	.95832	.33544	.28569	3.500
26	.95337	3.1588	.30182	3.313	26	.95849	.33616	.28513	3.507
28	.95354	3.1652	.30126	3.319	28	.95865	.33687	.28457	3.514
30	.95372	3.1716	.30071	3.325	30	.95882	.33759	.28402	3.521
32	.95389	3.1780	.30015	3.332	32	.95898	.33832	.28346	3.528
34	.95407	3.1845	.29960	3.338	34	.95915	.33904	.28290	3.535
36	.95424	3.1910	.29904	3.344	36	.95931	.33977	.28234	3.542
38	.95441	3.1975	.29849	3.350	38	.95948	.34050	.28178	3.549
40	.95459	3.2041	.29793	3.356	40	.95964	.34124	.28123	3.556
42	.95476	3.2106	.29737	3.363	42	.95981	.34197	.28067	3.563
44	.95493	3.2172	.29652	3.369	44	.95997	.34271	.28011	3.570
46	.95511	3.2238	.29626	3 375	46	.96013	.34346	.27955	3.577
48	.95528	3.2305	.29571	3.382	48	.96029	.34420	.27899	3.584
50	.95545	3.2371	.29515	3.388	50	.96046	.34495	.27843	3.591
52	.95562	3.2438	.29460	3.394	52	.96062	.34570	.27787	3.599
54	.95579	3.2505	.29404	3.401	54	.96078	.34646	.27731	3.606
56	.95596	3.2573	.29348	3.407	56	.96094	.34722	.27676	3.613
58	.95613	3.2641	.29293	3.414	58	.96110	.34798	.27620	3.621

NATURAL SINES, TANGENTS, COSINES AND SECANTS.

	74 Deg.					75 Deg.			
MIN	SINE.	TANG.	COSINE	SEC.	MIN	SINE.	TANG.	COSINE.	SEC.
0	.96126	3.4874	.27564	3.628	0	.96593	3.7320	.25882	3.864
2	.96142	6.4951	.27508	3.635	2	.96608	3.7407	.25826	3.872
4	.96158	3.5028	.27452	3.643	4	.96623	3.7495	.25769	3.880
6	.96174	3.5105	.27396	3.650	6	.96638	3.7583	.25713	3.899
8	.96190	3.5183	.27340	3.658	8	.96653	3.7671	.25657	3.898
10	.96206	3.5261	.27284	3.665	10	.96667	3.7759	.25601	3.906
12	.96222	3.5339	.27228	3.673	12	.96682	3.7848	.25545	3.915
14	.96238	3.5418	.27172	3.680	14	.96697	3.7938	.25488	3.923
16	.96253	3.5497	.27116	3.688	16	.96712	3.8028	.25432	3.932
18	.96269	3.5576	.27060	3.695	18	.96727	3.8118	.25376	3.941
20	.96285	3.5656	.27004	3.703	20	.96742	3.8208	.25320	3.949
22	.96301	3.5736	.26948	3.711	22	.96756	3.8299	.25263	3.958
24	.96316	3.5816	.26892	3.719	24	.96771	3.8391	.25207	3.967
26	.96332	3.5897	.26836	3.726	26	.96786	3.8482	.25151	3.976
28	.96347	3.5977	.26780	3.734	28	.96800	3.8574	.25094	3.985
30	.96363	3.6059	.26724	3.742	30	.96815	3.8667	.25038	3.994
32	.96379	3.6140	.26668	3.750	32	.96829	3.8760	.24982	4.003
34	.96394	3.6222	.26612	3.758	34	.96844	3.8854	.24925	4.012
36	.96410	3.6305	.26556	3.766	36	.96858	8.8947	.24869	4.021
38	.96425	3.6387	.26500	3.774	38	.96873	3.9042	.24813	4.030
40	.96440	3.6470	.26443	3.782	40	.96887	3.9136	.24756	4.039
42	.96456	3.6554	.26387	3.790	42	.96902	3.9232	.24700	4.049
44	.96471	3.6638	.26331	3.798	44	.96916	3.9327	.24644	4.058
46	.96486	3.6722	.26275	3.806	46	.96930	3.9423	.24587	4.067
48	.96502	3.6806	.26219	3.814	48	.96945	3.9520	.24531	4.076
50	.96517	3.6891	.26163	3.822	50	.96959	3.9616	.24474	4.086
52	.96532	3.6976	.26107	3.830	52	.96973	3.9714	.24418	4.095
54	.96547	3.7062	.26050	3.839	54	.96987	3.9812	.24362	4.105
56	.96562	3.7148	.25994	3.847	56	.97001	3.9910	.24305	4.114
58	.96578	3.7234	.25938	3.855	58	.97015	4.0009	.24249	4.124

NATURAL SINES, TANGENTS, COSINES AND SECANTS.

	76 Deg.				77 Deg.			
MIN	SINE.	TANG.	COSINE.	SEC.	MIN	SINE.	TANG.	COSINE.	SEC.
0	.97030	4.0108	.24192	4.134	0	.97437	4.3315	.22495	4.445
2	.97044	4.0207	.24136	4.143	2	.97450	4.3430	.22438	4 457
4	.97058	4.0307	.24079	4.153	4	.97463	4.3546	.22382	4.468
6	.97072	4.0408	.24023	4.163	6	.97476	4.3662	.22325	4.479
8	.97086	4.0509	.23966	4.172	8	.97489	4.3779	.22268	4.491
10	.97100	4.0611	.23910	4.182	10	.97502	4.3897	.22212	4.502
12	.97113	4.0713	.23853	4.192	12	.97515	4.4015	.22155	4.514
14	.97127	4.0815	.23797	4.202	14	.97528	4.4134	.22098	4.525
16	.97141	4.0918	.23740	4.212	16	.97541	4.4253	.22041	4.537
18	.97155	4.1022	.23684	4.222	18	.97553	4.4373	.21985	4.549
20	.97169	4.1126	.23627	4.232	20	.97566	4.4494	.21928	4.560
22	.97182	4.1230	.23571	4.242	22	.97579	4.4615	.21871	4.572
24	.97196	4.1335	.23514	4.253	24	.97592	4.4737	.21814	4.584
26	.97210	4.1440	.23458	4.263	26	.97604	4.4860	.21758	4.596
28	.97223	4.1546	.23401	4.273	28	.97617	4.4983	.21701	4.608
30	.97237	4.1653	.23345	4.284	30	.97630	4.5107	.21644	4.620
32	.97251	4.1760	.23288	4.294	32	.97642	4.5232	.21587	4.632
34	.97264	4.1867	.23231	4.304	34	.97655	4.5357	.21530	4.645
36	.97278	4.1976	.23175	4.315	36	.97667	4.5483	.21474	4.657
38	.97291	4.2084	.23118	4.326	38	.97680	4.5609	.21417	4.669
40	.97304	4.2193	.23062	4.336	40	.97692	4.5736	.21360	4.682
42	.97318	4.2303	.23005	4.347	42	.97705	4.5864	.21303	4.694
44	.97331	4.2413	.22948	4.358	44	.97717	4.5993	.21246	4.707
46	.97345	4.2524	.22892	4.368	46	.97729	4.6122	.21189	4.719
48	.97358	4.2635	.22835	4.379	48	.97742	4.6252	.21132	4.732
50	.97371	4.2747	.22778	4.390	50	.97754	4.6382	.21076	4.745
52	.97384	4.2859	.22722	4.401	52	.97766	4.6514	.21019	4.758
54	.97398	4.2972	.22665	4.412	54	.97778	4.6646	.20962	4.771
56	.97411	4.3086	.22608	4.423	56	.97791	4.6779	.20905	4.783
58	.97424	4.3200	.22552	4.434	58	.97803	4.6912	.20848	4.797

NATURAL SINES, TANGENTS, COSINES AND SECANTS.

	78 Deg.					79 Deg.			
MIN	SINE.	TANG.	COSINE.	SEC.	MIN	SINE.	TANG.	COSINE.	SEC.
0	.97815	4.7046	.20791	4.810	0	.98163	5.1445	.19081	5.241
2	.97827	4.7181	.20734	4.823	2	.98174	5.1606	.19024	5.257
4	.97839	4.7317	.20677	4.836	4	.98185	5.1767	.19067	5.272
6	.97851	4.7453	.20620	4.850	6	.96196	5.1929	.18909	5.288
8	97863	4.7591	.20563	4.863	8	.98207	5.2092	.18852	5.304
10	.97875	4.7729	.20506	4.876	10	.98218	5.2257	.18795	5.320
12	.97887	4.7867	.20449	4.890	12	.98229	5.2422	.18738	5.337
14	.97899	4.8007	.20393	4.904	14	.98240	5.2588	.18681	5.353
16	.97910	4.8147	.20336	4.917	16	.98250	5.2755	.18624	5.369
18	.97922	4.8288	.20279	4.931	18	.98261	5.2923	.18567	5.386
20	.97934	4.8430	.20222	4.945	20	.98272	5.3093	.18509	5.403
22	.97946	4.8573	.20165	4.959	22	.98283	5.3263	.18452	5.419
24	.97958	4.8716	.20108	4.973	24	.98294	5.3434	.18395	5.436
26	.97969	4.8860	.20051	4.987	26	.98304	5.3607	.18338	5.453
28	.97981	4.9006	.19994	5.001	28	.98315	5.3780	.18281	5.470
30	.97992	4.9152	.19937	5.016	30	.98325	5.3955	.18223	5.487
32	.98004	4.9298	.19880	5.030	32	.98336	5.4131	.18166	5.505
34	.98016	4.9446	.19823	5.045	34	.98347	5.4308	.18109	5.522
36	.98027	4.9594	.19766	5.059	36	.98357	5.4486	.18052	5.540
38	.98039	4.9744	.19709	5.074	38	.98368	5.4665	.17994	5.557
40	.98050	4.9894	.19652	5.089	40	.98378	5.4845	17937	5.575
42	.98061	5.0045	.19594	5.103	42	.98389	5.5026	.17880	5.593
44	.98073	5.0197	.19537	5.118	44	.98399	5.5209	.17823	5.611
46	.98084	5.0350	.19480	5.133	46	.98409	5.5393	.17766	5.629
48	.98096	5.0504	.19423	5.148	48	.98420	5.5578	.17708	5.647
50	.98107	5.0658	.19366	5.164	50	.98430	5.5764	.17651	5.665
52	.98118	5.0814	.19309	5.179	52	.98440	5.5951	.17594	5.684
54	.98129	5.0970	.19252	5.194	54	.98450	5.6139	.17536	5.702
56	.98140	5.1128	.19195	5.210	56	.98461	5.6329	.17479	5.721
58	.98152	5.1286	.19138	5.225	58	.98471	5.6520	.17422	5.740

NATURAL SINES, TANGENTS, COSINES AND SECANTS.

	80 DEG.					81 DEG.			
MIN	SINE.	TANG.	COSINE.	SEC.	MIN	SINE.	TANG.	COSINE.	SEC.
0	.98481	5.6713	.17365	5.759	0	.98769	.63137	.15643	6.392
2	.98491	5.6906	.17307	5.778	2	.98778	.63376	.15586	6.416
4	.98501	5.7101	.17250	5.797	4	.98787	.63616	.15528	6.440
6	.98511	5.7297	.17193	5.816	6	.98796	.63859	.15471	6.464
8	.98521	5.7495	.17135	5.836	8	.98805	.64103	.15413	6.488
10	.98531	5.7694	.17078	5.855	10	.98814	.64348	.15356	6.512
12	.98541	5.7894	.17021	5.875	12	.98823	.64596	.15298	6.536
14	.98551	5.8095	.16963	5.895	14	.98832	.64846	.15241	6.561
16	.98560	5.8298	.16906	5.915	16	.98840	.65097	.15183	6.586
18	.98570	5.8502	.16849	5.935	18	.98849	.65350	.15126	6.611
20	.98580	5.8708	.16791	5.955	20	.98858	.65605	.15068	6.636
22	.98590	5.8915	.16734	5.976	22	.98867	.65863	.15011	6.662
24	.98599	5.9124	.16677	5.996	24	.98875	.66122	.14953	6.687
26	.98609	5.9333	.16619	6.017	26	.98884	.66383	.14896	6.713
28	.98619	5.9545	.16562	6.038	28	.98893	.66646	.14838	6.739
30	.98628	5.9758	.16504	6.059	30	.98901	.66912	.14781	6.765
32	.98638	5.9972	.16447	6.080	32	.98910	.67179	.14723	6.792
34	.98647	6.0188	.16390	6.101	34	.98918	.67449	.14666	6.818
36	.98657	6.0405	.16332	6.123	36	.98927	.67720	.14608	6.845
38	.98666	6.0624	.16275	6.144	38	.98935	.67994	.14551	6.872
40	.98676	6.0844	.16218	6.166	40	.98944	.68269	.14493	6.900
42	.98685	6.1066	.16160	6.188	42	.98952	.68547	.14435	6.927
44	.98695	6.1290	.16103	6.210	44	.98961	.68828	.14378	6.955
46	.98704	6.1515	.16045	6.232	46	.98969	.69110	.14320	6.983
48	.98713	6.1742	.15988	6.255	48	.98977	.69395	.14263	7.011
50	.98723	6.1970	.15930	6.277	50	.98986	.69682	.14205	7.040
52	.98732	6.2200	.15873	6.300	52	.98994	.69972	.14148	7.068
54	.98741	6.2432	.15816	6.323	54	.99002	.70264	.14090	7.097
56	.98750	6.2665	.15758	6.346	56	.99010	.70558	.14032	7.126
58	.98759	6.2901	.15700	6.369	58	.99018	.70855	.13975	7.156

NATURAL SINES, TANGENTS, COSINES AND SECANTS.

	82 DEG.					83 DEG.			
MIN	SINE.	TANG.	COSINE.	SEC.	MIN	SINE.	TANG.	COSINE.	SEC.
0	.99027	7.1154	.13917	7.185	0	.99255	8.1443	.12187	8.205
2	.99035	7.1455	.13859	7.215	2	.99262	8.1837	.12129	8.245
4	.99043	7.1759	.13802	7.245	4	.99269	8.2234	.12071	8.284
6	.99051	7.2066	.13744	7.276	6	.99276	8.2635	.12014	8.324
8	.99059	7.2375	.13687	7.306	8	.99283	8.3041	.11956	8.364
10	.99067	7.2687	.13629	7.337	10	.99289	8.3450	.11898	8.405
12	.99075	7.3002	.13571	7.368	12	.99296	8.3862	.11840	8.446
14	.99082	7.3319	.13514	7.400	14	.99303	8.4279	.11782	8.487
16	.99090	7.3639	.13456	7.431	16	.99310	8.4701	.11725	8.529
18	.99098	7.3962	.13398	7.463	18	.99317	8.5126	.11667	8.571
20	.99106	7.4287	.13341	7.496	20	.99324	8.5555	.11609	8.614
22	.99114	7.4615	.13283	7.528	22	.99331	8.5989	.11551	8.657
24	.99121	7.4946	.13225	7.561	24	.99337	8.6427	.11494	8.700
26	.99129	7.5281	.13168	7.594	26	.99344	8.6870	.11436	8.744
28	.99137	7.5618	.13110	7.628	28	.99350	8.7317	.11378	8.789
30	.99144	7.5957	.13052	7.661	30	.99357	8.7769	.11320	8.834
32	.99152	7.6300	.12995	7.695	32	.99363	8.8225	.11262	8.879
34	.99159	7.6647	.12937	7.730	34	.99370	8.8686	.11205	8.925
36	.99167	7.6996	.12879	7.764	36	.99377	8.9152	.11147	8.971
38	.99174	7.7348	.12822	7.799	38	.99383	8.9623	.11089	9.018
40	.99182	7.7703	.12764	7.834	40	.99389	9.0098	.11031	9.065
42	.99189	7.8062	.12706	7.870	42	.99396	9.0579	.10973	9.113
44	.99197	7.8424	.12648	7.906	44	.99402	9.1065	.10915	9.161
46	.99204	7.8789	.12591	7.942	46	.99409	9.1555	.10857	9.210
48	.99211	7.9158	.12533	7.979	48	.99415	9.2052	.10800	9.259
50	.99219	7.9530	.12475	8.016	50	.99421	9.2553	.10742	9.309
52	.99226	7.9906	.12418	8.053	52	.99427	9.3060	.10684	9.360
54	.99233	8.0285	.12360	8.090	54	.99434	9.3572	.10626	9.410
56	.99240	8.0667	.12302	8.128	56	.99440	9.4090	.10568	9.462
58	.99247	8.1054	.12245	8.167	58	.99446	9.4614	.10511	9.514

NATURAL SINES, TANGENTS, COSINES AND SECANTS.

	84 Deg.					85 Deg.			
MIN	SINE.	TANG.	COSINE.	SEC.	MIN	SINE.	TANG.	COSINE.	SEC.
0	.99452	9.5144	.10453	9.567	0	.99619	11.4301	.08716	11.474
2	.99458	9.5679	.10395	9.620	2	.99624	11.5072	.08657	11 550
4	.99464	9.6220	.10337	9.674	4	.99629	11.5853	.08599	11.628
6	.99470	9.6768	.10279	9.728	6	.99634	11.6645	.08542	11.707
8	.99476	9.7322	.10221	9.783	8	.99639	11.7448	.08484	11.787
10	.99482	9.7882	.10163	9.839	10	.99644	11.8262	.08426	11.868
12	.99488	9.8448	.10105	9.895	12	.99649	11.9087	.08368	11.950
14	.99494	9.9021	.10047	9.952	14	.99654	11.9923	.08310	12.034
16	.99499	9.9601	.09990	10.010	16	.99659	12.0772	.08252	12.118
18	.99505	10.0187	.09932	10.068	18	.99664	12.1632	.08194	12.204
20	.99511	10.0780	.09874	10.127	20	.99668	12.2505	.08136	12.291
22	.99517	10.1381	.09816	10.187	22	.99673	12.3390	.08078	12.379
24	.99523	10.1988	.09758	10.248	24	.99678	12.4288	.08020	12.469
26	.99528	10.2602	.09700	10.309	26	.99682	12.5199	.07962	12.560
28	.99534	10.3224	.09642	10.371	28	.99687	12.6124	.07904	12.652
30	.99539	10.3854	.09584	10.433	30	.99692	12.7062	.07846	12.745
32	.99545	10.4491	.09526	10.497	32	.99696	12.8014	.07788	12.840
34	.99551	10.5136	.09468	10.561	34	.99701	12.8961	.07730	12.937
36	.99556	10.5789	.09411	10.626	36	.99705	12.9962	.07672	13.034
38	.99562	10.6450	.09353	10.692	38	.99709	13.0958	.07614	13.134
40	.99567	10.7119	.09295	10.758	40	.99714	13.1969	.07556	13.235
42	.99572	10.7797	.09237	10.826	42	.99718	13.2996	.07498	13.337
44	.99578	10.8483	.09179	10.894	44	.99723	13.4039	.07440	13.441
46	.99583	10.9178	.09121	10.963	46	.99727	13.5098	.07382	13.547
48	.99588	10.9882	.09063	11.033	48	.99731	13.6174	.07324	13.654
50	.99594	11.0594	.09005	11.105	50	.99736	13.7267	.07266	13.763
52	.99599	11.1316	.08947	11.176	52	.99740	13.8378	.07208	13.874
54	.99604	11.2048	.08889	11.249	54	.99744	13.9507	.07150	13.986
56	.99609	11.2789	.08831	11.323	56	.99748	14.0655	.07091	14.100
58	.99614	11.3540	.08773	11.398	58	.99752	14.1821	.07034	14.217

NATURAL SINES, TANGENTS, COSINES AND SECANTS.

	86 Deg.					87 Deg.			
MIN	SINE.	TANG.	COSINE.	SEC.	MIN	SINE.	TANG.	COSINE.	SEC.
0	.99756	14.3007	.06976	14.335	0	.99863	19.0811	.05234	19.108
2	.99760	14.4212	.06917	14.456	2	.99866	19.2959	.05175	19.322
4	.99764	14.5438	.06859	14.578	4	.99869	19.5156	.05117	19.541
6	.99768	14.6685	.06801	14.702	6	.99872	19.7403	.05059	19.766
8	.99772	14.7954	.06743	14.829	8	.99875	19.9702	.05001	19.995
10	.99776	14.9244	.06685	14.958	10	.99877	20.2056	.04943	20.230
12	.99780	15.0557	.06627	15.089	12	.99880	20.4465	.04885	20.471
14	.99784	15.1893	.06569	15.222	14	.99883	20.6932	.04827	20.717
16	.99788	15.3254	.06511	15.359	16	.99886	20.9460	.04768	20.970
18	.99791	15.4638	.06453	15.496	18	.99889	21.2049	.04711	21.228
20	.99795	15.6048	.06395	15.637	20	.99892	21.4704	.04652	21.494
22	.99799	15.7483	.06337	15.780	22	.99894	21.7426	.04594	21.765
24	.99803	15.8945	.06279	15.926	24	.99897	22.0217	.04536	22.044
26	.99806	16.0435	.06221	16.075	26	.99900	22.3081	.04478	22.330
28	.99810	16.1952	.06163	16.226	28	.99902	22.6020	.04420	22.624
30	.99813	16.3499	.06104	16.380	30	.99905	22.9038	.04362	22.925
32	.99817	16.5075	.06047	16.538	32	.99907	23.2137	.04304	23.235
34	.99820	16.6681	.05989	16.698	34	.99909	23.5321	.04245	23.553
36	.99824	16.8319	.05930	16.861	36	.99912	23.8593	.04187	23.880
38	.99827	16.9990	.05872	17.028	38	.99915	24.1957	.04129	24.216
40	.99831	17.1693	.05814	17.198	40	.99917	24.5418	.04071	24.562
42	.99834	17.3432	.05756	17.372	42	.99919	24.8978	.04013	24.918
44	.99837	17.5205	.05698	17.549	44	.99922	25.2644	.03955	25.284
46	.99841	17.7015	.05640	17.730	46	.99924	25.6418	.03897	25.661
48	.99844	17.8863	.05582	17.914	48	.99926	26.0307	.03839	26.050
50	.99847	18.0750	.05524	18.103	50	.99928	26.4316	.03780	26.450
52	.99850	18.2677	.05466	18.295	52	.99931	26.8450	.03722	26.864
54	.99853	18.4645	.05408	18.491	54	.99934	27.2715	.03664	27.290
56	.99857	18.6656	.05349	18.692	56	.99935	27.7117	.03606	27.730
58	.99859	18.8711	.05292	18.897	58	.99937	28.1664	.03548	28.184

NATURAL SINES, TANGENTS, COSINES
AND SECANTS.

88 Deg.				89 Deg.			
MIN	SINE.	TANG.	COSINE.	SEC·	MIN	SINE.	TANG.	COSINE.	SEC·

MIN	SINE.	TANG.	COSINE.	SEC·	MIN	SINE.	TANG.	COSINE.	SEC·
0	.99939	28.636	.03490	28.654	0	.99985	57.290	.01745	57.298
2	.99941	29.122	.03432	29.139	2	.99986	59.266	.01687	59 274
4	.99943	29.624	.03374	29.641	4	.99987	61.383	.01629	61.390
6	.99945	30.145	.03315	30.161	6	.99988	63.657	.01571	63.664
8	.99947	30.683	.03257	30.698	8	.99988	66.106	.01513	66.112
10	.99949	31.242	.03199	31.257	10	.99989	68.750	.01454	68.757
12	.99951	31.820	.03141	31.836	12	.99990	71.615	.01396	71.622
14	.99952	32.421	.03083	32.437	14	.99991	74.729	.01338	74.736
16	.99954	33.045	.03025	33.060	16	.99992	78.126	.01279	78.133
18	.99956	33.694	.02966	33.708	18	.99992	81.847	.01222	81.833
20	.99958	34.368	.02908	34.382	20	.99993	85.940	.01163	85.984
22	.99959	35.069	.02850	35.084	22	.99994	90.463	.01105	92.469
24	.99961	35.801	.02792	35.814	24	.99995	95.489	.01047	95.495
26	.99962	36.563	.02734	36.576	26	.99995	101.107	.00989	101.112
28	.99964	37.358	.02676	37.371	28	.99996	107.43	.00931	107.411
30	.99966	38.188	.02617	38.201	30	.99996	114.59	.00872	114.548
32	.99967	39.057	.02560	39.069	32	.99997	122.78	.00814	122.850
34	.99969	39.965	.02501	39.978	34	.99997	132.22	.00756	132.275
36	.99970	40.917	.02443	40.931	36	.99997	143.24	.00698	143.266
38	.99971	41.916	.02385	40.928	38	.99998	156.26	.00640	156.250
40	.99973	42.964	.02327	42.976	40	.99998	171.89	.00582	171.821
42	.99974	44.066	.02269	44.077	42	.99998	190.98	.00524	190.840
44	.99975	45.226	.02210	45.237	44	.99999	214.86	.00465	215.05
46	.99977	46.449	.02152	46.460	46	.99999	245.55	.00407	245.70
48	.99978	47.739	.02094	47.750	48	.99999	286.48	.00349	286.53
50	.99979	49.104	.02036	49.114	50	.99999	343.78	.00291	343.65
52	.99980	50.548	.01978	50.559	52	.99999	429.72	.00233	429.20
54	.99982	52.081	.01919	52.090	54	.99999	572.96	.00174	574.71
56	.99983	53.709	.01861	53.718	56	1.	859.44	.00116	862.0
58	.99984	55.441	.01803	55.450	58	1.	1718.87	.00058	1718.8

90 Deg.

Sine = 1.
Tangent = Infinite.
Cosine = 0.
Secant = Infinite.

The preceding Table of Sines, Tangents, Cosines and Secants is given for every two minutes of the Quadrant to a Radius of 1.

CHAPTER II.

GEARING.

In the transfer of motion from one axis to another gearing is the most important system that can be introduced, whether the shafts are to be parallel or at an angle to each other.

For this purpose when the shafts are parallel, we use spur gears, so called from their teeth being parallel with their axis. When the gears are not of the same size, the smaller one is usually called a pinion, although the name " spur gear " is also correct.

Bevel gears are used for transmitting motion between a pair of shafts that are at right angles to each other, and one wheel is always larger than the other.

Mitre gears are so called because the pitch line of their teeth are always at an angle of 45° from their axis. When we say a pair of mitre gears, we know that they are both alike, that the same cutter will cut both gears, and also that their shafts are to be at right angles to each other.

Thus it can be seen that a mitre is a bevel wheel (although we do not usually call it such), but a bevel wheel is never a mitre, except as stated that the pitch line is at an angle of 45° to its axis (or bore.)

Angle gears are also bevel gears, but they are so called from the fact that they are usually employed for transmitting motion between shafting that is less or greater than a right angle or 90°.

Internal gears also have their teeth, like spur gears, parallel to its axis, but the teeth of the internal gear are inside of the rim, while those of the spur gear are outside.

Spiral gears are so called from having their teeth formed like a screw of a very coarse pitch, and for this reason are sometimes called screw gears. A spiral gear, like a spiral milling cutter, runs smoother than with straight teeth, and sometimes can be used to greater advantage than a worm and worm wheel.

When a pair of spiral gears are required to connect a pair of shafts that are parallel to each other, one should be right hand and the other left hand; they may be one degree or twenty degrees, to suit, and whatever angle is given to one must also be given to the other, regardless of their size, but the pitch of the spiral will be in proportion to the number of teeth; thus in a spiral gear of twenty teeth 10 degrees angle and a certain pitch, another gear to mesh with it of 40 or 60 teeth, should also be cut at 10 degrees, but the pitch would be twice or three times as great, or in proportion to the number of their teeth.

If a pair of spiral gears are to connect at right angles to each other, then both wheels will be right hand or left hand, according to the direction they are to drive.

In spur gears when we say a 4-inch, an 8-inch or a 20-inch gear, it is always understood to be the pitch diameter, and if these gears were of 8 pitch then their diameters would be $4\frac{2}{8}$, $8\frac{2}{8}$ and $20\frac{2}{8}$ respectively; but if they were to be 10 pitch, then instead of adding eighths, you would add tenths, or if they were to be 2 pitch you would add ½'', or if 1 pitch you would then add inches. Thus a gear of 1 pitch, 20 teeth, would be 20 inches diameter on the pitch line and 22 inches outside diameter, or if you want a pair of gears, say 24 teeth and 30 teeth of six pitch, then the pair would be $\frac{24}{6}$ and $\frac{30}{6}$ respectively, or 4 inches and 5 inches diameter respectively on the pitch line or $4\frac{2}{6}$ and $5\frac{2}{6}$ inches outside diameter. In other words, the gear will measure on the pitch line as many 8ths, 10ths or 32ds as there are teeth; thus, in a wheel of 20 teeth, 8 pitch 20/8ths; 20 teeth 10 pitch, 20/10ths; 20 teeth 32 pitch, 20/32ds, etc. of inches, and two more eighths should be added if of 8 pitch, or 2/32 more if of 32 pitch, etc. This is called diametral pitch and means so many teeth per inch in diameter, measured on the pitch line.

Nearly all gears are now made on this system, for the reason that in building machinery the distances between two or more shafts that are to be driven by gears will always be so many 8ths apart if 8 pitch, or so many 10ths, if 10 pitch, etc., while in the old system of circular pitch it is common to have the distances so many inches and a sixty-fourth full or a thirty-second scant, etc.

The clearance at the bottoms of teeth should always be one-tenth (1/10) of the thickness of the tooth on the pitch line.

To find the thickness of a tooth on the pitch line, divide the circumference of the wheel on the pitch line by the number of teeth and spaces, or by twice the number of teeth, and one-tenth of this will be the depth of clearance at the bottom of the teeth.

Thus, to find the thickness of an 8 pitch tooth, as there are eight teeth to every inch in the diameter measured on the pitch line, then a wheel of one inch diameter = 3.1416″ in circumference, and divided by 16 = .196″ for the thickness, and one-tenth of this for clearance = .020 nearly, for any 8 pitch gear.

If this was a 6 pitch gear, we would divide by 12; thus, 3.1416 ÷ 12 = .262″ nearly, for the thickness of any 6 pitch tooth, and this divided by 10 = .026″ for the depth of the clearance of any 6 pitch gear.

If it was a 30 pitch gear, then 3.1416 ÷ 60 = .052″ for the thickness of the tooth on the pitch line, and one-tenth of this = .005″ for the depth of the clearance, etc.

In any gear of 8 pitch the depth of tooth is always one-eighth above the pitch line and one-eighth below the pitch line, and also the clearance; then 2/8 = .250 and added to .020 = .270″ for the total depth of any 8 pitch gear.

In a 6 pitch gear the depth of tooth is one-sixth of an inch above the pitch line and one-sixth of an inch below the pitch line, plus the clearance; thus we have explained that the clearance for a 6 pitch gear was .026″, then added to 2/6 of an inch = .359″ for the depth of the teeth for any 6 pitch gear, etc.

It must be remembered that in all cut gearing the width of space on the pitch line should always be the same as the thickness of the teeth, and consequently, the circular pitch of any gear is equal to twice the thickness of the tooth on the pitch line. Or, dividing the circumference of the gear on the pitch line by the number of teeth will be the same thing.

Thus, a wheel one inch diameter on the pitch line would be 3.1416″ in circumference, and if it was to be of 8 pitch, then there would be 8 teeth on the wheel; then 3.1416 ÷ 8 = .393″ nearly, for the circular pitch, or, if it was 10 pitch, then 3.1416 ÷ 10 = .314″ for the circular pitch, etc.

Remember, that in calculating the dimensions of gear teeth, as in the two examples just shown, as for instance dividing 3.1416 by 10, it is not necessary to go higher than thousandths, or three decimals, and we always take for the last figure the one nearest to a whole number.

Or we can find the diametral pitch in the following manner when the circular pitch is known:

The circular pitch of a gear is ⅞″; what is the diametral pitch? ⅞″ = .875″ and 3.1416 ÷ .875 = 3.59, the answer.

In other words 3.1416 divided by the circular pitch reduced to a decimal number, will be the diametral pitch.

If we have a pair of gears that are 12″ and 8″ respectively, pitch diameters, we know that the distance between centers will be equal to one-half of the diameters of the two gears; or, 12 + 8 = 20, and 20 ÷ 2 = 10″. Or we may have the two gears like the following example: Find the distance between centers of two gears in mesh of 28 and 24 teeth respectively and 32 pitch. 28 + 24 = 52, and 52 ÷ 32 = 1⅝ or 1.625; this divided by 2 = .8125, the answer.

Suppose we have a pair of gears of 26 and 32 teeth respectively and 8 pitch, what is the distance between centers of these wheels when in mesh? 26 + 32 = 58, and 58 ÷ 8 pitch = 7.25″, and this again divided by 2 = 3.625″, the answer.

Now let us examine a pair of gears in circular pitch. We

GEARING.—TOOTH DIMENSIONS.

Diametral Pitch.	Circular Pitch.	Thickness of Tooth on the Pitch Line.	Depth to Cut.	Working Depth.	Clearance.
1	3.1416	1.5708	2.157	2.000	.157
1¼	2.5132	1.2566	1.725	1.600	.125
1½	2.0944	1.0472	1.437	1.333	.104
1¾	1.7952	.8976	1.232	1.143	.089
2	1.5708	.7854	1.078	1.0	.078
2¼	1.3962	.6981	.958	.888	.070
2½	1.2566	.6283	.863	.800	.063
2¾	1.1423	.5711	.784	.727	.057
3	1.0470	.5235	.719	.666	.053
3¼	.9666	.4833	.664	.616	.048
3½	.8976	.4488	.616	.571	.045
4	.7854	.3927	.539	.500	.039
5	.6283	.3141	.431	.400	.031
6	.5236	.2618	.359	.333	.026
7	.4488	.2244	.308	.286	.022
8	.3927	.1964	.270	.250	.020
9	.3490	.1745	.240	.222	.018
10	.3141	.1570	.216	.200	.016
11	.2856	.1428	.196	.182	.014
12	.2618	.1309	.180	.167	.013
14	.2244	.1122	.154	.143	.011
16	.1963	.0982	.135	.125	.010
18	.1745	.0872	.120	.111	.009
20	.1570	.0785	.108	.100	.008
22	.1428	.0714	.098	.091	.007
24	.1309	.0654	.090	.083	.007
26	.1208	.0604	.083	.077	.006
28	.1122	.0561	.077	.071	.006
30	.1047	.0523	.072	.066	.006
32	.0982	.0491	.067	.062	.005
34	.0924	.0462	.063	.059	.004
36	.0872	.0436	.060	.055	.004
40	.0785	.0392	.054	.050	.004
42	.0748	.0374	.051	.048	.003
46	.0683	.0341	.047	.043	.004
50	.0628	.0314	.043	.040	.003
54	.0581	.0290	.040	.037	.003
60	.0523	.0261	.036	.033	.003

have a pair of gears of 24 and 30 teeth and ⅜ pitch; what is the distance between the centers of these two wheels when in mesh?

24 × ⅜″ (or .375″) = 9.000″, the circumference on the pitch line; 9 ÷ 3.1416 = 2.864+, the diameter on the pitch line. 30 × ⅜″ (or .375″) = 11.250″, or the circumference on the pitch line, and 11.250 ÷ 3.1416 = 3.581, nearly, for the diameter on the pitch line; and 2.864″ + 3.581″ = 6.445″, then divided by 2 = 3.2225 inches, or the answer.

This can also be found in a more simple manner as follows: Multiply the constant number .3183 by the circular pitch, and the result by one-half the number of teeth in both wheels; thus, in the same example, .3183 × .375 = .11936+, and one-half the number of teeth in both wheels = 27; then .11936 × 27 = 3.222″, the answer, or the distance between the centers of the two wheels. Any example in circular pitch can be done in the same manner.

The decimal .3183 is found by dividing one by 3.1416.

The depth of teeth in circular pitch is found in the following manner: Thus, for a gear of ½″ circular pitch 3.1416 divided by .5 (½) = 6.283, for the diametral pitch, and 1 divided by 6.283 = .159″, for one-half of the running depth of the tooth, and twice this, or, .318″ = the running depth. Now if the circular pitch is ½″, then the tooth is exactly ¼″ thick on the pitch line, and the clearance we said was one-tenth (1/10) of the thickness of the tooth on the pitch line; then 1/10 of ¼, (or .250″) = .025″ and added to .318″ = .343″ for the depth to cut any gear of ½″ circular pitch.

We can also find the depth of the teeth in a more simple manner, thus: Multiply the number (constant) .3183 by the circular pitch and this will give one-half of the running depth of the tooth; thus, in ½″ circular pitch ½″ = .5″; .3183 × .5 = .159, and doubled equals .318, and one-tenth of the thickness of the tooth = .343″, the answer, or total depth as before.

It can readily be seen that if we want to have a pair of gears in mesh, and the holes are bored to the proper distance for standard gears, and we then take a pair of gears that are 8 or 10 thousands too large or too small in the diameter, it will be too tight or too loose, and if the gear has 15 teeth and should be ten thousandths of an inch too small in the diameter, then it would be about 30 thousandths of an inch too small or to be divided into the 15 teeth, or about two thousandths of an inch for each tooth, etc.

In a great many instances this would never be known, and especially in a rough class of work, such as rolling mill machinery, etc. But in a fine class of work the greatest care should be taken to have the blanks turned to an exact size by means of the micrometer caliper or the vernier, as the case may be, and then if the gear cutter or milling machine is graduated correctly (some are not) we will have no trouble in getting good work.

In designing the shapes of teeth, it is well to remember that the teeth of a pair of wheels should always be in contact at least equal to the pitch. Or, in other words, if we have a pair of wheels in mesh with each other of 3″ pitch, the teeth should not separate from each other until the next pair of teeth are well in contact, otherwise the friction from the sliding motion will be very great and a uniform motion cannot be maintained.

It has also been demonstrated by practice that any describing curve rolled on the outside of one pitch line and on the inside of another will work correctly together.

An epicycloid is somewhat similar, except that it is traced by a point on the circumference of a circle, as shown in figure 7, rolling upon the pitch line of another, and, when rolling on the inside it is called a hypocycloid. The circle C is called the generating circle, because it generates (or forms) the curves for the shapes of the teeth.

This generating circle is usually made equal to the radius (half the diameter) of the smallest wheel in a train of gearing. Suppose this smallest wheel to be 3 pitch, 15 teeth or 5 inches in diameter, then the generating circle would be 2½″ diameter. This same circle would be used for all the wheels connecting in a train, rolled on the outside of the pitch line (figure 7) for generating the faces of the teeth, and on the inside (Figure 8) for the flanks of the teeth.

Now if we roll this 2½'' generating circle on the inside of a 5'' pitch circle, we will have a perfectly straight line from the pitch line through the center of the gear, or, as we call them, radial lines, for the flanks of the teeth of this 5'' gear.

It is not necessary that this size of generating circle should be used for this 5'' gear, but it is the size best adapted for general purposes.

If we use a generating circle that is less than one-half the diameter of the pitch circle, the flanks of the teeth will be more nearly parallel with each other, while the faces of the teeth will be more pointed than before, and the latter will naturally make the teeth crowd harder on each other, and, at the same time, if the flanks of the teeth are parallel, even for a short distance, the cutters will work hard, as there can be no clearance on the teeth of cutters when parallel. (This refers to formed cutters only.)

In the epicycloidal form of gear, one of the most simple, is shown at Figure 1, and is usually called pin gearing, so called because one of the gears is made of two discs a little larger than the outside of the pins which are inserted for the teeth, as shown at C, this wheel is made somewhat wider than the large wheel, otherwise they could not run together.

It must not be forgotten that the pitch lines G G, of both wheels must be in proportion to the numbers of teeth in the two wheels; thus, if the large wheel has 14 teeth, and the small one 7 teeth (or pins), the pitch diameter of one wheel must be just twice as great as the other.

In designing a pair of wheels of this kind we will suppose the pins C to be ⅜'' diameter; the distance between two holes on the pitch line should be ¾'' or ¾ circular pitch, and, if there were 7 pins in the small wheel, then the circumference of the pitch circle G would be 7 times ¾'' around it; this will, of course, make the teeth on the large wheel ⅜'' thick on the pitch line also.

To draw the teeth on the large wheel, first lay them out just ¾″ between centers on the pitch circle as shown, and draw the circles equal to the size of the pins for the bottom of the teeth, and, with the dividers set in one of these circles, H, and the other leg of the dividers touching the edge of the next circle, draw the addendum (or that part of the tooth outside the pitch circle) shown at I, etc.

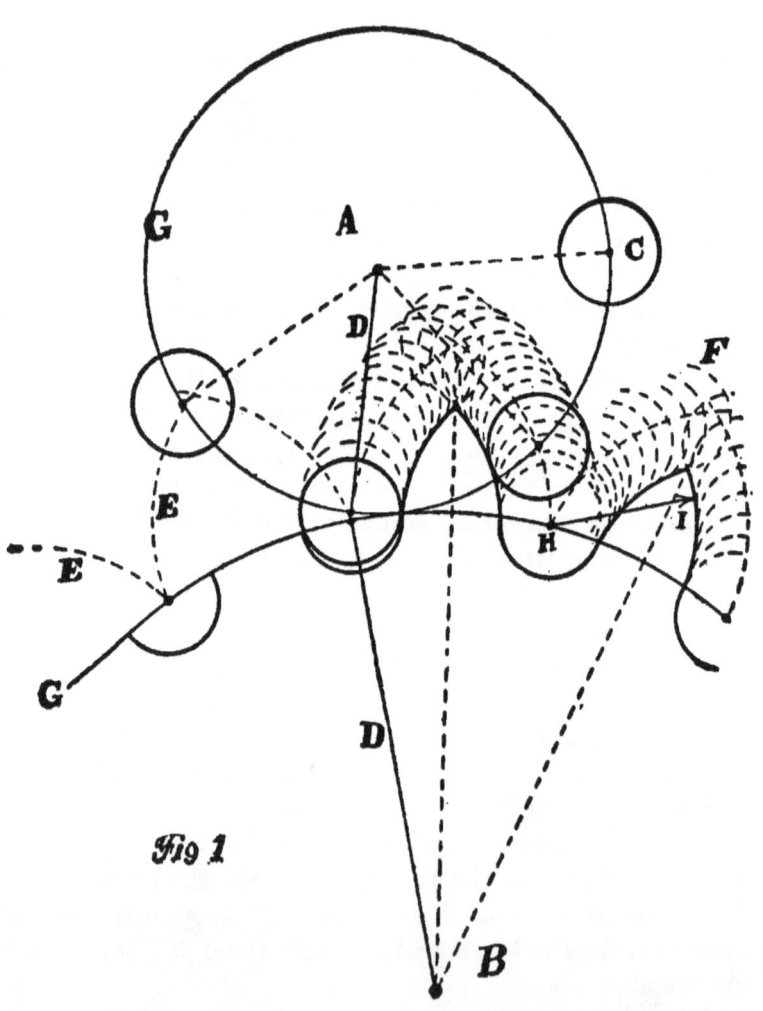

Fig 1

Figure 2 represents the single curve gear, and is of 4 pitch (diametral) 13 teeth, and consequently is 13-4ths or 3 ¼'' diameter on the pitch line A A, which should be drawn first, and as any 4 pitch gear is .393'' thick on the pitch line, lay out with the dividers several points equal to this distance on the line A A; then with bevel pro-

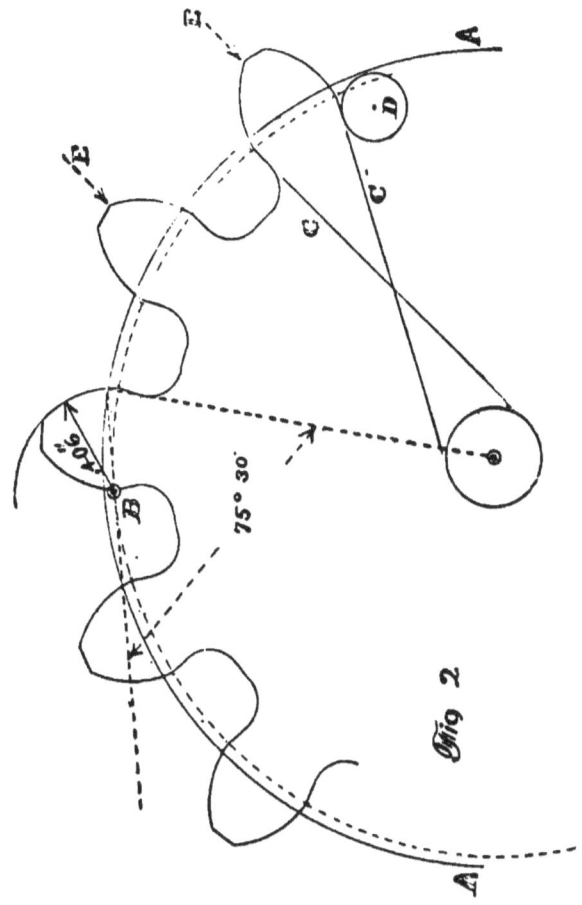

Fig 2

tractor, or what is better, a piece of thin sheet steel cut to an angle of 75° 30', and placing the corner of this template on the pitch line at one of these points as shown, and with one edge in line with the center, measure off on the other side from the corner of the template a distance equal to one-fourth (¼) of the radius, or from the pitch line to the center of the gear, which in this case is about .406″, as shown at B, and, with the dividers set in the center of this gear describe at B a circle, which is called the base circle, shown dotted in the figure. Having drawn the base circle, we do not have to use this template again on this gear for the reason that having spaced off on the pitch circle (not the base circle) as directed, and with the dividers set to .406″ as nearly as possible, we place one leg of the dividers on the base circle and the other on the pitch circle at one of these points stepped off and draw the curves for the faces of the teeth to the base circle only.

Now it has been found that for 12 and 13 teeth that parallel lines should be used for that portion of the teeth inside of the base circle, and drawing a circle at the center of the gear, as shown, for convenience, equal to the width of space at the base circle, draw lines C C, and for the fillets at the bottom of the teeth, the radius should be about one-sixth (1/6) of the distance E E. With gears having 20 teeth the curves may extend from the addendum to the fillets at the bottom (or two pitches deep.)

In all gears from 13 to 20 teeth, there should be parallel lines inside of the base circle for a portion of the distance. With a little practice in drawing the teeth of a pair of wheels in mesh with each other, and in different positions, making the lines as fine and accurate as possible, and also practicing on a wheel of very coarse pitch, you will soon learn how to form the inside or flanks of the teeth. Remember the outside should be made as described, and the inside, or that portion inside of the base circle to suit the outside or addendum of the teeth.

If you want to make a drawing at any time, say of a pair of gears of any pitch (in order to find the shapes of the teeth), draw the teeth as stated, in different positions, and make them five or ten times (for convenience) as large as required; this will be on the principle of a magnifying glass, and will show the errors very plainly; this refers to gears of any pitch, style, etc.

Remember that a gear of 60 pitch and any number of teeth is of the same shape as a gear of 2 pitch (or any other pitch) with the same number of teeth, and, of course, using the same style of a tooth.

That is, an involute tooth, of 32 pitch 15 teeth, is of the same shape as an involute tooth of 1 pitch 15 teeth; the only difference is, that one is much smaller or finer than the other.

I have had a great many cutters made by making the drawings of three or four teeth of a gear on smooth stiff paper and then cutting out with a sharp knife; but when regular standard cutters are wanted, it is cheaper and better to get them from parties who make a business of this class of work.

In Figure 3, I have shown a double curve gear of ½″ pitch, 40 teeth. There are no fillets shown at the bottom of these teeth, because they are strong enough without them; in gears with a small number of teeth, however, it will be necessary to have fillets the same as in a single curve.

This style of gear teeth was invented by Professor Willis, after a great deal of experimenting, and very nearly approaches a perfect epicycloid. It is drawn in the following manner

The example is 40 teeth ½″ pitch; therefore, 40 times ½″ around on the pitch line, or 20″ circumference, and divided by 3.1416 = 6.366 inches in diameter, on the pitch line A A, which should be drawn first; as the gear is ½ inch pitch, the tooth should be exactly ¼″ thick on this line. Now, having made several points on the pitch circle A A, ¼″ from each other (for ½″ pitch, or 5/16″ for ⅝″ pitch), with a bevel protractor, or what is better, a piece of thin sheet steel for a template, as shown at B C D of 75° placed at one of these points; we find in the table (that follows) for 40 teeth, ½″ pitch, the number 4; this means 4/20 of an inch, and is for the face of the teeth; then with the dividers set to 4/20 to the right of the corner of the template, make the point F, and from this point lay off the face of the tooth as shown by the small circle.

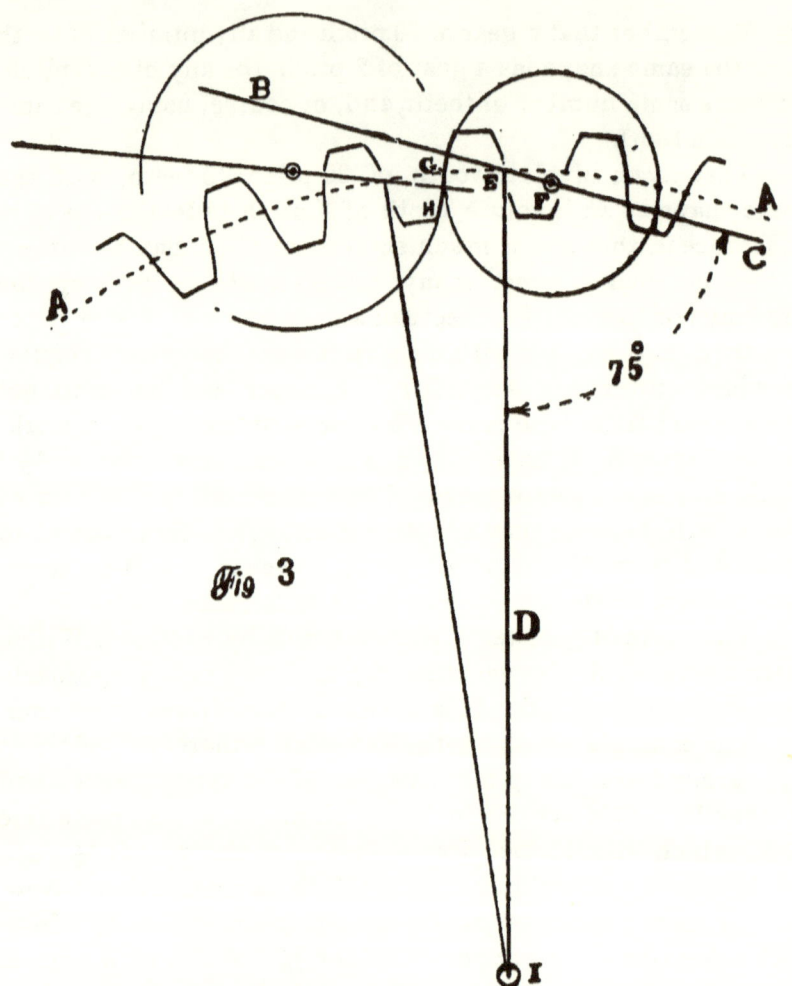

Fig 3

For the flank, or inside of the same tooth, we move the instrument one pitch, whatever it may be; in this case it is ½″ to the left, as shown, and in the table for the flanks of teeth we find the number 7 for 40 teeth ½″ pitch, and we now measure off 7/20″ to the left of the corner, and from this point describe the curve for the flank, as shown by the large circle.

It must be remembered that the numbers in the table are so many 20ths of inches. If you want to draw several of these

TABLE FOR DOUBLE CURVE GEAR TEETH.

(WILLIS SYSTEM.)

CENTERS FOR THE FLANKS OF THE TEETH.

PITCH IN INCHES AND PARTS.

NUMBER OF TEETH.	½	⅝	¾	1	1¼	1½	1¾	2	2¼	2½	3	3½
13	64	80	96	129	160	193	225	257	289	321	356	450
14	35	43	52	69	87	104	121	139	156	173	208	242
15	25	31	37	49	62	74	86	99	111	123	148	173
16	20	25	30	40	50	59	69	79	89	99	191	138
17	17	21	25	34	42	50	59	67	75	84	101	117
18	15	19	22	30	37	45	52	59	67	74	89	104
19	13	17	20	27	35	40	47	54	60	67	80	94
20	12	16	19	25	31	37	43	49	56	62	74	86
22	11	14	16	22	27	33	39	43	49	54	65	76
24	10	12	15	20	25	30	35	40	45	49	59	69
26	9	11	14	18	23	27	32	37	41	46	55	64
28			13		22	26	30	35	40	43	52	60
30	8	10	12	17	21	25	29	33	37	41	49	58
35		9	11	16	19	23	26	30	34	38	45	53
40	7			15	18	21	25	28	32	35	42	49
60	6	8	9	13	15	19	22	25	28	31	37	43
80		7		12		17	20	23	26	29	35	41
100			8	11	14			22	25	28	34	39
150	5				13	16	19	21	24	27	32	38
Rack.		6	7	10	12	15	17	20	22	25	30	34

CENTERS FOR THE FACES OF THE TEETH.

PITCH IN INCHES AND PARTS.

NUMBERS OF TEETH.	½	⅝	¾	1	1¼	1½	1¾	2	2¼	2½	3	3½
12	2	3	4	5	6	7	9	10	11	12	15	17
15	3				7	8	10	11	12	14	17	19
20		4	5	6	8	9	11	12	14	15	18	21
30	4			7	9	10	12	14	16	18	21	25
40			6	8		11	13	15	17	19	23	26
60		5			10	12	14	16	18	20	25	29
80				9	11	13	15	17	19	21	26	30
100			7					18	20	22		31
150	5	6				14	16	19	21	23	27	32
Rack.				10	12	15	17	20	22	25	30	34

For 4″ Pitch, double, 2″; For 5″ Pitch, double, 2½″, etc.

teeth, then with one leg of the dividers set to the center of the gear at I, draw arcs through the centers of these two circles shown in the figure, and you will not have to use the template again on this gear.

Figure 4 represents a perfect epicycloidal tooth, both on the pinion and the rack; they are of 4 pitch, and the pinion has 15 teeth, and were drawn in the following manner: For the pinion, turn up a block of wood with a radius equal to the radius of the pinion on the pitch line, also another piece (concave) to match the other. Now take the dividers and lay off the pitch circle on paper, and place one of these wood blocks (made as thin as possible) and with another round block turned up just one-half the diameter of the pitch circle of the pinion, and, holding a lead pencil close to the periphery, and rolling it on this circle, describe the curves, first on one side and then the other (inside and outside of the pitch circle); these curves will form a perfect epicycloid.

One straight block of wood will answer for the rack, placing it on the pitch line G D, and rolling the same block first on one side and then the other as before.

Two sizes of rolls can be used on a pair of gears, but whatever size is used for the outside, or face, of one gear must, in all cases, be used for the inside of its mate.

This rack and pinion can also be done in the same manner as described in the double curve gears; thus, for the rack, place the instrument with the corner touching the pitch line as shown to the left of the figure, and, as there is no center to a rack as in the pinion, the end A will have to be placed at 90° to the pitch line ; in the table find the number corresponding to the pitch required, and describe the curve for the face, and then move one pitch to the left, and describe the flank as already explained.

Figure 5 also shows a pinion of 15 teeth in mesh with an internal gear of 30 teeth, and was drawn in the same manner as in Figure 4. It will be seen that the teeth of the internal wheel are similar in shape to that of the rack, except that in

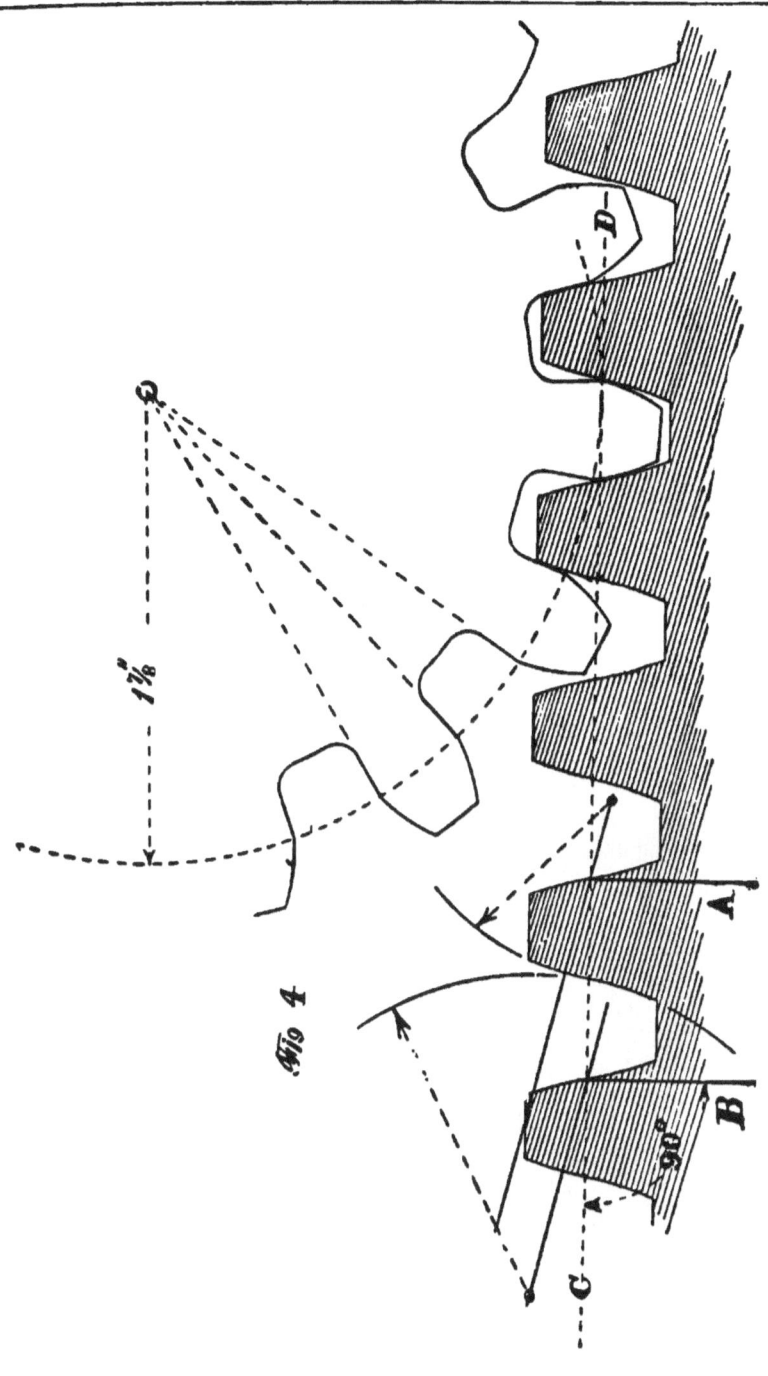

Fig. 4

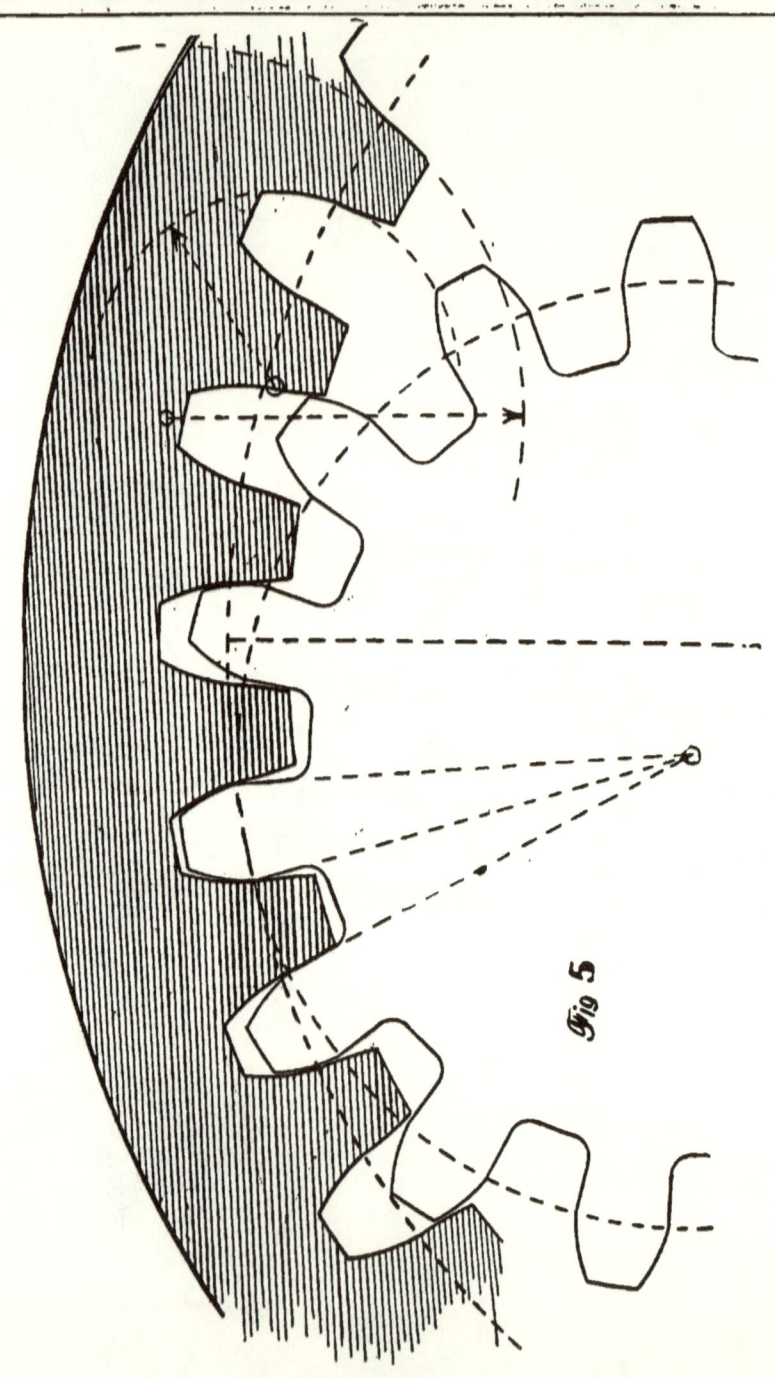

Fig 5

the internal wheel the teeth are thicker at the root than in the rack, this being due to the curve of the wheel.

An internal wheel can be drawn in the same manner as any other gear, the difference being that the teeth as drawn becomes the space and the space the teeth.

In figure 6 I have shown the manner of constructing the perfect involute shape of gear teeth, which is as follows: From the center D, describe the pitch circle A (a small portion only being seen) and on this circle step off points for the teeth as already explained; we then place our template or protractor of 75° 30' with the corner on the pitch line A and the edge in line with the center of the gear, measuring off one-fourth of the radius of the gear, which, in this example, is $\frac{3}{4}''$ (the radius being 3''). We now have a point from which with the dividers set (the other point in the center at D) we describe the arc C B, which is called the base circle.

Remember that the involute always extends from the base circle, and not the pitch circle, to the top of the tooth, while that portion of the tooth inside the base circle is the same as explained in single curve gears. We then lay out a number of radial lines, extending from the base line to the center; it is not necessary to start from any particular place in the figure. I have started nearly $\frac{3}{4}''$ from the side of the tooth. I could have made it $\frac{1}{4}''$; the more lines and the closer they are, if properly drawn, the more correct will be the tooth, but it can easily be seen that I have made them close enough for all purposes; but whatever distance you make 1 and 2, make the rest the same, or in other words, space them evenly. Next from these radial lines draw the lines marked 1' 2' 3', etc., exactly at 90° from the radial lines, and, with the dividers set with one point at 1 on the base line, and the other point at F, also on the base line, draw that portion of the tooth between F and 2', then open the dividers, and placing one leg at 2 on the base circle, and with the pencil at 2' extend the tooth to 3', then open again, and placing one point of the dividers at 3 on the base circle, and the pencil at 3' extend the tooth to 4', etc. Continue in this way until you

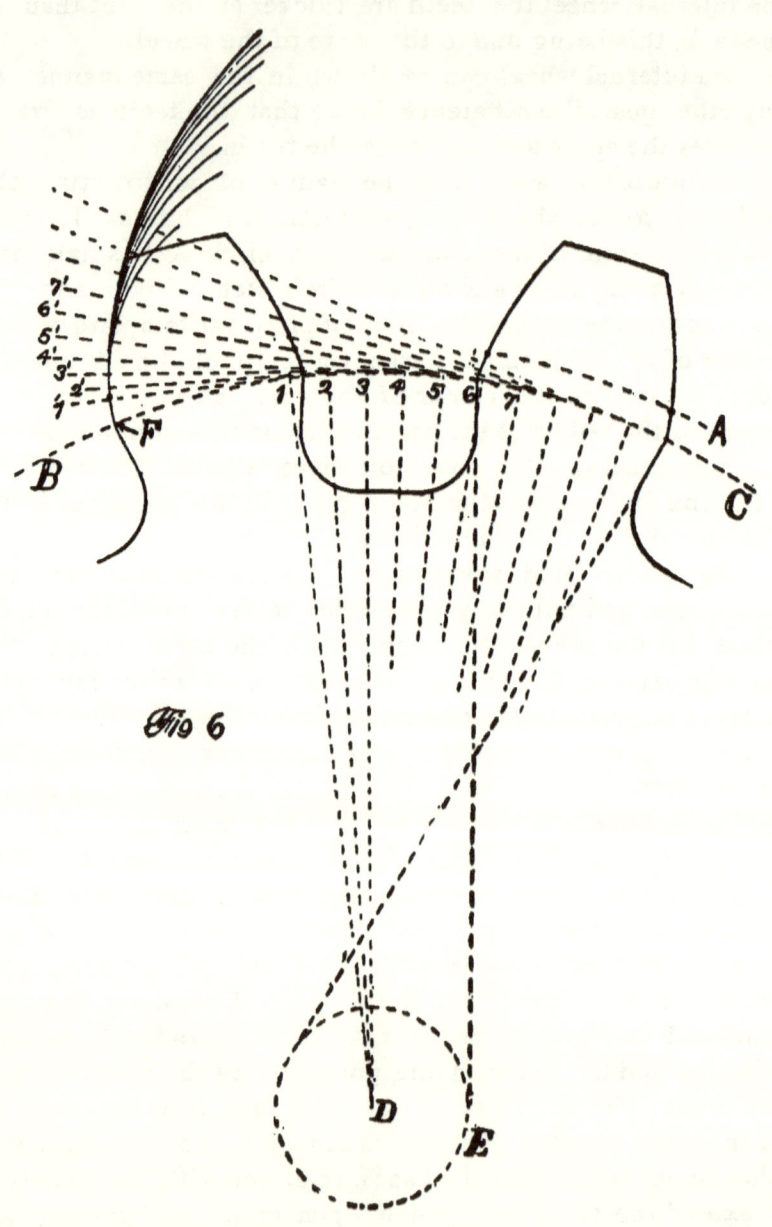

Fig 6

finish the tooth as shown.   It can easily be seen by the draw-
jug that a single arc struck from any position will not be an
involute.

The true involute tooth is the best by far for the shapes
of gear teeth for most purposes, for the reason that when the
distance between centers are not correct it will make no difference in their uniformity of speed, etc.

Figure 7 illustrates a method of drawing the perfect
epicycloid, as follows : B is the center of the gear E A, the
pitch circle, and C the generating circle, which in this case I
have made a little less in diameter than the radius of the gear,
in order to show a curve in the next figure, as both these
figures 7 and 8 show but one side of a tooth ; figure 7 the face
of a tooth, and figure 8 the flank of the same tooth.

In Figure 7 draw radial lines from the center B, through
the pitch circle A E, as shown; they must be produced fa
enough to reach the top of the tooth.   Make these lines uniform in their distance one from the other; it is not important
what the distance is, but do not get them too far apart.   Suppose them to be one-eighth of an inch starting from A, toward
E; then on the generating circle C, also commencing at A,
step off points exactly the same distance $\frac{1}{8}''$, as shown at 1, 2,
3, etc., and with the dividers set to the center of the circle at
B, draw arcs from these points on the generating circle, as
shown at 1, 2, 3, etc.   Remember to draw the arc from the
line F B to 1 on the generating circle ; next draw the arc from
the line F B to 2 on the generating circle; in the same manner draw all the arcs, and as there are 13 points on the generating circle, then the 13th arc will be continued through to
the 13th radial line.

Now to find the shape of the face of the tooth A D above
the pitch line, place one leg of the dividers on the 13 point on
the generating circle near I and the other leg at G, then remove the dividers to H, and mark the point I; next with one
leg of the dividers in the 12 space on the generating circle
and the other leg at J, remove as before to K, and describe
the point shown at L.   Continue in this way until you pro-

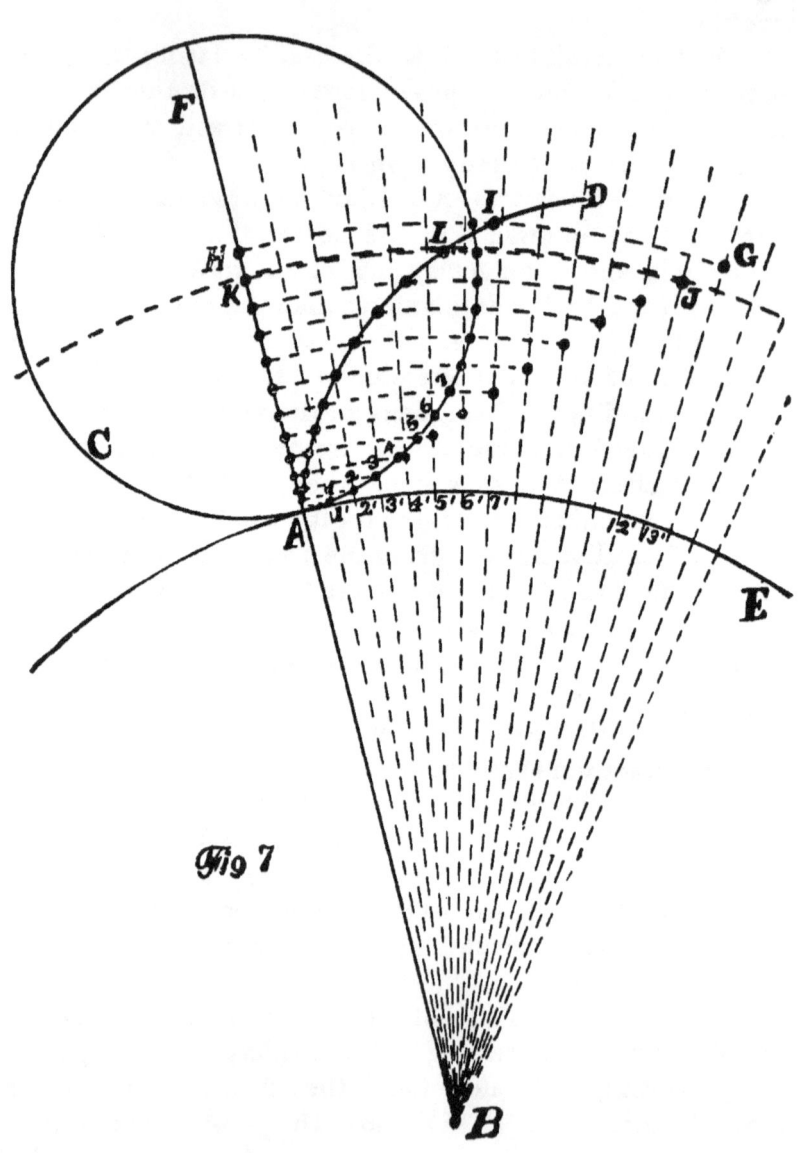

Fig 7

duce all the points shown on the arc A D, and a curve through these points will be an epicycloid.

Figure 8 shows the same system for drawing the flanks of the same tooth. B is the center of the gear, A E is the pitch circle, and C the generating circle. Draw radial lines from the center B to the pitch circle, as shown; as before stated the distance between points is not particular, except that what-

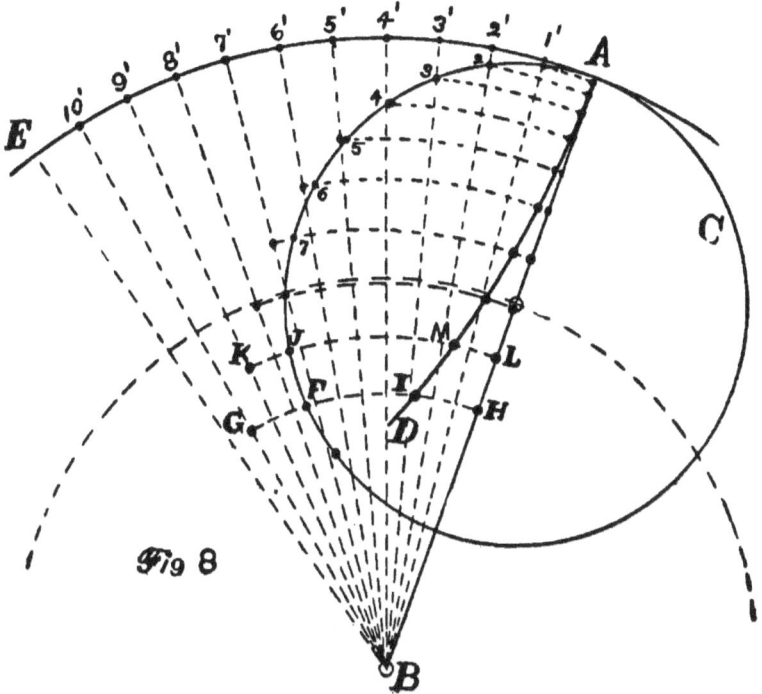

Fig 8

ever they may be in the circle E A, they must be stepped off the same on the generating circle C, and all must start from the same point A. Now with the dividers set at the center B describe arcs through the points 1, 2, 3, 4, etc., on the generating circle, the 10th arc passing through the 10 point on the generating circle to the 10th radial line; the 9th arc passing through the 9th point on the generating circle to the 9th radial line, etc. Then with one point of the dividers set at F, the 10th point on the circle, and the other at G, the 10th radial line, transfer to the line A B at H and produce I; and from J, the 9th point on the circle, to K, the 9th radial line, transfer to L, and produce M; continue in this manner as shown, and a curve drawn through these points, if not too far apart, will be an epicycloid for the flank of this gear.

As already explained, in a combination of gearing in which they are all to interchange, the generating circle is usually made ½ the diameter of the smallest gear in the set. But if you want a pair 24″ diameter, or one that is 24″ and the other 30″ diameter, on the pitch line, then I would use for either case a generating circle that was 12″ diameter for general purposes, but, if you want to increase the strength of the teeth, in these two latter cases I should make the generating circle a little less than one-half the diameter of the smallest of the pair, on the pitch circle.

The teeth of racks are sometimes made with straight faces; some parties make them at an angle of 15° on each side, and some make them 14½° on each side. I prefer the latter, as that is the angle (29°) of a worm thread.

BEVEL WHEELS.

I will now show you how to draw a pair of mitre wheels in gear. Figure 9 represents a pair of 6 pitch 18 teeth; $18 \div 6 = 3$ inches for the largest pitch diameter shown at A A; draw these two lines first as near as possible to the proper length and exactly at right angles (90°) to each other; next draw lines through the center of both these lines representing the axis of the gears and meeting at B, as shown. From the extreme ends of the largest pitch diameters draw the lines C, meeting at B. These lines (C) are the pitch lines of the teeth; at right angles to the lines C B, draw E F, the length of which depends on the pitch of the gear; if 4 pitch, draw one-fourth of an inch on the outside and one-fourth plus the clearance on the inside. The clearance on bevel gears of all kinds is the same depth on the large end of the gear as in spur gears; as the example is 6 pitch, then draw E F one-sixth of an inch, or .166″ on the outside of the line C shown at E

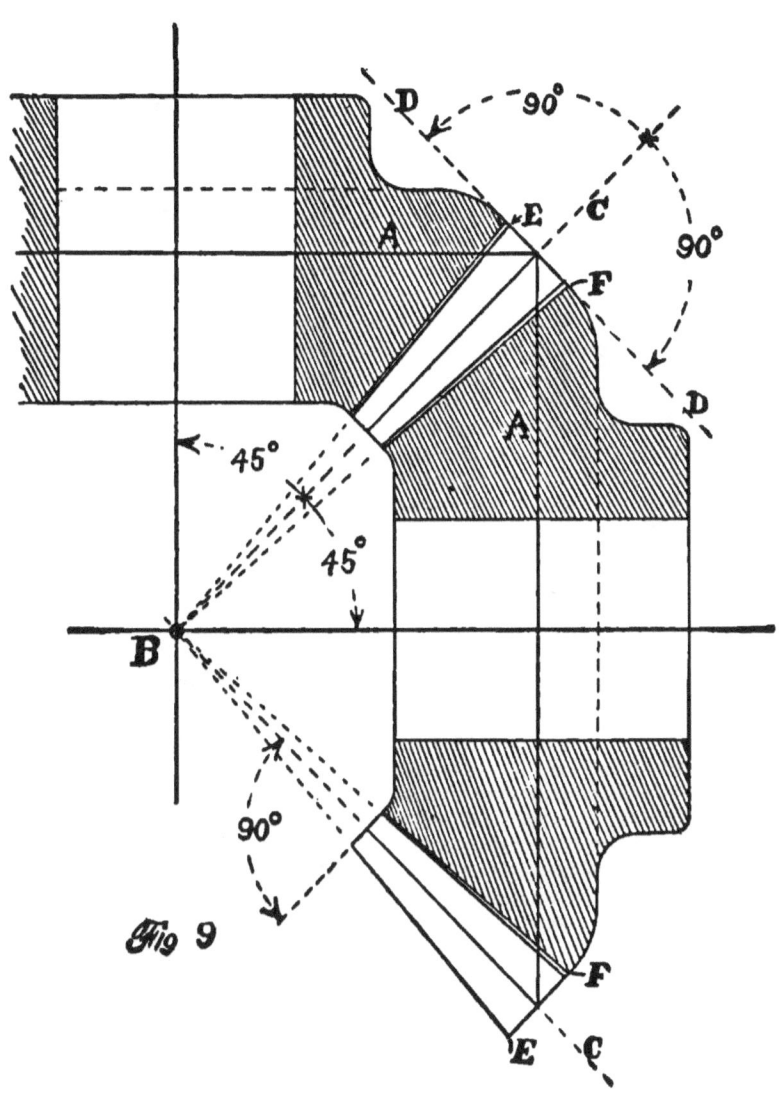

Fig. 9

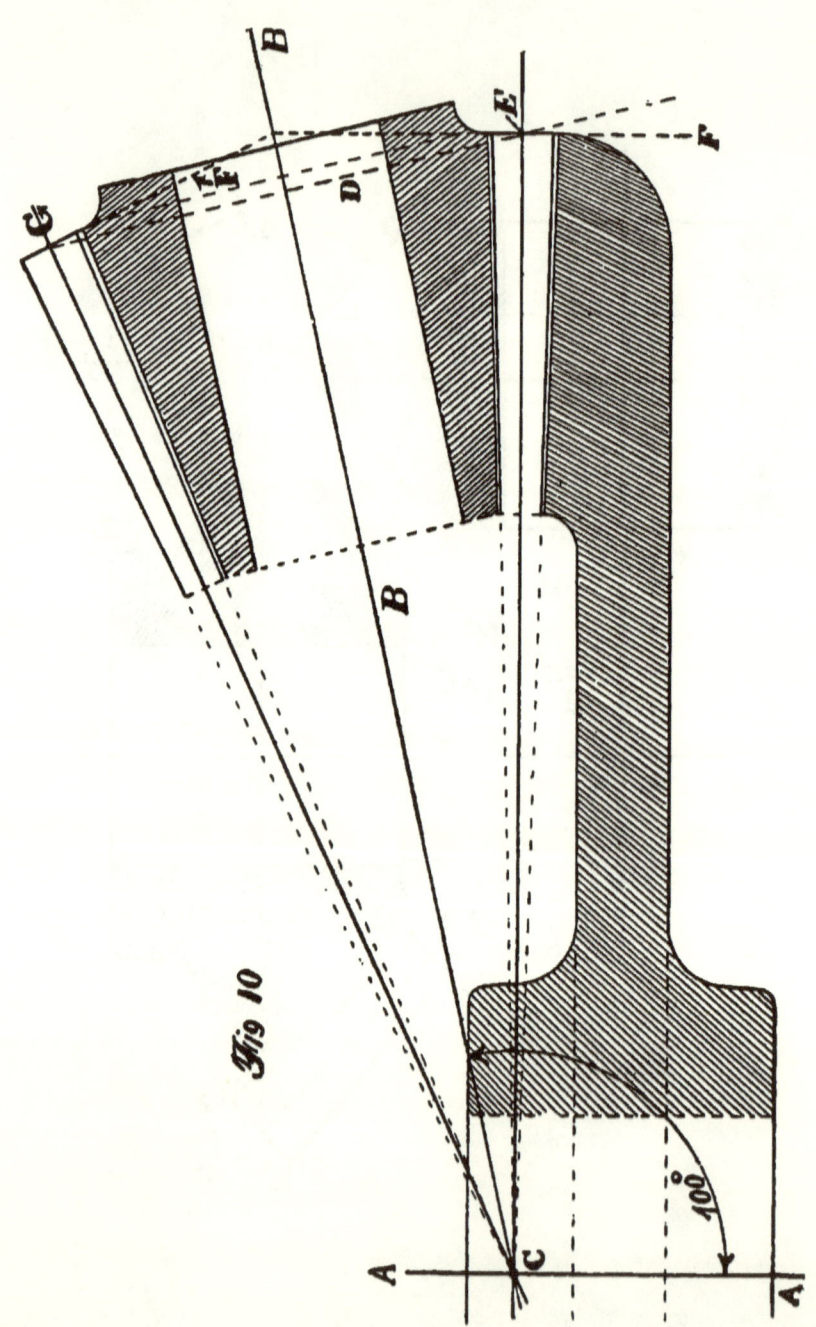

Fig 10

and one-sixth plus the clearance or .192 shown at F; next draw all these lines E F, according to the length of the face of the gear wanted, toward the center B; this length and also the general outlines of hub, etc., depend on circumstances. The center angle of a pair of mitre gears is always 45°, as shown.

It sometimes happens that we have to drive two shafts by gearing that are less or greater than a right angle (90°). In Figure 10 is an example of this kind, in which the shafts are at an angle of 100° from each other, as shown. The pinion has 16 teeth and the wheel 72, and are 8 pitch. First draw the lines A A and B B at an angle of 100°; at right angles to B B draw the line D, exactly 2 inches long (8 pitch 16 teeth) representing the largest pitch diameter of the pinion. The end of this line at E should be just 4½ inches from A A, because the large wheel has 72 teeth, and consequently is just 9 inches in diameter at the largest part (or 4½″ radius). At the intersection of the lines A A and B B shown at C, draw E C and G C; as the gears are 8 pitch, then the teeth will extend ⅛″ above the pitch line and also ⅛″ plus the clearance below the pitch line at the large end only, and at right angles to the pitch lines E C and G C; all these lines are drawn to the center at C. Draw the shape of the gears to suit circumstances.

Figure 11 shows the manner of constructing the teeth of bevel gears. At right angles to the pitch line and about one-third of the length of the tooth from the large end, draw the line B B extending to the axis of the gear E E, and, with the dividers set to this length, transfer to one side and draw the circle C C. As this gear is 4 pitch, then the tooth and space are each .393″ wide on the pitch line ; now space off three or four points on the line C, and with our template or protractor of 75° 30′, draw the shapes in the same manner as explained in spur gears, using for the circle A a radius equal to one-fourth of the line B B.

Remember that the shape and dimensions of these teeth on the circle C C are just the same as on a spur gear of the same diameter; this refers only to the extreme end of the bevel gear tooth at the largest pitch diameter, and from this point

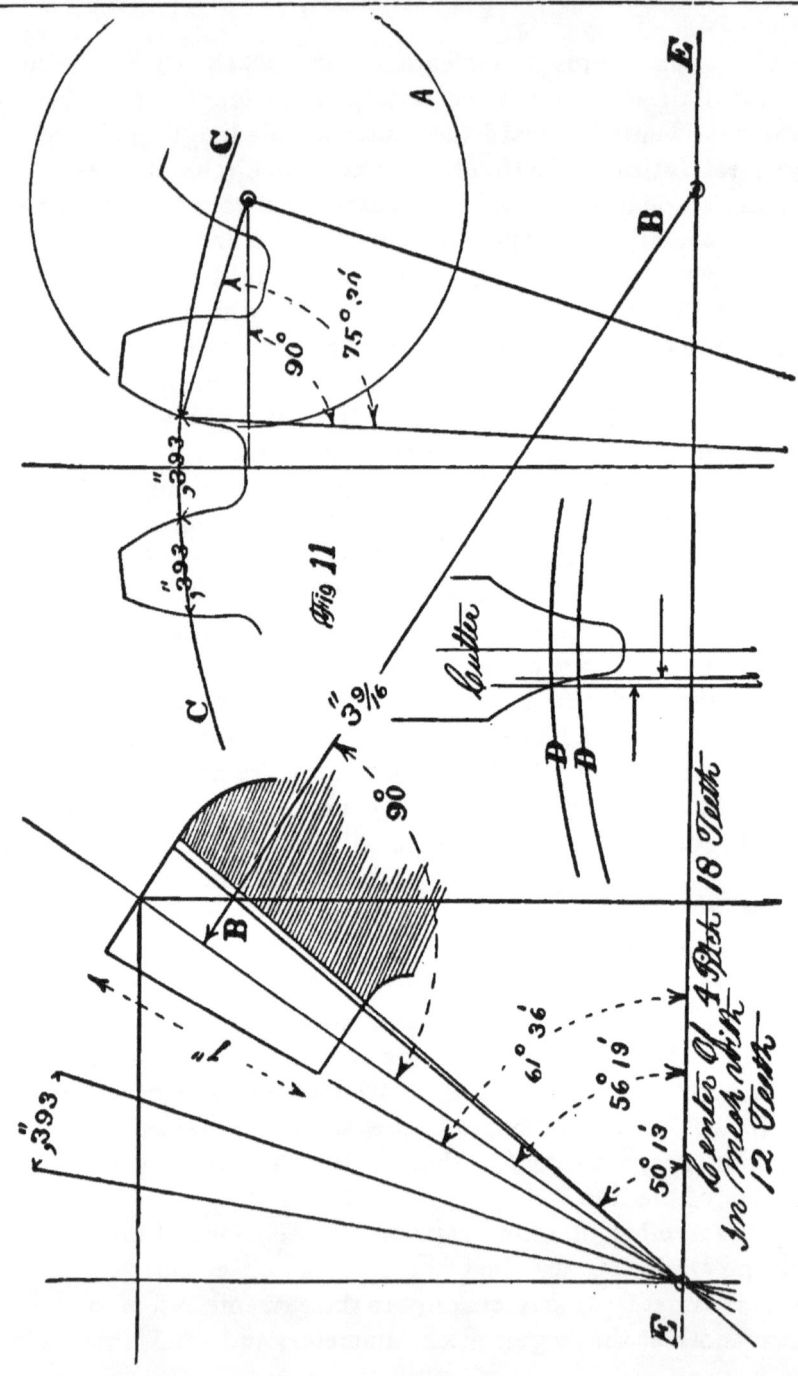

the teeth gradually get smaller in all dimensions, depending on the length of face, etc.

Now, we have found the shape of the teeth, but in cutting bevel gears the cutters will have to be made thin enough to cut through at the small end of the teeth, and the longer the face of the tooth, the thinner we will have to make our cutter. I have shown the shape of the cutter for this gear, and the arcs D D represent the pitch lines of the gear at the two extreme ends of the teeth. This will be more fully explained hereafter.

I will now explain the method of finding the angles of bevel gears. This is a very important matter for the reason that if we do not know the angles, we can neither turn nor cut them accurately.

Figure 12 represents a pair of bevel wheels of 4 pitch; O G is a line through the center of the large wheel which has 30 teeth, and O E, the center line through the pinion which has 12 teeth, a portion only is shown; the wheels are supposed to be in mesh, O I representing the pitch line between the two gears.

Now, as the large gear has 30 teeth, we know the radius (or one-half the diameter) is just 3¾″ which is radius to the angle B O E; we also know the radius of the pinion (or the length of B E), because it is one-half the diameter of the pinion on the pitch line, and, as the pinion has 12 teeth, dividing 12 by 4=3 inches diameter, or 1½″ radius; this 1½″ becomes tangent to the angle B O E, then 1.5″ divided by 3-¾″ = .400″, which is tangent to the radius of one inch. In the table of tangents we find the angle 21° 48′ to correspond with the decimal .400. 21° 48′ is then the center angle of the pinion on the pitch line as shown, and the difference between this and 90° or 68° 12′ is also the center angle of the large gear, also shown.

It must be remembered that the lines B O and I O are the pitch lines of the teeth, the latter for both the pinion and the large wheel as they are supposed to be in gear.

Now, the center angle of the gear being found on the

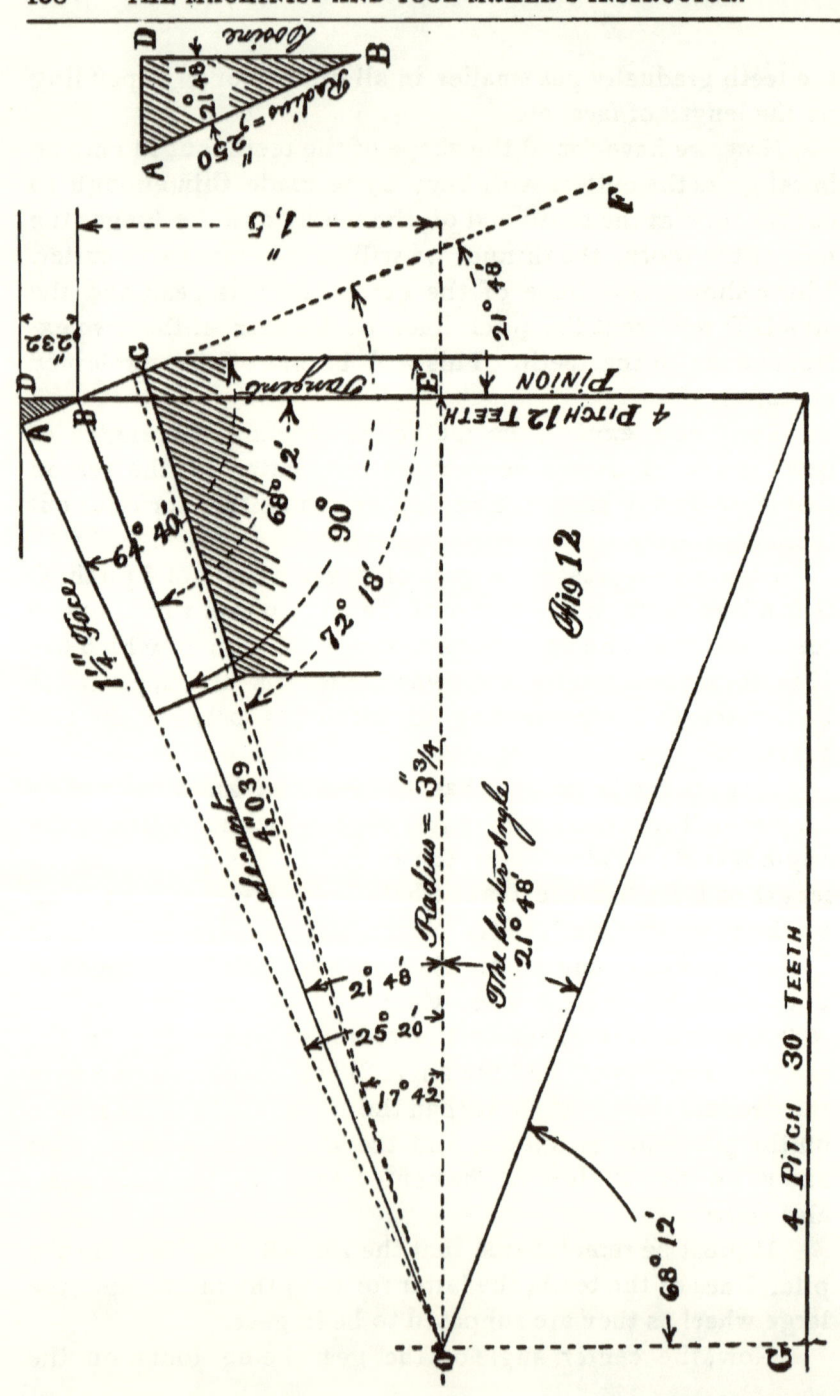

pitch line, then the complement of this angle, or 68° 12′, will be the proper angle to finish the teeth A C, measured from the back of the gear, because A F should always be made 90° from the pitch line B O as shown, and not from the outside or top of the teeth.

The outside diameter of bevel gears is found in a different manner from spur gears, because in bevel gears, if of 4 pitch, as in the example, we measure ¼″ (B A) at right angles to the pitch line B O.

For convenience I have shaded a small angle A B D at the top of this pinion, and, in order to show it more clearly have removed it to one side and have also enlarged it. This angle is for the purpose of finding the exact diameter of this pinion at the highest point shown at A.

In the angle A B D, the longest side A B is known, because it is always equal to the pitch. Thus in 10 pitch, it would be .100″; in 8 pitch, .125″, and in 4 pitch, .250″. As the example is 4 pitch, then A B is .250″. We also know the angle, because it is always the same as the center angle on the pitch line; thus, in the figure the angle is 21° 48′, and A D is sine and D B cosine to this angle. Now, in the table we find the cosine of 21° 48′ = .928, and, multiplied by the radius (.250) = .232″, and this is the distance D B to be added to the radius of the pinion; that is, the radius is 1.5″; then 1.5″ + .232 = 1.732″ for one side, and doubled = 3.4642″ for the largest diameter of the pinion.

Let us now find the angle to turn the face of this pinion. We have found the center angle at the pitch line, and for convenience we now want to know the length of this pitch line, (B O). As O E is radius and B E tangent, then B O is the secant of the angle B O E. In the table of secants we find opposite 21° 48′ the decimal 1.077, which, multiplied by the radius 3¾ = 4.0387, or say 4.039″ for the length O B, as shown. Now as A C is always at right angles to B O, then we have a right angled triangle A O B, figures 12 and 13. In the latter figure I have separated that portion of the tooth above the pitch line, and also that portion including the clearance

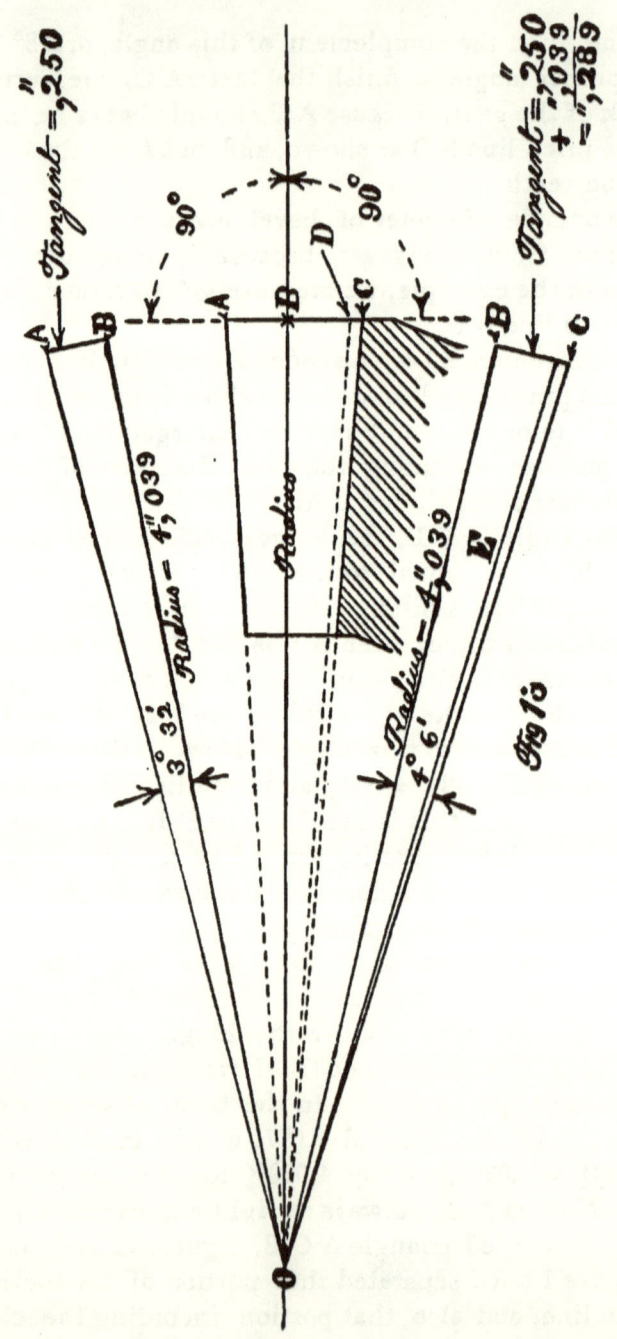

Fig 13

below the pitch line, forming two separate right angled triangles: the one above the pitch line for finding the angle to turn the pinion, and the one below the pitch line for finding the angle to cut the teeth.

As A C is 90° from O B and the length is also known to be 4.039″, also that A O is longer than B O, then A O is the secant to the angle A O B.

We know A B is .250″, and divided by the radius 4.039 = .0618+, or the tangent to the radius 1, and in the table of tangents this corresponds to the angle 3° 32′, which added to 21° 48′ = 25° 20′ for center angle; or 90° — 25° 20′ = 64° 40′ measured from the back as shown, for turning the face of the pinion.

For cutting the teeth the angle B O C is shown, and we have to add the clearance, which is always on the large end of bevel wheels the same as in spur wheels; in 4 pitch the clearance is .039″, and added to .250″ = .289″, which divided by 4.039 = .0715 + = tangent to radius 1, which corresponds to the angle 4° 6′, and 21° 48′ — 4° 6′ = 17° 42′, for the center angle; or 90° — 17° 42′ = 72° 18′, the angle to cut this gear, measured from the back as shown in Figure 12.

It is also necessary in making cutters for bevel gears to know the smallest pitch diameter of the gears in order that the cutters may be made of the proper thickness on the pitch line for cutting them.

Figure 14 shows the method of finding this diameter (figures 12, 13 and 14 representing the same gear.)

I have shown that the line B O is 4.039″, and in figure 12 the face is marked 1¼″; then 4.039 — 1.25″ = 2.790″ nearly.

In figure 14 I have shaded an angle A O C for the purpose of showing the method of finding the smallest pitch diameter of any mitre or bevel gear.

We have found the center angle on the cone pitch line to be 21° 48′, and as the longest line (A O) is radius, then A C becomes sine, and the sine of 21° 48′ = .371+, which multiplied by the radius (2.790″) = 1.036″ for the length of A C,

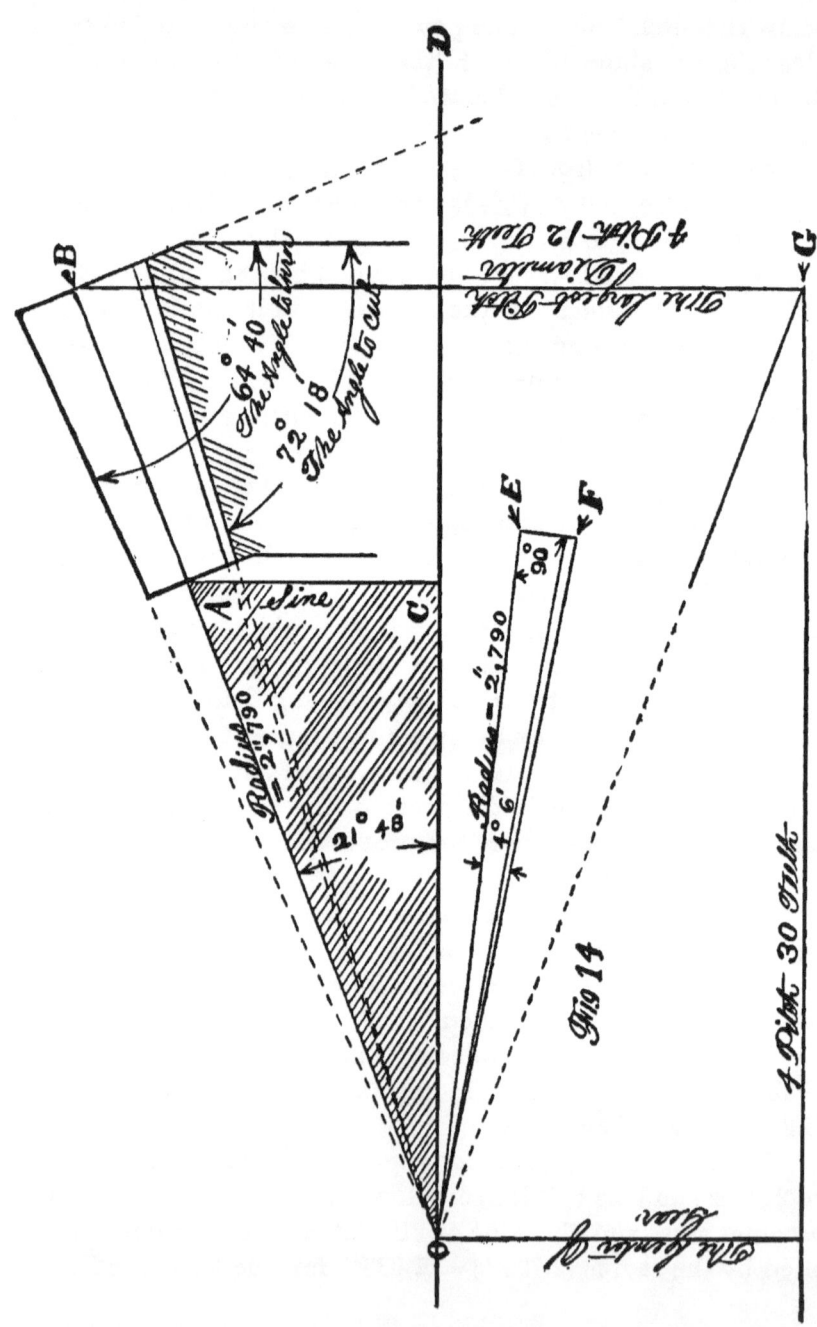

Fig 14

and twice this $= 2.072''$ for the smallest pitch diameter of the pinion.

$2.072'' \times 3.1416 = 6.509''$ for the circumference, and, divided by twice the number of teeth (24) $= .2712''$, for the thickness of the cutter or tooth on the pitch line.

It must not be forgotten that the cutter is made of the proper thickness to suit the teeth on the smallest pitch diameter, and, in making the cutter, it is also necessary to know the depth from the pitch line to the bottom of the tooth on the small end.

Referring back to Figure 14, I show a method of finding this depth by the angle E O F. I have shown A O to be $2.790''$ long, and this line is represented by E O. Now this angle is already explained in Figure 13, which is the same thing, and has been found to be 4° 6'; then as E O represents the pitch line, and E F at right angles to it the tangent, we multiply the tangent of 4° 6' by the radius 2.79; thus tangent 4° 6' $= .0717 \times 2.79 = .200''$ for the depth from the pitch line to the bottom of the teeth on the small end of the gear.

Now, as the teeth of bevel gears are of the same depth, thickness, etc., at the largest pitch diameter as those of spur gears, then this gear of 4 pitch will be $.289''$ from the pitch line to the bottom of the teeth on the large end, and only $.200''$ on the small end, a difference of $.089''$ in the depth from the pitch line, and of course, the cutter will be too thin for the large ends of the teeth.

To finish the teeth of bevel wheels correctly (or I might say approximately correct, for bevel gears cannot be made correct by rotary cutters) we will have to pass the cutter through each space at least twice.

There are two ways of cutting these teeth to get them of the proper thickness on the large end of the teeth, and, if possible, the wheels should always be on an arbor that is fitted in the taper hole of the index head spindle, no matter how slight the angle of the teeth may be, as otherwise the teeth may be thicker on one side than the other (or rather not spaced uniormly).

One way of cutting the teeth of bevel wheels to get them the right thickness on the large end of the teeth is to place the cutter central with the headstock spindle, and, having the wheel elevated to the proper angle, pass the cutter through, then rotate the wheel by the index crank, say two or three holes on the index plate, depending altogether on the gear you are cutting, that is, whether the cutter is much thinner than standard size.

Now, if you revolve the wheel as stated, but one hole, you will have to move the table slightly in or out depending upon which way you revolve it, so that the cutter will pass through the small end of the gear without touching the sides of the tooth, and, as the large end of the wheel will revolve through a greater space than the small end, so will the cutter passing through take out more and more as it reaches the large end of the teeth.

Remember that whatever the number of holes you turn one way, you must also turn the same number in the opposite direction, otherwise you will get crooked teeth.

It can easily be seen that the teeth will be rounded off a little too much unless the cutters have been made for cutting in this way.

The other way for cutting the teeth of bevel wheels is to set the Universal Head at the proper angle to the table, and cutting all the teeth in this position, then swivel the head to the same angle in the opposite direction and pass the cutter through the second time. The greatest care should be used to have the cutter central with the work.

I will now show you how to get the exact angle for swiveling the Universal Head to cut the teeth of a bevel wheel.

In figure 15, which also corresponds with Figure 11, but greatly enlarged, we have found the thickness of the tooth, or space at the pitch line on the small end of the gear to be .247″; we will also have to know the thickness of the cutter that touches the pitch line as it passes through the large end.

In figure 11 I have shown the position of the template of 75° 30′ on the pitch line, with the circle A equal to one-fourth

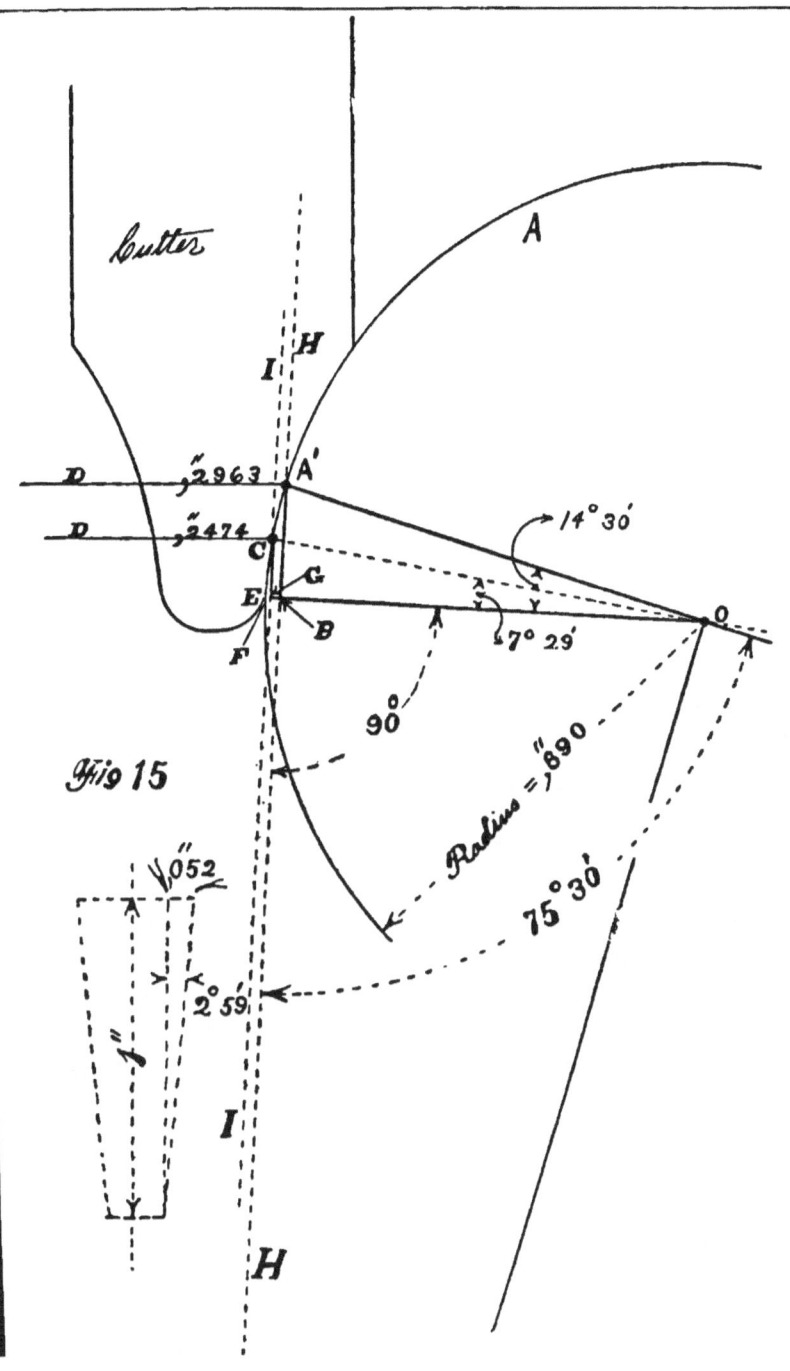

Cutter

A

H

I

D $\overset{''}{2963}$ A'

D $\overset{''}{2474}$

C

E   G

F   B

14° 30'

7° 29'

O

90°

Radius = $\overset{''}{890}$

75° 30'

Fig 15

$\overset{''}{052}$

1"

2° 59'

I

H

($\frac{1}{4}$) the radius, thus $39/16'' \div 4 = .890''$.   Now in Figure 15 the pitch line would touch at A^1, which corresponds with C C, Figure 11.   In Figure 15 H H represents the template of 75° 30' in line with the center of the gear and a right angled triangle (A^1 O representing the top of the template) with the vertex at O as shown, will be the complement of 75° 30' or 14° 30' as shown in the figure.   We have found the depth from the pitch line to the bottom of the tooth on the small end of the gear, which is .182'', and we know that the depth from the pitch line to the bottom of the tooth on the large end is the difference between the whole depth .539'' and .250'', or .289'' (for 4 pitch); then draw two lines D D on this cutter as shown, which represents the height of the pitch lines at the two ends of the teeth in the bevel gear.

We know how wide the space should be on the pitch line at the large end of the tooth, because it is the same as any tooth of a 4 pitch spur gear or .393''; as the cutter was made thin enough for the small end, we will have to find the width across the cutter that touches at the largest pitch diameter by the angles shown.   In other words, the object now is to find the distance between I I and H H.   As A^1 O is .890'' we call it radius, A^1 B the sine and B O cosine of the angle A^1 O B.

The cosine of 14° 30' = .968 + and multiplied by the radius (.890'') = .8626'' for the length of B O.   Now we have found the depth from the pitch line to the bottom of the small end of the gear (or the cutter) to be .182'' as stated, and the depth on the large end .289''; then the difference between these pitch lines, as represented by the lines D D, Figure 15 = .107''; we next find the distance A^1 B, or the sine of the angle A^1 O B.   The sine of 14° 30' = .2503 and multiplied by the radius (.890) = .223''; then subtracting the distance between D D which we said was .107'' from .223'', we have .116'' for the sine C G of the second angle (the line C O being dotted).

Now to find what this angle is we divide .116'' by .890 and we have .1301 for the sine to a radius of 1 inch, which in the table corresponds to the angle 7° 29'.

We have now found the degrees and minutes of these two

right angled triangles, and we now want to know the cosines of these two angles in order to know the distance between the two lines I I and H H. The cosine of 14° 30′ = .968, and multiplied by the radius (.890) = .861″. The cosine of 7° 29′ = .9915, and multiplied by the radius (.890) = .883. Now the difference between .861″ and .883″ = .022″, and this is the distance between I I and H H.

Now draw an angle as shown dotted at the bottom of figure 15, representing the length of the teeth (which in this case is one inch), one end equal in width to the thickness of the space between two teeth at the small end on the pitch line, the other end equal to the width of the space between two teeth on the large end on the pitch line, minus twice the width of space between the lines I I and H H ; this will be the correct angle for cutting the teeth of this bevel gear.

The angle for cutting any bevel gear or mitre wheel can also be found in a similar manner.

SPIRAL GEARS.

Figure 16 shows the manner of finding the correct diameter of gears when they are to be cut spiral and with regular standard cutters. Find the diameter of the gear on the pitch line in the usual manner and multiply it by the secant of the angle you wish to cut it, then add two pitches in the usual way. Thus, suppose you want a spiral gear of 8 pitch 24 teeth, or 10 pitch 30 teeth. The diameters for regular spur gears would be 3″ diameter on the pitch line. But if you want them cut at an angle of 10°, then multiply the secant of 10° = 1.0154 by 3″, and the result, 3.046″, will be the correct diameter on the pitch line; if 8 pitch, add two 8ths to this, making 3.296″ for the diameter of the outside. If the same gear was to be 10 pitch, then add two 10ths, making it 3.246″ outside diameter.

Now, if the same gear was to be cut at an angle of 23° 10′, then the secant of 23° 10′ = 1.0877, multiplied by 3″ = 3.263″ for the diameter on the pitch line.

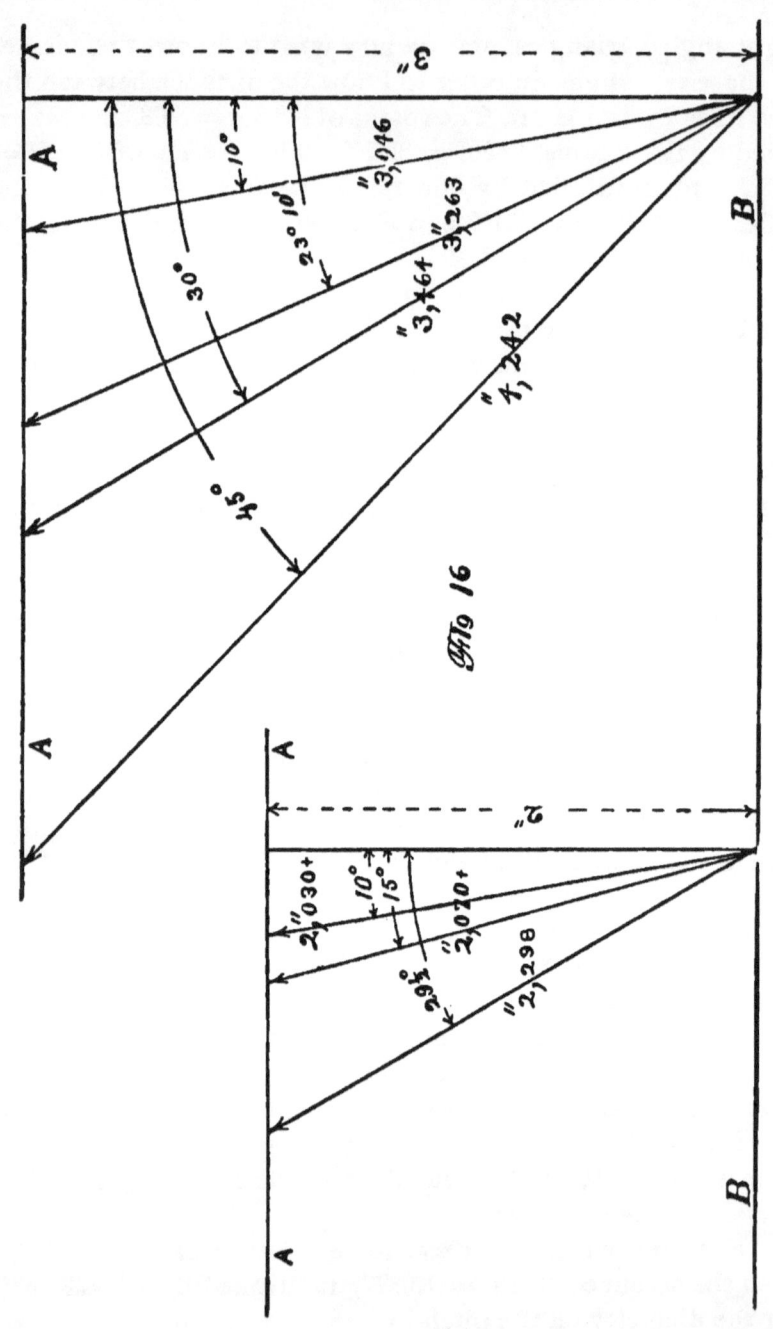

Fig 16

If they were to be cut at an angle of 45°, then the secant of 45° = 1.414 × 3″ = 4.242″ for the diameter at the pitch line.

Suppose you want a spiral gear of 4 pitch, 36 teeth and 10° angle. 36 ÷ 4 = 9, this multiplied by the secant of 10° = 9.1386″ for the pitch diameter and 2/4ths added = 9.6386″ for the outside diameter of the gear.

It sometimes happens, however, that we have a standard size blank, say 2¾″ diameter on the pitch line, and we want it to have 22 teeth; this would be right for an ordinary spur gear of 8 pitch. But if we should want to cut this gear at an angle of 45° (spiral), then we would have to make a special cutter,

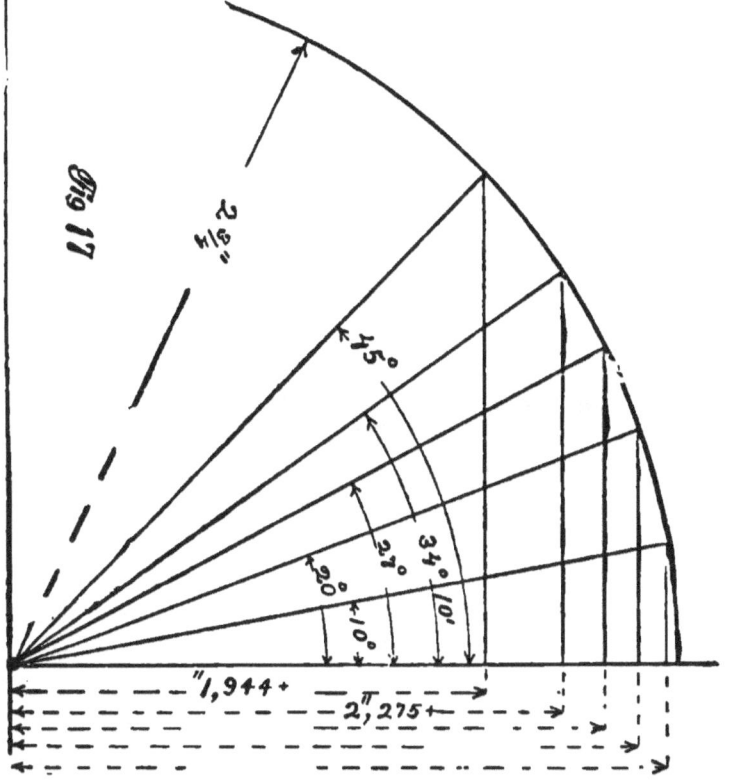

unless it would suit some other pitch. To find the thickness of the cutter on the pitch line when the diameter of the gear (on the pitch line) and the number of teeth is given, multiply the cosine of the angle you wish to cut it by the diameter of the gear on the pitch line, and this again by 3.1416, then divide the product by twice the number of teeth, and the result will be the thickness of the tooth on the pitch line, thus :

In the example, figure 17, suppose we have a gear blank 2¾″ diameter on the pitch line, and we want the teeth to be cut spiral at an angle of 45°, 22 teeth. The cosine of 45° = .707, and .707 × 2.75″ = 1.9442″, and this again multiplied by 3.1416 = 6.105″; then 6.105″ ÷ 44 = .138 +″ for the thickness of the cutter on the pitch line. This would be nearly right for a cutter of 11 pitch, and, when the difference is so slight, we can sometimes make the gear a little larger or smaller to suit circumstances. Thus, suppose instead of making it 11 pitch, which is a little thicker than in the example, we make the blank to suit a 12 pitch cutter, which is about .007″ thinner, then, as there are 22 teeth and 22 spaces, a 12 pitch cutter being .131″ thick on the pitch line, we multiply .131 by 44 = 5.764″; divide this by 3.1416 = 1.834″ which multiplied by the secant of 45° (1.414) = 2.593″, or the diameter.

Suppose a party came into the shop and ordered a pair of spiral gears, one of the gears to be twice as large as the other to connect or drive two spindles that were 6″ apart, and parallel, and the teeth to be cut at an angle of 10° from their axis. What will be the thickness of the cutters at the pitch line?

If the spindles are 6″ apart, and one twice as large as the other, then the radius of one gear will be 2″ and the other 4″, or the diameters 4″ and 8″. The cosine of 10° = .9848, and multiplied by 8″ (the large wheel) = 7.878″, and this again multiplied by 3.1416 = 24.738″; this divided by twice the number of teeth in the wheel will be the thickness of the cutter on the pitch line. Thus: suppose there are 48 teeth on the wheel, then $24.738 \div 96 = .257+''$, the answer; and this, of course, will be the thickness of cutter for the small wheel also.

Now as these shafts are to run parallel, then one of the wheels will be cut right hand and the other left hand. They, of course, will be of the same angle, 10°, but the pitch of the large wheel will be twice as great as the small one.

In cutting the teeth of spiral gears the angle is usually given, but sometimes, instead of the angle, the number of inches to one turn is given ; thus, suppose you have a spindle $2\frac{1}{2}''$ diameter, and you want to mill grooves on it that will have, say one turn in 30''. In doing work like this, it is necessary that we know the proper angle to swing the table, which is done as follows : Multiply the diameter by 3.1416 and divide the product by the number of inches to one turn of the groove, which will give the tangent. In the table of tangents the angle can be found. Thus, $2.5 \times 3.1416 = 7.850$; $7.850 \div 30 = .2617$, the tangent, which, in the table corresponds to the angle 14° 40', the answer.

In cutting spiral gears, standard cutters (as regards shape) can generally be used, excepting when the angle is very great and the wheel is very small. In the latter case the teeth will be rounded off too much. If the cutter is large in the diameter at the same time, it will also increase the trouble. Special cutters should be made for this class of work if accuracy is required.

It must be remembered that in milling most kinds of work when the angle is very great, that the shape of the groove will not be the same as the cutter that produced it, except when using end mills. In this case the table is not set over, but end mills, if small, are too slow and consequently expensive.

WORM GEARING.

In making worms and worm wheels it is more convenient to do so by circular pitch than diametral pitch, for the reason that a worm is nothing more or less than a screw with a special shape of thread, (29° angle, 14½° each side). As all lathes are geared to cut so many threads per inch, for instance 4 threads per inch, which means ¼″ pitch, then the worm wheel must also be cut to suit it, and for this reason we use circular pitch for this class of work.

If you want to cut a worm and worm wheel with 9 threads per inch, dividing 1 by 9, the result .111 + ″ would be the pitch of both the worm and worm wheel, and dividing by 2, the result, .0555″, will be the thickness of the thread and also the tooth on the pitch line.

Most parties in ordering worms and worm wheels will say 3 pitch, 4 pitch, 5 pitch, etc., but they simply mean so many threads per inch (called linear pitch), and means so many threads measured in a straight line.

Figure 18 represents a worm and worm wheel of ⅜″ circular pitch; the wheel has 84 teeth. When the distance between centers should be some even figure, say 6″, 8″, etc., we make the worm wheel the right diameter to suit the pitch and number of teeth required, and then the worm is made of the proper size to "fill out," as you would call it.

In the figure the distance between centers is not important, and I have shown the worm to be 4″ outside diameter.

As the wheel has 84 teeth and is ⅜″ pitch, we multiply ⅜ or .375 by 84, and we have 31.5 inches for the circumference, which, divided by 3.1416 = 10.0267 inches for the diameter on the pitch line, as shown at E; we find the working depth for ⅜″ pitch to be .238″, and one-half of this or .119″ added to each side will make the worm wheel 10.265″ diameter at the throat, as shown on the line H. This is the only thing about worm wheels of much importance, that is, to get the correct diameter at the throat.

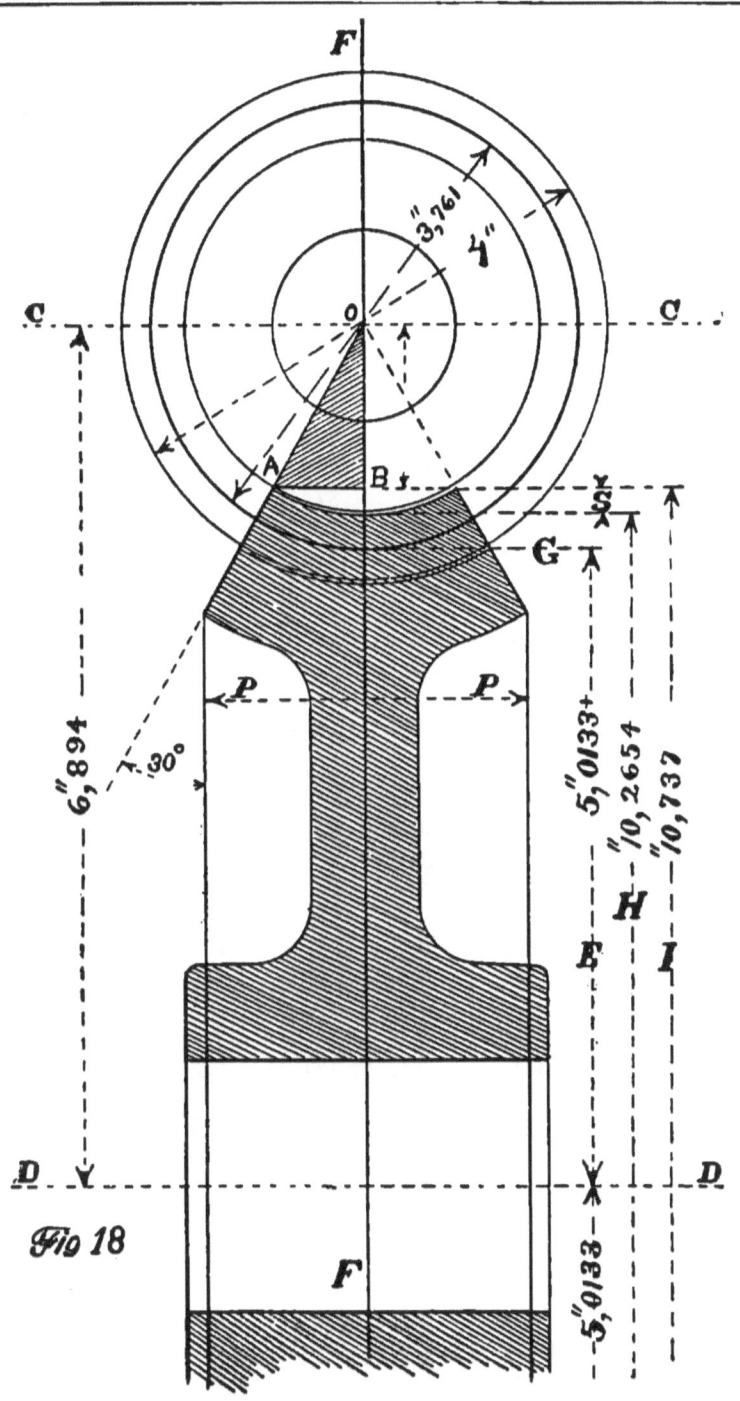

Fig 18

WORMS AND WORM WHEELS.

CIRCULAR PITCH.	THREADS PER INCH.	DIAMETRAL PITCH.	THICKNESS OF TOOTH ON PITCH LINE.	WORKING DEPTH OF TOOTH.	WHOLE DEPTH OF TOOTH.	WIDTH OF THREAD TOOL AT END.	WIDTH OF THREAD AT TOP.
3″	⅓	1.0472	1.5000	1.9098	2.0598	.9285	1.0061
2¾	4/11	1.1423	1.375	1.7506	1.8881	.8511	.9223
2½	2/5	1.2566	1.250	1.5915	1.7165	.7737	.8384
2¼	4/9	1.3962	1.125	1.4324	1.5449	.6963	.7545
2	½	1.5708	1.0	1.2732	1.3732	.6190	.6707
1⅞	8/15	1.6755	.9375	1.1936	1.2874	.5803	.6288
1¾	4/7	1.7952	.875	1.1141	1.2016	.5504	.5869
1⅝	8/13	1.9332	.8125	1.0345	1.1158	.5029	.5449
1½	⅔	2.0944	.750	.9549	1.0299	.4642	.5030
1⅜	8/11	2.2847	.6875	.8754	.9441	.4255	.4611
1¼	4/5	2.5132	.625	.7958	.8583	.3870	.4192
1⅛	8/9	2.7925	.5625	.7162	.7724	.3482	.3770
1	1	3.1416	.500	.6366	.6866	.3095	.3353
1 5/16	1 1/15	3.3510	.4687	.5968	.6437	.2902	.3144
⅞	1 1/7	3.5903	.4375	.5570	.6008	.2710	.2934
13/16	1 3/13	3.8664	.4062	.5173	.5579	.2514	.2724
¾	1⅓	4.1888	.375	.4774	.5149	.2321	.2515
11/16	1 5/11	4.5694	.3437	.4377	.4720	.2130	.2305
⅝	1 3/5	5.0264	.3125	.3978	.4290	.1935	.2096
9/16	1 7/9	5.5850	.2812	.3581	.3862	.1741	.1886
½	2	6.2831	.250	.3183	.3433	.1550	.1676
7/16	2 2/7	7.1806	.2187	.2788	.3006	.1353	.1466
2/5	2 ½	7.8540	.200	.2546	.2746	.1242	.1342
⅜	2 ⅔	8.3776	.1875	.2387	.2575	.1160	.1257
⅓	3	9.4248	.1666	.2122	.2289	.1032	.1116
5/16	3 1/5	10.0528	.1562	.1989	.2145	.0967	.1048
2/7	3 ½	10.9955	.1429	.1819	.1962	.0885	.0956
¼	4	12.5663	.125	.1591	.1716	.0799	.0838
2/9	4 ½	14.1371	.1111	.1415	.1526	.0686	.0741
1/5	5	15.7079	.100	.1273	.1372	.0620	.0670
3/16	5 ⅓	16.7552	.0937	.1193	.1287	.0580	.0628
1/6	6	18.8496	.0833	.1061	.1144	.0515	.0556
1/7	7	21.9912	.0714	.0910	.0981	.0442	.0478
1/8	8	25.1327	.0625	.0795	.0858	.0386	.0419
1/16	16	50.2654	.0312	.0398	.0429	.0193	.0209

This table refers to single threads only.
If double threads are required divide by 2.
If triple by 3, and if quadruple by 4, etc.

Now, if it was necessary that the distance between centers should be say 6″, then we would take one-half of the diameter or the radius of the worm wheel, as shown on the pitch line at G = 5.0133″, and subtracting it from 6″ we would have .9867″ for one-half the diameter of the worm on the pitch line, or 1.973″ for the whole diameter on the pitch line, and adding .238″ we would have 2.211″ for the outside diameter of the worm.

The exact diameter of any worm wheel at the largest part as shown on the line I, although not very important, can easily be found if we know the angle of the sides of the teeth; in the figure the angle is 30°, as shown.

For convenience I have shown a right angled triangle at the center of the worm A O B; the length O A is known, because it is one-half of the diameter of the worm, less the working depth (.238″) of the tooth ; then 2″ — .238+″ = 1.761″ for the radius A O ; the cosine of 30° = .866, which multiplied by the radius 1.761 = 1.525″, for the distance O B.

Now we know that from the center of the worm to the throat of the worm wheel it is 2″ —.238″, or 1.761″; then subtracting 1.525″ from 1.761″ = .236″ in a vertical direction from B to the throat of the wheel at the center ; then twice this, or .472″, added to 10.265″ = 10.737″ for the largest diameter of the worm wheel, as shown on the line I.

The dimensions of worm threads and the width of tools for cutting them are found in the following manner:

In the example the thread is 3/8″ circular pitch, and dividing 3.1416 by 3/8, or .375, we have 8.378 for the diametral pitch; then dividing 1 by 8.378 = .1193″ for one half of the working depth, or .238″, for the working depth of the tooth or thread ; as the pitch is 3/8″, then the tooth and also the space is one-half or 3/16″ thick on the pitch line; one-tenth of 3/16″, or .187″ = about .019″, and this added to twice .119″ = .257″, for the whole depth of any worm, worm wheel, or spur wheel of 3/8″ circular pitch.

The width of the top of thread and also the bottom of the space is found in the following manner:

Figure 18½ represents the side of this ⅜″ pitch tooth greatly enlarged, shown at A A. The angle of worm threads, as explained, is 14½° on each side, and drawing a line perpendicular to the pitch line, as shown, we produce a right angled triangle on each side of the pitch line, with the radius given. Then, as the tangent of 14½° = .2586, we multiply this by .119″, and the result, .0307″, is the distance B B, and twice this, or .0615, subtracted from the thickness of the tooth on the pitch line (.1875)″ = .125″ for the width of thread on top.

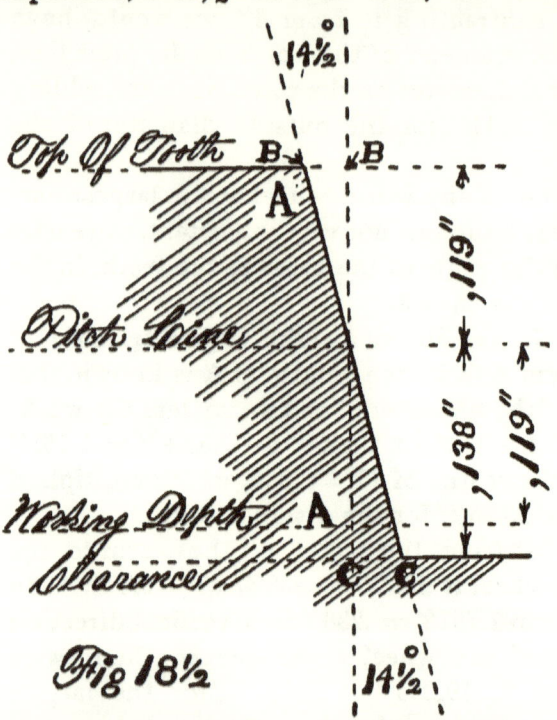

Fig. 18½

The tangent, .2586, multiplied by .138″, the distance from the pitch line to the bottom of the tooth, thus, .2586 × .138″ = .0356 for the distance C C; twice this, or .0713″, subtracted from the thickness of the tooth on the pitch line = .116″, nearly, for the width of space on the bottom, or the width of the tool for cutting the thread, etc., for a worm of ⅜″ circular pitch.

The dimensions of any worm thread can be found in the same manner.

In cutting the teeth of worm wheels they should first be driven on an arbor, and the table set over to the proper angle (corresponding to the angle of the worm thread), then select an ordinary spur gear cutter, not much, if any, larger in the diameter than the worm, and a little thinner on the tooth than the thread of the worm, and placing the worm wheel directly under the center of the cutter, raise the wheel up into the cutter sufficiently to cut it two-thirds or more of the whole depth, depending upon the size and shape of cutter, and also whether the angle is correct.   The teeth are roughed out only in this way by indexing; after which a hob, made like the worm, and with a diameter equal to that of the worm, plus twice the clearance added, is placed on the arbor of the milling machine, with the table set back to zero (right angled to the cutter arbor); the dog is then taken off the worm wheel arbor, and the wheel is then raised up into the hob as before.   The hob will revolve the worm wheel while it is gradually raised to the proper depth.

Now let us see what the angle should be in this worm wheel. As the worm is 3.761″ diameter on the pitch line, then the circumference would be about 11.809″, and dividing the pitch by the circumference, thus, $\frac{3}{8}″ = .375 \div 11.809″ = .0317″$ for the tangent (this will be more fully explained hereafter).   This tangent corresponds to the angle 1° 49″, which is the correct angle to swivel the table for roughing out the worm wheel.

Remember to take the circumference on the pitch diameter of the worm, and not the outside diameter.   The angle for roughing out any worm wheel is found in a similar manner.

It sometimes happens that when worm wheels are very small, or of a very coarse pitch, that it is necessary when commencing to hob the wheel (after it has been roughed out) to help revolve it by hand until it has made two or three turns, after which it will take care of itself.

In figure 19 I have shown an attachment to be used on the Universal Milling Machine for cutting the teeth of worm wheels complete, by hobbing, when a great many of one size are wanted, the details of which are as follows: A A is a spindle fitted at one end (shown at the left) to the milling machine spindle, the outer end projecting through the bearing B, which is held sidewise by the bevel wheel C on one side and a tight fitting nut and collars on the other, as shown.

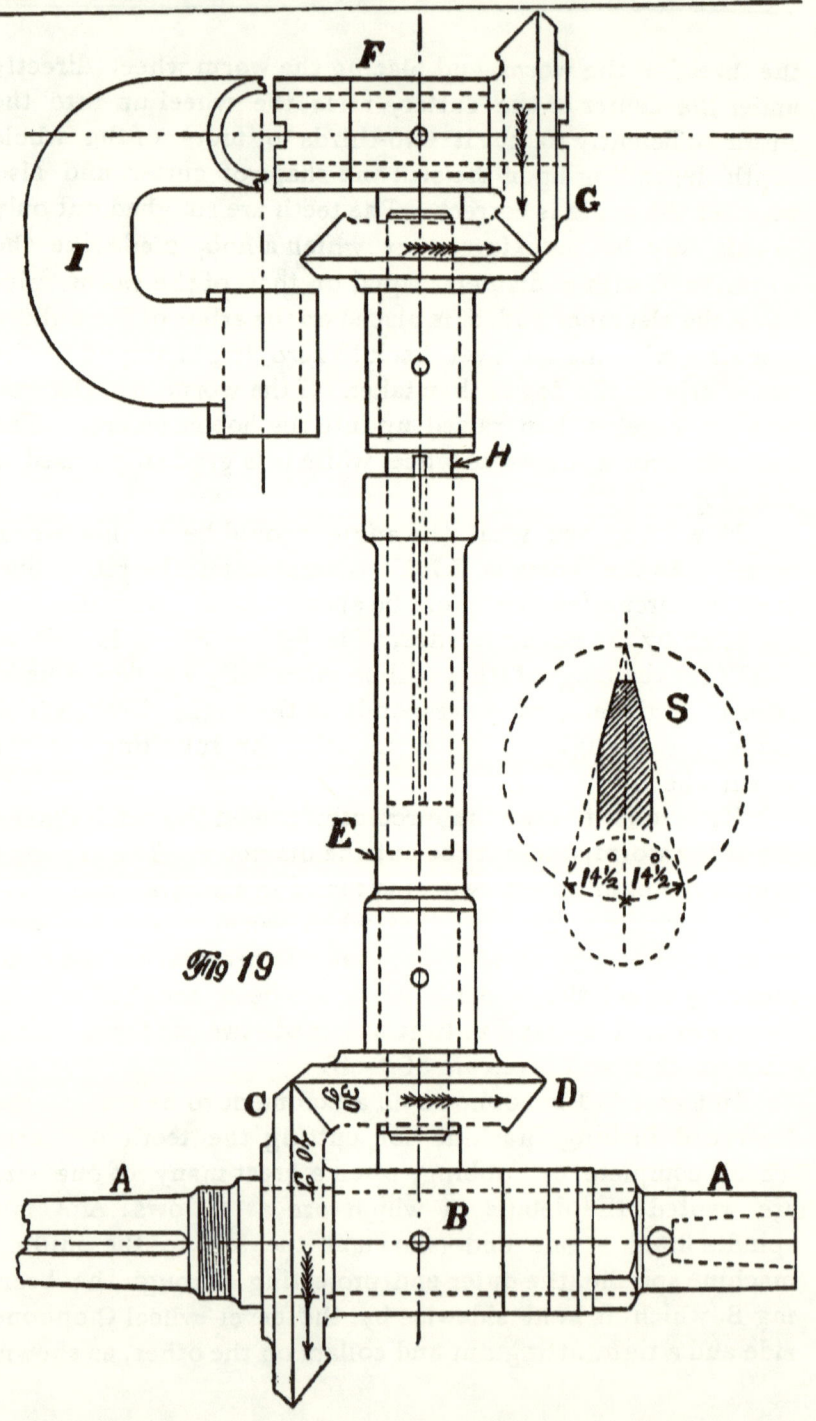

Fig 19

The outer end of this spindle is also bored taper to receive the shanks of small hobs, the outer end of the hob being supported by the center in the overhanging arm. The bevel wheel C meshes with D, which is screwed on the shaft E. The bearing F has a hollow shaft or sleeve passing through it, and is bored to slip over the worm shaft on the Universal Head, which it is to drive. The mitre wheel G is supposed to work on either side of the bearing F, in order to cut both right hand and left hand worm wheels as desired.

In the figure I have shown 40 teeth on the driving wheel C, and 30 teeth on the driven D. The pair at the other end are mitres, and can be made any size to suit circumstances (say 30 teeth each). As it takes 40 turns of the worm shaft to make one revolution of the spindle in the Universal Head, then, if we want to cut a worm wheel of 30 teeth, a pair of bevel wheels with 40 teeth for the driver, and 30 for the driven, as shown, will give the required number of teeth. If 32 teeth are wanted on the worm wheel, then a bevel wheel with 32 teeth should be placed at D, and if 50 teeth are wanted, then the wheel at D should have 50 teeth also. Of course, the other wheels need not be changed as regards the number of teeth.

The worm wheel to be cut is placed on an arbor between the centers in the usual way, and driven by a dog, the attachment being made long enough to suit the work. As the shaft H telescopes the shaft E, we are not limited to an exact length of the arbor on which the work is placed. Both bearings F and B are of the same design and better understood by the side elevation shown at I, partly broken off at one of the bearings for want of space.

CHAPTER III.

EXTRACTS FROM BROWN & SHARPE MANUFACTURING CO.'S
TREATISE ON MILLING MACHINES.

(PUBLISHED BY PERMISSION.)

MILLING MACHINES AND SKILL.

No one who has had sufficient experience with the Milling
Machine in its various forms to acquire a reasonably clear idea
of its capabilities, and who has an opportunity to see the machine in use in the various shops, can fail to see that in many
of them it is very imperfectly understood, and that, as a con-
sequence, comparatively poor results are obtained from its
use—results, we mean, which are very poor compared with
those which should be obtained, and are obtained in every
case where the legitimate functions of the machine are clearly
recognized, and the conditions necessary to its successful
operation secured.

The Milling Machine intelligently selected or constructed,
with reference to the work it is expected to do, provided with
well designed and well made special fixtures, where the nature
of the work calls for them, and then skillfully handled, is a
surprisingly efficient tool, but used as it is being used in many
shops today, it is a delusion, a failure and an injury alike to
the users, to the builders and to the good name of the milling machines generally.

While it is true that there is scarcely a machine tool in
use which will yield more satisfactory returns for a given out-
lay, when pains are taken to use it in the best possible manner, it is also true, we think, that there is no tool in common
use, the efficiency of which is so much reduced by careless or
ignorant handling and abuse. Considerable intelligence and
skill, as well as constant attention, must be bestowed upon
the milling machines in order to secure anything like a satisfactory performance from them, either in the quality of the
work done or in its quantity.

In some cases this skill and intelligence must be possessed and exercised by the man who actually handles the machine; in other cases by some one who, though he does not actually operate it, supervises its operation, and is responsible for the work done by it. But in any case, the skill, the intelligence and the careful attention must be exercised, or the results will be anything but satisfactory.

We hear a great deal about the comparatively cheap labor required to do milling machine work, and it is evident that too many shop proprietors have concluded from this that about all that is necessary to do such work is to buy the machine, hire a boy to run it, have him shown how for an hour or so by one of the lathe hands, and then let the boy and the machine work out their own salvation.

No greater mistake could possibly be made, and it is in such a shop that a milling machine man finds the machine working often at less than half of its capacity, with an apology for a cutter, ground by hand in every shape but the right one, two or three only of its superabundant teeth touching the work, and they, with a distinct thump and knock, indicating anything but a real cutting action, while the boy stands by, and occasionally—when it occurs to him to do so—squirting a few drops of black lubricating oil onto the chips with which the spaces between the teeth are tightly jammed. The proprietors of such shops are not usually very enthusiastic regarding the use of milling machines, and it would be a wonder if they were.

Where a Universal Milling Machine is used upon tool work or for other purposes requiring a constant change from one job to another, it is a mistake to suppose that there is economy in the employment of a boy or cheap man to operate it. Many of those who think they are saving money in that way would be greatly surprised to see the work turned out from such machines by good mechanics who thoroughly understand them, and are capable of earning good wages upon them.

Experience has proved that it pays as well to put first-class mechanics upon such machines as upon any other machine tools.

Where milling machines are used for regular manufacturing operations, and the same cycle of movements is to be repeated for a large number of pieces, boys or men who are not skilled mechanics, answer every purpose; but the skilled supervision must be there, and it must be seen to that the machine is as well taken care of, the cutters as well made and ground, and in fact, everything as well done as though a good mechanic actually operated the machines. In fact, in the shops in which the best results are obtained from the use of milling machines in regular manufacturing operations, all changes of the machines from one job to another, all adjustments, and the grinding and replacing of cutters, are done by, or at least under the direct supervision of, a skilled mechanic, responsible for the work of the machines, and who thoroughly understands and appreciates them. In this way only can the full benefits of the machine be realized.

It is far too common to go into the tool room and find a splendid Universal Milling Machine standing idle, while perhaps two or three men are doing at the shaper, planer or vise, jobs which could be done by an expert milling machine hand in one-fourth down to one-tenth of the time and a great deal better. One fault, which is far more common than would readily be believed in some quarters, is a failure to recognize the fact that a milling machine necessarily calls for some sort of a machine for grinding cutters, and that a machine upon which cutters are used, that are ground by holding the edges one after the other against an emery wheel by hand, is at a decided disadvantage, and will do no work which either in quality or cost will make a favorable showing when compared with that which is done by properly ground cutters.

It should be much more generally recognized that in milling machine practice, as in other things, there is a right way and a wrong way, and that skilled, intelligent labor pays best. When these facts are more generally recognized, it will be better for both the builders and for the users of the machines.

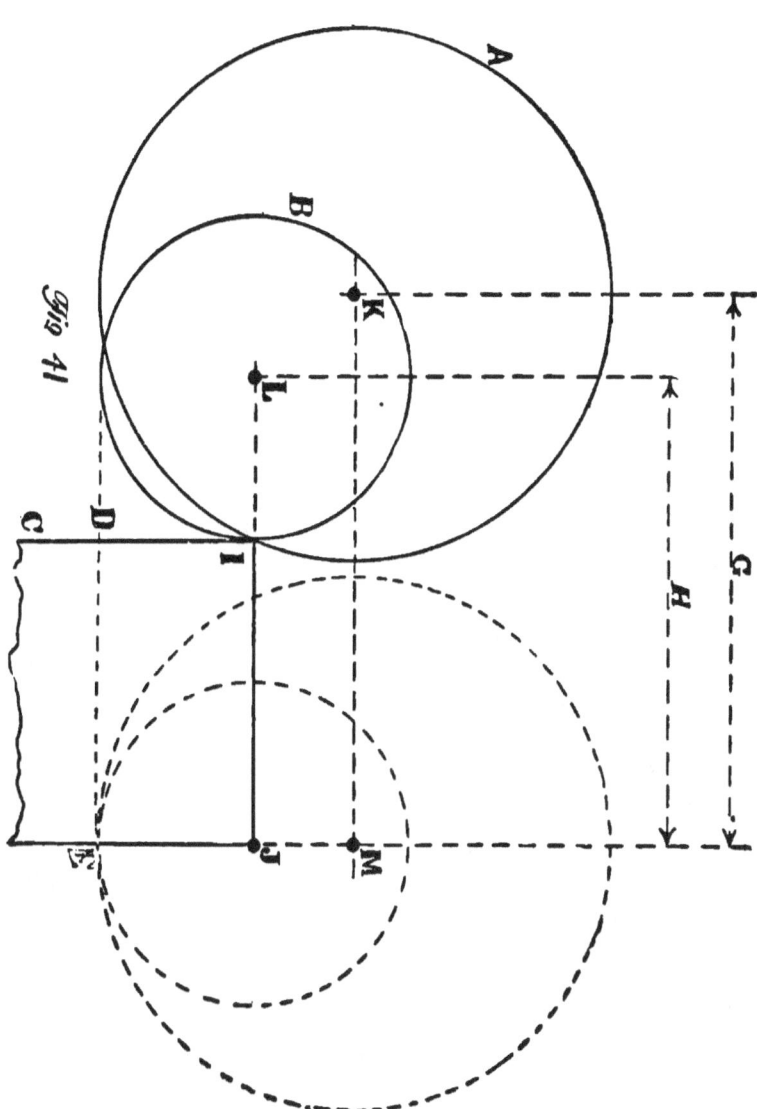

Fig 41

For most purposes, it is well to have mills or cutters as small in diameter as the work or their strength will admit. The reason is shown by figure 41. Suppose the piece I D C J E is to be cut from I J to D E. If the large mill A is used, it will strike the piece first at I, when its center is at K, and will finish its cut when its center is at M. The line G shows how far the mill must travel to cut off the stock I J D E. If the small mill B is used, however, it travels only the length of the line H. It can also be seen that a tooth of B travels through a shorter distance between the lines D E and I J than a tooth of A. This is true of all ordinary work, or where the depth of cut I D is not more than half the diameter of the small mill.

The advantage of small mills has been illustrated in our own works where a difference of $\frac{1}{2}$ an inch in the mills has made a difference of 10 % in the cost of the work.

In short, small mills do more and better work, cut more easily, keep sharp longer and cost less than large mills.

When it is possible the mill should be wider than the work, and the hole in the mill should be as small as the strength of the arbor will admit. The stock around the hole, however, should not be less than $\frac{3}{8}$ of an inch thick.

A mill is not necessarily too soft because it can be scratched with a file, for sometimes when cutters are too hard, or brittle, and trouble is caused by pieces breaking out of the teeth, they can be made to stand well and do good work by starting the temper.

Of late years mills have been made with coarser teeth than formerly; the advantages being more room for the chips and less friction between the teeth and the work. When the teeth are so fine that the mill drags, or the stock is powdered, the mill heats quickly and does not cut freely.

The friction may also be reduced, especially in large mills taking heavy cuts, by nicking or cutting away parts of the teeth, which breaks the chips and allows heavier cuts and feeds to be taken.

Knowing the conditions under which a mill is to be used, in our own practice, we modify the number of teeth as seems expedient, usually making the special mills coarser in pitch than the stock mills, for our observation indicates that there are more mills with too many teeth than with too few. But sometimes we relatively increase the number of teeth, as for instance, large mills, in some cases, can advantageously be designed to have more than one tooth cutting all the time on broad surfaces and in deep cuts.

The adoption of the most suitable cutting angle should receive the same close attention that is now universally bestowed upon the ordinary tools for turning and planing. But in practice, while in many instances adopting the angle according to the material to be used, yet taking into consideration all the conditions of using and caring for the cutters, we have generally found it satisfactory to make the cutting edges of the teeth radial.

The relief or clearance of mills we think should usually be about three degrees, and the land at the top of the teeth from .02 inches to .04 inches wide before the clearance is cut or ground.

Mills to cut grooves should be hollowed about five one-thousandths in one inch for clearance; that is, a grooving mill should be about one one-hundreth of an inch thinner at one inch from its edge or circumference than it is at the edge.

Our grooving mills are given a limit of two one-thousandths in thickness. Mills made to exact thickness are very expensive. In cutting grooves that are to have some parts of their sides nearly or quite parallel, it is well to leave considerable stock for the finishing cut, as mills, like taps, do better work when they get well into the stock.

A dull mill wears away rapidly and does poor work. Accordingly care must be taken to keep mills sharp. In sharpening them it is necessary to be very careful that the temper should not be drawn. The emery wheel should be of the proper grade as to hardness and as to the size of the emery. The wheel should be soft enough so that it can be easily scratched with a pocket-knife blade, and the emery should not be finer than 90, nor coarser than 60. As a rule, the coarser and softer the wheel, the faster it should run, although the periphery speed should not exceed 5,000 feet per minute. A wheel of the proper grade should be used with the face, not to exceed ¼″ wide. If the wheel glazes, the temper of the cutter will be drawn. In such a case, if the wheel is not altogether too hard, it can sometimes be remedied by reducing the face of the wheel to about ⅛″, or by reducing the speed, or by both.

Before using, a wheel should be turned off so that it will run true. A wheel that glazes immediately after it has been turned off, can sometimes be corrected by loosening the nut and allowing the wheel to assume a slightly different position, when it is again tightened.

Another method of preventing a wheel's glazing is to use a piece of emery wheel, a few grades harder than the wheel in use, on the face of the wheel, whereby the cutting surface of the wheel is made more open and less apt to glaze.

Mills that have their teeth ground for clearance are particularly apt to have their temper drawn in sharpening, especially at the edge of the teeth, and often when the temper has been drawn and the teeth are polished, they will look as usual after being ground.

Oil is used in milling to obtain smoother work, to make the cutters last longer, and where the nature of the work requires, to wash the chips from the work or from the teeth of the cutters. It is generally used in milling a large number of pieces of steel, wrought iron, malleable iron, or tough bronze. When only a few pieces are to be milled it frequently is not used, and some steel castings are milled without oil; also in cutting cast iron it is not used. For light, flat cuts it is put on the cutter with a brush, giving the work a thin covering like varnish; for heavy cuts it should be led to the cutter from the drip can sent with each machine, or it should be pumped upon or across the cutter in cutting deep grooves; in milling several grooves at one time, or indeed, in milling any work, where, if the chips should stick, they might catch between the teeth and sides of the groove and scratch or bend the work.

Generally we use lard oil in milling, but any animal or fish oils may be used. The oil may be separated from the chips by a centrifugal separator, or by the wet process, so that a large amount may be used with but little waste.

Some manufacturers prefer to mix mineral oil with lard or fish oil, and state the mixture is less expensive and works well. Prof. J. E. Denton has made experiments with mixtures and thinks that mineral or coal oil can be advantageously used.

An excellent lubricant to use with a pump is by mixing together and boiling for one-half hour, ¼ pound sal soda, ½ pint lard oil, ½ pint soft soap, and water enough to make ten quarts.

There is a difference of opinion as to whether the work should be moved against the cutter, or with it. But in most cases our experience and experiments show it is best for the work to move against the cutter, as shown at A, Figure 41½. When it moves in this way the teeth of the cutter, in com-

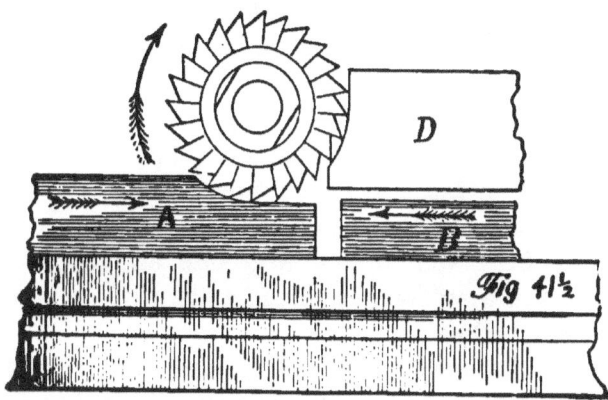

Fig 41½

mencing their work, as soon as the hard surface or scale is once broken, are immediately brought into contact with the softer metal, and when the scale is reached it is pried or broken off. Also when a piece moves in this way the cutter cannot dig into the work, as it is liable to do when the bed is moved in the direction indicated at B. When a piece is on the side of a cutter that is moving downwards, the piece should, as a rule, have a rigid support and be fed by raising the knee of the machine.

Some work, however, is better milled by moving with the cutter. For example: To dress both sides of a thick piece (D) with a pair of large straddle mills, it might be well to move the piece toward the left, as the cutters then tend to keep it down in place instead of lifting it.

Again, in milling deep slots with a thin cutter or saw, it may be better to move the work with the cutter, as the cutter is then less likely to crown sidewise and make a crooked slot.

When the work is moving with the cutter the table gib screws must be set up rather hard, for if the work moves too easily the cutter may catch, and the cutter or work be injured. A counter weight to hold back the table is excellent in such milling.

It is impossible to give definite rules for the speed and feed of cutters, and what is here said is only in the way of suggestions. The judgment of the foreman or man in charge of the machine should determine what is best in each instance.

The average speed on wrought iron and annealed steel is perhaps forty feet a minute, which gives about sixty turns a minute for mills $2\frac{1}{2}$ inches in diameter. The feed of the work for this surface speed of the mill can be about $1\frac{1}{2}$ inches a minute, and the depth of cut say 1/16 of an inch. In cast iron a mill can have a surface speed of about fifty feet a minute, while the feed is $1\frac{1}{2}$ inches a minute, and the cut 3/16 of an inch deep; in tough brass the speed may be eighty feet, the feed as before, and the chip 3/32 of an inch.

As a small mill cuts faster than a large one, an end mill, for example, $\frac{1}{2}$ inch in diameter, can be run about 400 revolutions with a feed of 4 inches a minute.

For example of what may regularly be done under suitable conditions, we may mention that cutters $2\frac{1}{2}$ inches in diameter used in cutting annealed cast iron in our works are run at more than 200 turns, or at a surface speed of more than 125 feet, while the work is fed more than 8 inches a minute. The cuts are light, not more than 1/32 of an inch deep, and the work is short, from $\frac{1}{2}$ inch to 1 inch long. Two side mills 5 inches in diameter running 50 turns a minute, dress both edges of cast iron bars $\frac{3}{4}$ of an inch thick, with a feed of more than 4 inches a minute.

An English authority, Mr. Geo. Addy, gives as safe speeds for cutters of 6 inches diameter and upwards:

Steel, 36 feet per minute, with feed of $\frac{1}{2}''$ per minute.

Wrought Iron, 48 feet per minute with feed of 1″ per minute.

Cast Iron, 60 feet per minute with feed of 1⅔″ per minute.

Brass, 120 feet per minute with feed of 2⅔″ per minute.

And he gives as a simple rule for obtaining the speed: Number of revolutions which the cutter spindle should make when working on cast iron = 240 divided by the diameter of the cutter in inches.

Mr. John H. Briggs, another English authority, states for cutting wrought iron with a milling cutter, taking a cut of one inch depth, which was a different thing from mere surface cutting, a circumferential speed of from 36 to 40 feet per minute was the highest that could be obtained with due consideration to economy, and to the time occupied in grinding and changing cutters; the feed would be at the rate of ⅝ inches per minute.

Upon soft, mild steel, about 30 feet per minute was the highest speed, with ¼ inch depth of cut and ¾ inch feed per minute. Upon tough gun metal, 80 feet per minute, with ½ inch depth of cut and ¾ inch feed.

For cutting cast iron gear wheels from blanks previously turned, and using in this case comparatively small milling cutters of only 3½ inches diameter, the speed was 26½ feet per minute, with ½ inch depth of cut and ¾ inch feed per minute.

Slotting cutters may often be run at a higher speed than other cutters of the same diameter, but with a wider face. Angular cutters must in some instances be used with a fine feed to prevent breaking the points of the teeth.

Castings that are to be milled should be free from sand. They should be well pickled, and in some cases it is an advantage to have them rattled after being pickled. Where they are small and are to be finished rapidly it is also well to have them annealed.

Forgings should be free from scale. They can be pickled in ten minutes in one part sulphuric acid and twenty-five parts boiling water, and if then rinsed in boiling water, they will dry before becoming rusty.

NUMBER OF DIVISIONS.	NUMBER OF HOLES IN THE INDEX CIRCLE.	NUMBER OF TURNS OF THE CRANK.		NUMBER OF DIVISIONS.	NUMBER OF HOLES IN THE INDEX CIRCLE.	NUMBER OF TURNS OF THE CRANK.	
2	ANY	20		65	39	24-39	
3	39	13	13-39	66	33		20-33
4	ANY	10		68	17	10-17	
5	ANY	8		70	49		28-49
6	39	6	26-39	72	27	15-27	
7	49	5	35-49	74	37		20-37
8	ANY	5		75	15	8-15	
9	27	4	12-27	76	19		10-19
10	ANY	4		78	39	20-39	
11	33	3	21-33	80	20		10-20
12	39	3	13-39	82	41	20-41	
13	39	3	3-39	84	21		10-21
14	49	2	42-49	85	17	8-17	
15	39	2	26-39	86	43		20-43
16	20	2	10-20	88	33	15-33	
17	17	2	6-17	90	27		12-27
18	27	2	6-27	92	23	10-23	
19	19	2	2-19	94	47		20-47
20	ANY	2		95	19	8-19	
21	21	1	19-21	98	49		20-49
22	33	1	27-33	100	20	8-20	
23	23	1	17-23	104	39		15-39
24	39	1	26-39	105	21	8-21	
25	20	1	12-20	108	27		10-27
26	39	1	21-39	110	33	12-33	
27	27	1	13-27	115	23		8-23
28	49	1	21-49	116	29	10-29	
29	29	1	11-29	120	39		13-39
30	39	1	13-39	124	31	10-31	
31	31	1	9-31	128	16		5-16
32	20	1	5-20	130	39	12-39	
33	33	1	7-33	132	33		10-33
34	17	1	3-17	135	27	8-27	
35	49	1	7-49	136	17		5-17
36	27	1	3-27	140	49	14-49	
37	37	1	3-37	144	18		5-18
38	19	1	1-19	145	29	8-29	
39	39	1	1-39	148	37		10-37
40	ANY	1		150	15	4-15	
41	41		40-41	152	19		5-19
42	21	20-21		155	31	8-31	
43	43		40-43	156	39		10-39
44	33	30-33		160	20	5-20	
45	27		24-27	164	41		10-41
46	23	20-23		165	33	8-33	
47	47		40-47	168	21		5-21
48	18	15-18		170	17	4-17	
49	49		40-49	172	43		10-43
50	20	16-20		180	27	6-27	
52	39		30-39	184	23		5-23
54	27	20-27		185	37	8-37	
55	33		24-33	188	47		10-47
56	49	35-49		190	19	4-19	
58	29		20-29	195	39		8-39
60	39	26-39		196	49	10-49	
62	31		20-31	200	20		4-20
64	16	10-16		205	41	8-41	

INDEXING.

The first office of the indexing head stock or spiral head is to divide the periphery of a piece of work into a number of equal parts, and in connection with the foot stock; it also enables the milling machine to be used for work sometimes done on planer centers and on gear cutting machines.

As the index spindle may be revolved by the crank, and as forty turns of the crank make one revolution of the spindle, to find how many turns of the crank are necessary for a certain division of the work, or, what is the same thing, for a certain division of a revolution of the spindle, forty is divided by the number of the divisions which are desired. The rule then may be said to be, divide forty by the number of the divisions to be made and the quotient will be the number of turns, or the part of a turn, of the crank, which will give each desired division. Applying this rule — to make forty divisions, the crank would be turned completely around once to obtain each division; or, to obtain twenty divisions, it would be turned twice. When, to obtain the necessary divisions, the crank has to be turned only part of the way around, an index plate is used. For example:—If the work is to be divided into eighty divisions, the crank must be turned one-half way around, and an index plate with an even number of holes in one of the circles would be selected, it being necessary only to have two holes opposite to each other in the plate. If the work is to be divided into three divisions an index plate should be selected which has a circle with a number of holes that can be divided by three, as fifteen, eighteen, twenty-seven, etc., the numbers on the index plates indicating the number of holes in the various circles.

The sector is of service in obviating the necessity of counting the holes at each partial rotation or turn of the crank, and to illustrate its use it may be supposed that it is desired to divide the work into 144 divisions. Dividing 40 by 144 the result, 5-18, shows that the index crank must be moved 5-18 of a turn to obtain each of the 144 divisions. An index plate with a circle containing eighteen holes or a multiple of eighteen, is selected and the sector is set to measure off five spaces, or the corresponding multiple, ten spaces for example, in a circle with thirty-six holes. In setting the sector it should be remembered that there must always be one more hole between the arms than there are spaces to be counted or measured off. The required number of turns of the crank for a large number of divisions may be readily ascertained from the accompanying index tables, which correspond to the Brown & Sharpe Manufacturing Company's Milling Machines.

If the angle of elevation of the spiral head spindle is changed during the progress of the work, the work must be rotated slightly to bring it back to the proper position, as when the spindle is elevated or depressed the worm wheel is rotated about the worm, and the effect is the same as if the worm were turned in the opposite direction.

CUTTING SPIRALS WITH UNIVERSAL MILLING MACHINES.

The indexing head stock or spiral head, as indicated in connection with the descriptions of the Universal Milling Machines, is used for cutting spirals, the flutes of twist drills, for example, as well as for indexing or dividing.

A positive rotary movement is given to the work while the spiral bed is being moved lengthways by the feed screw, and the velocity ratios of these movements are regulated by four change gears, shown in position in Figure 42 and known as the gear on worm or worm gear, first gear on stud, second gear on stud and gear on screw or screw gear.

The screw gear and first gear on stud are the drivers and the others the driven gears. Usually those gears are of such ratio that the work is advanced more than an inch while making one turn, and thus the spirals, cut on milling machines, are designated in terms of inches to one turn, rather than turns, or threads per inch; for instance, a spiral is said to be of 8 inches lead, not that its pitch is 1-8 turn per inch.

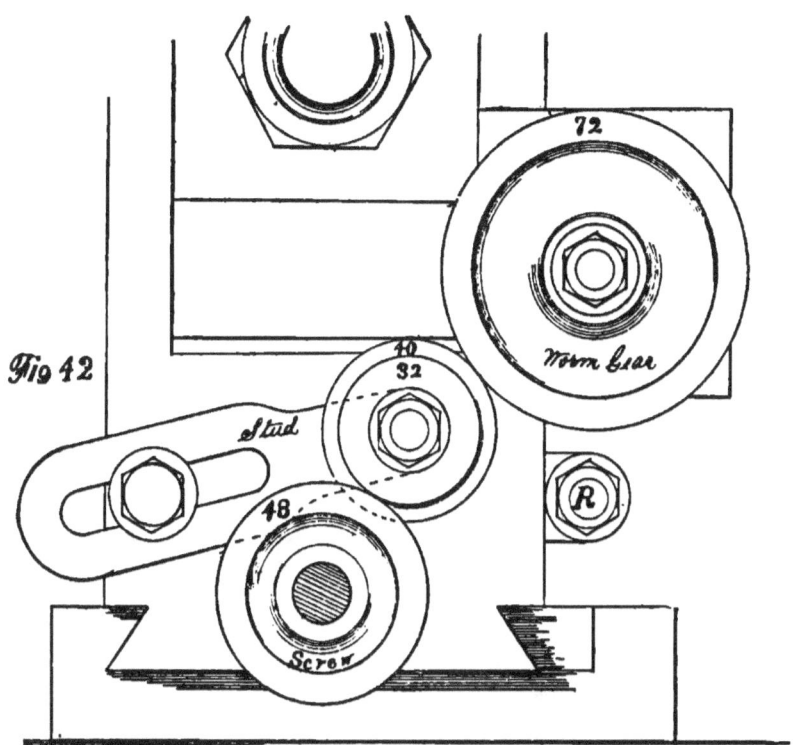

Fig 42

The feed screw of the spiral bed has four threads to the inch, and forty turns of the worm make one turn of the spiral head spindle; accordingly, if change gears of equal diameters are used, the work will make a complete turn while it is moved lengthways 10 inches; that is, the spiral will have a lead of 10 inches. But this lead is practically the lead of the machine, as it is the resultant of the action of the parts of the machine that are always employed in this work, and it is so regarded in making the calculations used in cut‑ting spirals.

In principle, these calculations are the same as for the change gears of a Screw Cutting Lathe. The compound ratio of the driven to the driving gears equals in all cases the ratio of the lead of the required spiral to the lead of the machine.   This can be readily understood by changing the diameters of the gears.

Gears of the same diameter produce, as explained above, a spiral with a lead of 10 inches, which is the same lead as the lead of the machine.   Three gears of equal diameter and a driven gear double this diameter produce a spiral with a lead of 20 inches, or twice the lead of the machine;   and with both driven gears twice the diameters of the drivers, the ratio being compound, a spiral is produced with a lead of 40 inches, or four times the machine's lead.   Conversely, driving gears twice the diameter of the driven produce a spiral with a lead equal to ¼ the lead of the machine or 2½ inches.

EXPRESSING THE RATIOS AS FRACTIONS.

$$\frac{\text{Driven Gears}}{\text{Driving Gears}} = \frac{\text{Lead of Required Spiral.}}{\text{Lead of Machine}}$$

; or, as the product of each class of gears determines the ratio, the head being double-geared, and as the lead of the machine is ten inches

$$\frac{\text{Product of Driven Gears}}{\text{Product of Driving Gears}} = \frac{\text{Lead of Required Spiral}}{10}$$

that is, the compound ratio of the driven to the driving gears may always be represented by a fraction whose numerator is the lead to be cut and whose denominator is 10; or, in other words, the ratio is as the required lead is to 10; that is, if the required lead is 20 the ratio is 20:10: or, to express this in units instead of tens, the ratio is always the same as one-tenth of the required lead is to one. Frequently this is a very convenient way to think of the ratio; for example, if the ratio of the lead is 40, the gears are 4:1. If the lead is 25, the gears are 2.5:1, etc.

To illustrate the usual calculations, assume that a spiral of 12-inch lead is to be cut.   The compound ratio of the driven to the driving gears equals the desired lead divided by 10, or it may be represented by the fraction 12-10. Resolving this into two factors to represent the two pairs of change gears, $\dfrac{12}{10} = \dfrac{3}{2} \times \dfrac{4}{5}$. Both terms of the first factor are multiplied by such a number (24 in this instance) that the resulting numerator and denominator will correspond with the number of teeth of two of the change gears furnished with the machine (such multiplications not affecting the value of a fraction), $\dfrac{3}{2} \times \dfrac{24}{24} = \dfrac{72}{48}$. The second factor is similarly treated, $\dfrac{4}{5} \times \dfrac{8}{8} = \dfrac{32}{40}$, and the gears with 72 and 32 and 48 and 40 teeth are selected, $\dfrac{12}{10} = \left\{ \dfrac{72 \times 32}{48 \times 40} \right\}$ The first two are the driven and the last two the drivers, the numerators of the fractions having represented the driven gears, and the 72 is placed as the worm gear, the 40 as the first on stud, 32 the second on stud and 48 as the screw gear. The two driving gears might be transposed and the two driven gears might also be transposed without changing the spiral. That is, the 72 could be used as second on stud and the 32 as the worm gear, if such an arrangement was more convenient.

From what has been said, the rules are plain. Note the ratio of the required lead to 10. This ratio is the compound ratio of the driven to the driving gears. Example:—If the lead of a required spiral is 12 inches, 12 to 10 will be the ratio of the gears, or divide the required lead by 10 and note the ratio between the quotient and 1. This ratio is usually the most simple form of the compound ratio of the driven to the driving gears. Example:—If the required lead is 40 inches the quotient, 40÷10 is 4, and the ratio 4 to 1. Having obtained the ratio between the required lead and 10 by one of the preceding rules, express the ratio in the form of a fraction, resolve this fraction into two factors; raise these factors to higher terms that correspond with the teeth of gears that can be conveniently used. The numerators will represent the driven and the denominators the driving gears that produce the required spiral. For example:—What gears shall be used to cut a lead of 27 inches?

$$27\text{-}10 = 3\text{-}2 \times 9\text{-}5 = \left\{ \frac{3}{2} \times \frac{16}{16} \right\} \times \left\{ \frac{9 \times 8}{5 \times 8} \right\} = \frac{48 \times 72}{32 \times 40}$$

From the fact that the product of the driven gears divided by the product of the drivers equals the lead divided by 10, or one-tenth of the lead, it is evident that ten times the product of the driven gears divided by the product of the drivers will equal the lead of the spiral. Hence, the rule:— Divide ten times the product of the driven gears by the product of the drivers, and the quotient is the lead of the resulting spiral in inches to one turn. For example:—What spiral will be cut by gears with 48, 72, 32 and 40 teeth, the first two being used as driven gears? Spiral to be cut equals

$$\frac{10 \times 48 \times 72}{32 \times 40} = 27 \text{ inches to one turn.}$$

Cuts that have one face radial are best made with an angular cutter, for cutters of this form readily clear the radial face of the cut, and so keep sharp longer and produce a smoother surface than when the radial face is cut in a vertical plane with a cutter where the teeth can have no side clearance from the work.

The setting for these cuts must also be made before swinging the spiral bed to the angle of the spiral.

THE UNIVERSAL MILLING MACHINE—Continued.

(BY THE AUTHOR)

From the preceding method of obtaining spirals as practiced by the Brown & Sharpe Manufacturing Company, we find that the same rule will also apply to the milling machine as constructed by others. For example:—Figure 43 is

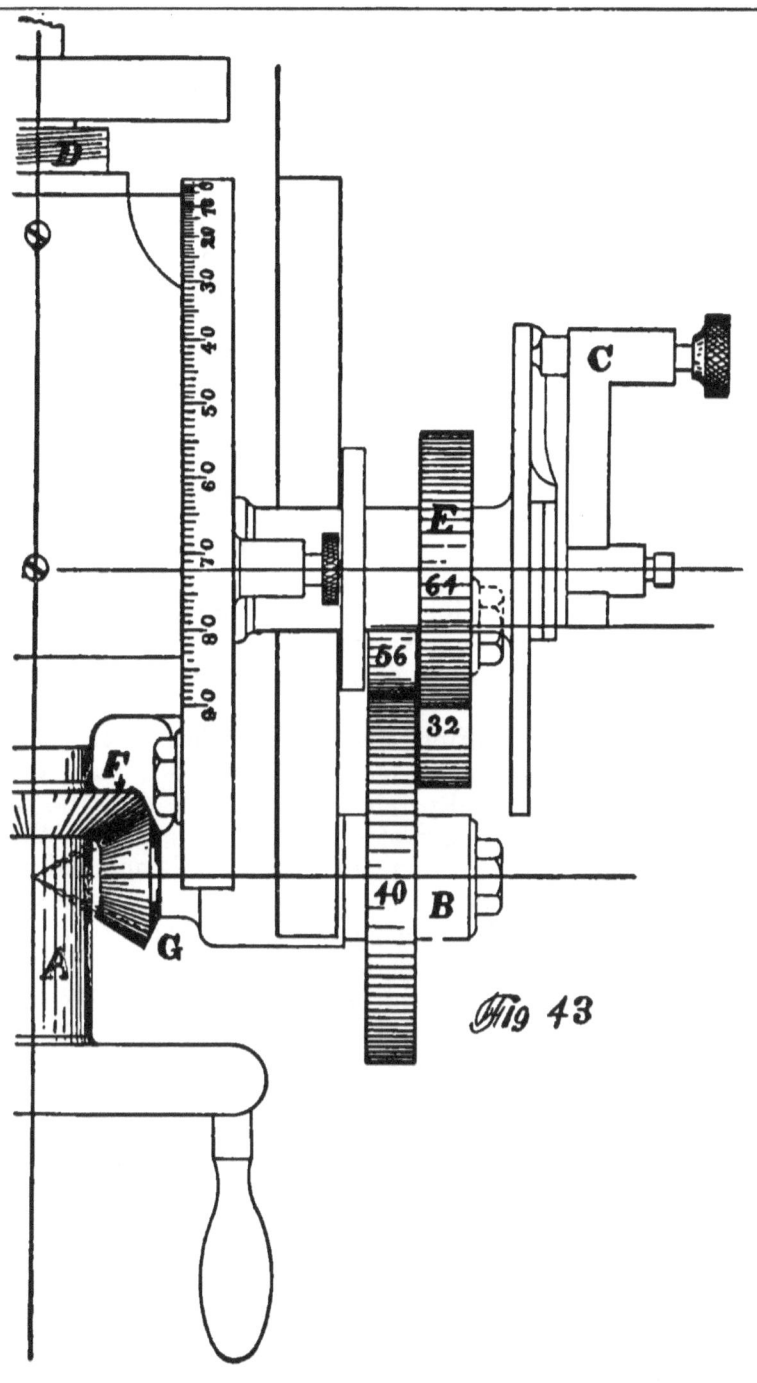

Fig 43

another style of the Universal Milling Machine, a portion of the index head only being shown. The feed screw A has two threads per inch, but there is a pair of bevel gears as shown at F G that drive the change gears, and F is twice as large as G; these bevel wheels are not to be changed, and B is called the screw gear. Now it can be seen that this gear near B will make four revolutions while the screw moves the table one inch, and as the index crank C makes forty turns to one turn of the spindle D, if all four of the change gears were of the same size, the table of the machine would move through a space of ten inches, while the index crank made 40 turns or the spindle of the Universal head made but one turn, and consequently, the lead of the machine (figure 43) is also ten inches.

Now, suppose we want to cut a spiral mill that is to have a lead of one turn in 60 inches; dividing 60 by 10 we have the ratio of the change gears, 6 to 1.

Now, if we select for one pair of these gears 12 and 36 or 24 and 72, or any number that is 3 to 1, dividing the ratio 6 by 3=2; then any pair of gears that is 2 to 1 will answer for the second pair.

In compound gearing always remember when you find the ratio of the gears wanted, and select one pair, that in order to find the second pair you must divide the ratio of the change gears by the ratio of the first pair selected; that is, we found the ratio of the gears were 6 to 1, and, taking 24 and 72 for the first pair, which is 3 to 1, we divide 6 by 3 and we have 2, which means that any number 2 to 1 will be right for the next pair, and therefore 64 and 32 will answer. Now, we can place the 32 on the screw and 64 on the stud to mesh with this gear, and the 72 on the worm with the 24 in gear with it; or, we can put the 24 on the screw and the 72 in mesh with it and the 64 on the worm with 32 to engage with it; either way will be right.

Let us take another example:—Suppose we want to mill a spiral of one turn in 28 inches, what gears should we use? We found the lead of the machine to be 10 inches, therefore dividing 28 by 10 we have 2 8-10, or 2 4-5, for the ratio of the gears. We will now try a pair that is 2 to 1, and see how we come out. Say 20 and 40, or 32 and 64 for the first pair of gears; now, 2 4-5=14-5, and any pair 2 to 1, or one gear being twice as large as its mate =2-1, which is equal to 10-5, and dividing 14-5 by 10-5 we have 1 4-10 for the ratio of the next pair, and taking 40 for one gear and multiplying this by 1 4-10, we have 56 for the next gear, so that 64 and 35 will answer for one pair and 56 and 40 for the other; these gears are shown in position in the figure (43). Now let us prove this to be one turn in 28 inches:—As the screw is the driver, so is 40 the driver of 56, and as 32 is on the same stud with 56, then 32 is the driver of 64; then multiplying the product of the two driven gears by 10 and dividing by the product of the drivers, will be the lead of the spiral, thus:

$$
\begin{array}{ll}
64=\text{Driven} & 32=\text{Driver} \\
56=\text{Driven} & 40=\text{Driver} \\
\hline
384 & 1280 \\
320 & \\
\hline
3584 & \\
10 & \\
\hline
\end{array}
$$

1280)35840(28″, the answer, or the lead of spiral.
2560

10240
10240

Example:—What spiral can we obtain from 72 and 48, as driven gears, and 28 and 40 as drivers?

$$
\begin{array}{ll}
72=\text{Driven} & 28=\text{Driver} \\
48=\text{Driven} & 40=\text{Driver} \\
\hline
576 & 1120 \\
288 & \\
\hline
3456 & \\
10 & \\
\hline
\end{array}
$$

1120)34560(30.86″, or nearly, the answer.
3360

9600
8960

6400
6720

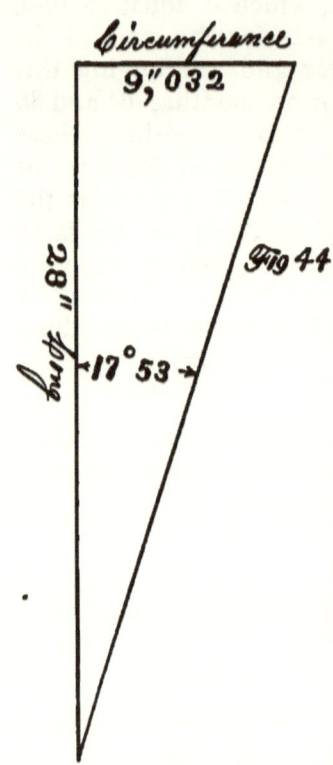

Circumference
9."032

28" *long*

←17° 53 →

Fig 44

The next thing is to find the angle to set the machine when cutting spirals, which is found in the following simple manner: Find the circumference of the work that is to be cut spiral, no matter what it is; take the outside diameter (except in case of a spiral gear, and then take the pitch diameter) and divide it by the length of the piece, which will give the tangent of the angle, and, in the table of tangents you will find the angle, or as follows: Figure 44 represents a piece of work that is 28" long and 2⅞" diameter, that is to have a spiral of one turn in its length. The circumference of 2⅞"=9.032", and divided by 28=.3225; in the table of tangents, we find the angle 17° 53' to correspond to this number, which is the correct angle to swivel the table. If the piece was 2½" in diameter and the same length, we should then have a circumference of 7.854", nearly, and, divided by 28, we should have a tangent of .2805, which would then be 15° 40', as per table. Remember that this is a right angled triangle, or, in other words, the two lines marked circumference and length, as in figure 44, should always be at right angles to each other.

A spiral mill 2½" diameter is large enough for ordinary work and should have from 22 to 24 teeth, and should have a spiral of about one turn in 36". A cutter of this size and number of teeth will have about ½" solid stock with a one-inch hole.

For a spiral mill 3½" diameter I should give about 26 teeth, and one turn in not less than 48 inches; a cutter of this size can be cut coarser than one of 2½" diameter, because there will be more stock around the hole.   If you want a good spiral mill for roughing purposes (that is, one that will cut fast), after the size has been finished in the lathe, take an ordinary cutting off tool, about one-eighth of an inch wide, with the corners rounded, and cut a thread of about two or three threads per inch in the opposite direction that you intend to mill the spiral.   That is, if you wish to have a right hand mill, then you should cut this coarse thread in the lathe left hand.   This is the best style of cutters we have for heavy or fast milling.

If a spiral mill of about 2″ diameter with a solid shank was required I should give it a spiral of about one turn in 36″, and should also make it right hand for the reason that, instead of pulling out of the spindle while finishing a cut, the tendency would be to force itself tighter in the spindle, and therefore less danger of marking the work.

An angle of 10° to 12° will answer for most any ordinary size of spiral mills.

In small end mills the teeth will have to be finer than large ones, to give them greater strength.

I should give in end mills of ½″ and ⅝″ diameter eight teeth each; ¾″, ⅞″ and 1″ ten teeth each; 1¼″ and 1½″ each twelve teeth, etc., and for a 1¼″ diameter thin cutter, say 3-16″ to ¼″ thick, not less than sixteen teeth.

If a pair of twin or straddle mills were wanted for general work, such as milling, bolt heads, etc., I would make them 4 inches diameter, ½″ thick and not more than 32 teeth, and for a pair of 5″ diameter for general work, I should give them 36 teeth and make them ⅝″ face; for a 60° angular cutter, 1½″ diameter at the large end, I should give it 12 teeth, or, one of the same kind (60°) 2¼″ largest diameter, 16 teeth; and one of 3″ largest diameter (60°), 20 teeth, etc.

Always remember to have the teeth of cutters coarse enough so that in grinding the clearance the emery wheel will not touch the cutting edge of the next tooth.   On most cutters the teeth on the periphery can be sharpened with wheels as large as 8" to 12" diameter, but on the sides of small cutters sometimes a wheel 2" diameter is too large.

Milling cutters larger than 4 inches diameter and one inch face, and larger than 2½ inches diameter and 4-inch face, should have key ways: ⅛" wide and 3-32" deep is large enough for most purposes; the key ways should be slightly rounded in the corners to lessen the danger of cracking while hardening.

I will now show you the shapes of cutters for a variety of purposes, and also the sizes, angles, etc., for ordinary work. I say ordinary, because we sometimes have to make a cutter twice the size or may be only one-half the size for some special class of work that we may have on hand. Figure 45 represents a cutter for cutting the teeth of spiral mills,

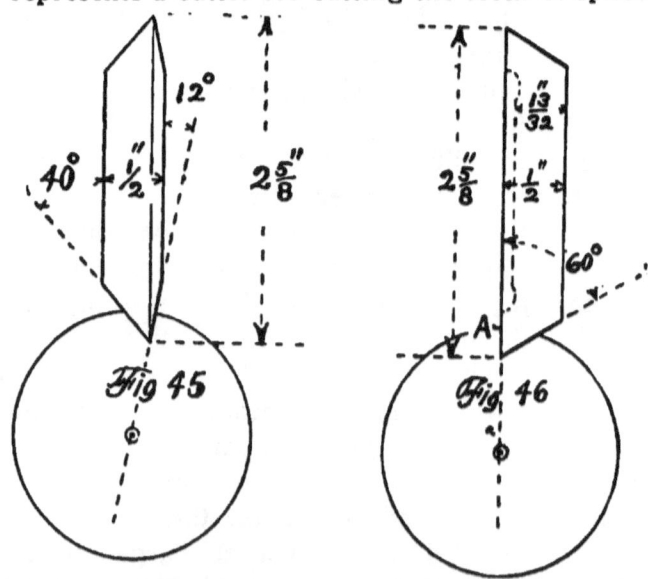

Fig 45   Fig 46

It is 12° on one side and 40° on the other side, as shown; the side marked 12° should always point to the center of the work, and, if two pieces having different diameters are to be milled, the table with the work will have to be moved in or out to suit that particular size, because setting it for any certain size it will not be right for any other diameter of work. The best way to set the work for this cutter is to raise the table until you think it high enough for the cutter when at the proper depth in the work, then, with a short scale or straight edge placed directly under the center of the cutter arbor and resting on the side marked 12°, with the center of tail stock also moved directly under the center of cutter arbor, the scale should point to the center of tail stock. The teeth of spiral mills on top should not be much over 1-32″ thick when milled.

Figure 46 represents an angular cutter of 60° for cutting the teeth in other cutters. This is generally used for cutting the teeth on the periphery of all ordinary cutters, except when the angles are very great. For instance, if the cutter shown at figure 48 was cut on both sides with a cutter of 60°, the teeth would be easily broken, and for this reason we will have to be governed accordingly. For the various shapes of cutters we use 60°, 65°, 70° and 75° cutters to cut them with, depending, as stated, on the acuteness of the angles. All cutters should have the teeth cut rather coarse when they are strong enough to stand it, for the reason that it will give more room for chips, and this is a very desirable matter with milling cutters. I would give the cutters (figures 45-46) each 26 teeth for the diameter as shown.

Figure 47 represents the neatest style of cutters for fluting taps; five sizes of cutters will answer for nearly all sizes. I would make them ⅜″, ½″, ⅝″, ¾″ and 1″ thick, and all of them 2⅝″ diameter, but the corner of the small one should be rounded very little and the large one about as shown in the figure; the others should have the corners proportioned between these two. I would also give them each 24 teeth. The width of land on all regular taps should be 1-32 inch wide to every ⅛″ in diameter, as shown at B. This refers to standard sizes only.

Figure 48 represents the shape of cutters for cutting the teeth in formed cutters, worm wheel-hobs, etc.

Figure 49, represents the best style of milling cutters for milling the teeth in screw machine dies. I would give the former (figure 48) 32 teeth and the latter (figure 49) 24 teeth, for the diameters given.

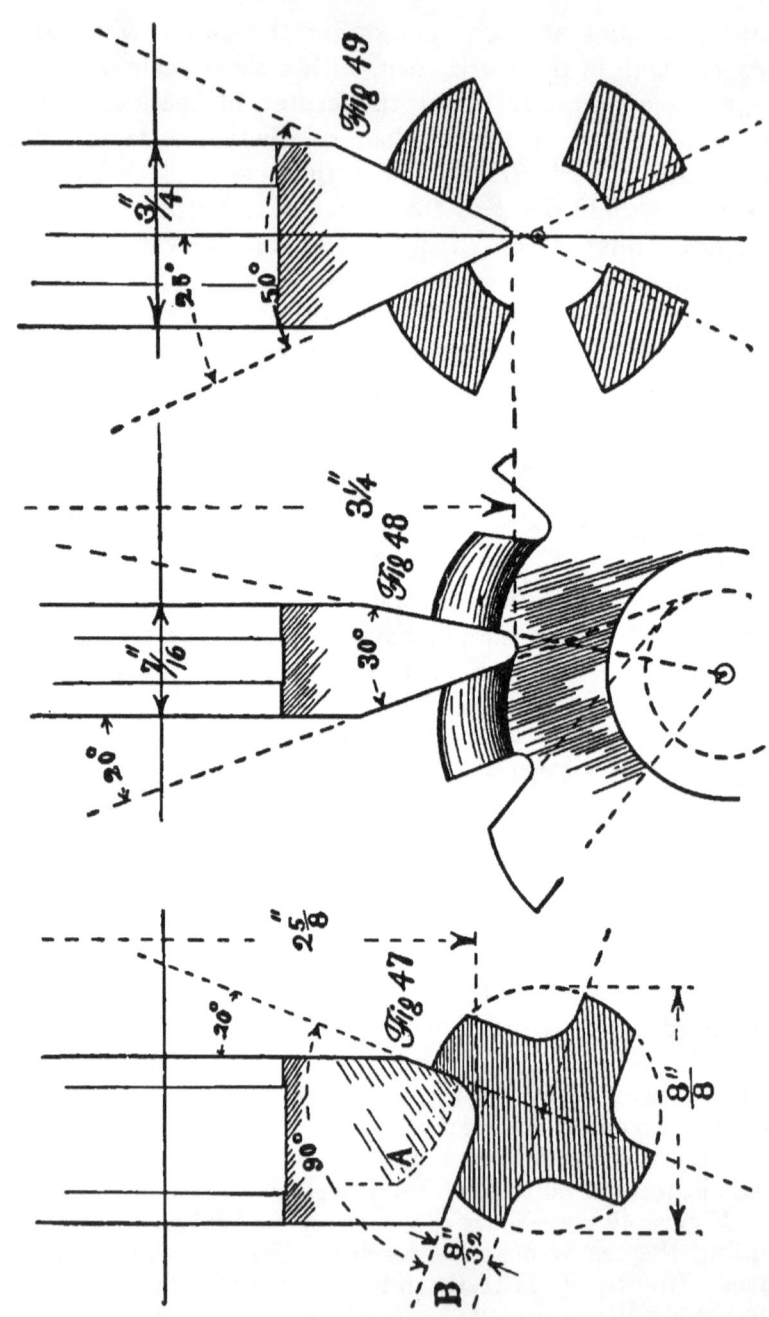

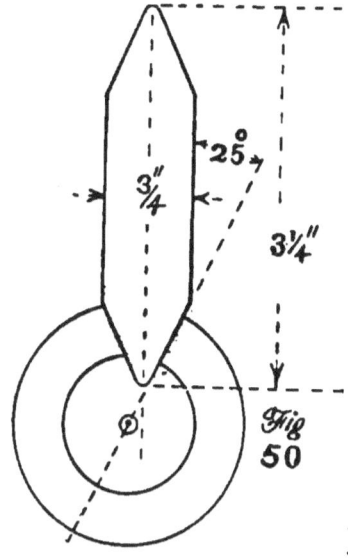

Figure 50, which is also the same as figure 49, is shown in position for milling a hollow mill for screw machines. After setting the cutter in position, as shown, the table should be swiveled from about 20° for a ½″ mill to about 30° for a 1⅛″ mill.

For fluting reamers we sometimes use the cutter shown at figure 47, but only when the flutes are to be very coarse. For hand reamers they should be shaped as shown by the dotted line at A. All milling cutters should have the holes ground after hardening, and for this purpose I always allow five one-thousandths of an inch in the diameter; the sides always should be ground, as otherwise they will not run true.

In these illustrations of cutters I have marked the thickness and also the diameters and angles as suitable for general purposes.

For small shank milling I use a chuck as shown at figure 51; it is composed of three pieces, A, B, C. The long taper of A is fitted to the machine spindle and bored large enough to suit a ¾″ shank mill nearly through. The back end is tapped ⅝″ and the spindle is bored large enough to admit a rod of that size extending from the back end to hold this chuck from any danger of slipping out and spoiling the work while in operation. These small mills are all made of Crescent tool steel (drill rods) and for a ½″ mill you have only to cut off a piece of ½″ stock, say 5 inches long, as this is quite long enough for most purposes; cut the teeth on one end, say 1½″, and, as the mills are parallel, you have the advantage of having them project just long enough for any particular class of work.

In order to suit the different sizes, however, you will have to have one of these pieces, shown at B, for each size mill. This piece is reamed parallel, as shown by the dotted lines, and turned taper to suit the body of chuck nearly three-fourths of its length, and from there to the front end it is tapered in the opposite direction and the nut C is also bored taper in front, in order to draw the shell B tight on the shank of the mill; this shell B is sawed in six equal spaces to within say

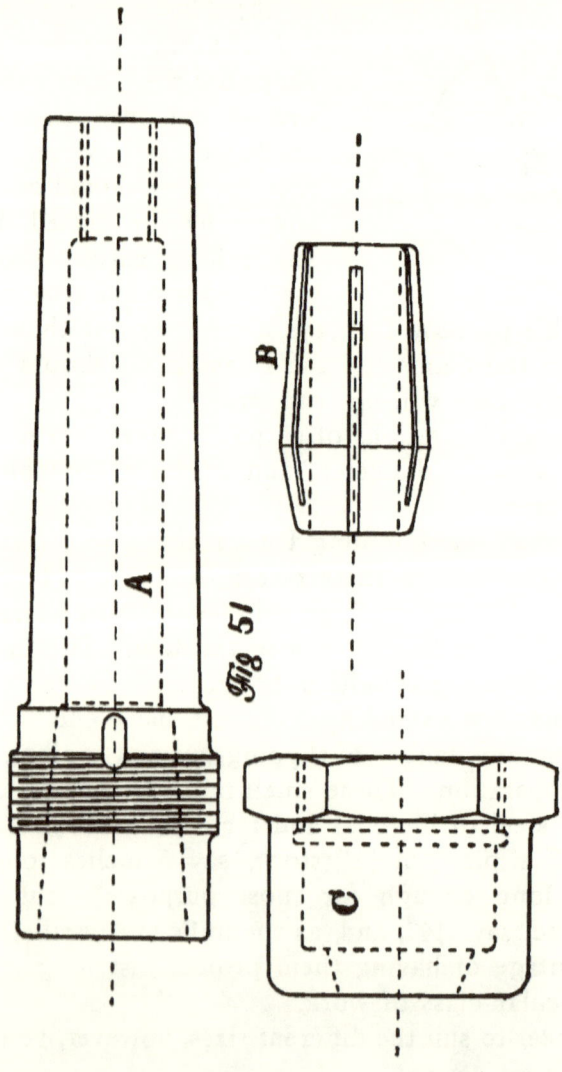

Fig 51

¼" from the end, each alternately starting from opposite ends, and in this manner the shell will close parallel on the work. The body of the chuck A and also the shell B should be made of tool steel.

Figure 52 represents a special chuck that I made several years ago for milling bolt heads. The body of the chuck, which is about 2½" through contains six 1¼" holes, a portion of which is cut off in the drawing for want of space. The lower portion of the chuck shown in dotted lines is screwed on the spindle of the Universal Head, and, being split, is held firmly in position by a screw. In order to get good results with this chuck it is necessary that the holes should be accurately spaced; this is quite an easy matter, as they can be drilled, bored and reamed by indexing on the milling machine. These holes are 1¼" and we have split bushes of different sizes, so that all sizes of bolts can be milled up to and including 1¼".

The bolts are held in position by the screw A and collar B, of which only one is shown. These collars and screws are all fitted in place before the holes C are bored, after which the bottom of B should have about one sixty-fourth of an inch taken off, so that they may clamp hard on the bush or bolt, as the case may be, so that they will not mark the work.

In using this chuck the spindle of the Universal Head is placed in a vertical position with the face of the chuck upright, as shown in the drawing, and six straddle mills about 3½" or 4" diameter are used. The manner of using is as follows: The bolts, six in number, are placed in position with the heads projecting a little above the face of the chuck and the cutters set to just pass over without marking the chuck. The bolts 1, 2 and 3 are now milled on one side as shown by the dotted lines, and one-sixth of a turn is then made to the next bolt, and numbers 1 and 2 will then be milled on two sides, after which another one-sixth of a turn is made, and by this time No. 1 will be finished. At every one-sixth of a turn we can now take out a finished bolt, and, of course,

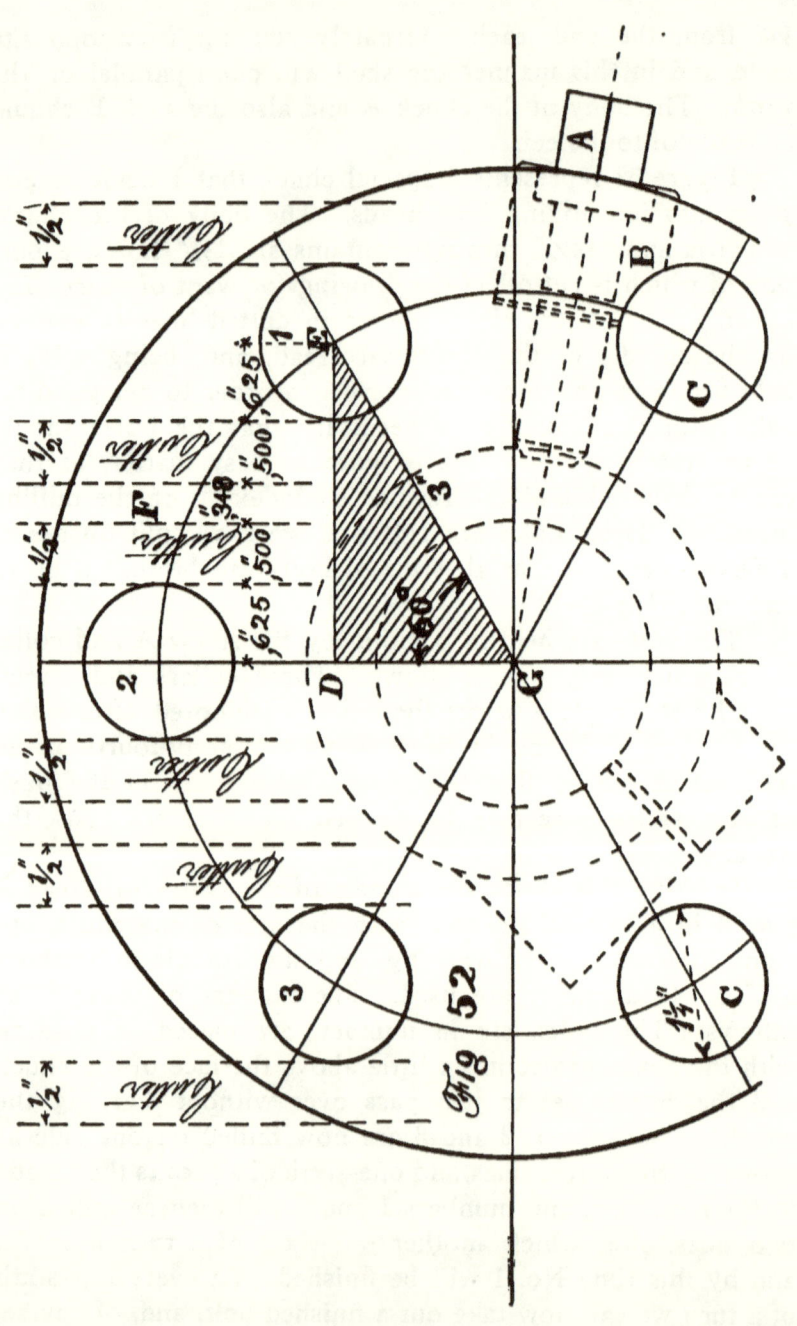

Fig. 52

we also put in a blank every time we take out a finished bolt.

Suppose that we want to mill some bolt heads 1¼" hexagon (which can be represented by the holes) and the cutters are ground just ½" hub and face alike in width. The next thing to do is to find a spacing collar that will be the right thickness to separate the two cutters shown at F. As there are six divisions represented by these holes, an angle, as shown, will be 60°, and G E being the radius of this angle, then D E is the sine of the angle of 60°, and the sine of 60°=.866 to a radius of 1"; then three times this would be the distance D E, or 2.598", and, taking from this the diameter of one of these bolts and the two one-half inch cutters, will leave .348" for the width of collar at F, as shown.

STRAIGHT LINE INDEX DRILLING.

It sometimes happens that we want a certain number of holes per inch drilled in a straight line; now, if it is possible to clamp this work on the milling machine bed or to hold it in the vise, we can very easily do a piece of work of this kind and know that it is right when done.

Suppose that we want some holes spaced off to be exactly four per inch. As the screw has four threads per inch we know that every time the screw makes just one turn or ¼" that it would be right for four holes, but in order to get this distance exact, we must gear up the machine similar to what we would if cutting a spiral, except that instead of turning the worm shaft crank for spacing we pull out the pin, being careful not to move it, but moving the index plate until the proper hole is reached and then securing it by the pin until the next move is to be made, etc. In other words, we move the table by compound gearing by the index plate, instead of the crank.

If we have five holes per inch to drill, dividing 5 by 4 threads on the screw, we have the ratio of the gears, or 1¼, which means that if we select a gear, say 40 teeth, and another one with 1¼ times 40=50 teeth, then the next pair will be alike, and just one turn of the index plate will be correct.

If we want to drill ten holes per inch, dividing 10 by 4 threads per inch, we have a ratio of 2½ for the gears. Now we will take 64 and 32 for one pair, which is 2 to 1, and dividing 2½ by 2 we have 1¼ for the ratio of the next pair, or say 48 and 60 teeth, etc.

If seven holes per inch were required, dividing 7 by 4, we have 1¾ for the compound ratio; now we will take 32 and 40 for one pair, which is a ratio of 1¼, or, in other words, one gear is one and one-quarter times as large as the other, or has a difference of one and one-quarter times as many teeth as the other; then for the next pair of gears we divide the compound ratio 1¾ by the ratio of the pair already selected and we have as follows: 1.75÷1.25=1.4 for the ratio of the next pair, then taking 40 for one of these gears and multiplying it by 1.4 we have 56 for the last gear, and one turn of the index plate will move the table 1-7 of an inch.

Suppose we prove this example. If we were to drill 100 holes we would turn the index plate 100 times around in order to get that number of holes, and we have two pair of gears 32 and 40 and 40 and 56. Now it is plain to see that the small gears are the drivers in both cases, and it makes no difference so long as we keep them in pairs as found, where we place them; then as we turn the index plate, we will put say the 40 tooth gear back of it for the first driver, and its mate, 56, on the stud in gear with it; then the next small gear, 32, on the same stud in mesh with the 40 tooth gear on the screw; then

$$100 \text{ holes}=100 \text{ turns.}$$
$$40=\text{first driver}$$

$$\text{First driven}=56)\overline{4000}(71.4285$$
$$\underline{392}$$
$$80$$
$$\underline{56}$$
$$240$$
$$\underline{224}$$

160
112
———
480
448
———
320
280
———

71.4285
32=second driver.
————————
1428570
2142855
————————
Second driven=40)2285.7120

Threads on screw=4)57.1428=revolutions of screw.
————————

14.2857=the number of inches the table has moved in drilling 100 holes.

Holes per inch=7)100=holes to be drilled.
————————

14.2857=the number of inches the table has moved.

In calculating the gears for drilling 14 holes per inch, we divide 14 by 4, which is 3½, or the compound ratio of gears; then if we take any pair that is 2 to 1, say 64 and 32, and divide the compound ratio 3½ by the ratio of the pair selected, which is 2 in this case, we have 1¾ as the ratio for the second pair, or say 48 and 84.

It can readily be seen that if we should gear up for drilling seven holes to the inch with one turn, that we could also drill fourteen holes to the inch if we moved the index plate but one-half of a turn, or fifty-six holes per inch if moved only ⅛ of a turn, etc. Graduations can also be done in the same manner, but great care would be necessary if accuracy was required to take up all back lash in the running parts, while the screw itself might not be in good condition to give the desired result.

EXTRACTS FROM THE BROWN & SHARPE MFG. CO.'S TREATISE ON THE UNIVERSAL GRINDING MACHINE.

(By permission).

As the durability of a machine depends very largely upon the care of the operator, however well a machine may be constructed, if it is not properly cared for it will soon become unreliable.

In all cases we recommend a good quality of oil in preference to one of low grade. Sperm oil should be used on the internal grinding fixtures.

The machine should be kept as clean as possible, and in no case should the bearings be allowed to "gum up." When bearings are opened and exposed for any purpose whatever, they should be carefully wiped off before they are closed again, to free them from any grit that may have found its way upon the surfaces.

A loose fit between the wheel spindle and its boxes will produce imperfect work, and when very fine work is required the bearings should run nearly, if not quite, metal to metal. This necessarily will cause the boxes to heat, but in this case the heat is not injurious, for as the bearings are hard and the boxes bronze, the belt will slip, unless it is exceedingly tight, before abrasion can occur.

All end motion should be taken out of the wheel spindle before the wheel is used on the work.

A satisfactory emery wheel is an important factor in the production of good work. Too much, however, must not be expected of one wheel. A variety of shapes, sizes and grades of wheels are necessary to bring out all the possibilities of the grinding machine, the same as a variety of shapes and sizes of tools are necessary to obtain the best results from the lathe or milling machine.

Our aim in grinding is usually to obtain an accurate or true surface, but as a true surface is almost always a good surface it should be remembered that generally the same methods are employed, whether an exact size or a fine finish is the object desired.

In selecting and using a wheel, we are governed by the character of the metal to be operated upon, the shape and size of the work and the degree of accuracy desired.   We have to consider the size of the particles of emery in the wheel, the hardness of the wheel and its width.

We also have to determine the speed at which the work is to travel or be revolved, and whether or not water is to be used.

For the sake of clearness we refer separately to the various characteristics of wheels, but it should be borne in mind that a wheel should not be selected for a single characteristic, but that each of the essential elements is importantly affected by the others, and that all should be considered in choosing or using a wheel for any desired work.

Wheels are numbered from coarse to fine; that is, a wheel made of No. 60 emery is coarser than one made of No. 100.   Within certain limits, and other things being equal, a coarse wheel is less liable to change the temperature of the work and less liable to glaze than a fine wheel.   As a rule, the harder the stock the coarser the wheel required to produce a given finish.   For example, coarser wheels are required to produce a given surface upon hardened steel than upon soft steel, while finer wheels are required to produce this surface upon brass or copper than upon either hardened or soft steel.

Wheels are graded from soft to hard and the grade is denoted by the letters of the alphabet, A denoting the softest grade.   A wheel is soft or hard chiefly on account of the amount and character of the material combined in its manufacture with emery or corundum, but other characteristics being equal, a wheel that is composed of fine emery is more compact and harder than one made of coarser emery.

For instance, a wheel of No. 100 emery, grade B, will be harder than one of No. 60 emery, same grade.

The softness of a wheel is generally its most important characteristic.

A soft wheel is less apt to cause a change of temperature in the work or to become glazed than a harder one. It is best for grinding hardened steel, cast iron, brass, copper and rubber, while a harder or more compact wheel is better for grinding soft steel and wrought iron. As a rule, other things being equal, the harder the stock the softer the wheel required to produce a given finish.

Generally speaking, a wheel should be softer as the surface in contact with the work is increased. For example, a wheel 1-16 inch face should be harder than one ½ inch face. If a wheel is hard and heats or chatters it can often be made somewhat more effective by turning off a part of its cutting surface; but it should be clearly understood that while this will sometimes prevent a hard wheel from heating or chattering the work, such a wheel will not prove as economical as one of the full width and proper grade, for it should be borne in mind that the grade should always bear the proper relation to the width.

The width should be in proportion to the amount of material to be removed with each revolution, and as a wheel cuts in proportion to the number of particles in contact with the work, less stock will ordinarily be removed by a narrow wheel than by one that is of full width. The feed will also have to be finer if a narrow wheel is used.

The quality of the work as a rule is improved by using a wheel of full width if the wheel is soft in proportion. Judgment should be exercised in deciding upon the width of wheel to be used, as sometimes the work is of such size and shape as to make it necessary to use a wheel with a narrow face. Where this is the case the wheel should, where strength will admit, be only that width throughout, and care should be taken that the grade is kept in the proper relation to the width.

A wheel is most efficient in grinding just at the point before it ceases to crumble. The faster it is run up to this point the more stock will be removed and the more economically the work will be produced. Occasionally, however, it is necessary to run a wheel rather slowly, as the more slowly it runs the coarser it cuts and the less likely it is to change the temperature of the work. As a general rule, on any stock, the softer the wheel the faster it should be run..

Should a wheel heat or glaze it can often be made somewhat more effective by being run more slowly. On the other hand, if it be too soft, it can often be made to somewhat better hold its size and grind straight by being run more rapidly.

The surface speed of the work should be proportional to the speed of the wheel, that is, other things being equal, if the speed of the wheel is reduced the speed of the work should be reduced also. The desire is to have the work revolve at such a speed as to allow time for the wheel to cut away the high points on the work. If the work is run so fast that there is no time given for the wheel to cut, but the work is simply crowded against the wheel, the tendency is for the wheel to follow the inequalities in the form of the work, and straight or round surfaces are not obtained. When the wheel is not free cutting and the pressure of the wheel against the work is sufficient to cause the work itself to spring cr to cause a slight movement of the oil upon the centers, the accuracy of the result is impaired.

The desire in accurate grinding is to have a free cutting wheel and to obtain the proper speeds so that the stock may be removed with the least possible amount of pressure, thus preventing a change of temperature in the work and allowing the high parts to be most speedily reduced.

Thus far we have had in mind the selection and use of wheels for the comparatively small or medium sized work ordinarily ground on our machines. The requirements in grinding extremely large or long pieces are somewhat different. For example, in grinding a piece of steel three inches long, one inch diameter, on a Universal Grinding Machine we have indicated that the most absolutely accurate work would be accomplished by selecting a wheel only just hard enough to retain its size while passing six or eight times over the surface of the piece, and we have suggested that such a wheel should be run at a high rate of speed. We have considered rapidity of production as more important than economy of emery. If, however, we should attempt to use such a wheel to grind a piece of steel one inch diameter and three feet long, it is clear that before the wheel had passed over two of the three feet it would have ceased to cut.

The problem now is to maintain the diameter of the wheel so as to take a uniform cut over a large area. Each particle of emery must be used as long as possible before being thrown away. The particles may be used a longer time and are not so rapidly thrown away in a hard as in a soft wheel. Accordingly, one expedient in grinding large areas is to increase the grade of the wheel as the area increases, the speed of the wheel being reduced as the grade is increased.

The loss of fine particles will not decrease the diameter of the wheel as rapidly as the loss of coarser or larger particles. Thus another expedient is to use a finer wheel.

A fine wheel can be relatively softer than a coarser wheel, and so with a fine one there need be less pressure between the wheel and the work, and there is more certainty of obtaining an accurate surface.

If a wheel is run rapidly the particles of emery soon become dull and have to be thrown away. To retard this loss it is well to run the wheel more slowly as the length or area of the work increases.

As the length or area of the work increases, the feed should be coarser, so that the wheel may travel the entire length or area of the piece while its diameter is practically unchanged.

Water should be used on such classes of work as are injuriously affected by a change in temperature caused by grinding.

It should be used upon work revolved upon centers, as in this work a slight change in temperature will cause the wheel to cut on one side of the piece, after it has been ground apparently round.

In very accurate grinding water is especially useful, for it should be remembered that the exactness of the work will be affected by a change in temperature which is not perceptible to the touch.

In very accurate grinding it is also well to use the water over and over again, as by so doing there is less difference between the temperature of the water and that of the work than if fresh water is used. For many purposes soda water is the most satisfactory, as it has less tendency to rust the work or the machine.

For internal grinding it is especially important that a wheel should be free cutting and the work revolved so slowly as to enable the wheel to readily do its work. The wheels should generally be softer than for external grinding, as a much larger portion of the periphery is in contact with the work. Their small diameters make it impossible for the proper periphery speed to be obtained, and this must be considered in regulating the speed of the work.

The wheels listed at the end of this chapter are those which our experience has shown to be suitable for the various purposes specified. Special cases may demand changes in the grade letter, but under ordinary circumstances the list should be accepted as a guide.

The speed, diameter and width of wheels, and the number of the emery cannot be changed without changing the grade and cutting qualities of the wheels.

In mounting emery wheels there should always be elastic washers placed between the wheel and the flanges. Sheet rubber is best for this purpose, but soft leather will answer very well.

In some cases manufacturers of emery wheels attach a thick, soft paper washer to each side of the wheel for this purpose, in which case no further attention is required in this direction.

In all kinds of grinding the work should move in a direction opposite to that of the wheel at the cutting point.

To obtain good results when the grinding is done on the

centers it must be remembered that true center holes in the work, as well as true centers, are absolutely necessary.

The face plates should be kept true. They can be readily ground in place on the machines.

When slight tapers are desired for either external or internal grindings, the swivel table is set to the proper angle.

When more abrupt tapers are wanted for work ground on centers or for internal surfaces, the wheel slide is set to the proper angle. By placing the wheel slide and the swivel table at the proper angles, two tapers, for either external or internal work, may be obtained without changing the settings of the machine, the one automatically by the longitudinal movement of the table, the other by operating the cross feed by hand.

When an abrupt taper, similar to that shown in Figure 1, is to be ground, the swivel table remains parallel to the ways of the bed as in plain grinding, but the wheel bed is set to the angle, which brings the line of motion of the wheel slide, when operated by the cross feed, parallel with the taper to be obtained The wheel platen is set at right angles with the line of movement of the wheel slide, indicated by the arrow, and the face of the wheel is thus brought parallel with the line of the desired taper. The work is revolved by the dead center pully, as shown in cut, and the wheel is moved over the surface of the work by the cross-feed.

The method of grinding two tapers with one setting of the machine when one of the tapers is not more than ten degrees is shown in Figure 2.

For grinding the slight taper the swivel table is set over, and for grinding the more abrupt taper the wheel bed is set as in Figure 1, but the wheel platen is here set to bring the face of the wheel parallel with the longest surface to be ground.

Were the abrupt taper longer than the slight taper it would be well to set the wheel platen as in Fgure 1, so that the face of the wheel would be parallel with the line of taper. In obtaining the angle at which the wheel bed is to be set

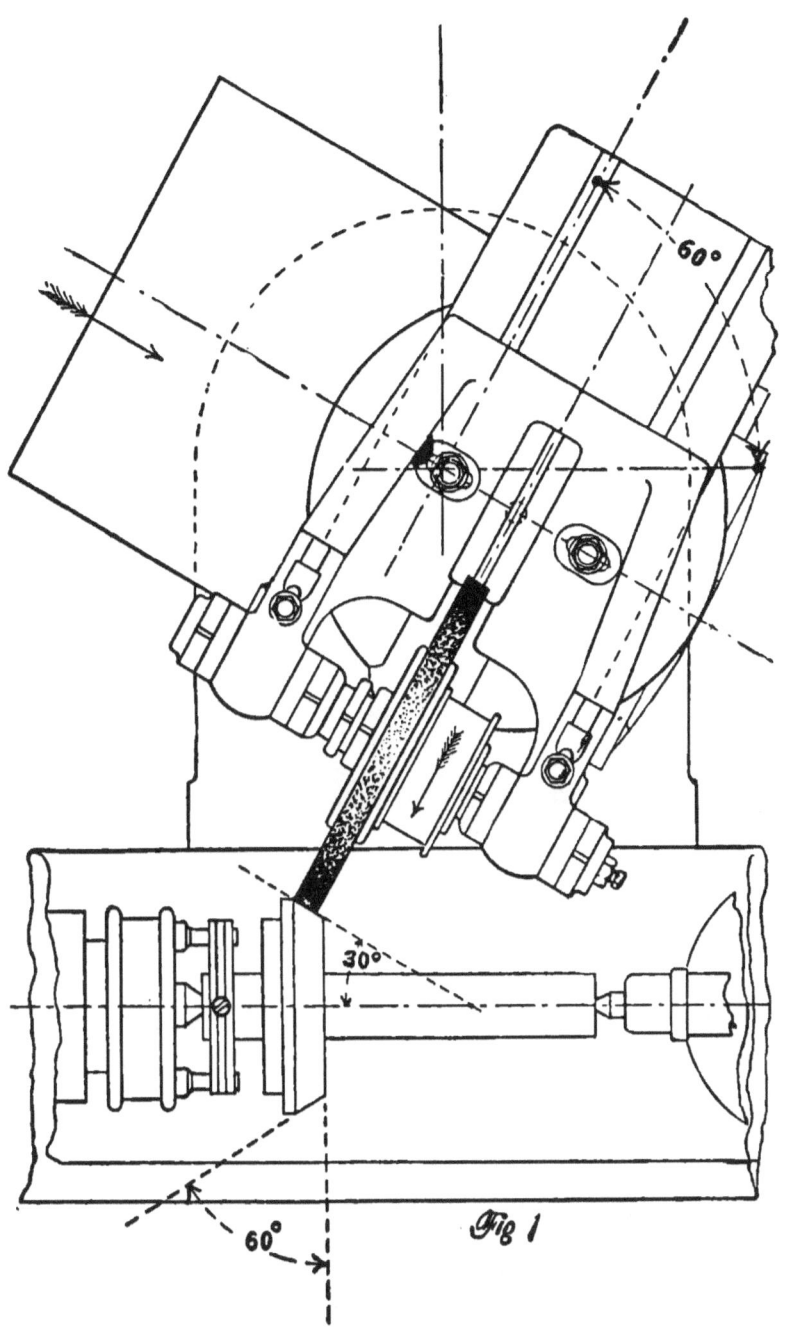

Fig 1

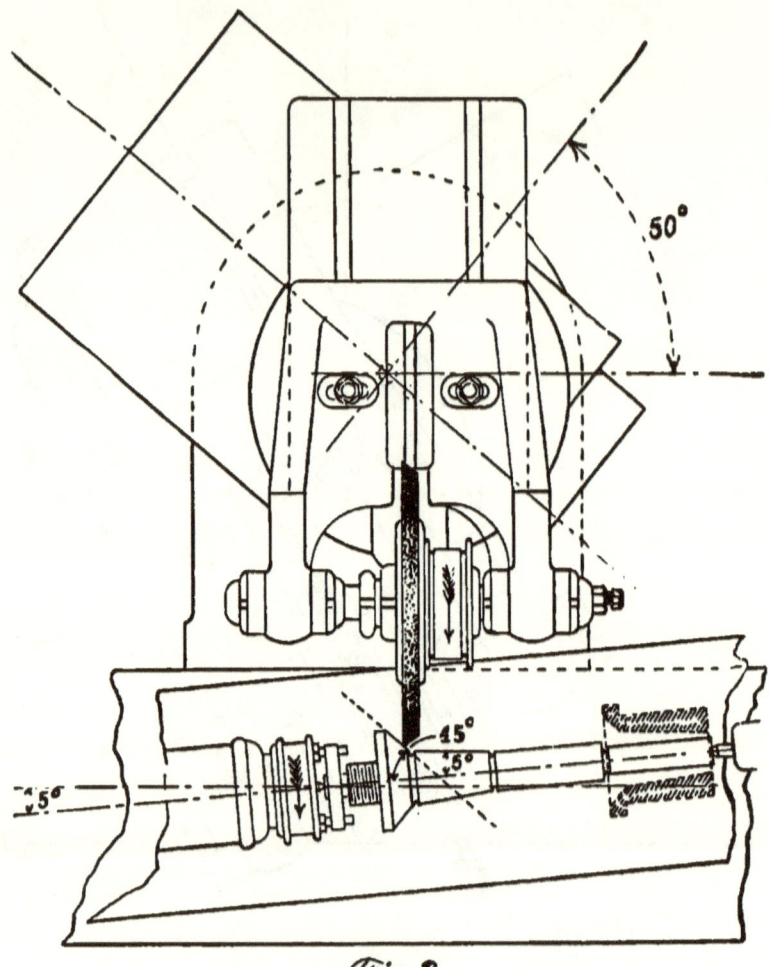

Fig 2

when the swivel table has been set over, it should be remembered that the angle must equal the sum of the two tapers. The abrupt taper is ground by feeding the wheel across the work by hand. The slight taper is ground while the table is fed automatically.

When, as suggested by the cut, a spindle and box are both to be ground, the box is ground first and the spindle is fitted to it. For convenience in fitting the work, the box may be placed as shown by the dotted lines and supported so that it will not touch the spindle as the latter revolves. The

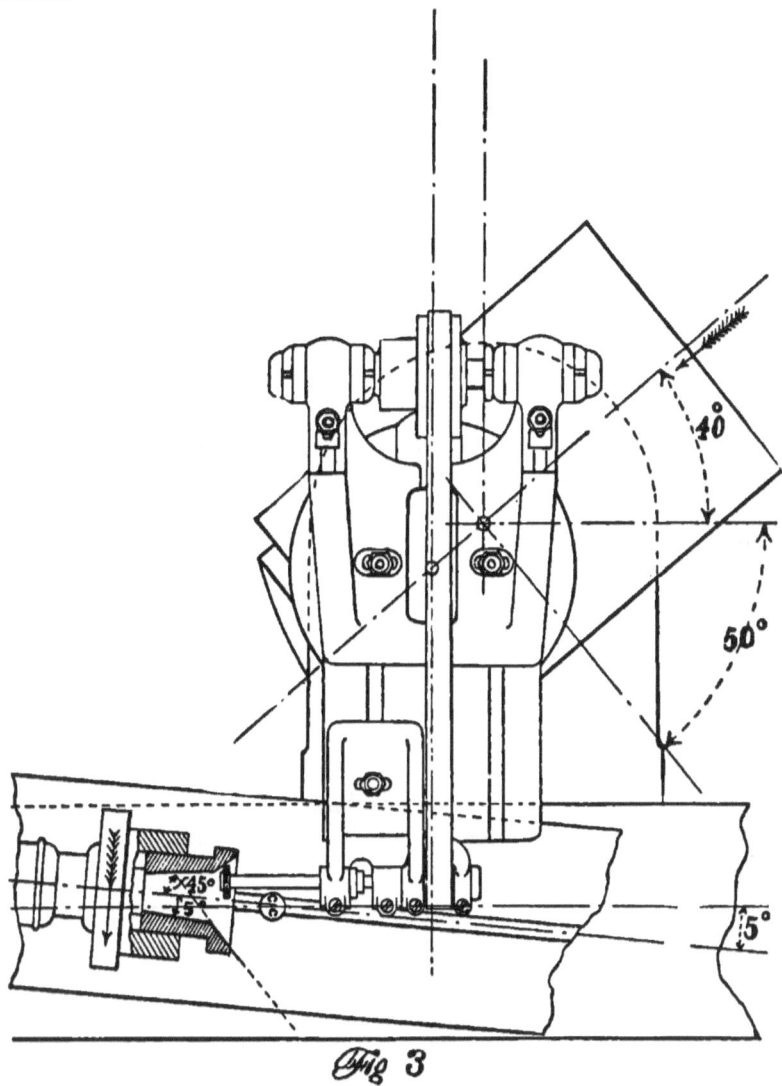

Fig 3

spindle thus need not be removed from the centers when it is necessary to try it in the box.

In grinding the box the machine is set as shown in Figure 3. Provision is made for grinding the slight taper by setting the swivel table, and for grinding the abrupt taper by swiveling the wheel bed.

Thin washers and cutters are conveniently mounted on a

special chuck furnished with the machine. This chuck holds the cutters by the hole in the center and should be used in all disk grinding where both sides of the pieces must be parallel. For most disk grinding it is also more convenient than a common chuck and more accurate results are generally obtained by its use. Thin saws are held this way and are ground concave or thinner at the center than at the teeth, to give the proper clearance.

Angular or taper cutters may be ground by holding them on a mandrel, but the swivel table must be set over for the proper taper. When the taper of the cutter is greater than two inches per foot, the feeding may be done with the cross feed, and the wheel set as shown and explained in connection with Figure 1.

The side teeth of straddle mills may be ground on a Universal Grinding Machine, but the machine is not recommended for such a purpose, as, in order to obtain the proper clearance, the wheel stand must be elevated so that the center of the wheel will be above the tooth rest, the tooth rest in this case having to be set as high as the center of the head stock spindle.

Where many cutters of this class have to be ground, or, in fact, for manufacturing establishments having a great deal of tool grinding, we would recommend the Brown & Sharpe's special tool and cutter grinding machines as more convenient and economical.

The following list of emery wheels, as made by the Norton Emery Wheel Company of Worcester, Massachusetts, to be used in connection with the Number 2 Universal Grinding Machine Improved (Brown & Sharpe), is recommended.

To grind hardened steel spindles, etc., shape 3 (plain 12" diameter, $\frac{1}{2}$" face), emery 60, grade K, mixture 14-A, speed 1,300 to 2,000; also emery 60, grade M, mixture 13-A, speed 1,300 to 2,000.

To grind soft steel, shape 3, emery 100, grade L, mixture 14-A, speed 2,000.

To grind long or large soft steel pieces, shape as before,

emery 100, grade N, mixture 5-A; also emery 100, grade O, mixture 6-A.

To grind collars, disks, saws, etc., shape 1, 13 or 14 (plain 6″ to 7″ diameter, and from ¼″ to ½″ face), Georgia corundum 36, grade J, mixture X-15-C, speed 3,000.

To grind cast iron spindles (solid), shape 3, (12″ diameter ½″ face), emery 60, grade M, mixture 13-A, speed 1,300 to 2,000.

To grind hollow cast iron rolls, shape 3, emery 60, grade F, mixture 15-A, speed 1,300 to 2,000.

WHEELS FOR INTERNAL GRINDING,

TO ROUGH OUT FOR ACCURATE WORK BUT CANNOT BE
CROWDED.   FOR HARD AND SOFT STEEL
AND CAST IRON.

Shapes 82, 83 and 84 (from ½″ to ¾″ diameter, ¼″ face and ¼″ hole), emery 46, grade G, mixture X-12-A, speed 13,400.

Shapes 84, 85 and 86, (from ¾″ to 1″ diameter, ¼″ hole and ¼″ face), emery 46, grade G, mixture X-12-A, speed 12,200.

Shapes 87, 88 and 89, (from 1″ to 1½″ diameter, ⅜″ face and from ¼″ to ⅝″ holes), emery 46, grade G, mixture X-12-A, speed 11,200.

Shapes 90 and 91, (from 2″ to 2½″ in diameter, ⅜″ face and ¾″ hole), emery 46, grade G, mixture X-12-A, speed 8,050.

To grind for finishing after roughing wheels have been used:

Shapes 82, 83 and 84, emery 120, grade F, mixture X-10-A, speed 13,400.

Shapes 84, 85 and 86, emery 120, grade F, mixture X-10-A, speed 12,200.

Shapes 87, 88 and 89, emery 120, grade F, mixture X-10-A, speed 11,200.

Shapes 90 and 91, emery 120, grade F, mixture X-10-A, speed 8,050.

For internal grinding the Special Fixtures are used.

CHAPTER V.

MECHANICS.

On this subject I shall treat more particularly on such matters as concern the mechanic in his surroundings.

QUESTIONS UPON THE PRINCIPLES OF THE LEVER.

At one extremity of a straight lever, whose length is 6 feet, a weight of 10 pounds is suspended; at the distance of 5 feet from the point of suspension a fulcrum is placed. What weight must be suspended from the other extremity of the lever to keep it in equilibrium (balanced)?

If 10 pounds is suspended 5 feet from the fulcrum, then at one foot from the fulcrum on the opposite end it will take 5 times as much to balance it, or 50 pounds, the answer.

A lever is 30 feet long; at what distance from the fulcrum must a weight of 200 pounds be placed so that it may be supported by a power able to sustain 50 pounds? 200÷50=4, then 30÷4=7½ feet, the answer.

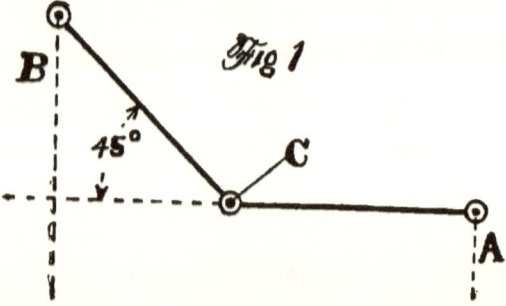

In a lever, as shown in figure 1, a weight of 100 pounds is suspended at A. What will be the required weight at B to hold this weight in equilibrium? Both arms being of the same length from the fulcrum C, but while A is horizontal B is inclined at an angle of 45°, as shown.

The cosine of 45°=.707, then 1÷.707×100=141.3 pounds, the answer.

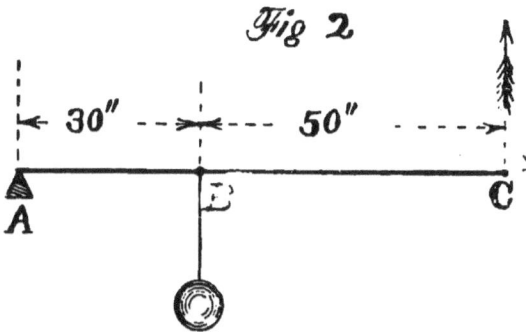

In the lever, as shown at figure 2, A is the fulcrum, B the weight, and the power is applied at C in the direction of the arrow. Required, the power at C to support a weight of 60 pounds in equilibrium at B, as shown.

In this case the weight at B multiplied by the distance A B must equal the power at C multiplied by the distance A C, or thus: Weight at B=60 pounds, distance A B= 30", then 60×30=1800; the distance A C is 30"+50", or 80", then 1800÷80"=22.5 pounds, the power at C to balance a weight of 60 pounds, as shown at B. The pressure on the fulcrum at A is equal to the difference between the weight suspended at B and the power at C; then, as the weight at B=60 pounds and the power at C=22.5 pounds, 60—22.5=37.5 pounds as the pressure on the fulcrum.

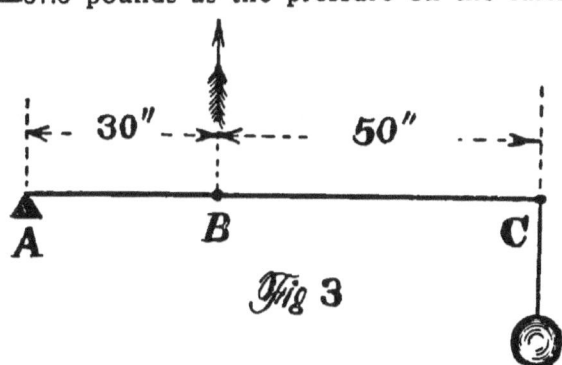

In figure 3 the power is represented between the fulcrum and the weight. Required, the power at B to support a weight of 60 pounds suspended at C, as shown.

In this, or similar examples, we multiply the weight by

the distance A C and divide by the power multiplied by the
distance A B; or thus: 60×80″=4800; now, as the power is
not known we divide 4800 by the distance A B, or 30″, thus:
4800÷30″=160 pounds, or the power at B to just balance a
weight of 60 pounds at C. In this example, as the power is
greater than the weight, the pressure at the fulcrum is upwards, and is equal to the difference between the power and
the weight, thus: 160—60=100 pounds.

The safety valve also comes under the head of levers, and
the calculations are similar to figure 3. In figure 4 let A be

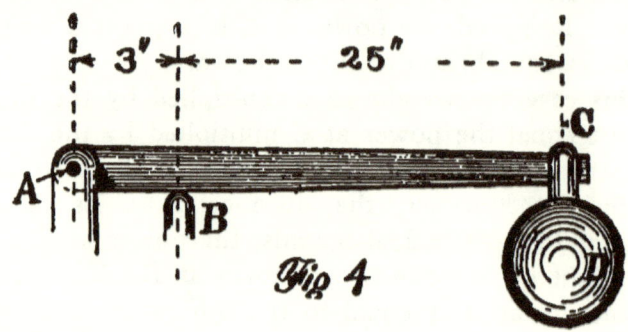

the fulcrum of the lever, B the valve, 3″ from the fulcrum,
and D a weight of 40 pounds suspended 25″ from the valve
or 28″ from the fulcrum; the valve is 3″ diameter. Required,
the steam pressure on the valve to just balance the weight.
(The weight of valve and lever is not taken into consideration). The distance A C is 28″, and the weight 40 pounds,
then 28×40=1120; the valve is 3″ in diameter, 3×3=9×.7854
=7.07 square inches, or the area of the valve; this being 3″
from the fulcrum, we multiply it thus: 7.07×3=21.21, and
1120÷21.21=53.2 pounds pressure, the answer.

Now, suppose that our safety valve is 4″ diameter and
3½″ from the fulcrum, and we want to blow off at 100 pounds
pressure, the weight is 90 pounds; how far from the fulcrum
will it have to be suspended?

The valve is 4″ diameter, then 4×4=16, and .7854×16=
12.56, or the number of square inches of area in the valve,
and this, multiplied by the distance from the fulcrum, 3½″,

thus: 12.56×3.5=43.9, and again by the pressure required, 43.9×100=4390; then 4390÷90=48.8 inches, nearly. This weight, of course, is supposed to balance the pressure on the valve, and any excess in the pressures will lift it. The weight of valve and lever has not been taken into consideration.

We have another safety valve 3½" diameter and placed 2¾" from the fulcrum, and we wish to maintain a boiler pressure of 65 pounds; the extreme length of lever from the fulcrum is 35 inches. Required, the weight, if suspended at the end of the lever.

The valve is 3.5" diameter, then 3.5"×3.5=12.25×.7854= 9.62, the area in square inches of the valve; then, 9.62×2.75, the distance from the fulcrum, =26.45, and multiplied by the pressure, 65 pounds, =1719.25; this divided by the length of lever 35"=49.1 pounds, as the required weight on the lever.

It must be remembered that the diameter of the valve in all cases must be taken from where the steam acts directly against it, and not from the largest part of the valve.

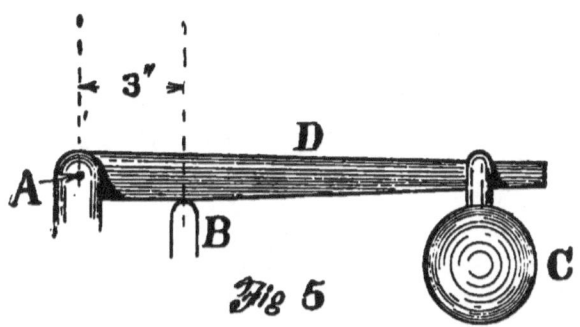

Fig 5

We have a safety valve (Fig. 5); the fulcrum A is 3 inches from the valve B, the weight C is 65 pounds, and the weight of the lever D is 10 pounds and its center of gravity (of the lever) is 9 inches from the fulcrum A; the valve is 3½ inches diameter at the point of pressure, and we wish it to lift when the pressure is 70 pounds per square inch; how far from the fulcrum will we have to place the weight?

The valve being 3½ inches diameter, then 3.5×3.5×.7854 =9.62 inches, area of the valve, or the number of square inches; then, 9.62×70, the steam pressure, and again by 3″, the distance A to B, =2020.2. The lever weighs 10 pounds, and its center of gravity is 9 inches from A; then, 10×9=90, and 2020.2—90=1930.2, and this divided by the weight, thus: 1930.2÷65=29.7 inches, nearly, the answer.

Or, if the lever had a notch filed into it 29.7″ from the fulcrum and our weight had been lost and we wished to know how large a weight would be required under the same conditions, we would divide 1930.2 by 29.7 inches, and this would give the answer, or the weight required.

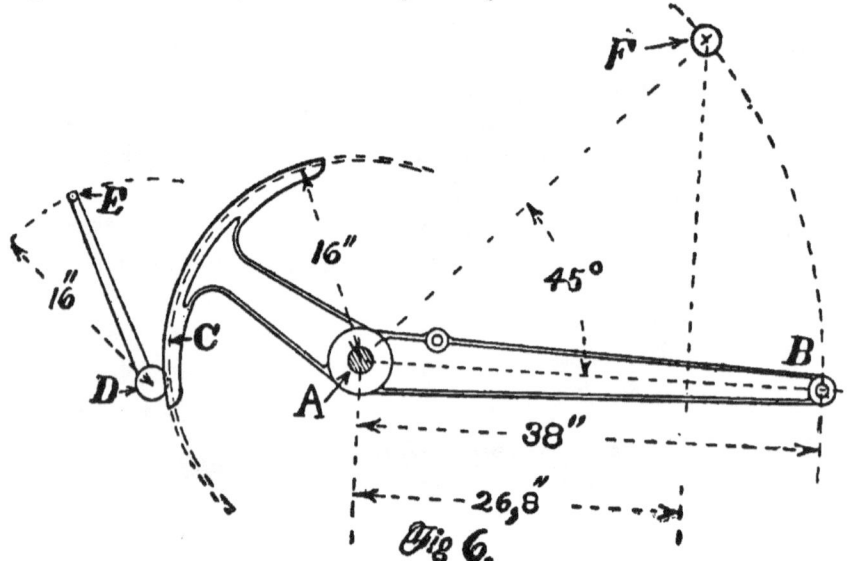

Fig 6.

We have a reel, attached to a lever at B, (Fig. 6), that swings on a stud shown at A, the long arm of which is 38″ from the fulcrum. The short arm is in the form of a segment of a gear and is 16″ from the pitch line to the fulcrum. To turn this lever, we have a crank attached to the pinion D, 16″ long; the pinion is 2 1-6″ diameter at the pitch line. What force will be required at E to balance a weight of 153 pounds suspended at B in a horizontal position, disregarding friction and weight of the moving parts?

In this example the force required at C will be as much greater than at B as the length from A B is greater than

A C; therefore, dividing 38 by 16, which is 2⅜, and, as the weight at B is 153 pounds, multiplying this by 2⅜ we have 363.4 pounds to be overcome at C. But as the crank E is 16″ long, and the pinion that it turns is but 1 1-12″ radius (one-half the diameter), we gain a leverage equal to the difference between the radius of the pinion and the radius of the crank; then, dividing 16″ by 1 1-12″, or 1.083″, and the result, 14.7, is the ratio of the power gained by the difference in the radius of the crank to that of the pinion; then, dividing 363.4 by 14.7 and the result, 24.7 pounds, will be the force required on the crank E to balance 153 pounds suspended at B. (Disregarding friction, etc.)

A force of 36 pounds would be a safe estimate in this case, including friction, to lift the weight.

It must be remembered that if the weight is in any other than a horizontal position from the fulcrum on which it moves that the distance A B, will be equal to the cosine of the angle, as shown in the figure. Thus, suppose that B was inclined at an angle of 45° (shown at F), then as the cosine of 45°=.707, and multiplied by 38″ will be 26.8″, for the distance to be considered for A B instead of 38″.

THE INCLINED PLANE.

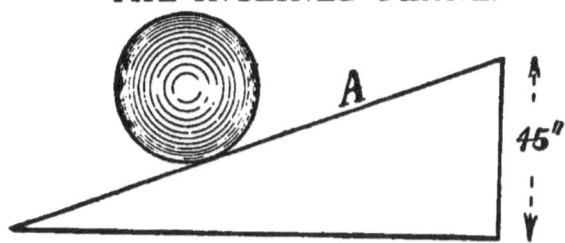

Fig 7

We have a barrel weighing 300 pounds, (Fig. 7), and we want to roll it into a wagon that is 45 inches high by using a plank (A) which is ten feet long; what force will be necessary to roll it up the inclined plane as shown when the pull is parallel with the line A?

300×45=13500 and 13500÷120″ (10 feet) =112.5 pounds.

This is the force necessary to hold the barrel on the plank, and if there was no friction, any excess of pressure over 112.5 pounds would roll the barrel. Or, multiply the weight by the perpendicular of the angle formed and dividing by the hypothenuse will give the answer.

From the preceding example, knowing how much force you could exert without fatigue, and having a barrel of oil, or anything similar, to roll into a wagon, if the weight was known, you would know how long a plank to select for the purpose. Suppose you were alone and wished to roll a barrel weighing 250 pounds into a wagon that was 45 inches high, and 100 pounds was about as much as you cared to exert; what would be the length of the board required?

$250 \div 100 = 2\frac{1}{2}$, then $45 \times 2\frac{1}{2} = 112.5$ inches, or nearly 10 feet. This would not be quite enough to overcome the friction, and we would get one a little longer for the purpose.

On the same principle, if you were to draw a wagon weighing 200 pounds up a hill that was 60 feet high in 300 feet in length, you would not only have the friction to overcome, the same as on a level road, but you would also add to this 60-300 of 200 pounds, or 40 pounds.

THE SCREW.

We have a screw, the pitch is 1 inch (or the distance between two threads) and a lever 30 inches long, measuring from the center of the screw (or its axis); what pressure can be produced by this screw, if we apply a force of 45 pounds at the end of the lever?

In this or similar examples we find the circumference of the circle described by the end of the lever, or where the power is applied, which in this case would be, thus: 30 inches radius $= 60$ inches diameter, then $60 \times 3.1416 = 188.5$, and 188.5×45, the force at the end of the lever, $= 8482.5$, and this divided by the pitch will give the answer. As the pitch in this case is one inch, then 8482.5 pounds is the answer. Now, if this screw was two inches pitch then we would have a pressure of one-half as much, or 4241.25 pounds. But if the screw was ¼ inch pitch, or four threads per inch, then we would have a pressure of four times as much, or 33930 pounds.

WHEEL AND AXLE.

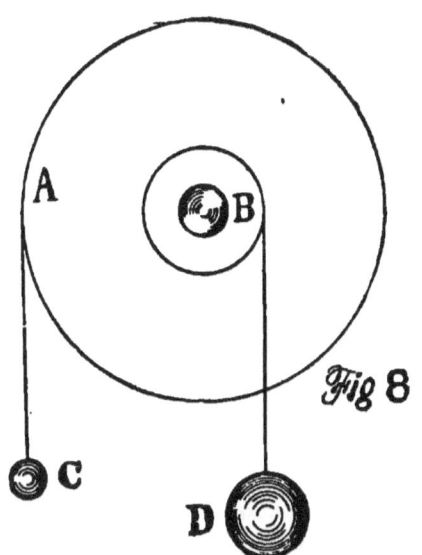

In this example, Fig. 8, we have two pulleys or drums on the same shaft. A is 24″ diameter and B is 7″ diameter; a weight of 40 pounds is suspended from the largest pulley, shown at C; what weight will be required at D to balance the weight at C? A being 24″ and B 7″, then 24÷7=3 3-7, and 40 times 3 3-7=about 137 pounds, the answer.

Fig 8

WHEEL GEARING.

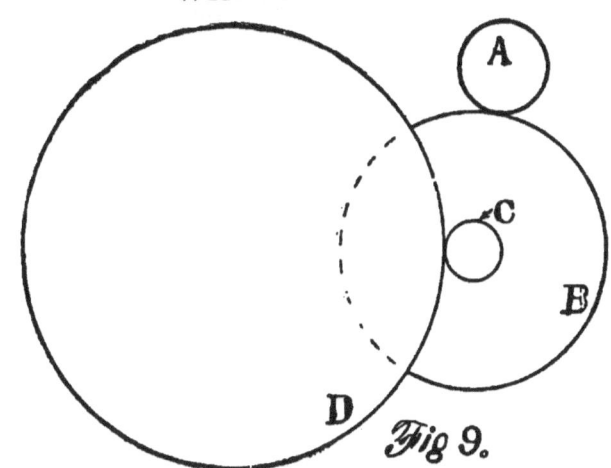

Fig 9.

In this example, Fig. 9, (compound gearing), A is the driving gear with 20 teeth, B 62 teeth and C 12 teeth

(B and C are both on the same shaft or stud), and D has 100 teeth; now if we turn the gear A with a force equal to 15 pounds on the pitch line, what will be the pressure on the pitch line of D?

If A exerts a pull of 15 pounds on the circumference of B, then the force acting on the circumference of D will be as 62 is to 12 times 15 pounds, thus: 62÷12=5 1-6, which multiplied by 15=77.5 pounds, nearly, the answer.

It can easily be seen that if the gear C was of the same diameter as B, that the force exerted on the periphery of D would not change. In other words, it would be 15 pounds, and if it was one-half as large we would double the leverage, and consequently would have a pressure of 30 pounds on D. But if C was twice as large as B, then we would have but one-half of 15 pounds, or 7½ pounds.

Suppose we have a machine on which there is a combination of gears, and also a drum operated by a crank, as follows: On the first shaft we have a pinion 4″ diameter and a crank 16″ long (or radius). On the second shaft there is a gear 15″ diameter and also a pinion 4″ diameter, and on the third shaft there is a gear 15″ diameter, and a drum 5 inches diameter, with a rope wound around it. These 4″ pinions in both cases mesh with the 15″ gears. If we exert a force of 50 pounds on the crank, what will be the weight that we could hold in suspension attached to the rope?

In this example we will first find the ratio between each pair of gears, thus: 15÷4=3¾, and as there are two pairs alike, then we multiply these two ratios together, thus: 3.75 ×3.75=about 14 for the compound ratio of the gears. We next find the difference between the radius of the crank and the radius of the drum, thus: 16÷2½=6.4, and multiplied by the compound ratio 14=89.6, and this again multiplied by 50, the force on the crank =4480 pounds, the answer.

Or, as follows, which is the usual way, 15″×15″=225″, and 4″×4″=16″; then 225″÷16″=14 ratio, which multiplied by 16″, the length of crank=224, and again by 50, the force on the crank=11200, divided by one half the diameter (radius) of the drum=4480 pounds.

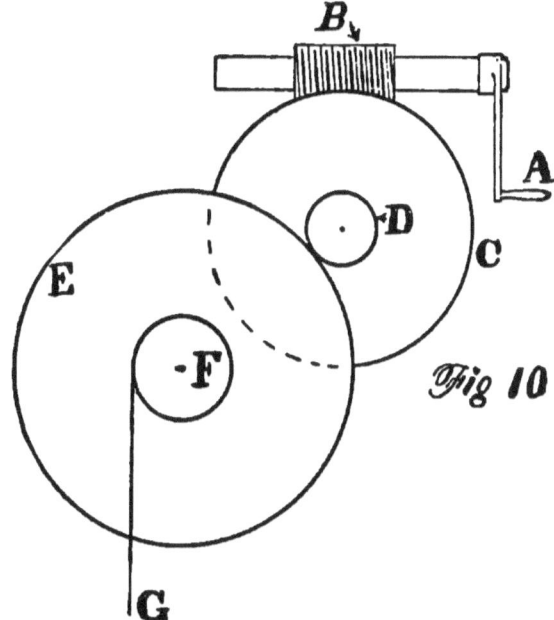

Fig 10

THE SCREW AND GEAR.

We have a machine combining the following parts, as shown in Fig. 10, in which A is a crank, 16″ radius, o⁻ length; B is a worm of 4 threads per inch; C a worm wheel 12 inches diameter on the pitch line. On the same shaft with the worm wheel is a pinion D, 3 inches diameter (pitch line) in mesh with the gear E, 16 inches in diameter. On the same shaft with this gear (E) is a small pulley F, 5 inches diameter, with a rope wound around it, as shown at G, making no allowance for either the friction or diameter of the rope; what weight can we support at G by a force of 30 pounds applied on the crank at A?

The crank A being 16″ long will describe a circle of 32″ in diameter, the circumference of which is 100.5 inches. Now, as the worm is ¼″ pitch (4 threads) then the crank A will pass through four times as great a distance, or 402 inches, while the worm, or what is the same thing, the worm wheel, moves but one inch (on the pitch line).

As the worm wheel C is 12″ diameter and the pinion D but 3″ diameter, we gain a leverage of 3 to 1; then 462×3=

1206.   It is plain that whatever may be the power gained at D will be imparted to E, since D drives E. But as E is 16 inches in diameter and F is but 5 inches, we gain accordingly; thus: 16÷5 =3 1-5; then 1206×3 1-5=3859.2, which multiplied by the force on the crank of 30 pounds=115776 pounds, the answer.

THE HYDRAULIC PRESS.

Suppose we have a small hydraulic press, the lever of which is 24 inches in length to the fulcrum; this lever is worked by hand and is attached to the plunger, which is but three inches from the fulcrum and also between it and the power. Suppose this plunger to be ¾ of an inch in diameter and the ram to be 12 inches diameter; by exerting a force of 40 pounds on the lever, what pressure can be obtained by the ram?

As the power applied is 24 inches from the fulcrum and the plunger is but 3 inches, we gain a ratio of 8 to 1   by moving the lever 8 inches to obtain 1 inch of plunger. The diameter of the plunger is ¾", then .75×.75×3.1416=442 thousandths of an inch (area of the plunger), and the ram 12"×12"×3.1416=113" (area of the ram); then 113÷.442= 255.6; or, in other words, the area of a cross section of the ram is more than 255 times as great as that of the plunger; then multiply 255.6 by the ratio of 8 and again by the force of 40 pounds on the lever, and we have as follows: 40×8× 255.6=81792 pounds, the answer.

TO FIND THE BRAKE HORSE-POWER OF AN ENGINE.

To find the brake horse-power of an engine proceed as follows: Clamp the friction brake on a pulley placed on the crank shaft of the engine with the arms A A in such a position that the ends B of the arms which meet will be in a horizontal position with the center of pulleys shown in figure 11; the end of arms at B are to rest on a scale blocked up in order to be in this position. Now we find that the pressure

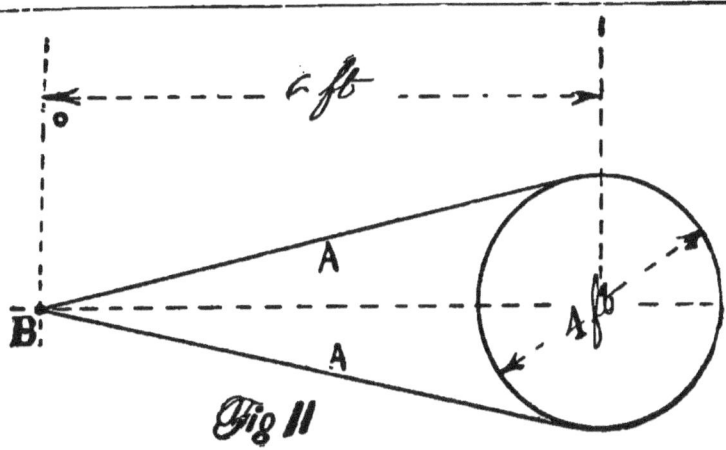

Fig. II

on the scale is just 700 pounds, and the distance from B to the center of pulley or brake is 6 feet; then multiplying together, thus: $700 \times 6 = 4200$, and dividing this by the radius of the pulley on which the brake is secured, we have as follows: $4200 \div 2 = 2100$; this is the resistance upon the circumference of the pulley. Now, if this pulley revolves 125 times per minute, we must find how many feet per minute the circumference of the pulley is making. Then $3.1416 \times 4 = 12.56$, the number of feet around the pulley, and this multiplied by the speed, thus: $12.56 \times 125 = 1570$; this equals the number of feet per minute the pulley travels at the circumference, and this again multiplied by the resistance on the pulley as follows: $1570 \times 2100 = 3297000$, or the foot pounds per minute; then dividing by 33000 we have as follows: $3297000 \div 33000 = 99.9$ horse-power of the engine (brake).

It must be remembered that the brake should be tightened sufficiently on the pulley until the speed of the engine is about to slack; this can easily be seen by the aid of a speed indicator.

HORSE-POWER.

The horse-power of an engine is found in the following manner. Example: We have an engine 24 inches diameter of cylinder, 40 inches stroke of piston, making 120 revolutions per minute, with steam at 75 pounds pressure per square inch; required, the horse-power. We first find the area of the piston by squaring the diameter and multiplying it by .7854, thus: 24×24×.7854=452, and multiplying this by the pressure of steam=33900; multiplying this again by the stroke in feet per minute, which is as follows: as the stroke is 40 inches, at every revolution of the engine the piston will travel 80 inches, then multiplying this by 120 (revolutions per minute) and we have 9600 inches, or 800 feet per minute; then 33900 ×800=27120000 foot pounds per minute. Then as a horse-power is equal to the work of 33000 pounds done in one minute, we divide 27120000 by 33000 and we have 822 horse-power for the answer. This is called the nominal horse-power; the indicated horse-power is found in the same manner, excepting that the steam pressure (the mean effective) is found by means of the indicator, which is always less than the boiler pressure.

PRESSURE ON THE GUIDES OF AN ENGINE.

Suppose we have an engine the cylinder of which is 30 inches bore, and 40 inches stroke, and we want to know the greatest pressure on the guides during a revolution, using 100 pounds pressure of steam per square inch and calling the connecting rod 10 feet long between centers.

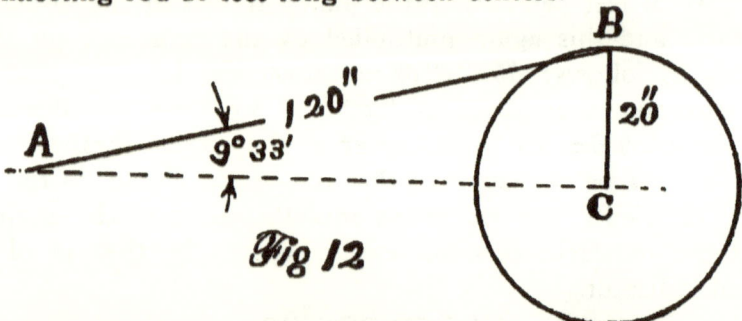

Fig 12

In figure 12, let A B, 10 feet or 120 inches be the connecting rod; B C=the length of crank, or one-half of the stroke. In the figure B C is drawn perpendicular to the line A C, because the greatest pressure is on the guides when the crank is at half stroke, as shown. Now, the cylinder is 30 inches bore, and consequently the area is 30×30×

7854=706 inches; multiplying this by the pressure of 100 pounds=70600 pounds pressure on the piston, and consequently on the line A C; 70600 multiplied by the distance (20") B C, and divided by the length A C, will give the pressure on the guides.

In the figure (12) we have a right angled triangle, as shown, the radius of which is 120 inches; B C is the sine of the angle B A C; then 20 inches (the sine) divided by the radius of 120 inches=.166, or the sine to a radius of 1 inch, and, in the table of sines, we find this to correspond with the angle of 9° 33'. The cosine of this angle=.986; then multiplying this by the radius of 120", thus: .986×120" =118.3 inches, or the length of A C. Then 70600×20= 1412000 and divided by 118.3=11935+ pounds, the answer.

TO FIND THE DIAMETER OF A SHAFT FOR TRANSMITTING POWER, WHEN THE HORSE-POWER OF THE ENGINE IS KNOWN.

Example: Suppose in a factory we have an engine 150 horse-power which is to run at a speed of 175 revolutions per minute. Required, the diameter of the main line of shafting.

```
175)150.00000(.857142
    140 0
    ─────
     10 00
      8 75
     ─────
      1 250
      1 225
      ─────
        250
        175
        ───
        750
        700
        ───
        500
```

$$.857142(.94+$$
$$729$$
$$\overline{128142}$$

$$9^2 \times 300 = 24300$$
$$9 \times 30 \times 4 = 1080$$
$$4^2 = \quad 16 \quad 101584$$

$$\overline{25396 \quad 26558}$$

$$.95+$$
$$2.9$$
$$\overline{855}$$
$$1\ 90$$

2.755 inches, the answer.

We first divide the horse-power of the engine by the revolutions it is to run per minute and extract the cube root, which in this case is .95, then multiply this by the constant 2.9, which gives about 2¾ inches for the diameter of the shaft. This is for good ordinary steel, but if it is to be of wrought iron, it should be one-eighth (⅛) larger, thus: ⅛ of 2.755″=.344″, and, added together =3.099″, the answer, if made of wrought iron.

IMPACT OR COLLISION OF BODIES.

Let us now for a moment examine into the force of a shot fired from one of our modern 12-inch guns. Suppose a solid shot, weighing 1,100 pounds, is fired at an object and strikes it with a velocity of 1,500 feet per second; then the mass of this body, which is the weight divided by 32.2, multiplied by the velocity in feet per second will be the answer, provided it takes just one second from the time the shot strikes the object until the momentum of the ball is stopped, or, as we say, destroyed; but we know that it does not take a second to stop it, and we will suppose that it takes but one-fiftieth (1-50) part of a second to stop it, then the force will be as follows: 1100÷32.2=34.16, which multiplied by the velocity equals 41240, which would be the answer, as explained if it required one second of time from the moment of striking until the momentum was destroyed; but if it only takes one-fiftieth of a second, then the force (average) will be 50 times as much, or 2062000 pounds, the answer. Or, if it takes the 1-100 part of a second, then the answer will be 41240×100= 4124000 pounds.

The force of a railway train or any other object can also be found in a similar manner if we know the weight (or mass) of the body, the velocity in feet per second, and the duration of the impact in time. Remember that the mass of any body is its weight divided by 32.2; that is, anything that weighs just 96.6 pounds, we would say that its mass was 3.

CENTRIFUGAL FORCE.

The centrifugal force of a fly wheel of an engine, or any-thing of similar shape, is the force exerted outward from the center, like the sparks from an emery wheel; the force of which can be found (approximately) as follows: We have an engine with a fly wheel, the rim of which weighs 60 tons, or 120000 pounds, is 18 feet in diameter at the center of the rim and has a velocity of 80 revolutions per minute. Required, the centrifugal force.

18 feet the diameter=56.5 feet in circumference, which multiplied by the number of revolutions 80=4520 feet per minute, and divided by 60=75.3 feet per second; 75.3 squared=5670, and multiplied by the weight in pounds= 680400000, and dividing this by the radius in feet, multiplied by 32.2, is the answer. Thus the radius of the wheel is 9 feet, which multiplied by 32.2=about 290; then 680400000 divided by 290=2346206 pounds, the answer.

CHAPTER VI.

SCREW CUTTING.

In nearly all modern lathes threads can be cut of most any pitch by simple gearing, by which we mean that there is one driver and one driven gear, and usually but one intermediate gear placed between them; but it makes no difference how many there are so long as they connect one with another in a direct train. The number of teeth in the intermediate gears also do not affect it; only the driver, as it is called, on the spindle and the driven on the leading screw are to be considered.

If the leading screw has eight threads per inch, and we wish to cut eight threads on a piece of work, then, as usually made, any two gears with the same numbers of teeth, one on the spindle and the other on the leading screw will cut it. If the leading screw has 4 threads per inch and we want to cut 8 threads, it is plain that the leading screw should turn only one-half as fast as the work, for the reason that while the leading screw makes four revolutions, and consequently the carriage travels one inch, the piece of work on the centers must make twice as many revolutions, or eight turns, in order to have eight threads per inch.

In simple gearing, then, if the leading screw has four threads per inch and we wish to cut four threads per inch on a piece of work, any two gears with the same numbers of teeth will answer.

And, if the leading screw has four threads and we want to cut five threads per inch, multiplying these numbers by any other number will answer, thus: $4 \times 6 = 24$ and $5 \times 6 = 30$; then 24 and 30 will answer; or, $4 \times 7 = 28$ and $5 \times 7 = 35$; then 28 and 35 will cut it, and so on.

Remember to multiply the number of threads on the leading screw and the number of threads you wish to cut by the same number, no matter what the number may be; if you have the gears, it will be correct.

Sometimes we find the pair of gears required thus: leading screw has two (2) threads per inch and we wish to cut six (6) threads per inch; then $2 \times 10\frac{1}{2} = 21$ and $6 \times 10\frac{1}{2} = 63$. It is plain to see that one is just three times as coarse as the other, and consequently, one gear must have just three times as many teeth as the other. It is also plain that if we are to cut threads finer than the leading screw that the largest gear should always be placed on the leading screw, and when coarser than the leading screw, the largest gear should go on the spindle.

SCREW CUTTING BY COMPOUND GEARING.

When cutting screws that are of a very coarse pitch or very fine it is usually done by compound gearing, for the reason that it is difficult to find a pair of gears in which the difference in the numbers of teeth is great enough to answer the purpose by simple gearing.

In compound gearing we generally have four (4) gears, arranged in two pairs as follows: Gear on spindle connects with one on stud, and this is one pair; by the side of this gear on the stud is another gear that meshes with the gear on the leading screw, this is the second pair. Always, in compound gearing, these four gears have to be considered both in regard to the numbers of teeth, as well as being placed in their proper positions.

Suppose, for instance, that the leading screw of a lathe has four (4) threads per inch and we want to cut a coarse thread on a worm, say one thread or one turn in three (3) inches; then, while the worm is making just one turn on the centers the screw will have to make twelve turns, and consequently, one is exactly twelve (12) times as coarse as the other, or, as we usually say, the compound ratio of the gears to cut this worm is 12 to 1.

Now we can take a pair, say 20 and 60 for one pair, which is a ratio of 3 to 1, and dividing the compound ratio 12 by the simple ratio of 3 we have four for the answer, which means that the next pair must be 4 to 1, and it makes no difference what the numbers of their teeth may be in either case so that they are kept in pairs and proportioned 3 to 1 and 4 to 1. It is plain to see, however, that in both cases the largest wheels are the drivers; thus 60 can be placed on the spindle and 20 on the stud for one pair, and 72 on the stud by the side of the 20 and 18 on the leading screw; or, 72 can be placed on the spindle connecting with 18 on the stud and 60 alongside of the 18 in mesh, with 20 on the leading screw. Or, we can take a pair of gears 2 to 1, say 40 and 80, and dividing 12 by 2, we have 6 for the ratio of the next pair; then any pair 20 and 120 or 30 and 180 will answer.

Suppose that the leading screw on a lathe has four (4) threads per inch and we want to cut a thread of ⅜ inch pitch. In a case of this kind we generally find how many threads there will be in a certain number of inches, both on the leading screw and the work that is to be threaded. Let us take three (3) inches in this example, and we find that there are 24 eighths, and the pitch is to be three-eighths; then there will be just eight full threads in three inches, while in the leading screw of four threads per inch there will be just twelve full threads in three inches, then the gears to cut this screw will be as 8 is to 12; that is, in simple gearing where only two gears are changed, multiply 8 and 12 by 2, 3, 4, 5, 6, or any other number, sometimes by 2½, 3½, 4½, and so on, and if you have such gears they will be correct. Or, if you compound the gears, take one pair alike, say 60 and 60 or 50 and 50, and the second pair will be as just described in simple gearing (8 to 12); for instance, 24 and 36.

Or, suppose you want to cut a screw of ⅞ inch pitch, the leading screw being four threads per inch; then we find that in 7 inches there are 56 eighths, and as each thread takes up a space of ⅞ inches, dividing 56 by 7 we have just eight full threads in the seven inches, while in the leading screw there will be 7 times 4, or 28 full threads; then our ratio will be as 8 is to 28, or 3½ to 1. In simple gearing we can take any gear, say 20 for one and 3½ times 20 for the next and so on, while in compound gearing we can take a pair of 2 to 1 and dividing 3½ by 2, thus: 3.5÷2=1.75, or 1¾ to 1, for the next pair; thus any pair 2 to 1, call it 30 and 60 for one pair, and 40 and 70 for the next.

Suppose the leading screw has three (3) threads per inch, and we want to cut a screw of ⅜ inch pitch. In three inches there are 24 eighths, and dividing 24 eighths by three-eighths we have eight full threads in three inches; while in the leading screw there would be 9 full threads in three inches, and the gear should be as 8 is to 9; then in simple gearing multiply these numbers by any other number, say 3, and we have 24 and 27; or, in compound gearing, these same gears will answer for one pair if the next pair are alike.

If we should want to cut 27 threads to the inch and the leading screw has 3 threads per inch, then 27÷3=9 for the ratio; then any pair 3 to 1, say 20 and 60 for one pair, and dividing the ratio of 9 by 3, we then have two pairs of gears 3 to 1; while if we should take for one pair 4 to 1, say 22 and 88, or 20 and 80, then dividing the ratio of 9 by 4, we have for the second pair 2¼ to 1; that is, any number in which one gear has 2¼ times as many teeth as the other, for instance, 24 and 54.

Again, suppose our leading screw has four threads per inch and we want to cut a coarse thread on a worm of 2⅝ inch pitch; then while the worm makes four revolutions the carriage will have to move four times 2⅝ inches or 10½ inches, and, as the leading screw has four threads per inch, it will turn four times 10½, or 42 revolutions; the compound ratio of the gears will then be 42 revolutions divided by 4 revolutions, or 10½; we will now take 30 and 90 for the one pair, which is 3 to 1, and dividing 10.5 by 3 and we will have thus: 10.5÷3=3.5, or 3½ to 1 for the second pair; thus 20 and 70 or 24 and 84 will answer.

CHAPTER VII.

A METHOD OF CALCULATING THE SPEED AND THE DIAME-
TER OF PULLEYS.

The countershaft of a lathe, or any other machine, has a pulley 16″ diameter and should run 80 revolutions per minute; the main shaft runs at 100 revolutions per minute. What should be the size of pulley on the main shaft?

Multiply the diameter of the driven pulley by the speed it should run per minute and divide the product by the speed of the main shaft, thus:

```
                    16″=di. of pulley on counter shaft.
                    80=revolutions per minute.
                    ──
Revolutions of
     main shaft=100)1280(12.8=diameter of pulley on
                    100             main shaft.
                    ──
                    280
                    200
                    ──
                    800
                    800
                    ──
```

We have an emery wheel that should run 3,600 revolutions per minute; the pulley on the emery wheel spindle is 3 inches diameter and the pulley on the countershaft is 14 inches diameter that is to drive the 3-inch pulley; alongside this 14″ pulley on the counter shaft is a pulley 6 inches in diameter; the main shaft runs at 120 revolutions per minute. Required, the diameter of pulley on main shaft.

Dividing the 14″ pulley on the countershaft by the 3″ pulley on the emery wheel spindle we have as follows: 14÷3=4 2-3, or 4.66, which means that the speed of the countershaft will be as 4.66 is contained in 3600, which is 772.5; then dividing 772.5 by 120, the speed of the main shaft, and we have 6.43, which means that the pulley on the main shaft should be 6.43 times as large as the pulley on the counter-shaft which it is to drive; then multiplying tne 6-inch pulley by 6.43 we have 38.5+, or 38½ inches for the size of the pulley required.

Another way: Multiply the speed required by the diameter of the driven pulley on the emery wheel spindle and divide by the driver on the countershaft; multiply this by the driven pulley on the countershaft and divide by the speed of the main shaft, thus: 3600×3=10800, and 10800÷14=771.4; 771.4×6=4628.4; then 4628.4÷120=38.5, the answer.

The countershaft of a machine has no pulley on it, and we want it to run at a speed of 240 revolutions per minute; the main shaft has a pulley 18 inches diameter and has a speed of 130 revolutions per minute. Required, the diameter of pulley on the countershaft. Multiply the diameter of the driver by its number of revolutions per minute and divide this by the number of revolutions required. Thus:

130 revolutions of main shaft.
18 diameter of pulley.

1040
130

240)2340(9.75 inches, the answer.
2160

1800
1680

1200
1200

We have a machine that should run at a speed of 800 revolutions per minute; the countershaft has no pulleys, but we have a pulley 20 inches diameter on the main shaft which runs at a speed of 130 revolutions per minute; our machine has a pulley 5 inches diameter on the spindle.   What size pulleys may we select for the countershaft in order to get the speed required?   \

Dividing the speed required for the machine by the 'speed

of the main shaft, thus: 800÷130=6.15, we find that the ratio of speed is as 6.15 to 1. Dividing the diameter of pulley on the main shaft by the one on the spindle, thus: 20 ÷5=4, and we find the ratio of the two pulleys is as 4 to 1. Therefore, dividing the ratio of the speed by the ratio of the pulleys, thus: 6.15÷4=1.53. Then we may select any pulley, say 16 inches for the large one, and dividing 16 bv 1.53= 10.4 inches, which will be the diameter of the other pulley. That is, a belt connecting a 20-inch pulley on the main shaft (130 per minute) with the 10.4 inch pulley on the countershaft, and another belt connecting the 16-inch pulley alongside of the 10.4″ pulley on the countershaft with the 5″ pulley on the machine will drive it with a speed of 800 revolutions per minute.

We have a machine that should run at a speed of 240 revolutions per minute; it has no pulley on the spindle, and we wish to use a countershaft that has two pulleys, one of 12 and the other 8″ diameter; there is also a pulley 14″ diameter on the main shaft, the speed of which is 140 revolutions per minute; required, the diameter of the pulley on the machine.

Dividing the speed of machine by the speed of the main shaft, thus: 240÷140=about 1.7 for the ratio of speed required.

As the speed of the machine should be greater than the main line, we will drive from the 14″ pulley on the main shaft to the 8″ pulley on the countershaft. Then dividing 14 by 8 we have a ratio of 1.75, and, as this is greater than what we want, (1.7), then the pulley on the machine should be a little larger than the one that is to drive it (the 12″) and dividing the ratio of speed that the 14″ pulley would drive the 8″ (1.75) by the ratio required (1.7), and the answer 1.03×12″=12.3″ about, for the size required. Or thus, 140×14=1960÷8= 245×12=2940÷12.3=239+, the speed of the machine per minute.

The simplest manner, then, to find the diameter of one or more pulleys when the speed of the main shaft and also the machine that you wish to drive is given, is as follows:

The main shaft revolves at a speed of 80 revolutions per minute, and we wish to drive the spindle of the machine with a velocity of 2300 revolutions per minute; required, the size of pulleys. 2300÷80=about 28.7. Now if we want only two (2) pulleys, one of them would be 28.7 times as large as the other; it would not make any difference what it was, so that the large one was 28.7 times the size of the small pulley. But it would be much better to use four pulleys, one on the main shaft, two on the countershaft and one on the spindle. In such a case we should try not to have them vary in size any more than possible, and, therefore, we would take for the first pair a ratio of 5 to 1; that is, say one of 6 inches and the other 30 inches diameter, for the one pair, and dividing 28.7 by the ratio of 5, we have for the next pair a ratio of 5.7+; that is, say the small pulley is 5 inches diameter, then the large pulley will be 5.7 times 5, or about 28.5 inches in diameter.

CHAPTER VIII.

CONDENSED SUGGESTIONS FOR STEEL WORKERS.

CRESCENT STEEL CO., PITTSBURG, PA.

(BY PERMISSION.)

ANNEALING.

Owing to the fact that the operations of rolling or hammering steel make it very hard, it is frequently necessary that the steel should be annealed before it can be conveniently cut into the required shapes for tools.

Annealing or softening is accomplished by heating steel to a red heat and then cooling it very slowly, to prevent it from getting hard again.

The higher the degree of heat the more will steel be softened, until the limit of softness is reached, when the steel is melted.

It does not follow that the higher a piece of steel is heated the softer it will be when cooled, no matter how slowly it may be cooled; this is proved by the fact that an ingot is always harder than a rolled or hammered bar made from it.

Therefore, there is nothing gained by heating a piece of steel hotter than a good, bright, cherry red; on the contrary, a higher heat has several disadvantages; first, if carried too far, it may leave the steel actually harder than a good red heat would leave it; second, if a scale is raised on the steel, this scale will be harsh, granular oxide of iron, and will spoil the tools used to cut it. It often occurs that steel is scalded in this way, and then because it does not cut well, it is customary to heat it again, and hotter still, to overcome the trouble, while the fact is, that the more this operation is repeated, the harder the steel will work, because of the hard scale and the harsh grain underneath; third, a high scaling heat, continued for a little time, changes the structure of the steel, destroys its crystalline property, makes it brittle, liable to crack in hardening and impossible to refine.

Again, it is common practice to put steel into a hot furnace at the close of a day's work and leave it there all night. This method always gets the steel too hot, always raises a scale on it, and worse than either, it leaves it soaking in the fire too long, and this is more injurious to steel than any other operation to which it can be subjected.

A good illustration of the destruction of crystalline structure by long continued heating may be had by operating on chilled cast iron.

If a chill be heated red hot and removed from the fire as soon as it is hot, it will, when cold, retain its peculiar crystalline structure; if now it be heated red hot, and left at a moderate heat for several hours—in short, if it be treated as steel often is, and be left in the furnace over night, it will be found when cold, to have a perfect amorphous structure, every trace of chill crystals will be gone and the whole piece will be noncrystalline gray cast iron. If this is the effect upon coarse cast iron, what better is to be expected from fine cast steel?

A piece of fine tap steel, after having been in a furnace over night, will act as follows:

It will be harsh in the lathe and spoil the cutting tools.

When hardened it will almost certainly crack; if it does

not crack it will be a remarkably good steel to begin with. When the temper is drawn to the proper color and the tap is put into use, the teeth will either crumble off or crush down like so much lead.

Upon breaking the tap, the grain will be coarse and the steel brittle.

To anneal any piece of steel, heat it red hot; heat it uniformly and heat it through, taking care not to let the ends and corners get too hot.

As soon as it is hot, take it out of the fire, the sooner the better, and cool it as slowly as possible. A good rule for heating is to heat it at so low a red that when the piece is cold it will still show the blue gloss of the oxide that was put there by the hammer or the rolls.

Steel annealed in this way will cut very soft; it will harden very hard, without cracking, and when tempered it will be very strong, nicely refined, and will hold a keen, strong edge.

HEATING TO FORGE.

Fully as much trouble and loss are caused by improper heating in the forge fire as in the tempering fire, although steel may be heated safely very hot for forging if it be done properly; but any high degree of heat, no matter how uniform it may be, is unsafe for hardening.

The trouble in the forge fire is usually uneven heat, and not too high heat. Suppose the piece to be forged has been put into a very hot fire, and forced as quickly as possible to a high yellow heat, so that it is almost up to the scintillating point. If this be done, in a few minutes the outside will be quite soft and in nice condition for forging, while the middle parts will be not more than red hot. The highly heated soft outside will have very little tenacity; that is to say, this part will be so far advanced toward fusion that the particles will slide easily over one another, while the less highly heated inside parts will be hard, possessed of high tenacity, and the particles will not slide so easily over each other.

The soft outside will yield so much more readily than

the hard inside that the outer particles will be torn asunder, while the inside will remain sound, and the piece will be pitched out and branded "burned."

Suppose the case to be reversed, and the inside to be much hotter than the outside; that is, that the inside shall be in a state of semi-fusion, while the outside is hard and firm.

If now the piece be forged, the outside will be all sound and the whole piece will appear perfectly good until it is cropped, and then it is found to be hollow inside, and it is pitched out and branded "burned."

In either case, if the piece had been heated soft all through, or if it had been only red hot all through, it would have forged perfectly sound and good.

If it be asked, why then is there ever any necessity for smiths to use a low heat in forging, when a uniform high heat will do as well? We answer:

In some cases a high heat is more desirable to save heavy labor, but in every case where a fine steel is to be used for cutting purposes, it must be borne in mind that very heavy forging refines the bars as they slowly cool, and if the smith heats such refined bars until they are soft, he raises the grain, makes them coarse, and he cannot get them fine again unless he has a very heavy steam hammer at command, and knows how to use it well.

In following the above hints there is a still greater danger to be avoided; that is by letting the steel lie in the fire after it is properly heated. When the steel is hot through it should be taken from the fire immediately and forged as quickly as possible.

"Soaking" in the fire causes steel to become dry and brittle, and does it more injury than any bad practice known to the most experienced.

HEATING.

Owing to the varying instructions on a great many different labels, we find at times a good deal of misapprehension as to the best way to heat steel; in some cases this causes too much work for the smith, and in other instances disasters follow the act of hardening.

There are three distinct stages or times of heating:

First, for forging,

Second, for hardening,

Third, for tempering.

The first requisite for a good heat for forging is a clean fire and plenty of fuel, so that jets of hot air will not strike the corners of the piece; next, the fire should be regular, and give a good uniform heat to the whole part to be forged. It should be keen enough to heat the piece as rapidly as may be, and allow it to be thoroughly heated through, without being so fierce as to overheat the corners.

Steel should not be left in the fire any longer than is necessary to heat it clear through, as "soaking" in fire is very injurious; and, on the other hand, it is necessary that it should be hot through to prevent surface cracks, which are caused by the reduced cohesion of the overheated parts, which overlie the colder center of an irregularly heated piece.

By observing these precautions a piece of steel may always be heated safely up to even a bright yellow heat when there is much forging to be done on it, and at this heat it will weld well.

The best and most economical of welding fluxes is clean, crude borax, which should be first thoroughly melted and then ground to a fine powder. Borax prepared in this way will not froth on the steel, and one-half of the usual quantity will do the work as well as the whole quantity unmelted.

After the steel is properly heated, it should be forged to shape as quickly as possible, and just as the red heat is leaving the parts intended for cutting edges these parts should be refined by rapid light blows, continued until the red disappears.

For the second stage of heating, for hardening, great care should be used; first, to protect the cutting edges and working parts from heating more rapidly than the body of the piece; next, that the whole part to be hardened be heated uniformly through, without any part becoming visibly hotter than the other. A uniform heat, as low as will give the required hardness, is the best for hardening.

BEAR IN MIND,

That for every variation of heat which is great enough to be seen there will result a variation in grain, which may be seen by breaking the piece; and for every such variation in temperature there is a very good chance for a crack to be seen; many a costly tool is ruined by inattention to this point,

The effect of too high heat is to open the grain; to make the steel coarse.

The effect of an irregular heat is to cause irregular grain, irregular strains and cracks.

As soon as the piece is properly heated for hardening, it should be promptly and thoroughly quenched in plenty of the cooling medium; water, brine, or oil, as the case may be. An abundance of the cooling bath, to do the work quickly and uniformly all over, is very necessary to good and safe work. To harden a large piece safely, a running stream should be used. Much uneven hardening is caused by the use of too small baths.

For the third stage of heating, to temper, the first important requisite is again uniformity. The next is time. The more slowly a piece is brought down to its temper, the better and safer is the operation.

When expensive tools, such as taps, reamers, etc., are to be made, it is a wise precaution, and one easily taken, to try small pieces of steel at different temperatures, so as to find out how low a heat will give the necessary hardness. The lowest heat is the best for any steel; the test costs nothing, takes very little time, and very often saves considerable loss.

TEMPER.

The word temper, as used by the steel maker, indicates the amount of carbon in steel; thus, steel of high temper is steel containing much carbon; steel of low temper is steel containing little carbon; steel of medium temper is steel containing carbon between these limits, etc., etc. Between the highest and the lowest we have some twenty divisions, each representing a definite content of carbon.

As the temper of steel can only be observed in the ingot, it is not necessary to the needs of the trade to attempt any description of the mode of observation, especially as this is purely a matter of education of the eye, only to be obtained by years of experience.

Likewise, the quality of steel cannot be determined from the appearance of the fracture of a bar as it comes from the hands of the manufacturer. This appearance is determined in the main, by the heat at which the bar is finished, and therefore, one end of a long bar (and especially of a hammered bar) may show a coarse, and the other end, a fine grain, where the whole bar will be well suited for the purpose intended. Two tools properly heated, forged and hardened (one from each end of such a bar) will, if broken, show fractures similar in color and grain.

The act of tempering steel is the act of giving to a piece of steel, after it has been shaped, the hardness necessary for the work it has to do. This is done by first hardening the piece, generally a good deal harder than is necessary, and then toughening it by slow heating and gradual softening, until it is just right for work.

A piece of steel properly tempered should always be finished finer in grain than the bar from which it is made. If it is necessary, in order to make the piece as hard as is required, to heat it so hot that after being hardened it will be as coarse, or coarser, in grain than the bar, then the steel itself is of too low temper for the desired work. In a case of this kind, the steel maker should at once be notified of the fact, and could immediately correct the trouble by furnishing higher steel.

Sometimes an effort is made to harden fine steel without removing (by grinding or other method) the scale formed in rolling, hammering or annealing. The result will generally be disappointing, as steel which would harden through such a coating would be of too high a temper where the scale was removed.

This surface scale is necessarily of irregular thickness and density, is oxide of iron—not steel—and, therefore, it will not harden, and is to a certain extent a bad conductor of heat. It should, therefore, be removed in every case to insure the best results.

If a great degree of hardness is not desired, as in the case of taps, and most tools of complicated form, and it is found that at a moderate heat the tools are too hard and are liable to crack, the smith should first use a lower heat in order to save the tools already made, and then notify the steel maker that his steel is too high, so as to prevent a recurrence of the trouble. In all cases where steel is used in large quantities for the same purpose, as in the making of taps, reamers, drills, etc., there is very little difficulty about temper, because, after one or two trials, the steel maker learns what his customer requires and can always furnish it to him.

In large general works, however, such as a rolling mill and nail factory, or large machine works, or large railroad shops, both the maker and worker of the steel labor under great disadvantages from want of a mutual understanding.

The steel maker receives his order and fills the sizes, of temper best adapted to general work, and the smith usually tries to harden all tools at about the same heat. The steel maker is right, because he is afraid to make the steel too high or too low, for fear it will not suit, and so he gives an average adapted to the size of the bar. The smith is right, because he is generally the most hurried and crowded man about the establishment. He must forge a tap for this man, a cold nail knife for that one, and a lathe tool for another, and so on; and each man is in a hurry. Under these circumstances he cannot be expected to stop and test every piece of steel he uses, and find out exactly at what heat it will harden best and refine properly. He needs steel that will all harden properly at the same heat, and this he usually gets from the general practice among steel makers of making each bar of a certain temper, according to its size.

But if it should happen that he were caught with only one bar of say, inch and a quarter octagon, and three men should come in a hurry, one for a tap, another for a punch and another for a chilled roll plug, he would find it very difficult to make one bar of steel answer for all of these purposes even if it were of the very best quality. The chances are that he would make one good tool and two bad tools; and when the steel maker came around to inquire, he would find one friend and two enemies, and the smith puzzled and in doubt.

There is a perfectly easy and simple way to avoid all of this trouble; and that is, to write after each size the purpose for which it is wanted, as for instance, lathe tools, taps, dies, hot or cold punches, shear knives, etc. This gives very little trouble in making the order, and it is the greatest relief to the steel maker. It is his delight to get hold of such an order, for he knows that when it is filled he will hardly ever hear a complaint.

Every steel maker worthy of the name knows exactly what temper to provide for any tool, or if it is a new case, one or two trials are enough to inform him, and as he always should have twenty odd tempers on hand, it is just as easy, and far more satisfactory to both parties, to have it made right as to have it made wrong.

For these reasons we urge all persons to specify the work the steel is to do, then the smith can harden all tools at about the same heat, and he will not be annoyed by complaints, or hints that he does not do his work well.

MISCELLANEOUS.

(From The Pratt & Whitney Co.)

For comprehensive information regarding the subject of standard pipe and pipe threads, as applied to American practice, we would refer all who may be interested to the Excerpt Minutes of Proceedings of the Institution of Civil Engineers of Great Britain, Vol. LXXI, Session 1882-3, Part I, containing the papers of the late Robert Briggs, C. E., presented and read after his death, on "American Practice in Warming Buildings by Steam."

The following extracts from the paper of Mr. Briggs (included more fully in the report of the committee on standard pipe and pipe threads, American Society of Mechanical Engineers, Vol. VIII, transactions,) are here presented, giving data upon which the Briggs standard pipe-thread sizes are based.

The taper employed for the conical tube ends is uniform with all makers of tubes or fittings, namely, an inclination of 1 in 32 to the axis. Custom has also established a particular length of screwed end for each different diameter of tube. Tubes of the several diameters are kept in stock by manufacturers and merchants, and form the basis of a regular trade in the apparatus for warming by steam. A knowledge of all these particulars is therefore essential for designing apparatus for the purpose. The ruling dimensions in wrought iron tube work is the external diameter of certain nominal sizes, which are designated roughly according to their internal diameter. These nominal sizes were mainly established in the English tube trade between 1820 and 1840, and certain pitches of screw-thread were adopted for them, the coarseness of the pitch carrying roughly with the diameter, but in an arbitrary way utterly devoid of regularity. The length of the screwed portion on the tube end varies with the external diameter of the tube according to an arbitrary rule of thumb, whence results, for each size of tube, a certain minimum of thickness of metal at the outer extremity of the tapering screwed tube-end. It is the determination of this minimum thickness of metal, for the tapering screwed end of a wrought-iron tube, which constitutes the question of mechanical interest.

The thread employed has an angle of 60°; it is slightly rounded off, both at the top and at the bottom, so that the height or depth of the thread, instead of being exactly equal to the pitch, is only four-fifths (4-5) of the pitch, or equal to 0.08 1/n, if n be the number of threads per inch. For the length of tube-end throughout which the screw-thread continues perfect, the empirical formula used is (0.8D+4.8) X 1/n, where D is the actual external diameter of the tube throughout its parallel length, and is expressed in inches. Farther back, beyond the perfect threads, come two having the same taper at the bottom, but imperfect at the top. The remaining imperfect portion of the screw-thread farthest back from the extremity of the tube is not essential in any way to this system of joint; and its imperfection is simply incidental to the process of cutting the thread at a single operation.

STANDARD DIMENSIONS OF WROUGHT IRON WELDED TUBES.

DIAMETER OF TUBE.   (BRIGGS STANDARD.)   SCREWED ENDS.

NOMINAL INSIDE.	ACTUAL INSIDE.	ACTUAL OUTSIDE.	THICKNESS OF METAL.	NO. OF THREADS PER INCH.	LENGTH OF PERFECT THREAD AT BOTTOM.
⅛ in.	0.270 in.	0.405 in.	0.068 in.	27	0.19 in.
¼ "	0.364 "	0.540 "	0.088 "	18	0.29 "
⅜ "	0.491 "	0.675 "	0.091 "	18	0.30 "
½ "	0 623 "	0.840 "	0.109 "	14	0 39 "
¾ "	0.824 "	1.050 "	0 113 "	14	0.40 "
1 "	1.048 "	1.315 "	0.134 "	11½	0.51 "
1¼ "	1.380 "	1.660 "	0.140 "	11½	0.54 "
1½ "	1.610 "	1.900 "	0.145 "	11½	0.55 "
2 "	2.067 "	2.375 "	0.154 "	11½	0.58 "
2½ "	2.468 "	2.875 "	0.204 "	8	0.89 "
3 "	3.067 "	3.500 "	.217 "	8	0.95 "
3½ "	3.548 "	4.000 "	.226 "	8	1.0 "
4 "	4.026 "	4.500 "	.237 "	8	1.05 "
4½ "	4.508 "	5.000 "	.246 "	8	1.10 "
5 "	5.045 "	5.563 "	.259 "	8	1.16 "
6 "	6.065 "	6.625 "	.280 "	8	1.26 "
7 "	7.023 "	7.625 "	.301 "	8	1.36 "
8 "	7.982 "	8.625 "	.322 "	8	1.46 "
*9 "	9.000 "	9.688 "	.344 "	8	1.57 "
10 "	10.019 "	10.750 "	.366 "	8	1.63 "

*By the action of the Manufacturers of Wrought Iron Pipe and Boiler Tubes, at a meeting held in New York, May 9, 1889, a change in size of actual outside diameter of 9 inch pipe was adopted, making the latter 9.625 instead of 9.688 inches, as given in the table of Briggs standard pipe diameters.

The sizes of Twist Drills to be used in boring holes to be reamed with Pipe Reamer, and threaded with Pipe Taps are as follows:

SIZE OF TAP.	DIAM. OF DRILL	SIZE OF TAP.	DIAM. OF DRILL.
⅛ inch.	21/64 inch.	1 inch.	$1\frac{3}{16}$ inch.
¼ "	29/64 "	1¼ "	$1\frac{15}{32}$ "
⅜ "	19/32 "	1½ "	$1\frac{23}{32}$ "
½ "	23/32 "	2 "	$2\frac{3}{16}$ "
¾ "	15/16 "	2½ "	$2\frac{11}{16}$ "
		3 "	$3\frac{5}{16}$ "

The angle for turning or grinding pipe taps and reamers is 1° 47'=(angle from center of axis.)

THE SELLERS SYSTEM.

Recommended by the Franklin Institute of Philadelphia, has been adopted by the United States Government, the Master Mechanics and Master Car Builders Associations, Locomotive Works, Machine Bolt Makers and by many manufacturing establishments throughout the country. The thread has an angle of 60 degrees, with flat top and bottom equal to one-eighth of the pitch. The advantages of this form of thread over the sharp V are that, in the tap, the edges of the thread are less liable to accidental injury, and will wear and retain their size and form longer, and, in the bolt, the flat top and bottom give increased strength and an improved appearance, while the greater facility with which practical uniformity and consequent interchangeability is now attained by it's use, as compared with tne Witworth form, will commend it to the attention of every user of taps and dies, wherever its application may be possible.

The accompanying table gives the standard diameter and number of threads per inch for all usual sizes, from one-quarter inch to six inches, inclusive.

SELLERS OR U. S. STANDARD.

Diameter...................... ¼ ⁵⁄₁₆ ⅜ ⁷⁄₁₆ ½ ⁹⁄₁₆ ⅝ ¾ ⅞
No. Threads per inch...... 20 18 16 14 13 12 11 10 9

Diameter...................... 1 1⅛ 1¼ 1⅜ 1½ 1⅝ 1¾ 1⅞ 2
No. Threads per inch...... 8 7 7 6 6 5½ 5 5 4½

Diameter...................... 2⅛ 2¼ 2⅜ 2½ 2⅝ 2¾ 2⅞ 3
No. Threads per inch...... 4½ 4½ 4 4 4 4 3½ 3½

Diameter...................... 3⅛ 3¼ 3⅜ 3½ 3⅝ 3¾ 3⅞ 4
No. Threads per inch.. .... 3½ 3½ 3¼ 3¼ 3¼ 3 3 3

Diameter...................... 4⅛ 4¼ 4⅜ 4½ 4⅝ 4¾ 4⅞ 5
No. Threads per inch...... 2⅞ 2⅞ 2¾ 2¾ 2⅝ 2⅝ 2⅝ 2½

Diameter...................... 5⅛ 5¼ 5⅜ 5½ 5⅝ 5¾ 5⅞ 6
No. Threads per inch...... 2½ 2½ 2⅜ 2⅜ 2⅜ 2⅜ 2¼ 2¼

¹⁄₁₆ 64, ³⁄₃₂ 50, ⅛ 40, ⁵⁄₃₂ 36, ³⁄₁₆ 32 and ⁷⁄₃₂ 28 are also according to
the Sellers system.

Screws and bolts 11-16, 13-16, and 15-16-inch diameter
are usually made, having 11, 10 and 9 threads per inch. respectively, but under the Sellers formula, strictly followed, they
should be 10, 9 and 8, respectively.

DIMENSIONS OF PRATT & WHITNEY CO. REAMERS
FOR MORSE STANDARD TAPER TWIST
DRILL SOCKET.

No	Diam. small end.	Diam. large end.	Gauge Diam. large end.	Gauge length.	Length of Flutes.	Total length	Taper per foot.	Center Angle or Angle to grind.
	in.	in.	in.	in.	in.	in.	in.	
1	0.365	0.525	0.475	2⅛	3	5¼	0.605=1°27′—
2	0.573	0.749	0.699	2½	3½	6¼	0.600=1°26′—
3	0.779	0.982	0.936	3⁵⁄₁₆	4	7½	0.605=1°27′—
4	1.026	1.283	1.231	4	5	8¾	0.615=1°28′
5	1.486	1.796	1.746	5	6	10	0.625=1°29′+
6	2.117	2.566	2.500	7¼	8½	12½	0.634=1°31′—

USEFUL INFORMATION.

STEAM.

(By permission of the Geo. F. Blake Mfg. Co., New York.)

A cubic inch of water evaporated under ordinary atmospheric pressure is converted into 1 cubic foot of steam (approximately).

The specific gravity of steam (at atmospheric pressure) is .411 that of air at 34° Fahrenheit, and .0006 that of water at the same temperature.

27.222 cubic feet of steam weigh one (1) pound; 13,817 cubic feet of air weight one (1) pound.

Locomotives average a consumption of 3000 gallons of water per 100 miles run.

The best designed boilers, well set, with good draft, and skillful firing, will evaporate from 7 to 10 pounds of water per pound of first class coal.

In calculating horse-power of tubular or flue boilers, consider 15 square feet of heating surface equivalent to one nominal horse-power.

On one square foot of grate can be burned on an average from 10 to 12 pounds of hard coal, or 18 to 20 pounds soft coal, per hour, with natural draft. With forced draft nearly double these amounts can be burned.

Steam engines, in economy, vary from 14 to 60 pounds of feed water and from 1½ to 7 pounds of coal per hour per indicated H.-P. See table following for duty of high grade engines.

Condensing engines require from 20 to 30 gallons of water at an average low temperature, to condense the steam represented by every gallon of water evaporated in the boilers supplying engines—approximately for most engines, we say, from 1 to 1½ gallons condensing water per minute per indicated horse-power.

Surface condensers should have about 2 square feet of tube (cooling) surface per horse-power for a compound steam engine. Ordinary engines will require more surface according to their economy in the use of steam. It is absolutely necessary to place air pumps below condensers to get satisfactory results.

RATIO OF VACUUM TO TEMPERATURE
(FAHRENHEIT) OF FEED WATER.

INCHES VACUUM.

00	212°
11	190°
18	170°
22½	150°
*25	135°
27½	112°
28½	92°
29	72°
29½	52°

*Usually considered the standard point of efficiency—Condenser and Air Pump being well proportioned.

WEIGHT AND COMPARATIVE FUEL VALUE OF WOOD.

1 cord air-dried hickory or hard maple weighs about 4,500 pounds, and is equal to about 2,000 pounds of coal.

1 cord air-dried white oak weighs about 3,850 pounds, and is equal to about 1,715 pounds of coal.

1 cord air-dried beech, red oak and black oak, weighs about 3,250 pounds, and is equal to about 1,450 pounds of coal.

1 cord air-dried poplar (white wood), chestnut and elm, weighs about 2,350 pounds, and is equal to about 1,050 pounds of coal.

1 cord air-dried average pine, weighs about 2,000 pounds and is equal to about 925 pounds of coal.

From the above it is safe to assume that 2¼ pounds of dry wood is equal to 1 pound average quality of soft coal, and that the full value of the same weight of different woods is very nearly the same; that is, a pound of hickory is worth no more for fuel than a pound of pine, assuming both to be dry. It is important that the wood be dry, as each 10 per cent. of water or moisture in wood will detract about 12 per cent. from its value as fuel.

DUTY OF STEAM ENGINES.

A well known engineer of high authority gives the following comparative figures, showing the economy of high grade steam engines in actual practice:

TYPE OF ENGINE.	Temperature of feed water	Pounds of water evaporated per lb. of Cumberland Coal.	Pounds of steam per I. H. P. used per hour.	Pounds of Cumberland Coal used per I. H. P. per hour.	Cost per I. H. P. per hour supposing coal at $6 per ton.
Non-Condensing,	210°	10.5	29.	2.75	$0.0073
Condensing,	100°	9.4	20.	2.12	0.0056
Compound Jacketed,	100°	9.4	17.	1.81	0.0045
Triple Expansion Jacketed,	100°	9.4	13.6	1.44	0.0036

The effect of a good condenser and air pump should be to make available about 10 pounds more mean effective pressure, with the same terminal pressure; or to give the same mean effective pressure with a correspondingly less terminal pressure. When the load on the engine requires 20 pounds M. E. P., the condenser does half the work; at 30 pounds, one-third of the work; at 40 pounds, one-fourth, and so on. It is safe to assume that practically the condenser will save from one-fourth to one-third of the fuel, and it can be applied to any engine, cut-off, or throttling, where a sufficient supply of water is available.

USEFUL INFORMATION.—WATER.

(Geo. F. Blake Mfg. Co.

Doubling the diameter of a pipe increases its capacity four times. Friction of liquids in pipes increases as the square of the velocity.

The mean pressure of the atmosphere is usually estimated at 14.7 pounds per square inch, so that with a perfect vacuum it will sustain a column of mercury 29.9 inches, or a column of water 33.9 feet high at sea level.

To find the pressure in pounds per square inch of a column of water, multiply the height of the column in feet by .434. Approximately, we say that every foot elevation is equal to ½ pound pressure per square inch; this allows for ordinary friction.

To find the diameter of a pump cylinder to move a given quantity of water per minute (100 feet of piston being the standard of speed) divide the number of gallons by 4, then extract the square root, and the product will be the diameter in inches of the pump cylinder.

To find quantity of water elevated in one minute running at 100 feet of piston speed per minute, square the diameter of the water cylinder in inches and multiply by 4. Example: Capacity of a 5-inch cylinder is desired. The square of the diameter (5 inches) is 25, which multiplied by 4 gives 100, the number of gallons per minute (approximately.)

To find the horse-power necessary to elevate water to a given height, multiply the weight of the water elevated per minute in pounds by the height in feet, and divide the product by 33,000 (an allowance should be added for water friction and a further allowance for loss in steam cylinder, say from 20 to 30 per cent.)

The area of the steam piston, multiplied by the steam pressure, gives the total amount of pressure that can be exerted. The area of the water piston multiplied by the pressure of water per square inch, gives the resistance. A margin must be made between the power and the resistance to move the pistons at the required speed—say from 20 to 40 per cent., according to speed and other conditions.

To find the capacity of a cylinder in gallons, multiplying the area in inches by the length of stroke in inches will give the total number of cubic inches; divide this amount by 231 (which is the cubical contents of a U. S. gallon in inches) and the product is the capacity in gallons.

WEIGHT AND CAPACITY OF DIFFERENT STANDARD GALLONS OF WATER.

	Cubic inches in a Gallon.	Weight of a Gallon in pounds.	Gallons in a Cubic Foot.
Imperial or English	277.274	10.00	6.232102
United States	231	8.33111	7.480519

Weight of a cubic foot of water, English Standard, 62.321 lbs. Avoirdupois.

Weight of Crude Petroleum, 6½ lbs. per U. S. gallon.

Weight of Refined   "   6½ lbs. per U. S. gallon.

42 gallons to the barrel.

A "miner's inch" of water is approximately equal to a supply of 12 U. S. gallons per minute.

TABLE OF SQUARES AND HEXAGONS, EXACT SIZE, ACROSS FLATS AND CORNERS.

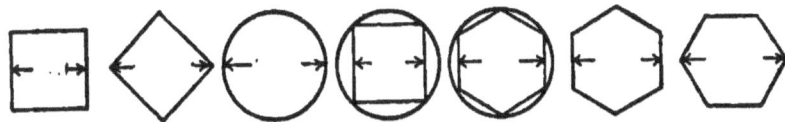

STANDARD SQUARE.	ACROSS CORNERS.	STANDARD ROUND.	LARGEST INSCRIBED SQUARE.	LARGEST INSCRIBED HEXAGON.	STANDARD HEXAGON.	ACROSS CORNERS.
1/8	.1767	1/8	.0883	.108	1/8	.1443
5/32	.2209	5/32	.1104	.1352	5/32	.1803
3/16	.2651	3/16	.1325	.1623	3/16	.2165
7/32	.3093	7/32	.1546	.1893	7/32	.2526
1/4	.3535	1/4	.1767	.2165	1/4	.2887
5/16	.4419	5/16	.2209	.2706	5/16	.3608
3/8	.5303	3/8	.2651	.3247	3/8	.4330
7/16	.6187	7/16	.3093	.3788	7/16	.5052
1/2	.7071	1/2	.3535	.4330	1/2	.5773
9/16	.7955	9/16	.3977	.4871	9/16	.6495
5/8	.8839	5/8	.4419	.5412	5/8	.7217
11/16	.9723	11/16	.4861	.5953	11/16	.7938
3/4	1.0606	3/4	.5303	.6495	3/4	.8660
13/16	1.1490	13/16	.5745	.7036	13/16	.9382
7/8	1.2374	7/8	.6187	.7577	7/8	1.0104
15/16	1.3258	15/16	.6629	.8118	15/16	1.0825
1	1.4142	1	.7071	.8660	1	1.1547
$1\frac{1}{16}$	1.5026	$1\frac{1}{16}$	.7513	.9201	$1\frac{1}{16}$	1.2269
$1\frac{1}{8}$	1.5910	$1\frac{1}{8}$	.7954	.9742	$1\frac{1}{8}$	1.2990
$1\frac{3}{16}$	1.6794	$1\frac{3}{16}$	.8396	1.0283	$1\frac{3}{16}$	1.3712

TABLE OF SQUARES AND HEXAGONS, EXACT SIZE, ACROSS FLATS AND CORNERS.

STANDARD SQUARE.	ACROSS CORNERS.	STANDARD ROUND.	LARGEST INSCRIBED SQUARE.	LARGEST INSCRIBED HEXAGON.	STANDARD HEXAGON	ACROSS CORNERS.
1¼	1.7677	1¼	.8838	1.0825	1¼	1.443
1 5/16	1.8561	1 5/16	.9280	1.1366	1 5/16	1.5155
1⅜	1.9445	1⅜	.9722	1.1907	1⅜	1.5877
1 7/16	2.0329	1 7/16	1.016	1.2448	1 7/16	1.6599
1½	2.1213	1½	1.060	1.2990	1½	1.7320
1 9/16	2.2097	1 9/16	1.104	1.3531	1 9/16	1.8042
1⅝	2.2981	1⅝	1.149	1.4072	1⅝	1.8764
1 11/16	2.3865	1 11/16	1.193	1.4613	1 11/16	1.9486
1¾	2.4748	1¾	1.237	1.5155	1¾	2.0207
1 13/16	2.5632	1 13/16	1.281	1.5696	1 13/16	2.0929
1⅞	2.6516	1⅞	1.325	1.6237	1⅞	2.1651
1 15/16	2.7400	1 15/16	1.370	1.6778	1 15/16	2.2372
2	2.8284	2	1.414	1.7320	2	2.3094
2⅛	3.0052	2⅛	1.502	1.8402	2⅛	2.4537
2¼	3.1819	2¼	1.590	1.9485	2¼	2.5980
2⅜	3.3587	2⅜	1.679	2.0567	2⅜	2.7424
2½	3.5355	2½	1.767	2.1650	2½	2.8867
2⅝	3.7123	2⅝	1.856	2.2732	2⅝	3.0311
2¾	3.8890	2¾	1.944	2.3815	2¾	3.1754
2⅞	4.0658	2⅞	2.033	2.4897	2⅞	3.3197
3	4.2426	3	2.121	2.5980	3	3.4641
3¼	4.5961	3¼	2.298	2.8145	3¼	3.7528
3½	4.9497	3½	2.474	3.0310	3½	4.0414
3¾	5.3032	3¾	2.651	3.2475	3¾	4.3301
4	5.6568	4	2.828	3.4640	4	4.6188

TAPERS PER INCH AND CORRESPONDING ANGLES, ALSO THE ANGLES TO TURN OR GRIND.

TAPER PER INCH.	INCLUDED ANGLE.	ANGLE TO TURN OR GRIND.	TAPER PER INCH.	INCLUDED ANGLE.	ANGLE TO TURN OR GRIND.
1-64"	0° 54'	0° 27'−	33-64"	28° 54'	14° 27'+
1-32"	1° 48'	0° 54'−	17-32	29° 46'	14° 53'−
3-64	2° 42'	1° 21'−	35-64	30° 36'	15° 18'−
1-16	3° 34'	1° 47'+	9-16	31° 24'	15° 42'+
5-64	4° 28'	2° 14'	37-64	32° 14'	16° 7'+
3-32"	5° 22'	2° 41'	19-32"	33° 4'	16° 32'+
7-64"	6° 16'	3° 8'−	39-64	33° 54'	16° 57'+
1-8	7° 10'	3° 35'−	5-8	34° 42'	17° 21'+
9-64	8° 2'	4° 1'+	41-64	35° 32'	17° 46'+
5-32	8° 56'	4° 28'	21-32	36° 20'	18° 10'−
11-64"	9° 50'	4° 55'−	43-64"	37° 8'	18° 34'+
3-16"	10° 42'	5° 21'+	11-16	37° 56'	18° 58'+
13-64	11° 36'	5° 48'−	45-64	38° 44'	19° 22'+
7-32	12° 28'	6° 14'+	23-32	39° 32'	19° 46'
15-64	13° 22'	6° 41'	47-64	40° 20'	20° 10'−
1-4 "	14° 16'	7° 8'−	3-4 "	41° 0'	20° 33'+
17-64"	15° 8'	7° 34'−	49-64	41° 54'	20° 57'−
9-32	16° 0'	8° 0'+	25-32	42° 40'	21° 20'+
19-64	16° 54'	8° 27'−	51-64	43° 26'	21° 43'+
5-16	17° 46'	8° 53'−	13-16	44° 14'	22° 7'−
21-64"	18° 38'	9° 19'+	53-64"	44° 58'	22° 29'+
11-32"	19° 30'	9° 45'+	27-32	45° 44'	22° 52'+
23-64	20° 22'	10° 11'+	55-64	46° 30'	23° 15'+
3-8	21° 14'	10° 37'+	7-8	47° 16'	23° 38'
25-64	22° 6'	11° 3'	57-64	48° 0'	24° 0'+
13-32"	22° 58'	11° 29'−	29-32"	48° 46'	24° 23'−
27-64"	23° 48'	11° 54'+	59-64	49° 30'	24° 45'−
7-16	24° 40'	12° 20'+	15-16	50° 14'	25° 7'−
29-64	25° 32'	12° 46'−	61-64	50° 58'	25° 29'−
15-32	26° 22'	13° 11'+	31-32	51° 42'	25° 51'−
31-64"	27° 14'	13° 37'−	63-64"	52° 24'	26° 12'+
1-2"	28° 4'	14° 2'+	1	53° 8'	26° 34'

TAPERS PER FOOT AND CORRESPONDING ANGLES, ALSO THE ANGLES TO TURN OR GRIND.

TAPER PER FOOT.	INCLUDED ANGLE.	ANGLE TO TURN OR GRIND.	TAPER PER FOOT.	INCLUDED ANGLE.	ANGLE TO TURN OR GRIND.
1-8 "	0° 34'	0° 17'+	1 "	4° 46'	2° 23'+
9-64"	0° 40'	0° 20'+	1 1-16	5° 4'	2° 32'+
5-32	0° 44'	0° 22'+	1 1-8	5° 22'	2° 41'
11-64	0° 50'	0° 25'—	1 3-16	5° 40'	2° 50'—
3-16	0° 54'	0° 27'—	1 1-4	5° 58'	2° 59'+
13-64"	0° 58'	0° 29'+	1 5-16"	6° 16'	3° 8'+
7-32"	1° 2'	0° 31'+	1 3-8	6° 34'	3° 17'—
15-64	1° 8'	0° 34'+	1 7-16	6° 52'	3° 26'—
1-4	1° 12'	0° 36'—	1 1-2	7° 10'	3° 35'—
17-64	1° 16'	0° 38'+	1 9-16	7° 26'	3° 43'+
9-32"	1° 20'	0° 40'+	1 5-8 "	7° 44'	3° 52'+
19-64"	1° 26'	0° 43'—	1 11-16	8° 2'	4° 1'—
5-16	1° 30'	0° 45'—	1 3-4	8° 20'	4° 10'—
21-64	1° 34'	0° 47'	1 13-16	8° 38'	4° 19'—
11-32	1° 38'	0° 49'+	1 7-8	8° 56'	4° 28'
3-8 "	1° 42'	0° 51'+	1 15-16"	9° 14'	4° 37'—
23-64"	1° 48'	0° 54'—	2	9° 32'	4° 46'—
25-64	1° 52'	0° 56'—	2 1-8	10° 8'	5° 4'—
13-32	1° 56'	0° 58'+	2 1-4	10° 42'	5° 21'+
27-64	2° 0'	1° 0'+	2 3-8	11° 18'	5° 39'+
7-16"	2° 4'	1° 2'+	2 1-2 "	11° 54'	5° 57'—
29-64"	2° 10'	1° 5'—	2 5-8	12° 30'	6° 15'—
15-32	2° 14'	1° 7'+	2 3-4	13° 4'	6° 32'+
31-64	2° 18'	1° 9'+	2 7-8	13° 40'	6° 50'—
1-2	2° 24'	1° 12'—	3	14° 16'	7° 8'—
17-32"	2° 32'	1° 16'+	3 1-8 "	14° 50'	7° 25'+
9-16"	2° 42'	1° 21'+	3 1-4	15° 26'	7° 43'—
19-32	2° 50'	1° 25'	3 3-8	16° 0'	8° 0'+
5-8	2° 58'	1° 29'+	3 1-2	16° 36'	8° 18'—
21-32	3° 8'	1° 34'—	3 5-8	17° 10'	8° 35'+
11-16"	3° 16'	1° 38'+	3 3-4 "	17° 46'	8° 53'—
23-32"	3° 26'	1° 43'—	3 7-8	18° 20'	9° 10'—
3-4	3° 34'	1° 47'+	4	18° 56'	9° 28'—
25-32	3° 41'	1° 52'—	4 1-8	19° 30'	9° 45'+
13-16	3° 52'	1° 56'+	4 1-4	20° 4'	10° 2'+
7-8 "	4° 2'	2° 1'—	4 1-2 "	21° 14'	10° 37'+
27-32"	4° 10'	2° 5'+	4 3-4	22° 24'	11° 12'—
29-32	4° 20'	2° 10'—	5	23° 32'	11° 46'
15-16	4° 28'	2° 14'+			
31-32	4° 38'	2° 19'—			

TAP DRILLS FOR SHARP V AND U. S. STANDARD THREADS.

The sizes of Twist Drills given in these Tables are correct for general purposes.

DIAMETER OF TAP.		NO. OF THREADS PER INCH	DIAMETER OF TAP AT BOTTOM OF V THREAD.	SIZE OF DRILL FOR V THREAD.	DIAMETER OF TAP AT BOTTOM OF U. S. STAND. THREAD.	SIZE OF DRILL FOR U. S. STAND. THREAD.
1-4″	{	16 18 20	.142″ .154 .163	11-64″ 3-16 3-16 }	.185″	No. 11.
9-32	{	16 18 20	.173 .185 .194	13-64 7-32 7-32		
5-16	{	16 18	.204 .216	15-64 1-4 }	.240	1-4″
11-32	{	16 18	.235 .247	17-64 9-32		
3-8	{	14 16 18	.251 .267 .279	19-64 19-64 5-16 }	.294	19-64
13-32	{	14 16 18	.282 .298 .310	21-64 21-64 11-32		
7-16	{	14 16	.313 .329	23-64 23-64 }	.344	23-64
15-32	{	14 16	.344 .360	25-64 25-64		
1-2	{	12 13 14	.356 .366 .376	13-32 27-64 27-64 }	.399	13-32
17-32	{	12 13 14	.387 .397 .407	7-16 7-16 29-64		
9-16	{	12 14	.418 .438	15-32 31-64 }	.454	15-32
19-32	{	12 14	.449 .469	1-2 33-64		
5-8	{	10 11 12	.452 .468 .481	1-2 33-64 17-32 }	.507	33-64
21-32	{	10 11 12	.483 .499 .512	17-32 35-64 9-16		

TAP DRILLS FOR SHARP V AND U. S. STANDARD THREADS.

[CONTINUED.]

DIAMETER OF TAP.	NO. OF THREADS PER INCH.	DIAMETER OF TAP AT BOTTOM OF V THREAD.	SIZE OF DRILL FOR V THREAD.	DIAMETER OF TAP AT BOTTOM OF U. S. STAND. THREAD.	SIZE OF DRILL FOR U.S. STAND THREAD.
11-16″	11	.530″	37-64″		
	12	.543	19-32		
3-4	10	.577	5-8		
	11	.593	41-64	.62	5-8″
	12	.606	21-32		
25-32	10	.608	21-32		
	11	.624	43-64		
	12	.637	11-16		
13-16	9	.620	43-64		
	10	.639	11-16		
7-8	9	.683	47-64	.731	47-64
	10	.702	3-4		
29-32	9	.714	49-64		
	10	.733	25-32		
15-16	8	.720	25-32		
	9	.745	51-64		
1	8	.783	27-32	.837	27-32
1⅛	7	.878	61-64	.940	61-64
	8	.908	31-32		
1 5/32	7	.909	63-64		
	8	.939	1		
1¼	7	1.003	1 5/64	1.065	1 5/64
1 9/32	7	1.034	1 7/64		
1⅜	6	1.086	1 11/64	1.158	1 11/64
1 13/32	6	1.117	1 13/64		
1½	6	1.211	1 19/64	1.283	1 19/64
1 17/32	6	1.242	1 21/64		
1⅝	5	1.279	1 25/64	1.389	1 13/32
	5½	1.311	1 13/32		
1¾	5	1.404	1 33/64	1.490	1½
1⅞	4½	1.491	1 39/64	1.615	1⅝
	5	1.529	1 41/64		
2	4½	1.616	1 47/64	1.712	1 23/32

TAP DRILLS FOR MACHINE SCREWS.

The sizes of Drills given in this Table correspond to the Brown & Sharpe Twist Drill and Steel Wire Gauge.

NUMBER OF TAP.	THREADS PER INCH.	DIAMETER OF TAP.	DIAMETER OF TAP AT BOTTOM OF THREAD.	SIZE OF DRILL FOR TAPPING.
4	32	.110	.056	No. 45
4	36	.110	.062	" 44
4	40	.110	.067	" 44
6	30	.137	.080	No. 37
6	32	.137	.083	" 35
6	36	.137	.089	" 35
6	40	.137	.094	" 33
8	24	.163	.091	No. 30
8	30	.163	.106	" 29
8	32	.163	.109	" 29
8	36	.163	.115	" 29
10	20	.189	.103	No. 29
10	22	.189	.111	" 28
10	24	.189	.117	" 24
10	30	.189	.132	" 22
10	32	.189	.135	" 20
12	20	.216	.130	No. 20
12	22	.216	.138	" 19
12	24	.216	.144	" 15
14	16	.242	.134	No. 19
14	18	.242	.146	" 16
14	20	.242	.156	" 13
14	22	.222	.164	" 10
14	24	.242	.170	" 5
16	16	.268	.160	No. 11
16	18	.268	.172	" 6
16	20	.268	.182	" 3
16	22	.268	.190	" 2
18	16	.295	.187	No. 2
18	18	.295	.199	" 1
18	20	.295	.209	" 15-64
20	16	.321	.213	No. 1-4
20	18	.321	.225	" 1-4
20	20	.321	.235	" 17-64
22	16	.347	.239	No. 17-64
22	18	.347	.251	" 9-32
24	14	.374	.250	No. 19-64
24	16	.374	.266	" 19-64
24	18	.374	.278	" 5-16
26	16	.400	.292	No. 21-64

TABLE OF DECIMAL EQUIVALENTS OF STUBS STEEL WIRE GAUGE.

The Crescent Drill Rods made by Miller, Metcalf and Parkin, Pittsburgh, Pa., also correspond to these sizes.

LETTER.	SIZE OF LETTER IN DECIMALS.	NO. OF WIRE GAUGE.	SIZE OF NUMBER IN DECIMALS.	NO. OF WIRE GAUGE.	SIZE OF NUMBER IN DECIMALS.	NO. OF WIRE GAUGE.	SIZE OF NUMBER IN DECIMALS.
Z	.413	1	.227	28	.139	55	.050
Y	.404	2	.219	29	.134	56	.045
X	.397	3	.212	30	.127	57	.042
W	.386	4	.207	31	.120	58	.041
V	.377	5	.204	32	.115	59	.040
U	.368	6	.201	33	.112	60	.039
T	.358	7	.199	34	.110	61	.038
S	.348	8	.197	35	.108	62	.037
R	.339	9	.194	36	.106	63	.036
Q	.332	10	.191	37	.103	64	.035
P	.323	11	.188	38	.101	65	.033
O	.316	12	.185	39	.099	66	.032
N	.302	13	.182	40	.097	67	.031
M	.295	14	.180	41	.095	68	.030
L	.290	15	.178	42	.092	69	.029
K	.281	16	.175	43	.088	70	.027
J	.277	17	.172	44	.085	71	.026
I	.272	18	.168	45	.081	72	.024
H	.266	19	.164	46	.079	73	.023
G	.261	20	.161	47	.077	74	.022
F	.257	21	.157	48	.075	75	.020
E	.250	22	.155	49	.072	76	.018
D	.246	23	.153	50	.069	77	.016
C	.242	24	.151	51	.066	78	.015
B	.238	25	.148	52	.063	79	.014
A	.234	26	.146	53	.058	80	.013
		27	.143	54	.055		

THE BROWN AND SHARPE TWIST DRILL AND STEEL WIRE GAUGE.

SIZE OF NUMBERS.

NO.	SIZE OF NUMBER IN DECIMALS.	NO.	SIZE OF NUMBER IN DECIMALS.	NO.	SIZE OF NUMBER IN DECIMALS.	NO.	SIZE OF NUMBER IN DECIMALS.
1	.2280	16	.1770	31	.1200	46	.0810
2	.2210	17	.1730	32	.1160	47	.0785
3	.2130	18	.1695	33	.1130	48	.0760
4	.2090	19	.1660	34	.1110	49	.0730
5	.2055	20	.1610	35	.1100	50	.0700
6	.2040	21	.1590	36	.1065	51	.0670
7	.2010	22	.1570	37	.1040	52	.0635
8	.1990	23	.1540	38	.1015	53	.0595
9	.1960	24	.1520	39	.0995	54	.0550
10	.1935	25	.1495	40	.0980	55	.0520
11	.1910	26	.1470	41	.0960	56	.0465
12	.1890	27	.1440	42	.0935	57	.0430
13	.1850	28	.1405	43	.0890	58	.0420
14	.1820	29	.1360	44	.0860	59	.0410
15	.1800	30	.1285	45	.0820	60	.0400

DIFFERENT STANDARDS FOR WIRE GAUGE IN USE IN THE UNITED STATES.

Dimensions of Sizes in Decimal Parts of an Inch.

(BROWN & SHARPE MFG. CO.)

NUMBER OF WIRE GAUGE.	AMERICAN OR BROWN & SHARPE.	BIRMINGHAM OR STUBS' WIRE.	WASHBURN & MOEN MFG. CO.	TRENTON IRON CO., TRENTON, N. J.	STUBS' STEEL W.RE.	U. S. STAND. FOR PLATE.
000000						.4687
00000				.45		.4375
0000	.46	.454	.3938	.4		.4062
000	.40964	.425	.3625	.36		.375
00	.3648	.38	.3310	.33		.3437
0	.32486	.34	.3065	.305		.3125
1	.2893	.3	.2830	.285	.227	.2812
2	.25763	.284	.2625	.265	.219	.2656
3	.22942	.259	.2437	.245	.212	.25
4	.20431	.238	.2253	.225	.207	.2343
5	.18194	.22	.2070	.205	.204	.2187
6	.16202	.203	.1920	.19	.201	.2031
7	.14428	.18	.1770	.175	.199	.1875
8	.12849	.165	.1620	.16	.197	.1718
9	.11443	.148	.1483	.145	.194	.1562
10	.10189	.134	.1350	.13	.191	.1406
11	.090742	.12	.1205	.1175	.188	.125
12	.080808	.109	.1055	.105	.185	.1093
13	.071961	.095	.0915	.0925	.182	.0937
14	.064084	.083	.0800	.08	.18)	.0781
15	.057068	.072	.0720	.07	.178	.0703
16	.05082	.065	.0625	.061	.175	.0625
17	.045257	.058	.0540	.0525	.172	.0562
18	.040303	.049	.0475	.045	.168	.05
19	.03589	.042	.0410	.04	.164	.0437
20	.031961	.035	.0348	.035	.161	.0375
21	.028462	.032	.03175	.031	.157	.0343
22	.025347	.028	.0286	.028	.155	.0312
23	.022571	.025	.0258	.025	.153	.0281
24	.0201	.022	.0230	.0225	.151	.025
25	.0179	.02	.0204	.02	.148	.0218
26	.01594	.018	.0181	.018	.146	.0187
27	.014195	.016	.0173	.017	.143	.0171
28	.012641	.014	.0162	.016	.139	.0156
29	.011257	.013	.0150	.015	.134	.0140
30	.010025	.012	.0140	.014	.127	.0125
31	.008928	.01	.0132	.013	.120	.0109
32	.00795	.009	.0128	.012	.115	.0101
33	.00708	.008	.0118	.011	.112	.0093
34	.006304	.007	.0104	.01	.110	.0086
35	.005614	.005	.0095	.0095	.108	.0078
36	.005	.004	.0090	.009	.106	.0070
37	.004453	....	....	.0085	.103	.0066
38	.003965	....	....	.008	.101	.0062
39	.003531	....	....	.0075	.099	....
40	.003144	....	....	.007	.097	....

The American Wire Gauge is the one commonly known as the English Standard Wire, or Birmingham Gauge, and designates the Stubs' soft wire sizes. The Stubs' Steel Wire Gauge is the one that is used in measuring drawn steel wire or drill rods of Stubs' make, and is also used by many makers of American drill rod.

CIRCUMFERENCES AND AREAS OF CIRCLES.

DIAMETER.	CIRCUMFER- ENCE.	AREA.	DIAMETER.	CIRCUMFER- ENCE.	AREA.
1/16	.1963	.00307	4	12.5664	12.5664
⅛	.3927	.01227	4⅛	12.9591	13.3641
¼	.7854	.04908	4¼	13.3518	14.1863
⅜	1.1781	.11045	4⅜	13.7445	15.0330
½	1.5708	.19635	4½	14.1372	15.9043
⅝	1.9635	.30679	4⅝	14.5299	16.8002
¾	2.3562	.44179	4¾	14.9226	17.7206
⅞	2.7489	.60132	4⅞	15.3153	18.6655
1	3.1416	.7854	5	15.7080	19.6350
1⅛	3.5343	.9940	5⅛	16.1007	20.6290
1¼	3.9270	1.2272	5¼	16.4934	21.6476
1⅜	4.3197	1.4849	5⅜	16.8861	22.6907
1½	4.7124	1.7671	5½	17.2788	23.7583
1⅝	5.1051	2.0739	5⅝	17.6715	24.8505
1¾	5.4978	2.4053	5¾	18.0642	25.9673
1⅞	5.8905	2.7612	5⅞	18.4569	27.1086
2	6.2832	3.1416	6	18.8496	28.2744
2⅛	6.6759	3.5466	6⅛	19.2423	29.4648
2¼	7.0686	3.9761	6¼	19.6350	30.6797
2⅜	7.4613	4.4301	6⅜	20.0277	31.9191
2½	7.8540	4.9087	6½	20.4204	33.1831
2⅝	8.2467	5.4119	6⅝	20.8131	34.4717
2¾	8.6394	5.9396	6¾	21.2058	35.7848
2⅞	9.0321	6.4918	6⅞	21.5985	37.1224
3	9.4248	7.0686	7	21.9912	38.4846
3⅛	9.8175	7.6699	7⅛	22.3839	39.8713
3¼	10.2102	8.2958	7¼	22.7766	41.2826
3⅜	10.6029	8.9462	7⅜	23.1693	42.7184
3½	10.9956	9.6211	7½	23.5620	44.1787
3⅝	11.3883	10.3206	7⅝	23.9547	45.6636
3¾	11.7810	11.0447	7¾	24.3174	47.1731
3⅞	12.1737	11.7933	7⅞	24.7401	48.7071

CIRCUMFERENCES AND AREAS OF CIRCLES

[CONTINUED.]

DIAMETER.	CIRCUMFER-ENCE.	AREA.	DIAMETER.	CIRCUMFER-ENCE.	AREA.
8	25.1328	50.2656	12	37.6992	113.097
8⅛	25.5255	51.8487	12⅛	38.0919	115.466
8¼	25.9182	53.4563	12¼	38.4846	117.859
8⅜	26.3109	55.0884	12⅜	38.8773	120.276
8½	26.7036	56.7451	12½	39.270	122.719
8⅝	27.0963	58.4264	12⅝	39.6627	125.185
8¾	27.4890	60.1322	12¾	40.0554	127.676
8⅞	27 8817	61.8625	12⅞	40.4481	130.192
9	28.2744	63.6174	13	40.8408	132.733
9⅛	28.6671	65.3968	13⅛	41.2335	135.297
9¼	29.0598	67.2008	13¼	41.6262	137.887
9⅜	29.4525	69.0293	13⅜	42.0189	140.501
9½	29.8452	70.8823	13½	42.4116	143.139
9⅝	30.2379	72.7599	13⅝	42.8043	145.802
9¾	30.6306	74.6621	13¾	43.1970	148.490
9⅞	31.0233	76.5888	13⅞	43.5897	151.202
10	31.4160	78.5400	14	43.9824	153.938
10⅛	31.8987	80.5188	14⅛	44.3751	156.698
10¼	32.2014	82.5161	14¼	44.7678	159.485
10⅜	32.5941	84.5409	14⅜	45.1605	162.296
10½	32.9868	86.5903	14½	45.5532	165.130
10⅝	33.3795	88.6643	14⅝	45.9459	167.990
10¾	33.7722	90.7628	14¾	46.3386	170.874
10⅞	34.1649	92.8858	14⅞	46.7313	173.782
11	34.5576	95.0334	15	47.1240	176.715
11⅛	34 9503	97.2055	15⅛	47.5167	179.673
11¼	35 3430	99.4022	15¼	47.9094	182.655
11⅜	35.7357	101.6234	15⅜	48.3021	185.661
11½	36.1284	103.8691	15½	48.6948	188.692
11⅝	36.5211	106.1394	15⅝	49.0875	191.748
11¾	36.9138	108.4343	15¾	49.4802	194.828
11⅞	37.3065	110.7537	15⅞	49.8729	197.933

CIRCUMFERENCES AND AREAS OF CIRCLES

[CONTINUED.]

DIAMETER.	CIRCUMFER-ENCE.	AREA.	DIAMETER.	CIRCUMFER-ENCE.	AREA.
16	50.2656	201.062	20	62.8320	314.160
16⅛	50.6583	204.216	20⅛	63.2247	318.099
16¼	51.0510	207.395	20¼	63.6174	322.063
16⅜	51.4437	210.598	20⅜	64.0101	326.051
16½	51.8364	213.825	20½	64.4028	330.064
16⅝	52.2291	217.077	20⅝	64.7955	334.102
16¾	52.6218	220.354	20¾	65.1882	338.164
16⅞	53.0145	223.655	20⅞	65.5809	342.249
17	53.4072	226.981	21	65.9736	346.361
17⅛	53.7999	230.331	21⅛	66.3663	350.497
17¼	54.1926	233.706	21¼	66.7590	354.657
17⅜	54.5853	237.105	21⅜	67.1517	358.842
17½	54.9780	240.529	21½	67.5444	363.051
17⅝	55.3707	243.977	21⅝	67.9371	367.285
17¾	55.7634	247.450	21¾	68.3298	371.543
17⅞	56.1561	250.948	21⅞	68.7225	375.826
18	56.5487	254.469	22	69.1152	380.134
18⅛	56.9415	258.016	22⅛	69.5079	384.466
18¼	57.3342	261.587	22¼	69.9006	388.822
18⅜	57.7269	265.183	22⅜	70.2933	393.203
18½	58.1196	268.803	22½	70.6860	397.609
18⅝	58.5123	272.448	22⅝	71.0787	402.038
18¾	58.9050	276.117	22¾	71.4714	406.494
18⅞	59.2977	279.811	22⅞	71.8641	410.973
19	59.6904	283.529	23	72.2568	415.477
19⅛	60.0831	287.272	23⅛	72.6495	420.004
19¼	60.4758	291.040	23¼	73.0422	424.558
19⅜	60.8685	294.832	23⅜	73.4349	429.135
19½	61.2612	298.648	23½	73.8276	433.737
19⅝	61.6539	302.489	23⅝	74.2203	438.364
19¾	62.0466	306.355	23¾	74.6130	443.015
19⅞	62.4393	310.245	23⅞	75.0056	447.690

CIRCUMFERENCES AND AREAS OF CIRCLES
[CONTINUED.]

DIAMETER.	CIRCUMFER-ENCE.	AREA.	DIAMETER.	CIRCUMFER-ENCE.	AREA.
24	75.3984	452.39	28	87.9648	615.754
24⅛	75.7911	457.115	28⅛	88.3575	621.264
24¼	76.1838	461.864	28¼	88.7502	626.798
24⅜	76.5765	466.638	28⅜	89.1429	632.357
24½	76.9692	471.436	28½	89.5356	637.941
24⅝	77.3619	476.259	28⅝	89.9283	643.549
24¾	77.7546	481.107	28¾	90.3210	649.182
24⅞	78.1473	485.979	28⅞	90.7137	654.840
25	78.540	490.875	29	91.1064	660.521
25⅛	78.9327	495.796	29⅛	91.4991	666.228
25¼	79.3254	500.742	29¼	91.8918	671.959
25⅜	79.7181	505.712	29⅜	92.2845	677.714
25½	80.1108	510.706	29½	92.6772	683.494
25⅝	80.5035	515.726	29⅝	93.0699	689.299
25¾	80.8962	520.769	29¾	93.4626	695.128
25⅞	81.2889	525.838	29⅞	93.8553	700.982
26	81.6816	530.930	30	94.2480	706.860
26⅛	82.0743	536.048	30⅛	94.6407	712.763
26¼	82.4670	541.190	30¼	95.0334	718.690
26⅜	82.8597	546.356	30⅜	95.4261	724.642
26½	83.2524	551.547	30½	95.8188	730.618
26⅝	83.6451	556.763	30⅝	96.2115	736.619
26¾	84.0378	562.003	30¾	96.6042	742.645
26⅞	84.4305	567.267	30⅞	96.9969	748.695
27	84.8232	572.557	31	97.3896	754.769
27⅛	85.2159	577.870	31⅛	97.7823	760.869
27¼	85.6086	583.209	31¼	98.1750	766.992
27⅜	86.0013	588.571	31⅜	98.5677	773.140
27½	86.3940	593.959	31½	98.9604	779.313
27⅝	86.7867	599.371	31⅝	99.3531	785.510
27¾	87.1794	604.807	31¾	99.7458	791.732
27⅞	87.5721	610 268	31⅞	100.1385	797.979

CIRCUMFERENCES AND AREAS OF CIRCLES.
[CONTINUED.]

DIAMETER.	CIRCUMFER-ENCE.	AREA.	DIAMETER.	CIRCUMFER-ENCE.	AREA.
32	100.5312	804.250	36	113.098	1017.878
32⅛	100.9239	810.545	36⅛	113.490	1024.960
32¼	101.3166	816.865	36¼	113.883	1032.065
32⅜	101.7093	823.210	36⅜	114.276	1039.195
32½	102.1020	829.579	36½	114.668	1046.349
32⅝	102.4947	835.972	36⅝	115.061	1053.528
32¾	102.8874	842.391	36¾	115.454	1060.732
32⅞	103.2801	848.833	36⅞	115.846	1067.960
33	103.6728	855.301	37	116.239	1075.213
33⅛	104.0655	861.792	37⅛	116.632	1082.490
33¼	104.4592	868.309	37¼	117.025	1089.792
33⅜	104.8509	874.850	37⅜	117.417	1097.118
33½	105.2436	881.415	37½	117.810	1104.469
33⅝	105.6363	888.005	37⅝	118.203	1111.844
33¾	106.0290	894.620	37¾	118.595	1119.244
33⅞	106.4217	901.259	37⅞	118.988	1126.669
34	106.814	907.922	38	119.381	1134.118
34⅛	107.207	914.611	38⅛	119.773	1141.591
34¼	107.600	921.323	38¼	120.166	1149.089
34⅜	107.992	928.061	38⅜	120.559	1156.612
34½	108.385	934.822	38½	120.952	1164.159
34⅝	108.778	941.609	38⅝	121.344	1171.731
34¾	109.171	948.420	38¾	121.737	1179.327
34⅞	109.563	955.255	38⅞	122.130	1186.948
35	109.956	962.115	39	122.522	1194.593
35⅛	110.349	969.	39⅛	122.915	1202.263
35¼	110.741	975.909	39¼	123.308	1209.958
35⅜	111.134	982.842	39⅜	123.700	1217.677
35½	111.527	989.800	39½	124.093	1225.420
35⅝	111.919	996.783	39⅝	124.486	1233.188
35¾	1133.312	1003.790	39¾	124.879	1240.981
35⅞	1110.705	1110.822	39⅞	125.271	1248.798

CIRCUMFERENCES AND AREAS OF CIRCLES
[CONTINUED.]

DIAMETER.	CIRCUMFERENCE.	AREA.	DIAMETER.	CIRCUMFERENCE.	AREA.
40	125.664	1256.64	44	138.230	1520.5
40⅛	126.057	1264.51	44⅛	138.623	1529.2
40¼	126.449	1272.40	44¼	139.016	1537.9
40⅜	126.842	1280.31	44⅜	139.408	1546.6
40½	127.235	1288.25	44½	139.801	1555.3
40⅝	127.627	1296.22	44⅝	140.194	1564.1
40¾	128.020	1304.21	44¾	140.587	1572.8
40⅞	128.413	1312.22	44⅞	140.979	1581.6
41	128.806	1320.26	45	141.372	1590.4
41⅛	129.198	1328.32	45⅛	141.765	1599.3
41¼	129.591	1336.41	45¼	142.157	1608.2
41⅜	129.984	1344.52	45⅜	142.550	1617.1
41½	130.376	1352.66	45½	142.943	1625.9
41⅝	130.769	1360.82	45⅝	143.335	1634.9
41¾	131.162	1369.00	45¾	143.728	1644.0
41⅞	131.554	1377.21	45⅞	144.121	1652.9
42	131.947	1385.5	46	144.514	1661.9
42⅛	132.340	1393.7	46⅛	144.906	1670.9
42¼	132.733	1401.9	46¼	145.299	1680.0
42⅜	133.125	1410.3	46⅜	145.692	1689.1
42½	133.518	1418.6	46½	146.084	1698.2
42⅝	133.911	1426.9	46⅝	146.477	1707.4
42¾	134.303	1435.4	46¾	146.870	1716.5
42⅞	134.696	1443.8	46⅞	147.262	1725.7
43	135.089	1452.2	47	147.655	1734.9
43⅛	135.481	1460.7	47⅛	148.048	1744.2
43¼	135.874	1469.1	47¼	148.441	1753.4
43⅜	136.267	1477.6	47⅜	148.833	1762.7
43½	136.660	1486.2	47½	149.226	1772.1
43⅝	137.052	1494.7	47⅝	149.619	1781.4
43¾	137.445	1503.3	47¾	150.011	1790.7
43⅞	137.838	1511.9	47⅞	150.404	1800.1

CIRCUMFERENCES AND AREAS OF CIRCLES.
[CONTINUED.]

DIAMETER.	CIRCUMFER-ENCE.	AREA.	DIAMETER.	CIRCUMFER-ENCE.	AREA.
48	150.796	1809.6	49	153.938	1885.7
48⅛	151.189	1819.0	49⅛	154.331	1895.4
48¼	151.582	1828.5	49¼	154.723	1905.0
48⅜	151.975	1837.9	49⅜	155.116	1914.7
48½	152.367	1847.5	49½	155.509	1924.4
48⅝	152.760	1856.9	49⅝	155.902	1934.2
48¾	153.153	1866.5	49¾	156.294	1944.0
48⅞	153.545	1876.1	49⅞	156.687	1953.7
			50	157.08	1963.5

INDEX.

CHAPTER II.

CHAPTER III.

CHAPTER IV.

CHAPTER V.

www.ingramcontent.com/pod-product-compliance
Lightning Source LLC
Chambersburg PA
CBHW020052030726
47498CB00006B/1751